The Summer House

The Summer House

Masashi Matsuie

*Translated from the Japanese
by Margaret Mitsutani*

Other Press
New York

Copyright © Masashi Matsuie 2012
First published in Japanese as 火山のふもとで *(Kazan no fumoto de)* in 2012 by Shinchosha Publishing Co., Ltd.

English translation copyright © Margaret Mitsutani 2025

This English edition is published by arrangement with the author in care of the Tuttle-Mori Agency, Inc., Tokyo.

Production editor: Yvonne E. Cárdenas
Text Designer: Patrice Sheridan
This book was typeset in Bembo Book and Helvetica by Alpha Design & Composition of Pittsfield, NH

10 9 8 7 6 5 4 3 2 1

All rights reserved. No part of this publication may be reproduced or transmitted in any form or by any means, electronic or mechanical, including photocopying, recording, or by any information storage and retrieval system, without written permission from Other Press LLC, except in the case of brief quotations in reviews for inclusion in a magazine, newspaper, or broadcast. Printed in the United States of America on acid-free paper. For information write to Other Press LLC, 267 Fifth Avenue, 6th Floor, New York, NY 10016. Or visit our Web site: www.otherpress.com

Library of Congress Cataloging-in-Publication Data
Names: Matsuie, Masashi, 1958- author. | Mitsutani, Margaret, translator.
Title: The summer house / Masashi Matsuie ; translated from the Japanese by Margaret Mitsutani.
Other titles: Kazan no fumoto de. English
Description: English edition. | New York : Other Press, 2025.
Identifiers: LCCN 2024044613 (print) | LCCN 2024044614 (ebook) |
 ISBN 9781635425178 (paperback) | ISBN 9781635425185 (ebook)
Subjects: LCGFT: Novels.
Classification: LCC PL873.A864 K3913 2025 (print) | LCC PL873.A864 (ebook) |
 DDC [Fic]—dc23
LC record available at https://lccn.loc.gov/2024044613
LC ebook record available at https://lccn.loc.gov/2024044614

Publisher's Note: This is a work of fiction. Names, characters, places, and incidents either are the product of the author's imagination or are used fictitiously, and any resemblance to actual persons, living or dead, events, or locales is entirely coincidental.

1

Sensei was always the first one up at the Summer House.

Just after dawn I was lying in bed, listening to him move around downstairs. I picked up my wristwatch from the bedside table. In the dim light, I saw that it was 5:05.

The library, just above the front entrance, had a small bed, where I slept. As day was breaking, muffled sounds would rise through the old wooden posts and walls.

I'd hear Sensei remove the bar and stand it against the wall. Then he'd slide the heavy inner door into its casing on the left, and open the outer one all the way until it reached the wall outside, where he'd fasten the brass doorknob with a loop of rope. That kept the wind from blowing it shut. Finally, closing the screen door behind him, he set out on his morning walk. Cold forest air blew softly through the screen door. Soon the Summer House was quiet again.

Here in the forest, over a thousand meters above sea level, the first to break the silence were the birds, starting before Sensei stirred. Woodpeckers, grosbeaks, thrushes, flycatchers... the names come quickly to mind. Some I can only remember by their song.

That morning, even before sunrise, the sky was an odd shade of blue, showing the silhouettes of trees that moments before had been sunk in darkness. All too soon, without waiting for the sun, morning broke.

I got out of bed and raised the blind on the small window that looked out onto the garden. Mist, thick clouds of it, veiled the leaves and branches of the katsura tree. The birds were quiet. I stuck my head out of the window to breathe in the mist. If that smell had a color, it wouldn't be white, but green. Careful not to make a sound, I raised the blind in the workshop next door. All I could see out of this much-wider window, facing south, was a stretch of white. The huge katsura in the garden floated in the mist. I wondered whether Sensei might get lost in the hazy woods.

But no matter how deep it seemed, the mist disappeared as soon as the sun rose. As though nothing had happened, the birds started singing again. He would soon be back. In an hour or so, everyone would be up.

The Murai Office of Architectural Design was in a quiet corner of a residential area in Tokyo called Kita-Aoyama, down an alley you'd miss if you weren't looking for it. It was a small concrete building with parking space under the eaves, just big enough for three cars. Every year, from late July to mid-September, it basically closed down and relocated to what everyone called the Summer House, in the mountain village of Aoguri in Kita-Asama, where there was an old colony of vacation homes owned by people who came to escape the city heat.

Once preparations for the move to the mountains started, the office suddenly got busier than usual. Meetings with clients were held almost daily to take care of any outstanding problems before we left. We also had to stock up on supplies to take with us. Styrene boards for study models. Staedtler Lumograph drafting pencils. Uni erasers. Tracing paper. Stationery. Some staff members got crew cuts so they wouldn't need the village barber, others went to the dentist to have their teeth checked. Having worked there for only four months, I couldn't think of anything special I'd need for this first summer in the mountains, beyond a cookbook for beginners I bought, knowing I'd have to take my turn at kitchen duty.

Ms. Yoshinaga, our accountant, stayed at the office in Kita-Aoyama, along with two other women who had families, and two men who had to oversee the construction of a building that had just begun. Sensei's wife, whose pediatrics clinic was at their home in Yoyogi-Uehara, never left Tokyo.

The company had a staff of thirteen, including Murai Sensei. While that was about average for a business headed by one individual architect, it was pretty small considering the mark he'd left on postwar Japanese architecture. He could have hired more people whenever he wanted to. Instead, he chose to tailor the projects he took on to the size of his staff, politely refusing work that didn't interest him, calmly letting chances for expansion pass him by.

During the 1960s the Murai Office had picked up quite a few commissions for public projects and large buildings in business districts, but by the 1970s its main focus was on private homes. An introduction was almost essential for a new client, but even then, Iguchi, the manager, would tell them, "It'll take at least two years, maybe even longer, to build your house," and then ask them frankly, "Are you willing to wait that long?" Few were discouraged. People who wanted to live in a house designed by Shunsuke Murai already knew it would take time. But there was another type of prospective client, with enough money to hire a famous architect but not very particular about which one. For them, Iguchi would raise the bar from "at least two" to "at least three" years. They were never that patient. Having decided to build a house, they wanted to see it completed as soon as possible, and unless it was some sort of vanity project, they weren't prepared to wait.

When I joined the office in 1982, Sensei was in his mid-seventies. While this is well beyond the normal retirement age, in the world of architecture, where people start out in their thirties and are still considered young in their forties, it's not unusual to stay active past seventy. Sensei not only designed the houses, but also would often go to the construction site to iron out details with his clients. There didn't seem to be any major problems either with his health or the company's finances. Nevertheless, although no one talked about it openly, everyone was wondering about the future, five or ten years down the road.

By the 1980s the Murai Office could already be said to be putting the brakes on, gradually slowing down in preparation for a final, quiet stop. The last staff member fresh out of university had been hired in 1979, and rumor had it that he would be the last. There were still students about to graduate who didn't let the rumors discourage them; one or two came hoping for a job interview the following year and the year after that, yet without success.

When I was in my last year at university, I knew I didn't want to go on to graduate school to study architecture, but doubted I'd fit into the tightly organized design department of a major construction company. In fact, I couldn't really see myself working anywhere. Postmodern design studios were popular, but I had no interest whatsoever in doing that sort of work.

I thought of apprenticing myself to a master carpenter and working my way up. In the summer vacation of my third year, I persuaded a small building contractor to let me help on two construction sites. But by that time contractors were simply a system for commissioning and supervising workers, while the best carpenters were lone wolves, in business for themselves, accepting work from any contractor who would hire them, with no time to take on trainees. In this new era, when houses could be quickly assembled from prefabricated materials without using planes, saws, or chisels, the building trade was becoming much less dependent on skilled craftsmen.

What I really wanted to do was to work independently from the start, without being attached to any company or design office. Unfortunately, that was virtually impossible. I wasn't a registered architect with a first-class license, and if I didn't go on to graduate school, I couldn't become one without at least two years of practical experience. I'd have to follow the normal route, joining some office of architectural design to get the practical training I needed, making do on a low salary for several years until I got my license.

There was only one architect I really respected, and that was Shunsuke Murai. He didn't design any of those strikingly modern buildings that sprang up between the 1964 Tokyo Olympics and the 1970 Osaka Expo. He didn't talk much either, and since he rarely strayed into areas outside his profession, only people especially interested in architecture were likely to know his name.

From the late 1960s to the early 1970s, Murai was probably better known in America than in Japan. When an exhibition on twentieth-century architecture was held at the Museum of Modern Art in New York in 1967, he was the only Japanese architect included. The catalogue credited him with grounding his work in traditional Asian forms while incorporating elements of modernism in innovative ways. As an example of "Japanese-style modernism," part of a major work of his from the 1960s, designed for the Komoriya, a Kyoto inn with a long history, was reconstructed in the museum courtyard, where it attracted a good deal of attention.

Visitors to the New York exhibition probably remembered having to take their shoes off at the entrance, and the smell of new tatami, rather than the name Shunsuke Murai. But he was not merely well-versed in the traditional architecture of his own country. As a young man he had made a firsthand study of older buildings in China, Korea, and Europe, becoming at the same time one of the first to grasp the simplicity and rationality of modernism, made possible by materials such as steel, glass, and concrete. From this he had developed a truly original style, of which certain connoisseurs soon took note.

At the opening party for the exhibition, one of the wealthiest men in the eastern United States asked him, without notice, to design a house for him. Jeffrey Hubert Thompson, whose grandfather had made a fortune from an East Coast railroad, taught anthropology at Harvard, his alma mater, but was better known as an art collector. He was also associated with an incident that occurred in his student days. Three months after disappearing while doing fieldwork along the White Nile in East Africa, he was found in a village several hundred kilometers away from the spot where he had last been seen. There was talk in the tabloids of a love affair with a local woman. Thompson himself never denied or confirmed it.

Twenty years later, still a bachelor, Thompson was among the guests at the private viewing. He read the article on the Komoriya in the catalogue while other guests chatted, and carefully examined the alcove, the decorative wooden panels above the sliding doors, the veranda, the doors and *fusuma*, made of wood and paper. He then approached Murai and asked him about the merits and drawbacks of using wood and concrete in the same structure, and how building on pliant, marshy land such as you'd find in Japan was different from working on hard, dry terrain.

Their conversation persuaded Murai to accept his proposal, and he spent several months supervising the construction of the Thompson House. It was his first long stay in America since before the war, when he had been apprenticed to Frank Lloyd Wright for two years. A sprawling project on land with a river flowing through it where deer came to drink, the result was widely featured in American architectural magazines. Though he was asked to design other houses on a similar scale, he refused on the grounds that he had too much work waiting back in Japan. "If I'd kept on building houses that big," he later told Iguchi quietly, "I'd have lost all sense of proportion."

Earlier in the 1960s, he had worked himself to exhaustion on a large-scale project commissioned by the government, only to end up clashing over his basic plan with the officials in charge. This experience must have made the recognition he later received in America all the more welcome, a hidden reserve of support. Many of his contemporaries who spoke eloquently on the future of urban planning were awarded contract after contract for major public projects. Sensei, on the other hand, stopped entering design competitions for public buildings; and since he'd never been one to hold forth on architectural theory, he didn't appear much in the media either.

But as I went around examining buildings he had designed ten or twenty years earlier, I realized how remarkable his work had been during those years of silence. Without getting caught up in the excesses of Japan's postwar economic boom, or indulging in any sort of flashy display, he had designed buildings that were simple and easy to use, yet with a beauty that didn't fade.

In the fall of my last year at university, as I became more and more anxious about my future, I decided to take a step toward something that had almost no chance of coming true.

It was late September. An unusually large number of red dragonflies, rarely seen in Tokyo, had flown in from the northwest, stopping on telephone wires or low concrete walls to rest their wings. I went out onto the upstairs veranda, where I saw several up close, on the pole I hung the washing from, and on the railing. Wings like paper-thin metal; deep-red bodies; the blurry brightness of their compound eyes. No human hand could create anything like this. In less than thirty minutes, they were gone. It was a dry, windless day.

After seeing the dragonflies off, I went back to my desk and wrote a letter to the Murai Office, asking politely but as briefly as possible if there was any chance of my working there. I enclosed a copy of my graduation project, a plan for a small house designed for a family with one member in a wheelchair. Days afterward I could still hear the sound of the envelope dropping down into the mailbox.

About a week later, I got a phone call from Hiroshi Iguchi, who told me he was the office manager. Although they had no plans to hire me, Murai Sensei was willing to give me a short interview.

On the appointed day, I headed for the office in Kita-Aoyama, having checked the location on a map. I met Sensei in his dimly lit office, facing north, on the second floor of a three-story building covered with green ivy.

"So you're Tōru Sakanishi." His voice was deeper than I expected. There was a lattice window to his left, casting a faint light on his cheek. Sturdily built, he looked serious—grim, even, though not in a nervous, high-strung way. He had the firm jaw one often sees on men who work with their hands. His tone was gentle, his face surprisingly expressive; as he listened to me, he would chuckle occasionally, or seem to be thinking about something I'd said. No one had ever listened to me more carefully.

"Does someone in your family use a wheelchair?" he asked.

"No."

"Then why design a house for one?"

"I wanted to see how a wheelchair would affect the proportions of an entire house."

Nodding slightly, he looked down at my plan, his hand resting on it as he asked more questions.

"What do you think is hardest about making the blueprint for a house?"

I thought for a while before answering.

"Maybe it's that you have to create a new space within limited boundaries, without adding or multiplying anything. It involves a lot of dividing and subtracting."

He nodded again, then looking straight at me asked, "Is that what you're best at?"

"I'm not sure, but I do think I'm good at that sort of thing."

"And what kind of architecture do you think is made by adding and multiplying?"

"I'm sure there's something of that in multistory apartments."

My meeting with Sensei over, still keyed up with excitement, I walked past the workshop on the same floor. No one spoke or even looked up from their work. Something about the old wooden desks, white walls, and wooden floor reminded me of Sensei's face, and his voice.

Shortly after that I got a call from Iguchi, telling me I had been accepted as a provisional employee. It sounded to me as if he couldn't quite believe it himself, though I may have been imagining this. Considering that there was a list of applicants on file in the office, many of them licensed architects with five to ten years of experience, it would have been natural for him to be surprised. I myself was amazed to hear I'd been hired, even provisionally.

When I turned up the next day, Sensei looked straight at me, just as he had before, and said, "While you're here, make sure you learn a lot and do good work."

After the New Year, I started going there in the early morning on Mondays, Wednesdays, and Saturdays, when I didn't have classes. I was assigned a desk in the farthest corner of the workshop. A guy named Uchida, who was about a decade older than me and had the desk next to mine, acted as my instructor. I spent my first days at the office doing the miscellaneous tasks he gave me, figuring out how things were done. Yet even with these small jobs, there seemed to be a reason for everything, down to minor details. After two or three weeks, I could see that the workings of the Murai Office were as clear as the cutaway drawing of a building. There were no unreasonable orders or wasted effort, which meant I had to stay alert.

During the early 1980s, in contrast to the hectic pace of architectural developments generally, the buildings Sensei designed tended to be seen almost as nostalgic, in the mode of Japanese tradition, but that's not how they seemed to me. There was nothing homespun about the logical framework I saw behind either his designs or the way things were done at the office.

There was a rational explanation for that old-fashioned, comforting feeling people got from Sensei's houses. It came from visual effects created by things like the height of a ceiling, or a light source in the floor, or a shoji lattice fitted into a window that faced south. There was nothing mysterious about it. Though he rarely tried to explain in public how he achieved these effects, he would show us in practice, not only on blueprints, by moving a ruler about on the workshop wall in relation to the ceiling, or sometimes by opening and shutting doors or windows. He was always logical, never emotional.

"You can sleep better in a small bedroom," he'd say, "because it's more relaxing. The ceiling shouldn't be too high. Too much space above the bed leaves room for ghosts to float around in." Here he would smile slightly. "The bed should be just close enough to the wall for you to be able to touch it when you have to go to the bathroom in the middle of the night." On kitchens he had this to say: "You only want to smell food before a meal—there's no point in it afterward. The height of the ceiling, and the position of the cooker and ventilator are the keys to controlling it." The way he sounded was like a craftsman simply explaining his techniques.

Spring came.

On the evening of April 1, when overcoats were no longer needed, a welcome party for me was held at an Italian restaurant near the office.

As we walked down the dark street, talking quietly, I smelled something sweet (Carolina jasmine, I was told by Yukiko Nakao, a staff member slightly older than me). I can remember that evening even now. I'd never eaten in a restaurant with Italian waiters and chefs before.

After the main course, a white, U-shaped cake with a square red candle in the middle was served. Uchida, my instructor, had asked the chef to make it from a drawing he'd done of the Summer House in Kita-Asama; the squat red candle was supposed to be the chimney. It was exactly one-fiftieth the size of the original, Uchida explained. "Couldn't calculate the next one, so I don't know how it'll compare with the original," he added. Just then, as if on a signal to the kitchen, another dessert was brought out. This one was a Mont Blanc, so big it had to be carried in both hands. The sides had been sculpted with a palette knife to make it look like Mt. Asama, and powdered sugar gave it a snowy summit. There were sighs of admiration from our group. Uchida frowned, looking embarrassed.

"Mountains don't have blueprints, so getting the shape right was harder than I thought it would be. I had to dig up some old snapshots, and maps with contour lines."

"It's good to have old pictures," Iguchi said cheerfully, "glad you found them." He was a little drunk.

"I asked the chef to let me help him. I've been looking at Mt. Asama from the Summer House for over ten years now, so I think we got it just about right."

"The back of the mountain, the Karuizawa side," Sensei said from where he was sitting. "This is how it looks from Oiwake or Komuro. Very impressive. Well done."

The cake was placed at the foot of the mountain. Uchida adjusted their positions. A flame rose from the chimney, along with a wisp of smoke. I'd already seen blueprints of the Summer House; now, I could imagine myself inside it.

Before the cakes were cut up, we had our picture taken, standing around them. Uchida peered through the lens of the Leica he always carried with him, then asked one of the waiters to press the button. "Ready? Everybody, smile!"

The office staff stood shoulder to shoulder against the wall, leaning over slightly. Sensei and I sat in the middle, the candle flame reflected in our glasses. Looking back, I realize that this is the only picture I have of myself with him. This grainy photograph, taken with a flash, would later bring back memories that meant more to all of us than we could say.

A month later, we heard on the office radio that Mt. Asama had erupted. This hadn't happened since 1973, nearly a decade earlier. Crops were covered in volcanic ash on the Gunma Prefecture side, and the west wind blew smoke as far away as the Bōsō Peninsula. Cinders, some small as grains of rice, others the size of peas, pelted the area around the Summer House. We heard from the caretakers' agency in Aoguri that although ash had fallen on the roof and clouded the windows, the glass wasn't broken, and the building itself was undamaged. Although immediately after the eruption some of us wondered if we'd be able to go to the Summer House that year, from May into June volcanic activity seemed to have stopped altogether.

Then came the last Thursday in July. After lunch, everyone at the office was busy packing blueprints, models, files full of materials and documents, including estimates and even records of conversations we'd had with clients, into cardboard boxes, which were then loaded into three station wagons. The boxes had obviously been used before, as some were reinforced with packing tape, and all had numbers on them, indicating the order in which they should be loaded. Tightly lined up in rows from the right, they fitted neatly into the luggage space.

The radio news now said that Typhoon 10 was on its way. The Kanto-Koshinetsu area was right in the path of the storm, at present a huge spiral over the Pacific. We set off from Kita-Aoyama, the three vehicles in single file, feeling the typhoon at our back as we headed for the northwest side of the Kanto Plain like stragglers lagging behind a flock of migrating birds.

After going over Usui Pass, we headed west on Route 18, then at Naka-Karuizawa made a right turn toward the north. When Mt. Asama appeared through gaps in the trees, I peered up at it as we climbed higher, navigating a series of hairpin turns. Then the whole scene opened up, and I saw the mountain looming over us, bathed in evening light, so huge it was startling. This was a live volcano that just three months earlier had been spewing cinders and ash. Had I watched the eruption from this spot, I would have felt a raw sense of danger, but now there were only wisps of steam rising from the crater, and they could have been mistaken for clouds.

Beyond the pass was the Asama Plain. From here the road to the north was perfectly straight. When we reached the heavily wooded area around the village of Aoguri, night was falling. At the intersection on the main road we turned east, and with the old Kita-Asama Station on our right, drove for several more minutes until we reached the main street through the oldest part of the village. The Summer House was just north of here.

With its two wings enclosing a large katsura tree, the house had a concrete base with two wooden floors above it. Hidden by deep-reddish-brown cedar siding, the concrete was a half-story high, lifting the lower level off the ground to protect the wood from the moisture that rose from the forest floor.

The three cars entered the yard from the left, then swung clockwise around the katsura tree for a half circle to the parking lot. Engines were switched off. As soon as the car door opened, I could sense that the air here was completely different. The sound of branches stirring along with birdsong and the chirring of cicadas drifted down from overhead. The breeze carried a faint odor of earth and leaves. I looked up to see patches of blue sky through the trees. It was nearly ten degrees colder than in Tokyo.

The village of Aoguri was high enough above sea level for the change in air pressure to affect your ears.

Water boiled at a lower temperature than down below. There weren't many people in the vicinity, and the night sky was full of stars, the forest home to nearly eighty types of birds, plus *kamoshika* (goat-antelopes), monkeys, flying squirrels, rabbits, foxes, and bears.

The Summer House was smaller than I'd imagined from that white cake. The cedarwood siding was probably just as it had been when the original house was built in 1956. With a round clock on the front, it might have been mistaken for a little country schoolhouse. The yard with the katsura tree in the center faced south; a short distance away from the main building, a Himalayan cedar, the tallest tree in the area, loomed over the garage.

The entrance was slightly off-center, and to the west. When Iguchi opened the door, the air inside was heavy and damp. We all started hauling boxes from the station wagons into the house. Several steps up from the entranceway, off to the right, was a spacious dining room. The workshop was on the second floor, at the top of the stairs. It was dark inside, and smelled of wood. The heavy wooden rain shutters were pulled back one after another to let in the last rays of sunlight, which reflected dully on the polished oak floor. As if she'd done this many times, Yukiko whisked the white cloth off the big oblong dining table and folded it up. Red-tinged light lay over the fine-grained maple tabletop.

Next to the dining room, on the eastern side, were the kitchen and a room for ironing and other household tasks. A right turn from there took you into a sort of service area, along one side of the U-shape, with the women's laundry room, a pantry, and a storehouse for gardening tools, from which you could go directly outside. To the west of the dining room was a place to keep blueprints in, and next to it, linen. From there you turned a corner into the opposite side of the U, where you found the men's laundry room, the boiler room, and more storage space, with a ping-pong table, a tall stack of garden chairs, two bicycles, and a motorcycle that belonged to Uchida, who had arrived ahead of the rest of us.

The women's bath was on the second floor, east of the workshop, and on the western side were the director's office, the library (where I slept), and the men's bath. In both wings, the second floor was lined with single rooms for staff members. The five rooms for women in the east wing faced the five for men in the west one, with a wide corridor and the yard with the katsura tree in between. Tables, chairs, sofas, and cabinets—all trial items made at the Tokyo office—were placed here and there in the corridor. We sat in the chairs and sofas to read, talk, or take afternoon naps. For Uchida, who was in charge of furniture, this was also storage space for samples, so that he could check on their size or other details. He repaired this furniture when needed, and kept it waxed, so all the pieces were in excellent condition.

After putting away my things in the library, I took off my socks. The cool wooden floor felt good under my bare feet. I remembered my childhood, when I used to go barefoot all summer. I pushed open the window looking out on the yard, to see the katsura tree right in front of me. Kawarazaki, one of the most important members of the team, was just driving past it into the parking lot.

All the windows were open. Slowly, the Summer House was beginning to breathe again.

2

When Sensei built a cottage here in the 1950s, it was a much longer trip from Tokyo to Aoguri. Without the expressway, it could take six hours just to get to Usui Pass. When it snowed heavily, a line of cars would get stuck on that winding mountain road. Though he was an experienced driver, Sensei preferred to take the Shinetsu Line from Ueno Station, then change to the Tanasaka Light Railway at Karuizawa.

This toylike train carried people and baggage from Shin-Karuizawa Station to Kita-Asama, then on to Kusatsu Hot Springs and back again, making six trips a day at its peak. Starting in 1914, it lasted fifty years, until the year of the Tokyo Olympics.

Shin-Karuizawa, where passengers boarded the light railway, was on the eastern side of the main station. Next to the big diesel locomotives on the Shinetsu Line, the little electric train, imported from America, where it had been used in mines, could have passed as a donkey engine. The pantograph sticking out of the roof above the driver's cabin looked like horns, giving it its nickname, "the Horned Beetle." It had one—two at most—passenger cars. From Shin-Karuizawa to Kita-Asama, about twenty-six kilometers, took an hour and a half. Kusatsu Hot Springs, the end of the line, was over three hours away. The Horned Beetle at best could only manage the average speed of a small car driving on level ground.

To save the time and money it would have taken to make tunnels, the track took a winding route through the forests of the Asama range. Also for economic reasons, railway bridges were kept to a bare minimum, with only a few small ones built over deep valleys that couldn't be circumvented. Skirting mountains, tracing the contours of the land, the track took more than two and a half times the distance to cover ten kilometers as the crow flies.

There weren't many motorcars in the village during the 1950s, and fewer than half as many summer houses as in the 1980s. As the trees were still young, the entire area was brighter and more open. Looking east from Kita-Asama Station, you had a view of the entire village, with all the surrounding hills and valleys. In late autumn, when the trees had shed their leaves, the Murai building, atop a gentle slope, would appear and disappear through the bare branches. On winter nights, if the lights were on, it shone down on the snow like a lighthouse in the deserted village.

Iguchi, the office manager, apparently remembered everything that had ever happened at the Summer House, and liked telling me, the newest employee, stories about the old days.

In the early 1960s, he had stopped working on construction sites to take charge of all the office work, including scheduling and financial negotiations with clients and contractors. Six years younger than Sensei, he was the same age as Hans Wegner, the furniture designer. He was born in March 1914, the month the Tokyo Station Building, designed by Kingo Tatsuno, was completed. Four months later, World War I broke out. But he always liked to say, "I was born exactly one week before the Tanasaka Light Railway started running." Though I couldn't tell whether he was talkative because Sensei said so little, or Sensei was quiet because Iguchi talked so much, as a pair they definitely complemented each other.

Most of his Horned Beetle stories were about how slow, unreliable, and generally lovable the little train was. He told me about the time the paper he'd been reading blew out of the window and he'd jumped off to retrieve it, then ran to catch up and hoisted himself aboard again; or about how they had to stop when lightning struck nearby one summer, and how cold it suddenly got when a gust of air blew down from the mountain while they waited for the storm to pass. One winter, when a huge snowdrift knocked the train off the track, the driver, the engineer, and the passengers all got out to clear the snow away and set it on the track again.

"That was a real blizzard—could've buried us alive. But we had our adrenaline pumping, and the train was pretty light. We made it to the station, but after that, nothing moved until the weather cleared." I never figured out how much of this was true.

Back then, people in Aoguri still rode in carts pulled by horses or oxen. The smell of manure hung in the air around the station. If you called from the public telephone at Shin-Karuizawa Station, a wagon would be waiting to take you to the Murai house, a half hour's walk from Kita-Asama Station on foot. As Sensei had often used horse-drawn carriages in America before the war, he was sad to see the last of these working animals disappear from Aoguri in the early 1960s.

Horizontal and vertical streets, like the lines on a *go* board, ran through the village. Just north of center was Firefly Pond. Despite the name "pond," it was actually a man-made lake, planned by the people who founded Aoguri. There was boating in the summer, ice-skating in winter, and for the children it was a favorite place to play. The oldest summer cottages, built in the village's first days, were in the area around Firefly Pond.

Sensei bought land in one of the best locations in Aoguri, within walking distance of Firefly Pond. He built a small house in the middle of his seven-hundred-*tsubo* plot (twenty-three-hundred square meters, about three-fifths of an acre), intentionally leaving lots of empty space around it. From the start he planned to use this summer residence as a model, to experiment with architectural techniques.

What started out in 1956 as a cottage where he and his wife could spend the hottest summer days had been expanded and reformed six times by 1982, and was now five times its original size. The entranceway and fireplace were about all that was left of the original interior; the wet areas—the kitchen and baths—had been moved and rebuilt. The two wings now lined with single rooms for men and women had been added so that he and a group of designers would be able to stay on there when they were working intensively on a project.

The years just before the Tanasaka Light Railway stopped running, from 1961 to 1963, were especially busy for the Murai Office. Most of the material concerning major projects was kept at the cottage in Aoguri, which had become a sort of fort for Sensei, where he could concentrate on his work without having to negotiate with people outside. "We'll be going to the hills today," he'd announce at the noon break, and by evening he and his staff would be on their way.

They would all pile into the one car on the Tanasaka Light Railway, making their way slowly northward through the trees toward Aoguri. From spring to summer, there were always lights on in the houses; even in the autumn and winter months, when the village was mostly dormant, someone was usually around.

As the train rounded each sharp curve, Mt. Asama would appear first on the right side, then on the left, switching so many times the passengers lost all sense of direction.

"It was kind of lonely, chugging up the mountain through the snow, getting farther and farther away from everything—sort of like heading into the afterlife," Iguchi said. "But Sensei liked being trundled along that way. 'Feels good,' he always used to say."

Yet rebuilding the railway bridges that typhoons washed away got too expensive, and the number of passengers plummeted due to the increase in buses and private cars, until finally, in 1964, the service was discontinued. This was also the year the Shinkansen, the bullet train, started running. Murai was even sadder than he had been to see the last horse-drawn cart disappear from the village.

Even so, these had been the village's most prosperous years. In the seventies, the owners of the summer houses started to die off. Their children would inherit a cottage, then promptly stop using it. A deserted house is like a peach forgotten on a kitchen shelf: it soon goes bad and starts to decompose. With no one to tend them, trees and bushes get overgrown in a year. Yards become choked with weeds, and with no air flowing through, buildings soon smell moldy. Various creatures move in to nest—ants and bees leave dark lumps in the attic, while birds lay their eggs in the casings for rain shutters. Woodpeckers drill holes in the outside walls, and if leaky roofs aren't repaired, mushrooms and ferns will sprout through cracks in the floor. During the sixties, you almost never saw such signs of neglect. Everyone came to Aoguri as often as they could to air out their cottages and work in their gardens.

In the Summer House kitchen there was a yellowing map taped to one side of the big refrigerator, showing the Aoguri residents from twenty years before. I loved looking at it. The owners' names, typed into the blocks where their houses were, included several I recognized, of well-known writers, painters, and musicians. Helped by this old map, I imagined the village when it was still quite young, the roads running through it still new. The embankments made to serve as fences would have been firm, and no garden overgrown with weeds or strewn with wet leaves. With the forests properly managed, there would have been a clear view of Mt. Asama through the trees. If you wanted to see the whole mountain now, you had to go to Firefly Pond, or climb the hill just north of it.

But you could still see Mt. Asama in the autumn, after the leaves had fallen, covered with powdery snow. Sensei liked this wintry scene, when the whole village seemed to go back in time. As cold winds began to blow, he would stock up on firewood, stacking enough logs by the wall to last until spring. The pile of firewood at the Summer House was a neater arrangement than anywhere else in the village.

"I'd never seen snow like it," Iguchi said, his face red from drinking.

In 1962, Sensei and his staff had worked at the Summer House until December 30, then after returning to

Tokyo from New Year's Eve until January 3, had come back to the mountain on January 4.

The following afternoon, flurries began silently to fall, gradually growing into a blizzard by evening. As the snow accumulated, Iguchi, who was already manager by this time, continued to work along with Sensei and the rest of the staff, turning the oil stove embedded in the floor all the way up, and making sure the fire in the fireplace didn't go out. They kept at it for hours, too absorbed in their blueprints for anyone to suggest stopping for a drink until finally, sometime past eleven, Sensei had murmured, "That's about enough for today." The only sounds were of pencils moving across paper and wood crackling in the fireplace. The smell of elm with a hint of sweet cherrywood was soothing. The small window on the north side of the house was blocked by snow, as if a white curtain had been drawn across it.

By the fifth day, alarmed to see how little firewood was left, and running out of food as well, they decided to call for a horse-drawn wagon so that Iguchi and the younger staff members could do some shopping in the village. The horse's white breath turned to frost that stuck to its muzzle and nose. From on top of the wagon, the entire village looked blindingly white. Here and there they saw branches that had broken under the weight of the snow.

Moving north along the main street, the wagon slowed down as it approached the intersection just beyond the shops in front of the station, and then stopped. The snow absorbed all sound. Looking to the right, they saw that one of the oldest houses in the village had been half destroyed when a Himalayan cedar had fallen on it. The roof had collapsed, revealing a pile of sparkling snow on the desk in the study. The owner of the house, a novelist named Harue Nomiya, who died in 1984 at the age of ninety-eight, was fortunately out when it happened.

When she came back and saw the damage, Nomiya apparently was unfazed. "Dying of some illness, getting crushed under a tree—it's all the same," she said, and without wasting any time mourning the loss, called a carpenter. "I'm getting old," she told him, "I don't need so much space anymore." She asked him to write off the ruined section, reducing the house to half its former size. As long as there was space for a small sofa in front of the fireplace and a table for four, the living room would be big enough. She squeezed her single bed into a corner of her now much smaller study.

Whether you admired her decisiveness or wondered how she could be so cold-blooded, the decision did still leave an old lady and her maid enough room to live in, and made the repair work a lot simpler. Without even a blueprint, and not having much to do in midwinter anyway, the carpenter and his team finished the job in a week. That was more than twenty years before my first summer in Aoguri. Since then this novelist, who spent more than half the year in her tiny cottage, had written four more books there.

The village of Aoguri had its own residents' association. As one of the founding members, Harue Nomiya served as its head from the age of eighty until her death. Anyone wanting to buy land and build a house in the area was screened by them. People who didn't mind the inconvenience of traveling for an hour and a half from Karuizawa on the Tanasaka Light Railway tended to be in a few similar professions, so most of the residents were either academics, translators, novelists, painters, actors, or musicians, showing how the village had developed through a network of personal connections.

As all these occupations came with long or practically permanent vacations, the residents' association was naturally pretty active, since its secondary work during the summer was to keep the children busy. Lots of activities were planned for them: excursions, bird-watching, campfires, and sports tournaments with a local youth club. Late in the season, concerts and lectures were held at the assembly hall in the center of the village.

Although Sensei sometimes showed up at concerts, he always went straight back to his cottage, skipping the party afterward. "Why should I have to be sociable when I'm here to get away from the heat?" he used to say, but as he rarely went to architectural gatherings in Tokyo, either, the bit about the heat was just an excuse. As if to make up for this unfriendliness, Iguchi, who loved a get-together, went to all of them.

The 1960s, when the village was still new and full of life, were followed by an even more active decade. The 1980s cast a shadow over the village, as the houses, now growing musty with age, were passed on to the next generation. Some were sold, and because the residents' association had no say in sales to individuals, the village gradually turned into a gathering of strangers.

But the original villagers kept the Aoguri of the past stored away in their memories, occasionally taking it out to reminisce over. As if recovered from a junkyard, the Tanasaka Light Railway would start moving on its vanished track again, over bright mountain slopes and primitive bridges, creaking very, very slowly along.

3

On Sunday, August 1, the fourth day after we arrived at the Summer House, the village was sucked into Typhoon 10.

It was a super typhoon, with wind speeds over thirty meters a second—nearly seventy miles an hour. We'd closed all the shutters the night before. The wind began howling from early morning, the clouds racing overhead like high-speed images in a film, trees bending ominously. By the time our afternoon break was over, it had grown in strength. Too restless to stay in the library, I went down to the dining room, where the others were all gathered. Sensei had come out of the director's office, grumbling, "The wind's so loud I can't even read, and all they talk about on the radio is millibars." Leaning down, he switched on the stereo by the fireplace and put Beethoven's Eighth Symphony on the turntable. Uchida made coffee, while Yukiko sliced up some leftover apple pie. People sat eating at the dining table, or lounged on the sofa by the fireplace drinking coffee as they leafed through architectural magazines. The music was almost drowned out by the storm.

The whole house creaked, the posts making a nasty, grating sound. Rain lashed at the walls like the spray from fire hoses. Katsura leaves slapped against the shutters. As the lights flickered, we heard a popping outside, like small explosions, and the electricity went off. The stereo was silent, and with the rain shutters closed the dining room was pitch-dark.

"A tree must've fallen on the wires," Uchida said calmly as he quickly fetched candles and holders. He set up five on the dining table and two on the mantel above the fireplace. He seemed used to this.

He then took a flashlight down to the boiler room, where we heard him turn on the generator. When the lights came back on in the dining room they seemed to waver, though I may have imagined this. Someone moved the needle, which had stopped in the middle of the third movement, back to the beginning.

On his return, Uchida told me we'd be fixing dinner together. On weekends the cooking was left to whoever felt like it, but it was usually Uchida, with either Yukiko or me helping out. As my instructor for the work we did, he also taught me how to cook.

I arranged onions and unpeeled potatoes and carrots, cut into large pieces, around a marinated leg of lamb, and put it in the oven. I then made some miso soup with tofu and watercress (which Sensei called horsecress). This was fairly simple, even for me. To Uchida, the secret to cooking a meal was doing everything in the right order. He'd start by washing the rice, then prepare the meat and vegetables, lining them up on the hot plate while he gathered the vegetable leavings and put them in a bucket for compost, before making the soup stock, stirring in the miso, and warming up the plates. He never hesitated; his hands were never idle. And because he washed the pots, bowls, and cutting boards in spare moments while the food was cooking, there was always plenty of room in the sink. "When you don't have a lot of time, it's best to either grill or steam things," he said, and sure enough, his meat and vegetables were done just before the rice was ready.

By the time we sat down to eat, the wind had died down, and it was quiet again. The Summer House was like a boat in the middle of a dark sea with the power still out. Someone suggested we dine by candlelight, so the lights were dimmed again. Perhaps because the worst of the typhoon was over, or simply because night had fallen, we could tell the temperature had dropped.

"A good fire sucks up all the moisture," Sensei said as he laid things in the fireplace. "On a day like today it's good to have a fire, even if it is summer."

He put some cedar chips on top of balls of newspaper, then formed elm logs into a square frame on top of the kindling. Lit by a match, with a whoosh the paper caught quickly, consuming the cedar chips almost immediately. The flames from the kindling lapped at the elm logs. I breathed in the smell. When the fire was burning well, he shifted the position of certain logs to show me how this affected it.

"Logs won't burn when they're too close together. Too far apart is no good either. When there's just a little space in between... See? Then they'll really burn."

I watched silently. Just as he'd said, the flames leapt up, dancing in the narrow space between two logs. The moment you separated them more, the red, glowing wood turned black and started giving off white smoke. Nudge them closer together and they caught again. Fire seemed fragile, coming to life only in alliance. I noticed that the wind and rain had stopped, and all I could hear was the crackling in the fireplace.

There were comfortable sofas and chairs in front of it. A wool carpet the color of dead leaves trapped any sparks that might fly out. After dinner, people who wanted to drink a bit more or listen to music stayed awhile, like cats or dogs finding a favorite place to curl up in.

A whiskey glass in his hand, Iguchi was sitting on the sofa in front of the fire. If Sensei hadn't been there, he would have been at the center of things, as he usually was on weekends, but tonight he seemed subdued. Perhaps drawn by their boss, now staring into the fire, Kawarazaki and Kobayashi, the two office veterans, sat quietly nearby.

Kawarazaki had a gentle-looking, roundish face, and although his hairline was receding, he still had a full head of soft, wavy hair. His horn-rimmed glasses suited him. Though he looked like a drinker, he never had more than one glass of wine, and went to bed early. Since I couldn't drink at all, I was glad there was someone like that on the staff. The oldest member of the team besides Iguchi, he seldom raised his voice, but wasn't the type to give much guidance to younger employees.

Kobayashi, the other veteran, was very pale, with a long, thin face and sharp features. Said to be one-eighth Russian on his mother's side, he was taciturn, and held his liquor so well that you could never tell whether he was drunk or not. He seemed slightly embarrassed by both his appearance and his height; seen in profile working at his desk, he always looked withdrawn. He was meticulous. His knack for catching even the smallest errors meant that problems with blueprints from the Murai Office rarely arose on construction sites. If you asked him about data or projects from the past, he would immediately tell you what you wanted to know. You felt there probably wasn't a speck of dust clouding his brain.

Despite the differences in appearance and personality, in the way they kept their attention quietly focused on Sensei these two were almost like twins.

Uchida, always calm and levelheaded, was maybe closer to Sensei. His attitude seemed more like Sensei's niece, Mariko, who worked part-time at the Summer House.

As I was in charge of buying food, Uchida had entrusted me with a list of wines he'd compiled after a good deal of careful research; his store of knowledge about food and drink amused Sensei. But Uchida was an avid reader, and would often retreat to his room right after dinner, taking a half-empty bottle of wine with him. Although he would stick around to talk for a while if he was in the mood, he rarely drank with Kawarazaki and Kobayashi, and didn't seem to get along with Iguchi either. The night after the typhoon, he headed straight for a bath when we'd finished eating.

Iguchi was the only one who got talkative in the evenings, and night after night Yukiko and I were his audience. Thanks to these after-dinner sessions, I learned a lot that summer about the history of Aoguri and the house we were living in.

"Harue Nomiya had a lover, didn't she?"

It was past eleven. The fire had died down to embers, glowing red. A short time before, Kawarazaki and Kobayashi had been tending the fire while Yukiko and Ms. Sasai drank tea at the dining table, but they had all gone to take a bath. Sensei had retreated upstairs quite a while ago. Perhaps because the typhoon had jogged his memory, Iguchi started talking about that snowstorm twenty years earlier. How, weighted down with snow, the Himalayan cedar had crashed through the roof of Harue Nomiya's cottage. Iguchi and I, along with Sensei's niece, were the only ones left in front of the fire. It was Mariko who mentioned Harue's lover. Iguchi looked a bit startled.

"She was already past seventy back then," he said. "Not that age rules it out."

"The house was wrecked just after her lover died," said Mariko. "That's probably why she thought she could make do with a much smaller place."

"That so?" Iguchi said with a vague smile, adding ice to his glass as he slowly poured himself more whiskey. Having nothing to add to this conversation, I watched the embers.

Mariko had gone to a music college, but didn't get a job after she graduated, and now lived with her parents in Yoyogi. Her father, Sensei's younger brother, managed a confectionery shop in Hongō that had been in the family for generations, and which Sensei, as the oldest son, should have taken over. Her mother gave private lessons on the tea ceremony at home.

Mariko was lively, and laughed a lot, showing a row of neat white teeth. Her long hair matched her long arms and legs. Apparently not worried about getting scratched by branches or bitten by insects outside, she usually wore sleeveless blouses with short skirts, reluctantly putting on a sweater and colorful knitted boots when the temperature dropped after sundown.

It was only while we were at the Summer House that she took over from Ms. Yoshinaga, who was in charge of accounting but stayed behind in Tokyo. As Mariko's family had an old cottage in Kyū-Karuizawa, she spent the weekends there, driving back and forth in her own car. Though she didn't seem to have anything else in common with Ms. Yoshinaga, they worked the same way—both fast, thorough, and accurate. What surprised me was that she used an abacus. "It's much faster than a calculator, and you never go wrong with one," she said as she flicked the little beads up and down with her long fingers. Her parents had had her learn it as a child, and when we did the shopping, she'd use the same technique to work out the total amount. According to Iguchi, "Mariko's an only child, so eventually her husband'll be adopted into the family, and she'll run the shop."

Interestingly, she gave a more serious impression when she was working, with her hair tied back and her head bowed over a notebook in which she kept the daily report she got from Ms. Yoshinaga by telephone. Fax machines cost about a million yen back then, so we didn't have one up there.

She had only started working at the Summer House the year before, and addressed her uncle as "Sensei," preferring not to let on that they were related. I figured she must be about three years older than me, since she'd been in England for further piano study after graduating from university. Among the five women on the office staff, the only one Mariko's age was Yukiko Nakao, which probably accounted for their always sitting together at meals, and for the unforced laughter we occasionally heard from Yukiko, who was the quieter of the two.

Mariko worked in the room next to the kitchen, where we did our ironing. Like the kitchen, it had a large open window facing east, making it light and airy, and a big table we used as an ironing board. There were telephones in the director's office, and on Iguchi's desk, but since Sensei disconnected his while he was working, Mariko answered all the calls. When staff members wanted to use the phone, they went to the ironing room.

Once she was done, Mariko put on the headphones of her new Walkman and listened to Al Jarreau or Michael Franks while she checked over what was stored in the refrigerator and the pantry. The sound of her Renault 5 would make me look up from a blueprint to watch the little black car pass beyond the katsura and its green leaves.

4

At first, I was like an ill-fitting rain shutter, but as I got used to things, I gradually settled into the groove and started working more smoothly.

The sound of Sensei leaving on his morning walk served as my alarm clock. I then went downstairs to get breakfast ready. I carefully wiped off the big table in the center of the dining room, the heart of the Summer House, and laid it with a new cloth, then put water on to boil, set out cups, saucers, and plates along with knives and forks, made some salad, filled the milk pitcher, got eggs, bacon, and sausages out of the refrigerator and lined them up on the counter, at which point Mariko would come down to help. We made hash browns, grilled the bacon and sausages, and fried the eggs on the four burners; for toast, there were two large toasters. While we were cooking, Sensei would return from his walk, and before long the rest of the staff drifted in. The food was laid out, but the rest was self-service, with each person coming to fetch his or her breakfast from the counter and pour a glass of orange or apple juice, and coffee or tea. I liked the mixture of breakfast smells when we were ready to start, forming a sort of central pillar with the nine of us sitting around it.

Breakfast officially began with Sensei's "Good morning," and a smattering of responses from around the table. His deep voice removed any last traces of sleepiness. The meal was much quieter than dinner. The big salad bowl, the jam, butter, salt, pepper, and the pitcher of milk were passed from hand to hand across the table in silence.

"There was a robbery at the Yamaguchi place the night before last," Sensei announced, making everyone look up.

"You mean Gen'ichiro Yamaguchi?" asked Uchida.

"That's right."

"What did they take?"

"Well, the canvas he'd almost finished was left untouched, but an envelope was missing from a kitchen drawer, with a hundred thousand yen in it."

"Money instead of the painting... Can't have known whose house it was."

"But if someone from around here stole a painting, who would they sell it to?"

"That's a point," said Uchida, eating a slice of tomato.

"We can't have any break-ins here. They'd aim for the bath or the laundry room, because they're deserted from late at night till early morning. It seems these guys got in through a window in the laundry room."

Gen'ichiro Yamaguchi had been a classmate of Sensei's at art school, one of his few close friends. Sensei had designed his atelier, his house, and his summer cottage. He was about the only person he saw socially in Aoguri. Iguchi was soon discussing the competition for the National Library of Modern Literature with the two older men. This was all they talked about, every morning. It was the first competition the Murai Office had been invited to enter in a decade. Our main target this summer was to come up with a basic plan; we would then sort out the details in time to submit the design in late November.

Kawarazaki, with his shock of wavy hair and horn-rimmed glasses, was nodding now and then as he listened. He looked somehow more defenseless at mealtimes, like a moon bear. Kobayashi, dipping his toast into the broken yolk of his egg, looked as pale and solemn as when he was working on a drawing.

Both men had been with the Murai Office for over twenty years. Though not all architects break away from where they've trained at the same sort of time, most are independent by their mid-thirties at the latest. Quite a few architects who had started out with Murai now had their own offices. These two, however, were already in their fifties. They had missed their chance to leave, or possibly had never intended to. As long as they were with Murai, they would have plenty of work, and since Iguchi was particular about the clients we took on, the work would be of a high quality. If the Murai Office were to win this competition, they would be involved in a major public structure. Also, the terms we worked under were a lot better than at other architectural offices ("The pay's lousy everywhere except here," Uchida was always saying), so if they didn't have much personal ambition it was natural to want to stay where they were.

According to Uchida, Kawarazaki was "more a cross-section than a floor-plan man." By this he meant that when designing a building, Kawarazaki thought first of its vertical structure. For him, the position of a staircase leading from the first to the second story had to grow out of necessity, because a flight of stairs could only be beautiful if it was where it absolutely had to be.

"Say you're drawing a plan for a large summer house," Uchida said, "and you want to put fireplaces in the living room, the bedroom, and the dining room." Having three separate chimneys would drive the cost up, increase the possibility of a leaky roof by three, and ruin the appearance of the house from the outside. That meant you'd need a plan where all three fireplaces would feed into a single chimney. One way to solve the problem of three rooms of different sizes, each with a different purpose, all with fireplaces, was to connect two rooms, either vertically—one above the other—or horizontally—back-to-back, with a wall between. But if you concentrated too much on that one chimney for the three fireplaces, you could knock the whole floor plan off-balance.

"In Kawarazaki's mind, the chimney's always there, right in the middle," Uchida said ruefully. "It comes before anything else, and he arranges the rest of the house around it. But you don't want to fuss so much about something like that. The chimney's something people should only notice after they've been living in the place awhile."

Kawarazaki's plans for a house, always starting with a cross section or cutaway, tended to follow the same pattern, often requiring later corrections.

For Kobayashi, on the other hand, a preoccupying factor was circulation. How would people move, make their way around the building? Were there any unnecessary or unnatural interruptions along the way? Sensei's designs tended to allow people to move easily through a house along a circular route: from the entranceway to the living room, then on to the dining room, the kitchen, and out through the back to return to the entrance. Kobayashi, influenced by the emphasis he placed on this, was about twice as concerned with the horizontal—the floor plan—as anyone else.

I remember him pointing at a plan for a seaside restaurant in a magazine. "There will be a bottleneck here," he said. "There's plenty of space for thirty customers, but if people get held up in this one spot it'll disrupt the service, and the place will feel cramped. Which might be hard on the stomach, spoil the food."

Between these two contrasting veterans, Uchida, though still in his thirties, was admired for his sense of detail. Methods for hiding indirect light sources, fittings for sliding doors, designs for tables, chairs, cabinets, or beds, bricklaying for fireplaces, combining tile with cypress in baths—his finishing touches, both visual and tactile, were sensitive and original. For anything to do with furniture, he was the one Sensei depended on.

As a child he had traveled in Europe several times with his father, who ran an import business with suppliers in Denmark and Sweden, and having also spent a year at high school in Paris, in some ways he had a head start. He originally wanted to be a painter, and you could see this in his drawings for furniture designs, any of which could have been framed and hung on the wall.

Anyone could see that Sensei relied heavily on the two people Uchida called "the cross-section and floor-plan men." Iguchi not only wanted their support now, but was getting ahead of himself, dreaming of a future for the Murai Office in which they would be the central figures. Believing that the business shouldn't come to an end with Murai himself, Iguchi was hoping to transform it into an institution that would keep the founder's ideals alive through changes in leadership, and he was counting on Kawarazaki and Kobayashi to be the first successors. Yet whether they felt pressured by Iguchi's enthusiasm, or just found the responsibility too heavy, neither seemed particularly keen for this plan to be realized.

What Iguchi had in mind was Taliesin, the studio Frank Lloyd Wright had created, which included vocational training for apprentices.

Though over twenty years had passed since Wright's death in 1959, his style and spirit were still very much alive at Taliesin. Iguchi believed that by learning from its aims and methods, the Murai Office could continue to operate for several decades more. Sensei had gone to America in 1939 to study under Wright, and if the war hadn't broken out, he might have stayed on at Taliesin. When he started bringing his staff to the Summer House, he may have had Taliesin in mind. Iguchi, at least, was sure of it.

At a point in his late thirties, when he felt he'd reached an impasse both in his work and his private life, Frank Lloyd Wright fell in love with the wife of one of his clients. In 1909, at the age of forty-two, he left his wife and children in Chicago and traveled to Europe with his lover, returning two years later. But social hostility in Chicago made them move to Wisconsin, Wright's birthplace, where he decided to build a new home and worksite on a hill he called Taliesin. Proud of his Welsh roots, Wright used the Welsh word, meaning "Shining Brow."

On August 15, 1914, soon after the outbreak of World War I, Wright, who was then away on business, got some shocking news. A handyman at Taliesin had set fire to the place, then taken a hatchet and killed Wright's lover, her son and daughter, a staff member, a carpenter, and a foreman. The man responsible was found barely alive, hiding inside a boiler after swallowing hydrochloric acid, and he died two days later. His motive for the killing remains unknown.

The harsh, staccato cry of the gray nightjar Wright heard the night he returned to Taliesin haunted him, plunging him into despair whenever he heard it again for the rest of his long life.

What saved Wright from the deep depression that followed was the building of the Imperial Hotel in Tokyo. Consultation on the project had begun in Japan in 1913, a year before the murders, and from 1918 he spent four years there overseeing the site. During that period, however, construction costs rose to six times the original estimate. When friction between Wright and the hotel concerning his frequent changes to the original plan reached a breaking point, the general manager stepped down, and Wright, suffering from a chronic stomach ailment, left Japan before the hotel was completed.

On September 1, 1923, nine years after the tragedy at Taliesin, the Imperial Hotel was finally finished under the direction of a Japanese architect who had studied with Wright. That morning, at 11:58, just as the completion ceremony was about to begin, the city was rocked by the Great Kanto Earthquake. Hundreds of thousands died or were missing, and buildings that hadn't collapsed fell victim to the fires that broke out all over Tokyo. When communication with the outside world was finally restored, Wright received a telegram: HOTEL STANDS UNDAMAGED STOP A MONUMENT TO YOUR GENIUS STOP.

The survival of his work at a time when Wright was again discouraged turned his reputation around. While Taliesin was buried in snow, a commission came from

Arizona to design a hotel at a deluxe resort. He drove there in the convertible he'd just bought. The great expanse of desert and the shapes of the mountains were a new stimulus. But again his luck didn't hold. In 1929, the onset of the Great Depression wiped out his client's funds, and the project remained an illusion.

Three years later, at the Modern Architecture: International Exhibition held at the Museum of Modern Art in New York, younger men like Le Corbusier, Gropius, and Mies van der Rohe were hailed as the architects of the future; Wright, at sixty-five, was regarded as a man of the past, partly because he'd spent so much time abroad.

His interest had already shifted from architecture itself to educating the next generation. He started a fellowship through which he gathered apprentices at Taliesin, collected tuition from them, and taught them architecture via a form of communal living. Cows and chickens were kept on the grounds, and crops were grown so that they could be self-sufficient. He had the trainees do everything themselves, from buying and sawing the lumber to constructing whatever they designed. In the small theater at Taliesin, classical music concerts were held, movies were shown, and guests were invited to give lectures. This system, it seemed, would allow Wright to spend his last years as an educator while covering the costs needed to keep Taliesin going.

But in 1937, at the age of seventy, Wright once again startled the architectural world with the Kaufmann House, built across a mountain stream in the forest at

Bear Run, Pennsylvania. A natural waterfall flows below a white, oblong balcony, which Wright liked to say resembled "a tray held by a waiter." The house, also called Fallingwater, is clearly one of his masterpieces. Wright, who saw nature as the architect's mentor, made it work for him as an actor on the stage he built, and in doing so, with this one project, he claimed victory over those who had tried to bury him in the past.

The following year, the Museum of Modern Art in New York reversed its position, holding a special exhibition devoted to Fallingwater. Architectural magazines came out with special issues on it, Wright appeared on the cover of *Time*, and requests for lectures never stopped coming. In 1940 another exhibition was held at the Museum of Modern Art. Entitled "Two Great Americans," it featured Wright and his contemporary D. W. Griffith, the director of films such as *Intolerance* and *Orphans of the Storm*.

The price Wright paid for all this attention was a severe case of pneumonia, probably brought on by exhaustion. Advised by his doctor to leave the bitter cold of Wisconsin winters behind, Wright went to Arizona, and this return to the desert gave him the idea of building a second Taliesin. This was when he started yearly treks to Taliesin West in Arizona for the Christmas season, and back to the original Taliesin in Wisconsin when spring came.

A large red truck loaded with food, followed by a string of station wagons and convertibles, formed a caravan that made these three-thousand-kilometer journeys across the country. Murai Sensei came to Taliesin just as these trips began.

Murai experienced the Great Kanto Earthquake as a third-year student in middle school. Although the confectionery shop his family ran escaped with minor damage, he never forgot the destruction he saw in Tokyo. The following year, his parents took him to dinner at the Imperial Hotel. I once read a short essay in which he said the occasion was the first time he became conscious of wanting to be an architect. While he was working in his professor's design office after graduating from art school, he went to Kobe to meet a Japanese architect who had studied under Wright and asked him for a letter of introduction, then wrote directly to Wright, asking to be taken on as an apprentice. This was in 1939. Several months later, he got a picture postcard with the simple message "You are accepted." Slipping the postcard between the pages of his copy of Wright's *An Organic Architecture*, which he packed in his suitcase, he boarded a ship for America from Yokohama.

In December 1941, Japan attacked Pearl Harbor. Encouraged by Wright to stay, Murai joined the caravan to Arizona late that year. The war didn't change the atmosphere at Taliesin much at all. Some apprentices became conscientious objectors and were jailed, but there was no flag-waving either at Taliesin or by Wright himself. In a natural environment remote from politics, studying architecture under a man who tended toward the "art for art's sake" school of thought, the idea of going off to fight an unknown enemy made little sense.

As a commune, Taliesin was inevitably seen as a breeding ground for draft dodgers. The tragedy in Wright's past—an incident unlikely to happen to any normal, law-abiding citizen—only fueled suspicion, attracting the FBI's attention.

With spring approaching, rumors reached Taliesin that internment camps for Japanese Americans were being built in California and Arizona. After talking to Wright, Murai returned to Wisconsin with the spring caravan, and in late April said goodbye to his colleagues and traveled on to New York by himself. There, along with Japanese diplomats, students, and businessmen in a reciprocal exchange, he boarded a vessel headed back to Japan.

The Murai Office of Architectural Design opened in a single room in a building in the Kōjimachi district of Tokyo, three months after his return. Murai and Iguchi, a younger friend from art school, were the entire staff; there was no one else to celebrate the beginning of their new venture.

Sensei didn't seem to encourage or resist Iguchi's plan to turn the office into another Taliesin, choosing instead simply to stand by and watch. He must have known that the competition for the new National Library of Modern Literature would affect their future, but at this point things carried on as calmly as they usually did at the Summer House every year.

The actual work of designing a building was much quieter than I'd thought. Once you had decided on a plan, you did the calculations, drew lines and more lines, redrew those lines, had them checked, reexamined your plan, drew more lines, then repeated the whole process. As Iguchi was the only chatty person in the group, when he was gone there wasn't much conversation, even during the afternoon tea break. I was still pretty nervous, so Uchida's monologues, switching from one topic to the next, with Yukiko laughing sometimes, were a relief. When Mariko joined us, she made our meals a lot livelier.

The workshop in Tokyo, where talks with clients were held in a separate room, was even quieter. Once a basic plan was finished, discussions with the client became a vital part of the job. Sensei often emphasized this point. "Even the smallest problem with your basic plan—something the client isn't comfortable with—is bound to flare up again when you get to a later stage," he said. "So it's best to keep hashing it out till they're completely satisfied." Although not expansive, his way of using words had a more direct effect than some fluent exposé.

"A house is a success when the client remembers how you explained the design, and talks about the new house to a friend in the same way. The architect's language now belongs to someone living in the place he designed. That's a sure sign you've got it right."

The next step is to make a model, necessary because it's hard to imagine a three-dimensional structure just from a blueprint. But explaining the model, with the blueprint spread out in front of you, isn't easy either. Clients will sometimes quote your comments back at you as evidence to support their case if a problem crops up. So you don't just say anything that pops into your head.

Uchida was amazingly good at making drawings and models, and at getting them across. He would hold the model in both hands, shifting it around to show it from various angles, sometimes taking the roof off to allow a client to peer inside. He would go back and forth between the model and the drawing, throwing in a comment now and then, always in language that was easy to understand. When he was finished, the client would have a clear idea of the whole package: the scene from each window, whether winter light would reach as far as the back of a room. This wasn't something he had learned from Sensei, but if you watched them carefully, you could see that they clearly had something in common. Neither used abstract or theoretical language. Both aimed to be as specific as possible, never trying to mystify clients with technical terms.

Let's say that your final design, model, and presentation have all been up to scratch. Even then, the chances are that things won't proceed smoothly. The client may suddenly come up with a new demand, something completely unrelated to everything you've gone over with him again and again.

This sometimes won't fit in with the plan at all, and when it threatens to delay the schedule and drive construction costs way up, you may have to rethink the whole scheme, looking at each element in turn. In cases like this, it's best to have the client explain specifically what he wants, in as much detail as possible. The architect mustn't interrupt to promote his own point of view. Trying to reason with the client is like telling him you think he's ignorant. The most important thing to do is listen. It takes patience to clear the way so that they can eventually see the contradictions in their proposals. It can become a battle of wills.

What I really admired about Yukiko was her ability to win these battles. While never seeming assertive, she invariably got her clients to accept her plan in the end. Most of them were prejudiced against a female architect in her mid-twenties, but one good conversation with her was all it took to put them at ease. Once, I heard her talking on the phone to a particularly difficult client. She didn't sound at all as if she were trying to convince him of anything. In a quiet, clear voice, she cheerfully responded to whatever was said, leading him to feel as if he'd found a solution of his own.

There's something mysterious about the human voice. It reveals a person's hidden feelings and intentions. Everything about Yukiko seemed to be in her voice, though no one knew exactly what that "everything" was. She was easy to listen to, the content never overcomplicated, yet there was still something else to it. That was what drew people to her. I began to wonder if it might not be the sound rather than words or meaning that moved people.

Everyone trusted Yukiko, from Sensei on down. You could hear the steadiness and competence in her voice. Without actually looking at her, I found myself listening carefully whenever I heard her speak.

5

By nine in the morning everyone would be sitting at their desks, sharpening their pencils. Most of us used Staedtler Lumograph 2H, though some preferred H or 3H. This was long before the introduction of CAD software, which allowed designers to draw on a computer, but as most architects had already switched to mechanical drafting pencils, it was unusual to still be using ordinary lead ones.

New employees were given an Opinel folding knife with their name carved on it to sharpen them with. There was a stock of Lyra holders for when the pencils got too short, and when the lead had worn down to under two centimeters, they were tossed into a huge glass jar of the kind they make plum wine in. When the jar was full, it would be added to others lined up along the shelf by the Summer House fireplace—seven of them already.

Both in the Kita-Aoyama office and Aoguri the day began with the sound of pencils being sharpened. It wasn't a bad way to start. When your brain is still half asleep, the smell of wood being whittled wakes you up almost like the smell of fresh-brewed coffee. That *whisk, whisk, whisk* of metal scraping against wood turns a switch on in your ears as well. There was only one of those manual sharpeners with a handle at the Summer House, in the ironing room that served as Mariko's workplace.

On my first day at the office, Sensei had me make a full-scale drawing of the handrail for a staircase. I got it checked when I'd finished it, and when I was given the okay, proceeded to make a blueprint, which I completed by early evening. With nothing else to do, I took out my knife and started sharpening my pencils, which by then were blunt. Uchida looked up from the desk next to mine.

"Uh, I see you're sharpening your pencils."

"That's right," I replied, stopping as I turned toward him.

"Guess I forgot to tell you. We only do it in the morning and afternoon, never in the evening. And I see yours don't have your name on them yet. Label them, like this," he added, showing me his blue Staedtler. He had scraped the paint off the wood near the end, where he'd written UCHIDA in roman letters.

"They say if you cut your fingernails at night you won't make it to your parents' deathbeds," he said, grinning. "You can't ignore superstitions." Then, to end the chitchat, he turned back to his work. Later I asked Yukiko about it and was told that sharpening no more than ten pencils, morning and afternoon, was a way of checking whether you were doing the work properly. Over this amount meant that you were either pressing too hard, being careless, or drawing too fast—that you'd stopped thinking, in other words. "Sometimes you lose your concentration while drawing so many lines," she said. "That leaves room for mistakes to creep in, so the pencils matter."

Kobayashi, the floor-plan man, missed an error in his first drawing of the incline leading down to the nave in the Asakayama Church, on which construction had begun two years earlier, and developed an ulcer during the week he spent redrawing the blueprint. When Kawarazaki casually said, "Guess your pencil wasn't sharp enough," he refused to speak to him for quite a while afterward. It was this sort of mistake that gave rise to our unwritten rule: take a break now and then while you're working on your plan.

Right after I joined the staff, it was officially decided that the Murai Office would enter the competition for the National Library of Modern Literature. It was Iguchi who made the announcement. Until then, everyone had been wondering why, for instance, one guy who'd been planning to leave in the spring had been asked to stay on for another six months, and why I had been taken on as a provisional employee. Learning that these decisions had been made with the competition in mind caused quite a stir in a normally quiet office.

Opposed on principle to competitions as a way of selecting an architect, Sensei had stopped participating in them. Although they appear to be fair, they are often simply camouflage, staged after the winner has already been chosen. The same is true of more limited contests; even with only a few participants, generally someone's way has already been paved. Where public buildings are concerned, the selection committee may not be fairly balanced, turning the competition into an empty ceremony. Sensei only accepted such commissions in exceptional cases, where he was the only architect from the start.

For this new library, the minister of education had apparently contacted Sensei informally, strongly urging him to get involved. The minister was not a career politician; in fact, he was the philosopher Michio Kajiki, whom Sensei had met on the return voyage from America after studying under Frank Lloyd Wright. Since Kajiki lived in Minami-Aoyama, they sometimes bumped into each other in the supermarket or at concerts; although not close, they had been on friendly terms for a long time.

Something Uchida told me made our reason for entering this competition clearer. Back in 1970, when the whole country was caught up in Osaka Expo '70 fever, Sensei was up north in Hokkaido, working on a detailed design for the new campus of a public university there. On the spacious grounds, the building he put the most effort into was the library. Aiming for something that would lure the students into the building during the bitterly cold winters, he designed a large area with a round, open fireplace in the center, and a hearth you stepped down into after taking off your shoes, so that students could read there, sitting or lying down in warm surroundings. Aside from the tatami children's corners you sometimes see in public libraries, this homelike sort of reading room was very unusual.

When the library was finished, the university administration made an arrangement with its Department of Agriculture to provide the library with logs from a woodland where forestry students were trained. Early every morning the fire was lit by the librarian, and kept going by any students available to throw on some wood. The result was a dramatic increase in the number of people using the place during the winter months. Indeed, the growing enrollment in Hokkaido University's Department of Literature, at a time when that subject was becoming less popular among university students, was attributed to the fireplace in the library. "Why not? No other school has that sort of thing," Sensei once said, looking rather pleased with himself.

He himself was an avid reader. Having designed many houses with private libraries—not just for scholars, but for clients who loved books as much as he did—he was interested in working on another large-scale facility. Unlike the National Diet Library, the Library of Modern Literature would allow people into the stacks, and it would have large reading rooms in addition to a restaurant, a day care facility, and an auditorium that would also serve as a film center. The library itself was to be a learning center where anyone would feel welcome, rather than primarily an archive for storing research materials like the Diet Library.

Furthermore, it was to house only books that were published after World War II—a guiding principle that provoked controversy among both publishers and politicians. But the advisory council, in response to a Ministry of Education inquiry, made it clear that it intended the library to be a public institution with a very different role. To put it simply, the place didn't need a definitive collection or oppressively official-looking architecture. If problems arose, the users—the public—could discuss them freely and suggest their own solutions. The function of the library, in other words, might change with the times. It wasn't hard to imagine the looks of dismay, or delight, this approach produced in different quarters.

After Kajiki had contacted him about the project, Sensei had apparently discussed it with him over a meal at that Italian restaurant near the office—the Ristorante Hana, where we later held my welcome party—without telling even Iguchi.

I couldn't see why Uchida knew all about this while Iguchi didn't. Anyway, his view was that Sensei's individualism made him a likely bet in what would only be a limited competition. But then, late in June, about a month before we went to the Summer House, we found out that the Kei'ichi Funayama Office had also entered the competition. Funayama had designed one large public building after another, and with him in the running we could no longer assume that our boss would be chosen as a matter of course. We had to treat it as a real competition. The tension clearly showed in Iguchi's face.

6

After I'd done some shopping for groceries in Kyū-Karuizawa, Uchida, who normally would have been reading in his room, asked me to have coffee with him in the garden. It was just three o'clock, time for our afternoon break. Sensei insisted that everyone take an hour's rest then.

"What made you pick the Murai Office anyway?" Uchida asked casually. Now that I thought of it, we had never talked about my reasons for joining.

Images of buildings Sensei had designed rose in my mind, one after another. The Hokkaido Folklore Museum, the Cloth Institute in Okinawa, the Ariyoshi House in Kumamoto, the Gen'ichiro Yamaguchi House in Yokohama... so many private homes, I couldn't remember them all. The last one I thought of was the Asukayama Church in Kita Ward, completed in 1980.

As it happened, this was the first church he had designed. After the blueprints appeared in an architectural magazine, I pored over them often enough to see them even now, page by page. By putting the floor plan, the cross section, and the elevation view together, I could re-create a good three-dimensional picture of it in my head. Since the church was in Tokyo, I'd thought I could go there anytime, but partly because it was in a part of the city I wasn't familiar with, I didn't actually get to see it until six months after it was finished. The afternoon I spent examining it turned the vague feelings I'd had until then into a definite desire to work under his guidance. If not for what I saw that day, I might still be undecided, without any plan ahead.

I visited the Asukayama Church on a bright, crisp autumn day, when a dry wind was blowing through the city.

The church, a combination of concrete and wood, was on a gentle slope in a quiet residential neighborhood beyond a shopping district. It was as fine as any of Sensei's recent works. Although not a showy building, it drew the viewer's attention. The façade made room for a porte cochere, with a semicircular area in front of it where some mountain cherry trees stood.

Being on a slope, the entrance led into the upper area. From there you walked down into the nave. Seen from the front, the building looked as if it were all on one floor, shaped like a big, gray cat curled up for a nap—quite unlike those Gothic churches that tower over the landscape like huge gravestones.

The curve of the driveway drew people into the church grounds as naturally as water. That day I watched an old man with his Shiba dog stroll up the drive and pass by the entrance, stepping on the shadows of the cherry trees as he left on the other side.

Although the exterior was architectural concrete, you could see through the polished glass door how much wood was used inside. Pushing the door open, you went in to see a larch-wood ceiling and an oak floor, with the grain leading toward the main area. The natural flooring created a sort of quiet tension with the white plaster walls, which seemed to purify the air as it passed over the wood. You walked through the vestibule to another door, beyond which an incline led down to the altar. With no sense of barriers, the line leading from the driveway to the entrance and on inside was as smooth as a cat's belly. As with all Sensei's buildings, this one had a silently inviting sort of atmosphere.

The white walls in the vestibule curved gently on both sides, to mirror the shape of the driveway. There were open spaces for people to gather here on the left and right, with cloth-covered sofas encircling a low, round table. People would naturally congregate in this area before and after the service.

My sneakers made a light, dry sound as I moved across the polished floor. Suppressing a desire to sit down on a sofa, I headed toward the back. I had written to the minister, telling him that I was an architectural student. When I knocked softly on his door it immediately opened to show a gaunt, graying figure, looking somewhat surprised through plastic-framed glasses. After I introduced myself, he smiled. "Yes, I read your letter," he said. "You're welcome to look at whatever you like." With permission to begin my survey, I took my measuring tape and notebook out of my knapsack.

Just six months before, this church didn't even exist. Instead there had been a large old house, long left vacant, surrounded by a dense bamboo grove. After receiving the land, the church had commissioned the Murai Office through an intermediary. An article in an architectural magazine described how, after the old house had been torn down and the deep-rooted bamboo removed, construction on the church had taken nearly a year.

Feeling the eyes of the minister on me, I started sketching the details around the inner door in the tentative way of a doctor poking around a patient's stomach. The door, made of cherrywood, was slightly redder than the oak floor. The curved handle was easy to grasp; the teak wood smooth to the touch. After holding it several times as if shaking hands, I drew it in my notebook. In under two years I had filled seventeen of these things with data from more than fifty different buildings. Although I sometimes wondered what the point of this was, I probably kept at it because no one had told me to.

I spent a long time surveying and sketching the interior. There were so many details typical of Shunsuke Murai I hadn't noticed at first, and once I'd found one, I kept seeing them everywhere. I was especially struck by the beauty of the slope leading down to the altar. I had no idea at the time that this was the part Kobayashi had had to do again.

There were horizontal rows of chairs on either side of the slope, with a shallow step between each row. There might have been a step at the end of each row as well, where the floor met the aisle; an elderly person on shaky legs or someone with poor eyesight might have stumbled there when they walked out. Yet looking closely, I saw that the end also sloped down to join the aisle, as smooth as water flowing down into a hollow.

Squatting down, I ran my fingers over the curved wood—the same oak as the floor. It felt like the slight bulge on the soundboard of a violin. If the horizontal surfaces on which the chairs were placed and the angle of the slope had been identical—that is, if the plan had been done accurately—then wood of the same measurements could have been used all the way down. Even so, you could hardly tell that this curved surface had been put in afterward, which showed how carefully the carpenters had done their job. What had they thought of Murai's attention to detail as they went about their work? I would never know, but it probably appealed to their craftsmanship.

I couldn't find the slightest fault elsewhere. The furnishings were a pleasure to touch, and there wasn't a single trowel mark on the plaster walls. A blind person with memories of other Murai buildings in his hands would probably have been able to tell just by touching here and there that this church had been designed by the same architect.

The row of windows near the ceiling opened and closed automatically, but as the mechanism was located behind the minister's room, the sound couldn't be heard. With the windows open, you could hear the noise of the city outside, along with the sound of birds, a breeze in the trees, and cars passing by. When they were closed, though, it was almost quiet enough to hear your own heart beating.

People's movements during the service had also been carefully considered. For instance, enough space had been left between the rows of chairs for worshippers not to have to raise the seats every time they stood up. The chairs themselves, with their rounded backrests, would comfortably accommodate anyone, and the top of each backrest folded over like the flap on a sailor blouse to form a bookrest for the person in the row behind. Without looking closely, you couldn't see the crack where the shelves were attached. Having them tilt slightly downward rather than stick straight out allowed more space in what was really a quite restricted area.

Most people probably never noticed these little touches, but they would be affected by them, nonetheless. Sensei left his mark in places that didn't appear in photographs or blueprints; in how surfaces felt to the touch, or the way a building was easy to use. Those were the things I'd wanted to see, feel, sketch, and record. With each survey I was coming closer to understanding his way of thinking, closer to finding the traces left by his hands.

I walked back up the aisle to the vestibule and set about measuring the height of the ceiling at the entrance and where the sofas were. Seeing I was having a hard time with the tape measure, the minister came over and held it flat against the wall for me.

I thanked him, feeling a bit flustered.

His hand still raised, he said, "Have you ever met Mr. Murai?"

"No. I've only seen him once, when he was giving a lecture."

"There's something almost intimidating about him." His hand was now down at his side. "I remember something that happened when we were about to move into this church. After all the chairs had been placed in the nave, he came and sat down in several of them. He seemed to be testing them. After a while he called his staff over. I was too far away to hear him, but I could tell how nervous everyone was, standing there with their notepads. That evening, the same four trucks that had delivered the chairs in the morning came and took them all away again."

"You mean they had to be redone?"

"Yes. I'd tried sitting in them myself, but couldn't find anything wrong with them. They were returned about a week later."

Something occurred to me. "Is it better for the chairs in a church to be a bit cramped, or uncomfortable?"

"Not at all," he replied. "It wouldn't do us any good if people thought of a church as a place that you left with a sore bottom. Of course if we switched to armchairs everyone would nod off, and I'd be left talking to myself. Can't have that either." He folded his hands in front of his chest and smiled again. "Sorry, I've got to go now. You carry on," he said as he hurried off.

Before I left, I took a last look at the nave. As the blueprint showed, the rectangular seating area was sandwiched between two semicircles, like the central part of a sports stadium. Three central larch-wood ceiling boards stretched all the way to the white wall behind the altar, where they bent downward and melded into cherrywood of the same width, which formed the vertical part of a cross. The arms of the cross were also cherrywood, the whole seeming to grow out of the curved plaster.

Traditional bentwood and plastering methods had been used to achieve this effect. Unusually for Shunsuke Murai, the details here were prominent. Whereas plain, untreated wood would normally be considered best for a symbol like a cross, he had tried a novel, carefully crafted design, which not only suited the bright, airy atmosphere but served as a stationary vanishing point for the whole interior.

Having finished my surveying and sketching, I went to say goodbye to the minister. "You're welcome back any time," he assured me. I thought of asking his impression of the cross, but in the end, didn't.

Outside, I looked through the glass door again. I could sense an invitation to prayer in this building, into which an unbelieving architect had poured all his skill and experience. The sanctity it embodied would calm, or encourage, or move the people who gathered here. As I turned my back on the church and walked away, I felt as though I were being pushed from behind by the admiration this architect, Shunsuke Murai, had inspired in me.

"Yes, that church is a superb piece of work," Uchida said. "Definitely one of his top recent projects... Those chairs that had to be done again—that was my fault," he added with a shamefaced laugh. "There was trouble with the hinges, where you raise the seat. Some were tight and others loose—not uniform. There were so many chairs, and Tagawa was worried about the delivery date. When I asked him about it later, he said he'd assumed they'd settle down in time. I thought something that minor could be overlooked, but was I wrong. Sensei insisted on all the hinges being replaced. He asked me how I could have failed to check them when I'd got everything else right."

Tagawa was one of the furniture makers who handled orders from the Murai Office, with a workshop in Yatsugatake, a mountainous area north of Tokyo. I tried to imagine the expression on his face when he saw the four truckloads of chairs come back, all the way from Kita Ward.

With his hands clasped behind his head, Uchida changed the subject. "There's a sort of sibling thing with Kei'ichi Funayama. You know the cathedral Funayama designed, just about a year before the Asukayama Church was built? The one that's opposite in every way?"

For a while everyone was talking about it. The Nishihara St. Peter's Cathedral was a huge building designed to resemble Noah's ark, its shiny stainless-steel exterior looming over its surroundings. Pictures of it were everywhere, not only on the covers of architectural magazines, but in full spreads in the popular weeklies as well. It was constructed on the former campus of Tokyo University of Education, on a hill overlooking Nishi-Shinjuku; from its bell tower, corresponding to a ship's pilothouse, you looked straight across at a skyscraper that Funayama had also designed. Seen from the latter, the cathedral looked like something out of a science fiction movie, a gigantic silver ship stranded on top of a hill.

In sheer volume, the cathedral dwarfed the Asukayama Church. Its hull seemed determined to expand outward. When the flood came, it would float on the water and set sail, while the Asukayama Church, curled like a sleeping cat, would quietly sink to the bottom.

Funayama had been three years behind Murai Sensei at the same college of art. From the early 1960s, when preparations for the first Tokyo Olympics had begun and new roads and buildings were being produced at fever pitch, wrapping the city in a cloud of dust, Funayama was always in the spotlight. Winning competition after competition, he designed monumental buildings that had everyone craning their necks to look up at them, in locations where they were most likely to attract attention. Murai never built anything that pushed outward or rose straight up into the sky. He consciously avoided exteriors that looked conspicuous, preferring designs that would fit into a neighborhood rather than stand out.

"I heard that it leaked just after they finished the cathedral, and the cost of heating it in winter and air-conditioning in summer is through the roof," Uchida said. "A church in the shape of Noah's ark is like putting a picture of a pig in a chef's hat in front of a BBQ joint. That design must have stretched the church's finances to the limit—I doubt he'd have been able to pull that off in Europe. But of course it was wildly successful, both for the architect and the client. Lots of people went to gawk at it, and it made Funayama chums with Catholic businessmen and politicians. There's a Catholic Diet member who when he was minister of foreign affairs took the prime minister of Italy to see the cathedral. Of course, Funayama was there waiting for them, and even showed them around the bell tower... Some say the pipe organ sounds wonderful, just like the one at Chartres. Well, I went to hear it once, and the reverberations lasted so long they sounded like *noise* after a while. Everything in that place is just too much. I'd much rather listen to a low, muffled tone, like the organ at Asukayama."

The pipe organ he mentioned was tucked into the wall off to the right of the altar. When I was getting ready to leave that day, a young woman was trying it out, pushing and pulling the stops—they reminded me of chess pieces. It had a soothing tone, but with some depth. There was almost no reverberation. A simple, friendly sort of sound, not at all like the music that seems to pound down onto the congregation's heads from above. This one started in your hands and feet, then traveled through you to your eardrums, rather than bouncing off the walls.

"It kind of surprised me," I said, "but while I was looking over the Asukayama Church, I felt there was a simple kind of humor in some of the details. I got the same impression from that pipe organ. As if Sensei, the usually serious one, suddenly came out with a joke."

"Humor...Maybe so."

"Lots of architects want to be heard, right? With him, it's as if the voice is so quiet it doesn't really matter whether you hear it or not."

"Same with religion. In the beginning it may have been something people had to keep quiet about. Early Christians were often persecuted, so they lay low, talked in whispers. But after Christianity was officially recognized, churches started getting bigger, and worshippers didn't have to worry about making a noise. The priest raised his voice, church architecture got grander, and organs got louder and louder. Modern architecture—especially skyscrapers—has pretty much followed the same path, wouldn't you say?"

"You don't want to talk loudly in one of Sensei's houses. There's something relaxing about the textures, the way the light comes in, delicate touches people don't even notice till they've lived there for a while. As if the building's speaking to them softly, so they follow suit. Those details in the Asukayama Church are like low voices."

"Yeah, but if they're too quiet *nobody's* going to notice. Cicadas make a racket because they need to find a mate—if they kept it down, the ladies would pass them by. If the plan for the library competition is too subtle, we might lose. Sensei's acting as if everything's normal, but even though he still gets up at five, his morning walks are getting shorter, and he's usually in his office before six."

I'd assumed Uchida would be sound asleep at that hour, so I was surprised he knew when Sensei got up.

"This is your first summer here," he went on, "but it's definitely going to be a turning point for all of us." He said he'd noticed a change in Sensei after we found out Funayama would be in the competition. If we got the library commission, things at the Murai Office would have to change.

That was when I finally noticed the tension behind our boss's calm exterior.

7

I'd been pruning branches off trees and chopping them up for firewood all morning when I heard Mariko Murai's voice behind me.

"We have to go shopping this afternoon, so let me know when you're done."

"I'm almost finished now."

She smiled and headed back into the kitchen through the back door. Mariko was always, somehow, brimming with energy. You could hear it in her voice, and see it in her smile and the whirl of her skirt as she turned around. She shone like the skin of the only orange in a bowl of fruit. Above her white deck shoes—she wasn't wearing socks—her long legs moved gracefully as she walked away.

On Monday, Wednesday, and Friday afternoons, she and I went down to Kyū-Karuizawa to do the shopping. Iguchi sometimes went with us when he needed to go to the bank or the post office, or to take some books out of the library. Leaving the forest for the town gave a sense of freedom you couldn't feel at the Summer House.

Mariko drove. On our first shopping trip I had driven the Volvo, but the way I'd handled the hairpin turns on the way down and parked in the lot at the supermarket apparently hadn't passed muster. Having only just gotten my license, I wasn't good enough for a big Volvo. This hurt a bit at first, but when I saw how much better she was than me, I settled down to enjoy the ride as a passenger.

We'd gone upstairs to the workshop before leaving, to ask Iguchi if he needed anything. "We're off now," Mariko had announced to no one in particular. "Have a good time," Yukiko said in her clear voice as she watched us go.

Five vehicles were parked in the wooden garage next to the east wing, where the women's rooms were. First, the cream-colored Volvo 240 station wagon Sensei used for long trips, which we borrowed when we went shopping. Next to it was Iguchi's dark-gray Mercedes station wagon 300TD. Then came Kawarazaki's metallic-blue Citroen DS21 and Kobayashi's Peugeot 305 liftback. At the far end was Mariko's black Renault 5, so small there was plenty of empty space around it.

Mariko headed not for Sensei's station wagon but her own car.

"Iguchi's not coming, so we'll have plenty of room in mine for what we buy today. I don't like the Volvo—too big and clunky."

I had never been in Mariko's car before. While I was wondering what I'd do if she offered to let me take the wheel, she opened the left-hand door and got into the driver's seat, tossing her leather shoulder bag into the back. Trying to look casual, I sat down next to her. As soon as the engine started, loud music I wasn't used to—soul music—filled the car. Mariko apparently didn't bother to turn the stereo off every time she cut the engine.

The steering on the Renault was on the left, and the transmission was manual. Tucking her long legs into the narrow space below the steering wheel, she quickly changed gears, and we were off. It felt as if we were skimming along the pavement, the body of the Renault being much lower than the Volvo. None of the guys I knew in our department at university had listened to this kind of music, but I grew to like the steady beat of the synthesizer and bass on later trips into town. What I caught of the lyrics were phrases like "I'm so lonely without you," or "It was love at first sight," or "I'm dying 'cos we're far apart," but however miserable the wording, the sound was warm and lively. Mariko said the tape she had on now was Teddy Pendergrass.

There was a sweet smell, too, in the little car. With Mariko's bare arms and legs much too close, I kept staring out the window at nothing in particular. The music, the sound of the engine, the whole atmosphere—everything about this car was different from the Volvo. And the difference was all down to her. I kept wavering between a desire to stay in the passenger seat forever, sitting next to her listening to songs about love and someone's beautiful eyes, and the awkward feeling that I didn't really belong there.

"Would you like to try driving this car sometime?"

"No, it's manual, so I think I'd better give it a pass."

"Why? You practiced on a manual at driving school, didn't you? If you managed a hill start and parallel parking with a bigger car like that, you should be able to handle anything, from a two-ton truck to this little number."

"You sure?"

"Sure I'm sure. You've got to try or you'll never get any better."

I watched the fingers of her right hand move the gearshift, then lightly rest on the steering wheel again, and thought of those fingers moving across a keyboard. Had piano study in England been the sort of cultural window-dressing expected of a girl from a well-off family, and nothing more?

"You're good at sharpening pencils," she said suddenly, looking straight ahead as she made the left turn from Aoguri onto the highway.

"Huh?"

"You're so careful. There aren't a lot of shavings left over when you're done. Someone that good with his hands should be a good driver too."

"I'm not sure I should take that as a compliment." This talk had caught me off-balance.

"Why not? What aren't you sure about?"

"All I did was copy Uchida."

She laughed out loud. "It takes skill to copy someone, you know."

Once on the highway, she stepped on the accelerator.

"When did you get your license?" I asked her.

"When I was eighteen. My mother was dead set against it, though. She said I should find a man to drive me around." She crinkled up her nose. "Kind of makes you wonder what century she's living in. I want to drive things myself—horse-drawn buggy, dogsled, even a tractor."

At the end of the highway we began descending from the pass, with all its hairpin turns. Downshifting, but rarely using the foot brake, Mariko took the car so neatly around the curves it looked no harder than breathing.

When Uchida was sharpening his pencils, his hands moved like a craftsman making furniture, lightly scraping the knife across the wood. Due to the shallow angle of the blade, the shavings were very thin. The tip of the pencil seemed to enjoy being sharpened.

In his role as my instructor, Uchida always explained things concretely, with a logic that was easy to follow. He'd been watching Kawarazaki and Kobayashi for a long time, and knew all about their separate talents, so what he told me about them immediately made sense. His comments about Mariko, on the other hand, were more opaque, making it hard to grasp what he was really trying to say. This had been bothering me for some time now. The day I'd arrived at the Summer House, Uchida took me up to the library on the second floor, where I was to sleep.

"Maruko Murai, the girl I introduced you to downstairs," he said, letting his eyes wander over the books lining the shelves without actually reading the titles. "Well, she's Sensei's niece. She doesn't look at all like him, though."

Since they had the same last name, I'd figured they were related, but as Uchida said, her manner was completely different from her uncle's.

"She's very competent. And as you'll soon see, she's a great cook. She's fluent in English, and speaks a little French too, apparently. Plays the piano well, and is an expert driver. Having someone like her around really brightens things up here. I wonder if she's okay with spending the whole summer in the mountains, but she goes to her parents' place in Kyū-Karuizawa on the weekend, so I guess she has ways to amuse herself there. But then again, there's something..." He didn't seem to know what to say, which was unusual for him. "It's hard to know what she's thinking sometimes."

Not knowing what to say myself, I gave a vague sort of nod.

"And one more thing, just to be clear," he added. "Not because she's Sensei's niece, but don't get involved with her. An office romance is out. If you got into a relationship, and rumors started, you could be asked to leave, so be careful. In an outfit this small, one needs a rule like that or the work could be disrupted, and it'd be hard on our relationships with each other too. Of course, if you decided to quit, you could move in on her right away in the time you had left."

Seeing that his little joke had fallen flat, he laughed to make up for it.

Kinokuniya Supermarket, open only during the summer, was crowded with tourists and people staying at their summer houses. I pushed the big shopping cart while Mariko, checking her list from time to time, filled it. I could tell she was thinking about what she'd cook while she shopped. It made her interesting to watch. She picked up a shiny green zucchini.

"That zucchini pasta you made was really good," I said.

"It's simple. All you need is garlic, olive oil, and salt. A friend from Chile taught me when I was in London. Her mother's recipe." She waited a beat. "My mother hates to cook. By the time I was in junior high I realized food tasted better if I made it myself, so I started fixing my own lunch every morning. And in England I never felt like eating out... You're going to get better and better at it."

I did in fact feel I was gradually getting the hang of how to cook breakfast for the nine of us at the Summer House—how to prepare things in order, so that everything would be hot when people were ready to eat. I'd picked this up from Uchida and her.

"Oh, I forgot to get rhubarb," Mariko said. "I want to make some jam. I'll be back in a minute." She hurried off to the vegetable section near the entrance.

When we loaded the back seats of the Renault with six big shopping bags, plus the six bottles of wine Uchida had asked us to get, the tires seemed to sink down slightly. Mariko let in the clutch more slowly than before. As a driver she was decisive, but also careful about details. Along with her perfume, the car was now filled with the smell of fresh bread and coffee beans, which made me suddenly realize how hungry I was.

"I'm going to stop off at my place. Do you mind?" Without waiting for an answer, she turned in the opposite direction from the way we usually went back to Kita-Asama. Past the Kyū-Karuizawa roundabout, we took the road leading to the old Mampei Hotel, but left it to climb a gentle slope until we were high enough to see the hotel below us on the right. The area was dotted with old summer residences, many with their shutters closed. This must have been one of the first bits of Karuizawa to be developed for city dwellers wanting to escape the summer heat.

The Renault slipped between the pillars of a low gate made of piled stones. I could tell at a glance that Sensei had designed the wooden building in front of us. It must have been built at around the same time as the Summer House. The cedar siding was the same, but apparently nothing had been added on.

Mariko parked the car under a huge maple tree that covered half the front yard, and before switching the engine off, opened all the windows. Besides our shopping for the Summer House there was a small paper bag on the back seat; she twisted around to get it, then got out. I followed her.

The key in the brass doorknob turned with a sharp, metallic click. A rather dark wooden corridor stretched out beyond.

"Have some tea while you're here. I'll go make it."

"What about the food? Is it okay to leave it in the car?"

"It'll be fine. They put in two hours' worth of dry ice, and the car's in the shade with the windows open."

She slipped out of her deck shoes and stepped up into the hallway. I silently took off my own shoes.

"You mind opening the windows for me? They're the same as at the Summer House. When you're done, you can sit on the sofa over there."

Mariko spoke without hesitation, leaving no time for the atmosphere to get awkward. That was a relief. Leaving her words to float behind her, she marched straight into the kitchen. I slid back the curtains and twisted the bronze lock to open first the tall glass sliding door and then the low window looking out onto the garden. The lawn was well tended. There was the smell of strong sunlight on summer grass. The chirring of cicadas was almost oppressive.

Though old, this was a living, breathing house that had been well taken care of over the years. The light-caramel-colored floor shone. Mariko's father must polish it regularly, rubbing good-quality wax into the wood. The glass in the windows, still in their old wooden frames, was starting to get a little wavy with age; the panes probably hadn't been changed since the house was built. For some reason, I didn't sense the presence of a mother in these rooms.

Since Sensei had designed it, I wanted to take a closer look, but somehow couldn't bring myself to walk around examining the house where Mariko stayed on weekends. I sat on the living room sofa and stared into the fireplace. A pair of fire tongs hung next to it, the wooden handle dark and shiny. They must have kept the chimney clean, because the white wall around the fireplace wasn't discolored. The fireplace itself was black only at the back, a sign that the chimney was drawing well.

There was a painting by Gen'ichiro Yamaguchi on the wall to the left, where the firewood was stacked: a sunlit beach with footsteps being washed away by the foam of a wave. The footsteps seemed to be a child's. Hadn't Yamaguchi's only son died of some illness?

I left the sofa and went over to look out at the garden. Though there wasn't the slightest breeze, I saw a patch of yellow moving among the green. A narcissus flycatcher was perched on the branch of a prickly ash. This was a bird I had seen only once in Tokyo. It was bright yellow from throat to breast. Above its black eye was a strip of the same yellow, like an eyebrow. With its head tilted to one side, the bird was looking this way. The narcissus flycatcher has a lovely song, but this one didn't seem in the mood for singing. I held my breath and stood very still, but it must have felt my eyes on it, for it flew off, showing the white pattern on the underside of its wings.

From the kitchen I heard the sound of the refrigerator opening and closing, and of something being mixed in a metal bowl. Then it was quiet, and Mariko came into the living room.

"Sorry. It'll be ready soon, so how about some music? The records are all my father's, but go ahead—put one on."

"Can I look through them?"

"Of course." She went back to the kitchen.

All the audio equipment was British. Quad amplifiers, a Linn player, Tannoy speakers. What would soul music sound like on this stereo set? The record rack, longer than my arm, was filled with a well-ordered collection of LPs, mostly classical, with a little jazz.

After pulling out several for a look, I finally settled on one with a well-worn sleeve that had apparently been listened to over and over again. Clifford Curzon playing Brahms's Second Piano Concerto. I gently lowered the arm onto the B-side. The slight scratch of the needle, and music with a tinge of loneliness like autumn sunlight came from the speakers.

While I sat on the sofa listening, I felt increasingly uneasy, as if Mariko's father was there, and I had barged into his house without permission. Two sons born into a family that ran a confectionery shop; the older one had become an architect, the younger took over the shop.

The older Murai later designed a summer house for his younger brother, who had his daughter work part-time in his brother's office. If they didn't get along, things probably wouldn't have worked out that way.

Emerging from the kitchen, Mariko put a brown teapot, a milk pitcher, and two plain white cups on the table in front of the sofa. Just then, as if it had been waiting for the music to end, the oven chimed from the kitchen, and a delicious smell filled the air. I lifted the arm on the record player. I wanted to listen to the second movement again from the beginning. Bringing in some freshly baked scones with jars of cream and jam, Mariko sat on the sofa across from me.

"I saw some scones in Kinokuniya and suddenly felt like making some."

"You did it so quickly, like magic."

"All I had to do was mix and bake. Go ahead, have one while they're hot."

"Thank you."

The fresh scone had a sunny smell, like the outdoors. I ate it spread with cold clotted cream and strawberry jam. The warmth, texture, and flaky sweetness mixed in my mouth.

I thought of Mariko's skin: firm and healthy, with no flab, so smooth I could have drawn its outline with a fine F pencil. It would have ended at her fingers, now holding a scone. Almost laughing, she looked at me.

"You're obstinate, aren't you?"

This was so sudden I almost choked on the food.

"That's probably what Sensei liked about you," she added, still smiling. I quickly took a sip of tea. I felt split between the taste of the scone and something I remembered.

My father hadn't liked the idea of my studying architecture at university. "I don't know much about architects," he'd said, "but aren't most of them stuck-up, would-be artist types? Join one of those architectural offices and you'll end up doing a lot of fiddly work for very little money. You won't be able to marry and start a family for years and years." The Murai Office paid well, and I wasn't doing fiddly work, but generally speaking, he may have been right. He himself was an engineer, and I couldn't figure out where this negative image of architects came from. When I didn't change course, he'd said, "You're too obstinate. You'll head off in a fixed direction, but it won't be as easy as you think."

The last time I'd been called that was about a year before. My adviser had suggested I take the exam for one of the major construction companies, but I'd refused. Sitting in his office, expressionless, I'd been told with a sour smile that I was "obstinate." My father might have accepted my joining a major construction company. By the time I actually joined the Murai Office he seemed to have given up on me, and showed little interest.

"People tell me I'm obstinate too," Mariko said with a grin, her arms around her knees. Below them, her legs were perfectly straight.

"When, for instance?"

"Whenever I don't like something and come out and say so."

"Is that all? Must be annoying."

"Girls who don't go along with the crowd, and say exactly what they think, get labeled. How about you? Do you always say what you think?"

"I guess it depends on the time and place."

She crossed her legs and looked straight at me. Embarrassed, I looked down at her shiny toenails. I tried to come up with a witty comment, but couldn't think of one. What would Uchida have said at a time like this?

Mariko looked at the clock. "We'd better be going," she said, sounding slightly tense. "I'll wrap these up for you, so wait just a minute." As if to put an end to the conversation, she stood up and went into the kitchen, then came back with the scones in a red paper box. "Take this tea bag and the little teapot. It's just big enough for one cup. There's some more jam and clotted cream as well." She shoved everything into a canvas bag that she handed over, stretching out a slender arm.

Not knowing what else to say, I thanked her. "I'll return the bag later."

"That's all right. Keep it."

The well-used bag, with the logo of a London deli in one corner, felt soft in my hand. It had been washed so often I could barely read the shop's phone number. This bag had spent time with Mariko long before I met her.

I went into the kitchen to help with the washing up. Standing next to her, I could sense the warmth of her body. Neither of us said anything. Not because we felt awkward, though we weren't relaxed, either—just a vague sort of reticence. I remembered what Uchida had told me. When I'd finished drying the dishes, she said, "We can't stay longer," looking straight at me, as if I were a rookie actor who'd forgotten his lines.

Neither of us said anything as we got into the Renault. With the windows still open, a bee, drawn by the smell, was hovering persistently above the shopping bags, making a low buzz that disappeared when she started the engine.

Though we hadn't done anything to keep secret about, I had the feeling I shouldn't mention stopping by at Mariko's summer house to the others. Without music this time, she drove silently under the trees with patches of sunlight shining through them, down the back roads of Kyū-Karuizawa. I had no idea how deep in I was, in a sea of my own dullness and ignorance. Had I just made a mistake that would have consequences? The more I thought about it the less I understood what had happened, and afraid I'd let out a groan or something, decided to stop thinking. I looked into the forest that lined the road, not focusing on anything, letting the trees and bushes race by.

The engine was humming smoothly. The Renault had been built to travel over stones or gravel, so this mountain road didn't give it any trouble. Earlier than I expected, we reached the old, weather-beaten Hoshino Hot Springs, and from there turned smoothly onto the highway. The rest of the way was due north, toward

Aoguri. The music started up again. I relaxed, realizing now how tense my shoulders had been.

"I've never listened to this kind of thing—it's really nice."

"You like it? Anything simple and honest is okay with me."

Mariko's reply came from an unexpected angle, and feeling somehow inadequate again, I kept quiet. She stepped on the accelerator. The tires hugged the road around the curves as we climbed.

"I like songs that tell you a person's feelings straight. Anything too complicated or so subtle you can't tell what they're getting at leaves me cold. Birds sing for simple reasons—to let other birds know this is their territory, or to find a mate. That's why their voices are so clear."

After a series of tight bends, the road was now straight. Mariko stepped lightly on the gas.

"Some birds don't sound so clear," I said.

"Really?"

"The kogera, for example. Its song is so quiet most people probably wouldn't even notice it. Sounds something like *khii*."

"Kogera?"

"It's a kind of woodpecker."

"Are there any in Aoguri?"

"Sure. I saw one this morning, hopping up the trunk of the katsura tree."

"You seem to know a lot about birds. I've never even heard of that one."

"When I was a kid in elementary school I used to go to Mt. Takao or the grounds of Meiji Shrine on Sundays with the Bird Searchers." My enthusiasm for birds lasted only through grade school. No one used the term "bird-watching" back then.

"The Bird Searchers? Never heard of them either."

"It's a kids' club, sponsored by the Wild Bird Society."

"Now that I do know." Laughing, she took one hand off the steering wheel and gave me a pat on the arm. On a piano it would have been staccato.

"Did I say something funny?"

"No, not really. Bird-watching just sounds like the kind of hobby you'd have."

"In what way?"

"No way at all, really... So, when you wanted to see rare birds, what did you do?"

"Search for them." I laughed for the first time. "That's why we were called the Bird Searchers."

"Sounds like you went to a lot of trouble," she said, impressed, and I suddenly felt more at ease.

"There's a really colorful bird called the ruddy kingfisher. They migrate, and spend the summers around Tokyo. They have a big red bill, and their bodies are sort of rust colored. You see them on Mt. Takao during the summer, probably around Aoguri too. They're hard to find, though. It's more common to hear them in a forest, a clear song that starts high and comes down, something like *quirr* or *pyorr*."

"Have you ever seen one?"

"When I was a kid out with the Bird Searchers, I was usually the first to make a sighting."

"How did you find them?"

"They seemed to come to me somehow. I'd just see one, right where I was looking, perched on a branch. It would stay there, as if resigned to it."

I remembered how amazed I was as a child to see this beautiful bird; it gave me the shivers, the red of the bill and the terra-cotta wings.

"How about that other bird you like... what was it called?"

"The kogera?"

"That's right—kogera. You said its song is a quiet *khii*."

"The wings have black and white spots, so the effect is gray, just the opposite of the ruddy kingfisher. I mean they don't stand out at all. And very small for a woodpecker. The English name is 'Japanese pygmy woodpecker.' The song doesn't stand out either."

"Do they migrate?"

"No, they stick around all year long. In Kita-Aoyama and Aoguri too. Not a rare bird at all, really, but to see one darting up the trunk of a tree is always exciting. Like the quote 'rare and strange.'"

"Strange?"

"Unlikely, liable to disappear anytime. When you see a great spotted woodpecker with that red head pounding away at a tree trunk it looks like a red-faced lunatic, but the kogera is quite different, shy and unassuming."

"Respectable."

"It makes the hole for its nest so carefully, a perfect circle, trimmed around the edges. Makes other woodpeckers' nests look down-market."

"But birds must have their own reasons for making their nests the way they do, neat or messy."

Mariko was a good listener who didn't miss anything. In profile she looked perfectly serious. So much so, in fact, that I swallowed the joke I'd been planning to make.

"The next time you see a kogera, let me know, will you?"

"Of course."

The awkwardness between us when we left her parents' cottage was now gone.

As the car traveled up the slope, I saw Mt. Asama through the windshield, so hulking one was looking straight up at it. It was hard to believe that the reddish earth of the mountainside, barren of plant life, was on the same planet as the road we were on. Asama's broad ridgeline was formed by lava that had been pushed up from the depths of the earth eons ago. That tremendous power had left this scar, over 2,500 meters high. Totally amazing, when you thought about it. Had the earth sunk somewhere, in proportion to the amount that had been forced up? What form had it taken deep in the earth, before it moved?

The conversation had stopped, and the cassette was over. There was only the sound of the engine. Mt. Asama had retreated far enough for me to have to turn around to see it. With the volcano, a wisp of steam coming from the crater, now behind us, we were back in the Kita-Asama area, still over a thousand meters high.

"We're exactly an hour late," Mariko said in a joking tone as she slowed down and turned right toward the village. The black Renault slid into the familiar road through the forest as if drawn by a magnet.

When we arrived at the Summer House, it was four o'clock, just after the tea break. The evening had already begun, and people were starting to unwind. Beyond the big window in the workshop, facing south, late-afternoon sunlight bathed the leaves on the trees. The cicadas were even noisier than before. The temperature was dropping. When Mariko appeared on the scene, you could feel the way attention was drawn in her direction. Iguchi looked up.

"You took a long time. Was it crowded down there?"

"The roads were jammed and so was the supermarket," Mariko replied evenly. "Sorry to be late."

"No problem. Just so long as everyone's here tonight."

Yukiko and Uchida looked up, taking in this exchange. Yukiko's eyes were on Mariko; she didn't even glance my way. Mariko gave Iguchi a perfect smile before heading down to the ironing room on the first floor. I silently followed her. From behind, over to one side, I felt Uchida's eyes trained on me.

I took two of the shopping bags we'd left in the entranceway in each arm and carried them into the kitchen. "Thanks," Mariko said, "I'll do the rest." I went back to the car to get the canvas bag she'd given me, then ran up the stairs to my bedroom in the library and put it on top of the cabinet where I kept my clean pajamas and sheets.

When I went back to the workshop, Uchida seemed to be waiting to speak to me. Compared to the almost oppressive atmosphere in Tokyo, where nobody talked, there was an easier feeling at the Summer House, where the windows were open, letting in a combination of sounds: birds and insects, the rustling of leaves, and the faraway hum of lawn mowers. Quiet, but not too quiet. I liked that. Uchida's soft voice mingled with the rasp of cicadas on the oak tree outside, so I was probably the only one who could hear him.

"After dinner, Kawarazaki and Kobayashi are going to present their plans for the Library of Modern Literature," he said.

That must have been why Iguchi seemed excited.

"So we'd better finish dinner early," Uchida added. "I'll help. Let's make something quick and easy. Since you're just back from shopping, we have plenty to work with, right?" The topic now being food, his voice returned to normal, and he grinned at me like an actor onstage. Uchida was a complicated man. You'd see him looking nervous, lost in thought, and then suddenly he'd smile as if life was a bundle of fun. These smiles of his were like cutoffs, making it impossible to go back to whatever you'd been talking about, or to reach that unknowable part of him, which no one ever got close to. I rather liked those dramatic smiles, though.

"We'll steam lots of vegetables, and use the sirloin for roast beef. There's vichyssoise chilling in the refrigerator. That'll be plenty. And we've got baguettes and *pain de campagne*. You bought both kinds today, didn't you?"

"Yes, we did."

"Since the bread's fresh," he said casually, "let's make an olive oil and balsamic vinegar dip for it, with freshly ground pepper. That way even if our bellies are full, our brains will still be working." Uchida believed there was a gap between the mental stamina of Japanese and Europeans, due to the difference in the staple diet. Japanese didn't think things through because they ate too much soft rice—their minds were especially foggy after dinner.

I had several of his recipes in my kitchen notebook. He began vichyssoise by making chicken stock (he called it *fond de volaille*), which he put on the stove around noon. But it wasn't his only cold soup—he also made one with corn or edamame, and gazpacho. The roast beef we were having tonight was one of his specialties. He had asked me to buy some horseradish to go with it.

Iguchi couldn't understand this enthusiasm for cooking, and grumbled and sighed about "foreign grub," suggesting Uchida should save his energy for his blueprints. Although not really a gourmet, Sensei was nevertheless interested enough to wander into the kitchen when Uchida was in charge of the evening meal, something he never did with anyone else. The occasional question he asked was answered by a cook looking rather pleased by the attention. Uchida himself considered a knowledge of good food and skill in cooking to be requisite for any architect. The first time I was on kitchen duty there, while he was washing up (he had his own rules for this as well, such as always starting with the raised ridge on the bottom of Japanese-style dishes, which is often overlooked), he said, "You know that old story about the man who named his son Eating-Sleeping-Living so the kid would never have any trouble with any of those things when he grew up? Well, I think he got it right. It *should* be thought of as one word. If you design a place for people to live in, but you skip over eating and sleeping, you end up with an empty shell. I would never ask someone who doesn't cook or do the laundry or clean his own house to design mine."

Up here, we took turns cooking and cleaning, and naturally everyone did their own laundry. We also had a field out back where we grew our own vegetables. And though not everyone was as good at it as Uchida, we could all come up with a decent meal when we had to. As I'd only started to live on my own in May of that year, my repertoire was limited, but Uchida had all sorts of newfangled kitchen utensils, such as a salad spinner that used centrifugal force to dry vegetables, and a rotary cheese grater; I had as much fun getting the hang of these gadgets as I had learning how to cook, so all in all I found kitchen duty a lot more interesting than I'd thought it would be.

"Anyway, how was Mariko's summer place?" Uchida whispered in a voice only I could hear as he bent over to pick up an eraser he'd dropped. I felt I'd been tripped up. I could tell I was blushing.

"Sensei designed it, didn't he?" I answered, trying to sound as calm as possible. "It isn't in the catalogue of his works—I found out for the first time today."

"There are others that aren't in the catalogue either. Mariko's place was built in 1960, so four years later than this house, but you can tell just by looking that they're both from around the same period... So, how was it?" he repeated, pretending not to notice how flustered I was. The question was more about Mariko, most likely. It helped that he didn't look all that interested. The way out, it occurred to me, was to tell him how much of the house I'd actually seen.

"I only saw the entranceway and the living room, but I noticed it has several details in common with this place. Inside, it's been taken good care of, and outside, the siding—probably from the time it was built—looked clean. The front door had obviously been in frequent use, the brass doorknob was shiny..."

"Island kitchens were modern back then—it's very well done, wouldn't you say?"

He must have sensed somehow that I had stood next to Mariko at the kitchen sink, drying the plates we'd used. I could feel my ears turning red. Uchida had clearly been there himself. Now that I thought of it, Mariko seemed more brusque toward him than she needed to be. I was starting to get really confused.

    Mariko came back upstairs. Without so much as a glance toward us, she went straight to Sensei's office, knocked, and didn't come out for quite a while. Uchida turned back to his desk, while I went to work on a full-scale drawing I had to finish.

8

Though the power outage was over, several wires that had been damaged in the typhoon had to be replaced. That afternoon the electricity was off, due to the repair work. The generator was running, but in the evening we lined the dining table with candles and ate by candlelight again. There were steamed vegetables fresh from the garden—eggplant, tomatoes, pimiento, and okra—along with the roast beef and vichyssoise. For a dressing we had walnut oil and lemon wedges, and an olive oil and balsamic vinegar dip with the baguettes. The big pepper and salt mills were passed around the table.

When we were almost finished, Iguchi said he'd seen Harue Nomiya for the first time in a while that afternoon, at a meeting of the residents' association. She looked as if she'd shrunk a size or two, and although she normally would have brought up some thorny problem, bringing the proceedings to a halt, today she simply noted her concern about the sudden decrease in the firefly population around the pond, announced that she intended to have her nephew's daughter, a graduate student at the Tokyo

Institute of Technology, look into the matter, and left before the meeting was adjourned.

"I hate to say it," Iguchi said, "but I'm afraid Nomiya Sensei won't be with us much longer."

"Then you shouldn't say it," said Mariko, looking at Yukiko as if she hoped she agreed. Yukiko smiled back, then frowned.

"She's right about the fireflies—you don't see many these days," she said. "I don't think pollution's the problem. There are more fish now, so maybe they're eating the larvae."

"There are lots of carp in Firefly Pond," Sensei agreed as he sipped his after-dinner coffee. "And I've heard that they eat firefly larvae."

Yukiko was knowledgeable where the names of flora and fauna were concerned. She went hiking with Ms. Sasai, another staff member, on weekends, and had climbed Mt. Asama, all 2,568 meters of it. I first learned the names alpine azalea, snowy aster, and lupine clover from a sketchbook in which she kept drawings of alpine flowers.

Kobayashi and Kawarazaki were discussing something Kei'ichi Funayama had designed that had been featured in the latest issue of *Modern Architecture*. It was a palace commissioned by the ruler of Qatar, the oil-rich country that had gained its independence from England about a decade earlier; the construction fee wasn't mentioned in the magazine, so no one had any idea how much it cost. Rumor had it that not only Qatar but other countries in the region were eager to have Funayama design grand public buildings for them. Apparently he had negotiated directly with the emir, who offered him unlimited resources without any provisos on how they were used.

Ms. Sasai broke in: "Well, then," she said, "he doesn't need to compete for a commission here. We've got lots of restrictions and a lot less money." This livened the conversation up. A showpiece like a palace was just up Funayama's alley, everyone agreed. Determined to be in the center of things, he would definitely want to participate in any sort of competition that would attract attention. In that sense, it was perfectly natural for him to aim for the National Library of Modern Literature.

Sitting at the same table, Sensei showed no sign of hearing any of this. As soon as the word "palace" was tossed around, Uchida, turning toward me, launched into a lecture on beehives. It wasn't uncommon for him to go off on odd tangents, but tonight he was clearly trying to steer the talk away from Funayama.

"There've always been ways to capture animals by making something they can use as a nest," he said, "octopus pots are one example. But the one with the best design is undoubtedly the wooden box for bees. It's just frames with rows of hexagons, so it's easy and cheap to make, the structure's strong enough to hold up under shocks from the outside, and the spaces inside are multipurpose, so the same thing can be used as a honey super, a brood chamber, or to store food. Two frames, placed back-to-back, make up one set, and several sets are lined up inside the box, hanging straight down. Between the frames there's what's called a bee space, just big enough for a bee to fit through, so worker bees or the queen can move about, and the hive holds in the heat like a panel heater, which allows bees to survive even in places where the temperature drops below zero." He explained all this as smoothly as a biology teacher. While giving the impression that it would lead on to architecture, he never actually made the connection.

"They imitate the structure of the nests bees make for themselves, don't they?" said Sensei, who'd been listening with some interest.

"That's right, but the big difference is that you can remove the lid and take the frames out whenever you like." He explained that until the nineteenth century, if people wanted honey, they had to destroy a nest to get it. Except in warm places like Southeast Asia, bees always seal their nest with a thin layer of sap and propolis, a kind of bee glue, to protect it from the weather and predators like hornets or yellow jackets. At least part of that seal had to be broken to get at the honey. Considering the demand for a regular supply of it, this was a disaster for the insects, and not very efficient for people either. A nineteenth-century American clergyman named Lorenzo Lorraine Langstroth—the difficult name rolled off Uchida's tongue as if he was used to saying it—was looking for a way to harvest honey without destroying the habitat. The hanging honeycombs he saw in the nests reminded him of files hanging vertically in a cabinet, which gave him an idea—why not make a box with a similar format, so you could get the honey without wrecking the nest?

"Langstroth was obviously a very observant, inventive guy," Uchida said, "but I think his being a Protestant minister had a lot to do with why he was the one to come up with a neat solution."

"How so?" I asked.

"Well, Protestants seem to have a knack for improving things, making devices more efficient, easier to use. That's really how Protestantism got its start. Luther's Reformation spread so quickly in Europe because he thought of ways to make religious teachings generally accessible. He used the new printing press Gutenberg invented to print the Bible hundreds of times faster than copying each one by hand, as they'd had to do before. Besides, at a time when Bibles were so heavy they had to be laid on a lectern, Luther came out with a compact edition people could carry around with them. And not in Latin, which most people couldn't and didn't want to read, but translated into German, which in those days was considered inferior. The result was that the Bible was much more widely read. This is where the Protestant belief in practical solutions begins."

Although Uchida must have picked up a good deal of this from books, listening to him, you got the impression he'd thought it up by himself.

"What you say applies to Shaker furniture too," Sensei said. "It's simple, yet beautiful in its simplicity."

"Absolutely. Though the Shakers are gone now, we still have their furniture. Langstroth died, but by the early twentieth century his hive boxes had spread all over America and Europe. Gutenberg was sued for failing to pay debts, and his workshop and all the machinery in it were confiscated, yet in no time his printing press was being used throughout Europe. Both inventions are simple enough to copy. We all know what Max Weber said about Protestantism being the driving force behind capitalism, but I think the Protestants' real strength is their ability to make things anyone can figure out how to use."

I thought I saw Iguchi give Uchida an irritated glance. These lectures seemed to bore him, even to be a bit frivolous. Someone as sensitive as Uchida must have been aware of this.

"Anyway," he went on, "simple, compact things are good because there's no need to explain how they work. And it's best if the occupants of a house discover for themselves the special features an architect has put in. A well-made house shouldn't need a user's manual."

At this point, Sensei stood up, saying we had to get started on the library presentations. Kobayashi and Kawarazaki went up to the workshop before anyone else. There was no idle chatter as the rest of us cleared the table.

When I got upstairs, the two men were seated at the big table talking quietly together. With everyone present, Sensei then appeared from his office with a brown leather notebook in one hand. Kobayashi was at the head of the table, the others along both sides. Using large croquis whiteboards, he began his explanation, flipping the panels over one by one with his long fingers as he went. I opened my own notebook to a new page and wrote down what he said in pencil. Yukiko was also taking notes.

Kobayashi's plan was a square building with five floors, two underground and three above. There was a smaller building, also square, to the south, which was to house the restaurant, café, childcare center, and auditorium. The two buildings were connected by a glass corridor overlooking a courtyard. This marked a clear division between the library itself and the annex containing the other facilities.

The most distinctive feature was the placement of the bookshelves in the library. These curved in a broad S-shaped pattern, so that seen from above, the effect was of a river flowing through the square space. It reminded me of Ogata Kōrin's screen, *Red and White Plum Blossoms*, except the curve was much broader. Because the bookcase-river didn't flow straight across the square but diagonally, from north–northwest to south–southeast, some space was left in the southeast and northwest corners. Here Kobayashi had placed reading tables.

Also, when you looked closely, you saw that there were breaks in the middle of the S-shaped curve for people to walk through. He hadn't forgotten the circulation route.

"The most important thing we have to aim for," he said, "is making it fun for the users. If the building were designed from management's point of view, the bookshelves would be arranged to make the librarians' job easier. And standard classification methods would leave the shelves looking dull and lifeless. I want this library to be a place where people not only come to find a specific book, but can also enjoy wandering through the open stacks. A riverbank that twists and turns is nicer than one that's been reinforced with concrete in a straight line." For all his talk of fun and enjoyment, Kobayashi himself looked as solemn as ever, his brow furrowed, without even the hint of a smile on his face.

He'd arranged the two buildings this way, with the library to the north and the smaller annex to the south, so that they would fit neatly into the long, rectangular plot of land, and because he wanted to leave the restaurant, which he'd placed on the first floor of the annex, facing a public road. That, he felt, would lower the library's psychological threshold, make it more accessible. He thought the library would seem more stable with the curving bookshelves enclosed in a simple square, which was why he had made both buildings that shape.

"Why did you put the restaurant and childcare center in a separate building?" Sensei asked.

"For one thing," Kobayashi said, "children's voices and the smell of food would be out of place in a library. Besides, I thought moving from a quiet, more dimly lit library into the much brighter annex should give people a cheerful, open feeling."

"I see you've kept the windows in the main building small."

"That's partly to protect the books from direct sunlight, but I also think it's easier to settle down in a library with quiet lighting. There will be lights like the ones in art museums among the bookshelves, and reading lights on the tables, so users won't have any trouble reading. But for the restaurant, I've made the windows nice and big."

"Well, what do you think?" Sensei asked, turning to us. "Any questions?"

The windows in the workshop were open, just as they had been in the afternoon. The insects were even louder now. I could see lots of them, of all sizes, flitting around the light trap under the katsura tree.

"You're going to use some kind of library classification system, aren't you?" Uchida said. "If so, with these wavy bookcases, how will you set off the various categories of books? Say, for instance, you line up fiction by the authors' names from left to right, starting on the top shelf—where will one series end and another begin? I'd also like to know more about what you're going to have on each floor."

"This is something I discussed with Kawarazaki. I'd like to have special themes for the open stacks, with the books chosen and arranged accordingly. The two floors below ground level will serve as storage space for closed stack materials, just as in ordinary libraries. But I want some part of the upper three floors to be a sort of showcase, with a different display for each new theme. This can be something like a museum exhibition, with the librarians acting as curators, deciding which books to put out and how to arrange them. Collecting and archiving is the role of the Diet Library, but we have to make this new library a place to bring people and books together. Otherwise, it won't serve a different purpose."

"But won't it be hard to find librarians who are capable of doing that?" asked Uchida. "They're professionals when it comes to classifying and administration, but can you really ask them to serve as curators as well? Isn't that beyond their purview?"

"You may be right," Kobayashi said, unfazed. "If so, it might be best to have people from outside at first, to form a kind of selection committee. The themes should be easy to understand; for instance, you could have a retrospective for a certain writer on the anniversary of his death. TV programs the writer appeared on could be shown in the auditorium during that time, or movies based on his work. Since the library will have only books published after the war, coming up with topics worth exploring in depth shouldn't be too difficult. For example, a skillfully done display with both cookbooks and essays on food from books and magazines could give an overall view of how our diet has changed since the war, and how various dishes were introduced from abroad."

"Arranging books by theme," Sensei said, "is an idea worth considering. Up to now, libraries have generally been passive, letting the users choose what to read from what's available. But with so many books coming out now, if you stick to the nineteenth-century idea of what a library is for, you'll end up accumulating more and more stuff that nobody reads. We need a brand-new concept that users will find convincing. Just explaining it verbally won't be enough, though. The building has to be designed to actually show them what you're getting at." Nothing is more persuasive than design itself—this was central to his own work.

"Will users be able to borrow books and take them home?" asked Yukiko, who must have been thinking of the Diet Library, which doesn't lend out books.

"No, they can't be taken out," Kobayashi answered. "That's already been decided, as a basic principle. This library is meant to be a place where you can discover books you wouldn't come across elsewhere. Once you've found something you want to have at home, you can maybe get it in a public library, or buy it at a secondhand bookstore. If we put in comfortable chairs and tables, people will look forward to sitting there reading, and may keep coming back till they've finished a book. I want the Library of Modern Literature to be somewhere you happen to encounter something new, as well as being somewhere to enjoy the company of books."

Kawarazaki's plan was much bolder. His library was a cylinder, situated on the northern side of the oblong plot of land, large enough to skim its boundaries. As with

Kobayashi's plan, there were two floors below ground level and three above, but there was more space on each floor. The restaurant and childcare center were to be on the first floor, with the auditorium below, and storage space on the floor below that, while the open stacks and reading rooms were all on the second and third floors.

These two floors were round, like the shape of the building, with four concentric rows of bookcases starting from the outside wall, moving toward the center. The outermost row had five breaks for users to walk through, followed by four for the next, then three, then two for the innermost, so that people could make their way easily through the bookcases in either direction. It looked a bit like that little handheld toy where you have to maneuver silver balls toward the center of a maze.

The passage along the outer wall turned into a gradient that led from the second to the third floor. You could start in the center on the second floor, looking at the bookcases as you made your way toward the outside, then climb the slope to the third floor, where you would start from the outside, circling toward the center.

Kawarazaki looked around from face to face, trying to read our reactions as he talked.

"The Stockholm Public Library, which Gunnar Asplund designed, is one example of a cylindrical library," he said. "The open stacks of the British Library are in one huge, dome-shaped, round reading room. And the National Library of France, in Paris, also has round reading rooms. But in all these libraries, the books are lined up along the wall. Since my plan has four rows of concentric bookcases, you can't see all the books continuously as you can in Asplund's Stockholm library. It's more like a circular maze.

"But I've placed a skylight in the middle, and since the bookcases are only two meters high, the space as a whole shouldn't feel closed in. The clear ceiling should make it bright enough. Though it looks like a maze, the purpose isn't to get people lost—at each break in the bookshelves there'll be a sign showing exactly where you are.

"The second and third floors are connected by a gradient. Wright's Guggenheim Museum has a circular one, but there you're supposed to take the elevator to the fifth floor and then come down along the slope, like a one-way street. With my plan, people will be able to go either up or down, and there'll be a spiral staircase in the center as well, so it should be easy to move around as you please."

"I see you use a lot of plate glass, but only on the first floor," Sensei said.

"Yes, the ceiling height on the first floor is four and a half meters, which should make for a free, open feeling. As in Kobayashi's plan, you can see into the restaurant from the outside. The reason I've made the ceiling so high is partly to make the restaurant feel spacious, but also because I want to split the opposite side of the first floor in two, with the childcare center on the mezzanine, in an area with a lower ceiling, where toddlers and those looking after them can be close together. I don't have any children of my own, but I did a little research, and it seems babies aren't generally very fond of wide-open spaces. And if you want to hang mobiles and things up for them, a low ceiling is best."

Ms. Sasai giggled at the mention of mobiles.

Sensei said: "If you were to have the kind of exhibitions on a certain theme that Kobayashi was talking about, how would you distinguish the exhibition area from the bookshelves?" He had his left arm on the table, with his chin resting on his right hand. Uchida had told me that this was the position he adopted when he was interested, and that he leaned back in his chair with his arms folded when he wasn't.

"Depending on the scale of the exhibition, one whole floor can be used, or for something smaller, just the two rows in the center—the space can be divided up in all sorts of ways."

"It looks like it would be hard to remove books and replace them with new ones," Uchida said, his arms folded across his chest.

"There's plenty of storage space below," Kawarazaki replied, "so at first there should be lots of extra room in the stacks. The lower part of the bookcases, from the waist down, can be cabinets that serve as cubbyholes for books when an exhibition is being set up. That way things should go pretty smoothly. If, for instance, the theme is that of a particular writer, you can use the bookshelves in the center as a showcase for manuscripts or photographs. And using part of both the second and third floors would allow lots of different things to be shown."

"How about it?" Sensei asked, leaning back in his chair. "Any questions?"

"What material are you planning to use for the bookcases?"

Looking at Kobayashi, Kawarazaki said, "We're both thinking of laminated beechwood."

"Of course there's the cost to think of, but wouldn't everyday maintenance be easier if it was melamine resin?"

"Well, the pulp that paper is made of comes from wood. Books line up nicely on wood, and they don't slip around either. Even taking the problems of mold and termites into account, there's just no comparison. And when dust collects on melamine, it gets a kind of dingy, dirty look."

Sensei turned to Iguchi. "Remember that time we made movable steel bookcases? That was a big mistake. The books were always sliding down, and got dusty and moldy too. Books need to breathe."

There followed various questions and answers about details, such as what sort of lighting or air-conditioning were being considered, materials for flooring, where the power plant and offices would be, and the size of the parking lot. Looking rather sleepy, Mariko served tea in the midst of this discussion, then went off to take a bath, after which she must have retired to her room. I looked at the clock and saw that it was past midnight.

"It's getting late," Sensei said. "Let's call it a day. Both plans we heard about tonight were bold and confident. I've been wavering between the two, trying out different ideas. A number of things need further thinking about. I should be able to come up with something by next week. Thanks for all your hard work. Who's in charge of breakfast tomorrow morning?"

"Sakanishi and me," Yukiko answered immediately. I looked over at her, but she didn't look back.

"Since it's past midnight, why don't we have breakfast an hour later than usual? From, say, eight o'clock?"

"But won't people get hungry?" I said. "We'll have things ready by seven thirty. Anyone who wants to sleep in can come down at eight."

"That sounds good to me." Sounding cheerful, this time Yukiko glanced at me and said, "See you at seven tomorrow morning in the kitchen."

Uchida and I shared the hot tub that night.

Because the tub had just been replaced, the fragrance of cypress wood filled the air. I felt it deep in my nostrils, waking me up. The smoothness of the new wood felt good under my hands and feet.

"Which plan did you find more interesting?" Uchida asked, his voice echoing in the room. Relaxing in the hot water, I told him frankly what I thought. Kawarazaki's plan had seemed clear and rather beautiful, but actually filling a round space with circular bookcases might make you sort of dizzy—when I'd visited the Guggenheim for the first time the year before, walking down that spiral slope with no horizontal part at all had left me feeling a bit woozy.

"The Guggenheim is as much a monument Wright left to the world as it is an art museum. And it had to be on Fifth Avenue—he wanted to put a squat, round building in the middle of all those square skyscrapers. I'm sure the impact that shape would have was very much on his mind."

As Uchida saw it, the trouble with Kawarazaki's plan was that from the start it focused on a cylinder—both the building and the bookcases *had* to be that shape—which meant adjusting everything else in the floor plan to fit into a round space. The reading rooms were clear enough, but the offices and auditorium didn't really fit, and would be hard to use. If he'd at least made the first floor square, with a round structure on top of it, the proportions would have been much more stable.

After smoothly rolling out his objections, he asked me what I'd thought of Kobayashi's plan.

"That S-shaped curve looked startlingly new on the blueprint, and I think his bookshelves may feel more stable than the concentric rows. The breaks in the middle make it easy to move around, and you can look through them too. With Kawarazaki's plan you have circles within circles, which might end up feeling kind of oppressive. Kobayashi's gives a quieter, gentler impression," I said, then quickly added, "not that I'm qualified to judge."

"The idea of having two squares is not bad—not bad at all. With the buildings set back that way, there's space around them, so it doesn't look so crammed in. The only trouble is, it's not very exciting."

"I wonder what Sensei thought…"

"You'll be able to tell next week, when he presents his own plan."

"I thought the idea of having exhibitions, and arranging the books by theme, was interesting. Can you include that kind of program in a presentation for a competition?"

"As Sensei said, you have to show it in the design. But it would take money to set up a selection committee—and yes, it would definitely be unusual in a competition. Iguchi didn't say anything, but you could tell he was dead set against it."

"It would be great if you could have someone who runs a used bookstore and really knows books on the selection committee."

"If he could hear you now, Iguchi would be fuming. 'Leave that stuff for later,' he'd say, 'You're an architect, not a social planner.'"

After the bath, Uchida, flashlight in hand, made sure everyone had gone back to their rooms, then turned off the generator and went to bed. I felt hungry. Taking the red box with the scones in it, I groped my way through the dark, holding on to the handrail as I went downstairs to the kitchen.

In the moonlight I could see two white candles on the table. I struck a match and lit one. The clock on the kitchen wall showed that it was past one. Since the electricity was off, the contents of the refrigerator were being stored in two big coolers. If it didn't come back on tomorrow, we'd have to get more ice or freezer packs.

Mariko's Tupperware wasn't hard to find. I opened the lid to find a soufflé cup full of clotted cream, a small jar of jam, and two wooden spoons. I took the scones out of the box and put them on a plate. The time I'd spent at Mariko's place that afternoon didn't seem real. It had been a long day. I sat by the edge of the big table and stared into space.

Just then, I heard someone behind me. I turned to see Mariko, a short distance away. She was wearing a baggy pullover shirt that covered most of her, with woolen knee socks. She stood there in the moonlight, and ignoring the surprise on my face, asked, "Were you hungry?" Too startled to speak, I nodded.

In a slightly raspy voice, as if she'd just woken up, she said, "You mind?" as she pulled out the chair to my right and quietly sat down. I could smell her freshly washed hair. She took the cup of clotted cream out of the Tupperware, scooped up a bit with her index finger, and stuck it in her mouth—a gesture too quick to make anything out of. Then she opened the jar of blueberry jam. Silently she handed me the wooden spoon. As if to put a lid on my confusion, I split a scone in two and spread it with clotted cream and then jam, opened my mouth wide, and bit into it. I nearly choked, making the candle flame flicker.

"You need something to drink," she said. She stood up, got some milk from the cooler, and poured me half a glassful. "Shall I make some tea?"

"No thanks. This is fine."

The milk soothed my throat. Getting a cut-glass cup out of the cupboard, she poured a little Calvados into it. A strong, fruity smell floated in the air.

"Too bad you can't drink."

"Sometimes I wish I could."

She laughed silently, her lips to the glass, sending out that fruity odor, stronger than before.

"Why don't you try going to a bar sometime? There are plenty of nonalcoholic drinks. A watermelon cocktail tastes great."

"Really?"

"Sure. And sitting next to someone a bit tipsy like me might make you feel a bit tipsy yourself."

I liked watching people enjoying a drink. And I'd never minded the smell of sherry or brandy.

"There's a bar within walking distance of the office in Aoyama. Let's go when we get back to Tokyo."

My mouth too full to talk, I simply nodded again. I knew Mariko liked things to be honest and straight, so I should believe anything she said, but I felt more jittery than ever.

We sat there awhile without saying anything.

Slowly draining the glass, she murmured, "I hope everything goes well with the library."

"So do I."

"I'm going back to my room. Good night."
"Good night."
She stood up. After quickly washing and drying the glass and returning the bottle to the cupboard, she spun around and headed straight for her room upstairs without looking back.

I was left in the kitchen with the candle flame. While finishing the rest of the milk, I spread a load of cream and jam on another scone and wolfed it down.

Even when I'd blown the candles out, the kitchen wasn't completely dark. Moonlight streamed across the table and floor. Taking the red box, now empty, I returned to my bed in the library. I looked over at the windows in the west wing and saw a single light, in Uchida's room. The entire east wing was dark.

9

The next morning, I woke up at a little past five.

I pushed open the window that looked out onto the yard, then crept back to bed. I felt the crisp morning air deep inside my nose.

After I heard Sensei going out for his morning walk, I went downstairs to the kitchen. A low hum was coming from the refrigerator. The electricity was back on. I took the food out of the coolers and put it in the refrigerator, then lined up enough eggs on the counter for everyone and went to the pantry, where I filled a basket with vegetables and oranges.

"Good morning," Yukiko said as she came into the kitchen, looking as if she'd been up for hours. Her smile was always friendlier when we were alone. She was wearing jeans and a white T-shirt. And as usual, no makeup. Her T-shirts were sometimes olive green, or gray with a white or navy-blue border around the collar; or she wore a gingham check shirt. She obviously had her own taste in clothes, and even the most casual outfits looked as if they'd been made for her. The day before we left Tokyo, she'd had her long hair cut very short, but that didn't really change her overall impression. It might just as well have been short to start with.

The only child of a small building contractor in Higashi-Kitazawa, she had a deep respect for Murai Sensei. On a trip with her parents when she was in high school, she was very impressed by the inn where they'd stayed, and wanted to know who had designed it. It was Shunsuke Murai, her father had told her, naming several other projects of his. He, too, must have had an interest in Sensei's work. It was around then that Yukiko had decided she wanted to be an architect.

"We didn't really need to get up this early, did we?" she said. "Breakfast doesn't start till seven thirty."

"I'll make us some coffee." I opened a window facing east and put the kettle on.

The leaves of the big weeping cherry tree outside were now a deeper green. Cherry trees attract insects, along with the redheaded and pygmy woodpeckers that feed on them. Though I hadn't seen any birds this morning, the cicadas were already sawing away. Small ones, yellowish brown in color. I hadn't been able to find this type in the *Illustrated Guide to Insects* in the library, so I asked Yukiko, who said they were called *Ezo-haru-zemi*.

"Are they from Hokkaido?" I asked, remembering that Ezo is the old name for it.

"They only survive in cool forests, or at high altitudes," she told me. "So even in Hokkaido you never see them in cities. They seem to like beech trees. This is their peak season around here."

"You're quite an expert."

"One of the local farmers told me."

While listening to her, I ground enough coffee beans for two cups, and by the time I was done the kettle was boiling. The beans made a soft, murmuring sound as I slowly poured hot water into the filter in a circular motion. This was what morning smelled like. I watched the beans rise, silently counting off the seconds as Uchida had advised me to do.

Back from his walk, Sensei stood at the kitchen door. "Mt. Asama is belching smoke this morning," he said. "The lava must be rising. There might be a small eruption," he added before heading upstairs. He would be using the short time until breakfast to work on his plan.

As a cook, Yukiko was very thorough. When she deveined shrimp or took the fibrous roots off some bean sprouts, the shrimp looked as if they'd never had those black veins, or the sprouts those roots. If she made two eggs sunny-side up, each would neatly take up half the frying pan, with its yolk right in the center. After she tossed a salad there was dressing on every leaf, and her steaks were always perfect—well done for Sensei, medium rare for everybody else. Yet while she was working, she never seemed hurried or nervous. The way she used her hands, the tempo—everything about her was precisely the opposite of Mariko. Maybe they got along so well because they were so different.

Ms. Sasai was the first to appear in the dining room. She'd been Yukiko's instructor when she first joined the office, and still gave her advice from time to time. She was in her late thirties, which placed her between the two veterans and Uchida, who had been on the staff for just over ten years. Having studied calligraphy from a young age, she produced brushwork that was better than anyone else's, and it was her neat, delicate writing on most of the invitations, or on bottles of sake offered at celebrations for the completion of the framework for a new house, or envelopes of money given at funerals. Like Yukiko, she was quiet, independent.

"Did you hear the horned owl last night?" she said sounding unusually enthusiastic. Yukiko turned to look at her.

I asked her where, about what time.

"I heard it hooting—quite low. It sounded very close...maybe in the katsura tree," she said hesitantly. "I'm not sure about the time, but anyway, it was late at night." Though she seemed surprised by a lot of questions from me, there was laughter in her voice.

The sky had been very clear during the night, the moon nearly full. If only I'd looked out of the window, I might have seen that bird. I was disappointed to have missed it.

Kobayashi came into the dining room next, followed by Kawarazaki. Then Uchida, looking rather dazed, carrying the glass he'd taken up to his room. Soon Sensei came down, so even though we'd decided to start later, by seven, almost everyone was there. Mariko and Iguchi were the only ones absent.

    The meal started as usual, with Sensei's greeting. He was more talkative than usual, asking about the two presentations we'd heard the night before, and getting answers from a much more relaxed-looking pair this morning. The salad bowl was empty in no time, so Yukiko got up to make some more. That was when Mariko finally appeared.

    "Sorry—I overslept."

    "No problem," Yukiko replied, smiling at her. Mariko's place was on the opposite side of the long table from me, near the kitchen and ironing room, so she could answer the phone if it rang. She looked slightly pale. Uchida, sitting to my right, didn't seem to be in very good shape either.

    "I wonder if the library offices should really be in the back, away from the books," Yukiko said as she put the salad bowl back in the center of the table. She must have been listening to Sensei and the two veterans. It was unusual for her to break into a conversation this way. "The idea of having displays in the open stacks, changing the books with each new theme, is big enough to make us rethink the overall layout, isn't it?"

    Kobayashi and Kawarazaki, sitting across from her, seemed surprised. She was unfazed. Sensei was also looking at her. For the first time I noticed that her eyes were tinged with brown.

"Do you have anything specific in mind?" Sensei asked as he tore a piece off a baguette.

"No, but having the librarians and outside people talk about new displays behind a wall, way at the back where they can't even see the books, seems like a waste. I thought maybe we could make somewhere for them to meet where the reading rooms are."

"You mean aside from the regular offices?" Kobayashi sounded as if he'd found a line on a form that he'd forgotten to fill in.

"That's right. When you're talking about which books to choose, wouldn't it be better to be where you can actually see them?"

"You may have a point there," Sensei said.

"But they won't need to discuss new exhibitions every day," said Kawarazaki, looking a bit mischievous, "and besides, what would those meetings mean to the library users? We're not talking about one of those soba shops where you can watch the chef make his noodles from scratch behind a glass panel."

"I was actually thinking of a room with glass walls," Yukiko said, looking straight at him. "It could be used not only for staff meetings, but for lectures or seminars as well, so on one floor of this big, quiet library there'd be a lively corner where you can hear people's voices."

The usually quiet breakfast table was turning into a continuation of last night's meeting. I looked at Uchida. Normally he would have broken in with a comment around this time, but he was just sitting there gloomily eating his fried eggs.

"With the Kawarazaki plan, for instance, where would you put this meeting room?" asked Sensei, putting down his fork.

"How about in the middle of one of the circles? Last night we heard that the middle areas could be used for exhibitions."

Just then Iguchi came in, his hair rumpled, as if he'd just gotten up. He gave Yukiko a "What's-with-her?" sort of look. Like Uchida, Yukiko spent most of her spare time reading, so it was natural for her to be interested in the plans for the library. Her warmth of feeling, though, seemed out of character.

"I don't know," Uchida said, still looking disgruntled. "When there wasn't a meeting you'd have a pretty sizable empty space with rows of chairs. Not very inspiring. Unless you're trying to show everyone what a vacuum looks like."

Yukiko fell silent. Something had occurred to me as I listened, so I decided to say it out loud.

"Couldn't the meeting room be a multipurpose area? Normally used for reading in, but with folding or stacking chairs, so it could be available for all sorts of things, like..."

Iguchi cut me off. "It's fine to start the morning with a serious discussion, but let's not muddy up the general plan with details. Don't forget—a library built under the auspices of the Ministry of Education is completely different from a church or a concert hall." Sounding more forceful than usual, he went on. "Government officials don't want to hear about things like folding chairs. Wander too far into the forest looking for mushrooms and someone's going to shoot you.

"Take the cabinets in offices—they're almost all ready-made, because the makers know exactly what's needed for storing stuff and getting at it easily. Our job is to think about the space where the cabinets go. Talking about special furniture is missing the forest for the trees."

"Fair enough," Sensei said to him, "but the question was whether it's best to have all the office work done in the back, or to move some of it nearer the reading rooms. I think that's worth considering."

"Yes, of course. Sorry—I came in in the middle and didn't hear that part," he said with a strained smile. "I was just trying to say it's too early to be thinking about furniture. I know it's one of our specialties, and if we get the commission, we can make all we want as long as we stay within the budget. But we should save it to have fun with later." He took a sip of coffee.

I had gone too far off track. Iguchi was merely playing his role as pilot, steering me back in. He always worried about whether the trouble it took to produce new original furniture was worth the cost, because when Sensei ordered something to be redone after a final check, it was often the furniture. Iguchi disapproved of messing around with such a small part of a construction project, and wanted to show it, while to Sensei, details were important precisely because they weren't obvious. Since Iguchi respected Sensei's work, this tug-of-war between them was rarely openly expressed. Still, when he saw a younger employee heading too far in Sensei's direction, as office manager he couldn't let it pass.

Quiet returned to the breakfast table. Yukiko caught my eye and smiled slightly, then picked up her orange juice and drained about half the glass.

"Public buildings like this library," Sensei said quietly, "aren't something people ask for directly. Government officials are always involved, and there's a budget. Members of the selection committee naturally have their own agenda. But a library has to be for the people who use it. It's nonsense to build it for national prestige, and when a bureaucrat sees this sort of project as a culmination of his personal connections and political savvy, the result's a can of worms. The public pay for it with their taxes, so if they end up thinking the thing looks impressive but is a pain to use, the architect has failed.

"And one more thing, if buildings aren't remembered for generations, the architect hasn't really done his job. That holds true whether he's working for the government or a construction company. You sometimes find amazingly good work in post offices or telephone exchange buildings. It's great if people go into an everyday sort of place like that and feel so at home there that they start wondering when and how it was designed, even if nobody knows who the architect was.

"We don't know who's actually going to build this new library yet, but either way, our plan won't disappear. Even if we don't get the commission, I want it to be so good that young architects will wish ours had been used instead. Some buildings aren't finished until after the architect dies, you know."

The Guggenheim Museum was completed in 1959, about six months after the death of Frank Lloyd Wright. That was a full sixteen years after he had been asked to design it.

When Sensei had finished talking, I watched Mariko take the empty salad bowl to the kitchen. This prompted the rest of us to clear the other breakfast things away.

10

It was warm the following morning, and kept getting hotter. Even with all the windows open, I could feel the sweat on my palms as I worked on my blueprint. The cicadas were at it more shrilly than usual, and the humidity was rising along with the heat. On days like this, there was always a heavy shower in the evening.

The workshop on the second floor had two windows: a big French window on the south side, and a long, horizontal one to the north. I remember the architecture professor at university referring to windows as "orifices," which made me giggle. In time, though, I got used to it, and could say it myself without cracking a smile. Something I never quite got used to, however, was the way many architects write 解, the Chinese character for "solution," on their plans in places where they've met a client's demand. Unlike mathematics, in architecture there are no correct answers, or 正解 (*seikai*). It might have started as a way to show that although you've solved the problem, the outcome isn't perfect, but it still seemed strange to me.

And oddly enough, Japanese architects often refer to their clients as "patrons." That was another thing I'd picked up at university, but the first time I came out with it at the Murai Office, Uchida corrected me.

"You mean client," he said. "I wonder when architects started using 'patron.' Even the big builders call their customers that. It must be because at one time we only had work when either the state or the church needed a building, so we were firmly on the receiving end. And when you think about it, until twenty or thirty years ago having a house built for you personally was a luxury only the very rich could afford, so I guess it was natural to think in terms of the poor architect having a patron." He laughed. "Anyway, we don't use that word here. We have clients."

At the Murai Office, we didn't use "solution" either. We did call our windows orifices, though. So, for instance, if I was asked what was best about the Summer House, I would definitely include those two orifices in the workshop.

With the French window to the south opened all the way, it was almost like working outdoors. The first time I sat at the desk I'd been assigned, it seemed a privilege to have a view of the katsura tree, its branches spreading out over the garden. Whether the sun was out or not, the roundish yellow-green leaves always looked fresh. Looking down on them made one almost feel afloat. When Mariko drove her Renault out of the yard, or a taxi went past toward a cottage belonging to a professor of Russian literature that was south of the Summer House, the cars appeared and disappeared through the leaves. If not for that tree, locals walking past might have felt they were being spied on from our second floor. I wondered what it would look like in the fall when the leaves turned, or in winter, when it was bare. I imagined the sun's rays, much lower than now, reaching to the very back of the workshop, shining on the wooden floor while the desks and chairs cast long shadows.

Kobayashi and Kawarazaki sat with their backs to the horizontal window to the north, with enough space between their desks for people to pass through. There were three pairs of desks in front of them, facing the garden. Ms. Sasai and Yukiko sat in front of the two veterans, followed by a couple of empty desks, and Uchida and I had the two nearest the French window. Iguchi's desk was placed diagonally in the eastern corner so that he could take in the whole workshop. The entire left-hand wall was bookcases, in which almost all the documents we'd brought from Tokyo were kept. Parallel to these was the long table where we set up our models or held meetings.

The office was now working on four private homes. On the table were models of two of these: an Ogikubo house, which was Uchida's project, and one in Matsubara, which Ms. Sasai was handling. After discussing their models with Sensei a while before, they had left them there. The scale model I'd made for the Ogikubo house, with help from Uchida, was much better than any I'd produced at university. He had given me tips on how to hold the cutter knife, keeping it at the right angle, and how to spread the glue thinly and evenly. Those parts of the house that would be made of wood could be removed to reveal the concrete semibasement. There was a baby grand piano in the music room, made of black styrene board. This was the only part of the model that Uchida had contributed.

We had to finish the Ogikubo house this summer. The nice couple who were commissioning it told us they needed a library big enough to hold more than eight thousand books, with an adjoining study, and a soundproof room for their piano. We were expecting a series of smaller demands to follow, but so far these were all they had asked for.

Uchida had already finished his plan for the entire house. The work on the thin tracing paper was finely balanced. It looked as good on the final blueprint, too, capturing every detail. His lines were sensitive, yet showed speed and decisiveness. A man who drew this skillfully, it seemed to me, would handle women just as well.

The week before, we had started working on the furniture. Uchida would do sketches, and after Sensei had checked them, I made full-scale drawings of the details on each piece. Many of these were necessary for things we were making for the first time. I referred both to the sketches that had already been approved and others Uchida gave me, with his notes scrawled on them.

The Murai Office always provided craftsmen with full-scale, detailed drawings of any area someone's fingers or the palm of their hand would touch. Whereas most architects used ready-made metal handles for cabinets, it was Sensei's standard practice to have them made of natural wood, either black walnut or rosewood. And with a vertical door handle, depending on how skillfully the inner curve is carved, the feeling of pulling the door open and the amount of force it takes will be quite different. "Except for the front doorknob," Sensei said, "it's best for a hand to touch wood. Metal is cold, and makes you tense up a bit, so it's just right for the front door—the boundary between inside and out. Using wood there would make it seem like a bit of the innards was sticking out—kind of embarrassing."

In addition to contractors, the office hired craftsmen who specialized in furniture. As most of them were in business for themselves but working mainly for the Murai Office, they didn't really need accurate drawings for different pieces made to the same specifications; but since Uchida had taken charge of this feature, there was a lot more variety. Sensei was pleased with Uchida's drawings for the furniture in the Ogikubo house, so after he'd made a few changes, that was it. In certain places, Sensei seemed to be roughening up the original drawings rather than refining them, but when I saw the finished product, I realized that he had actually made the furniture more rational, easier to use. What is the difference between being careful and being fussy? I felt as if I'd found the answer in the lines that were added to Uchida's work.

At university I'd always had confidence in my drawings. Then Uchida taught me how to use a Staedtler drawing pencil from scratch, and I recognized that I'd been doing things my way rather than the right way. After I started working at the office, I practiced drawing lines two millimeters apart within a one-centimeter space. This gradually turned into a musical staff without the notes—a staff composed of three kinds of lines: normal, thin, and thick. I'd show them to Uchida, who would tell me how to adjust the angle of the lead when it touched the tracing paper, and how I should move my arm. If I was careful about these two things, I could regulate the thickness and darkness of the lines I drew. Watching his hand skim across the paper, I couldn't tell how much force he was using, or where. His lines were taut, they almost shone. As he drew, the pencil sounded light, then firm, then soft—like no one else's.

"You instinctively hold your breath when you start to draw," Uchida said once when he saw me sitting there with my pencil, looking rather lost. "That's where you go wrong. It's a mistake anyone can make. When you do that, your muscles tense up. But if you slowly exhale, you loosen up. That's what people mean when they say take a deep breath. So your arm will be steadier if you breathe nice and slow while you're drawing. Have you ever seen Shikō Munakata doing his woodblock prints?"

I thought of programs showing that artist peering through glasses with thick lenses, energetically carving away, his nose practically touching the wood.

"When he's feeling good he hums to himself the whole time. Or sometimes he grunts out Beethoven's 'Ode to Joy' in that raspy voice of his," he added, giving his own imitation of him. "It looks like he's furiously gouging the wood out, but he's not. He's singing, which means he's breathing out, so the movement of his hand is actually much lighter than it looks. Even when someone's just sitting in a chair, there's some tension in the shoulders. Exhale, and it goes away. Keep breathing slow and easy and your shoulders will never get stiff."

Uchida's bright-red T-shirt had LESS IS MORE in small white letters across the front. On the back, in the same position, it said LESS IS A BORE. (The slogan on the front is Mies van der Rohe's, the other Robert Venturi's parody.) Uchida didn't really seem to subscribe to either, but, concentrating, he demonstrated his method of breathing for me, the red shirt gently rising and falling.

"It isn't something you should be conscious of," he said. "People used to sing together while they worked in the fields, or pulled in their fishing nets. That helped keep their muscles from tensing up too much. If they were quiet, and straining, somebody was bound to get hurt. Singing together gave them a sense of companionship, and got everybody working at the same rhythm. It probably made them more efficient—kept them from getting too tired as well."

During the four months before we came to the Summer House, I drew thousands of lines on tracing paper, and erased just as many. Laid end to end, they would be longer than all the lines I'd drawn in nearly four years at university.

    For lunch that day we had cold noodles topped with lots of myoga ginger and shiso leaves, and salad with summer vegetables and tofu. For the tea break there was ice cream, thin rice crackers, and chilled watermelon. Mariko half-heartedly helped Uchida prepare both. The rest of the time she spent in the ironing room, listening to music or writing letters to friends. She seemed to write lots of them; when I was called to the phone, I often saw her writing on pretty stationery or postcards with her Montblanc pen. Her handwriting was light and lively, sort of like a rabbit hopping along.
    Toward evening, the sky began to look threatening. The sun that had been beating down on us most of the day was now hidden, and heavy rain clouds rolled in from the direction of Mt. Asama. I remembered the laundry I'd left hanging out in the back garden. During the summer in Aoguri, it wasn't unusual to have sunny weather followed by an evening storm. That's why it was safer to hang your clothes in the laundry room, but I still preferred to do mine in the sunlight outside. Besides thunder and lightning, though, one had to check to see if any bees had crept into one's socks or undershirts. Iguchi, who had once been stung on the forehead while taking in his washing, now always hung it up indoors. My remedy was to hook the laundry basket over one arm and give

each piece of clothing a good shake with the other as I took it off the line.

When I went out into the garden, with the chirring of cicadas on all sides, Mariko was sitting on a bench gazing vaguely into space, with her Walkman headphones on. You had a clear view of Mt. Asama from where she was sitting, but she didn't seem to notice. Assuming she wouldn't be able to hear my voice, I raised a hand and waved. She responded with a vague sort of smile. I set about taking in my washing.

"What're you doing this weekend?" she asked, with the headphones off.

"Working in the garden with some of the others. The tomato plants need trimming, and we have to put nets over the corn so the raccoons can't get at it. There's some weeding to do too."

"Sounds like a lot of work," she said, sounding bored.

"How about you?"

"I'll be in Kyū-Karuizawa."

"Will your parents be coming?"

"Don't think they'll be able to until after O-Bon."

"They must be busy."

"Are you going to stay with the Murai Office?"

"I'll be here all summer anyway," I answered, not quite understanding what she meant.

"I know that. I mean are you going to strike out on your own sometime or not?" The question came out of the blue.

"I don't really know yet. At the moment it's all I can do to keep up with everyone else."

"Keep thinking that way and before you know it you'll be forty." I had never heard her sound so harsh. I couldn't imagine myself being forty. And not seeing why I should think that far into the future, I said nothing.

"A shop like my family's makes the same stuff year in year out. That's what our reputation's based on. If we put out something new once every four or five years it'll sell at first, because of the novelty, but what our customers really want is the same old things we've been selling for generations. People think it takes skill and good taste to keep a traditional confectioner's going, but it's really more about perseverance. I have to admire my father for sticking with it all this time. But I'm sure he envies Sensei, the brother who got to do what he wants."

This reminded me of my own brother. "Tōru, you're really lucky," he was always saying. He had wanted to go to art school, to study sculpture, but was persuaded by our father to choose engineering. After failing his entrance exams the first time, he did an extra year, got into a national university, then landed a job as an engineer with a manufacturing firm, just as our father had done.

The folklore museum in Hokkaido that Sensei had designed had a sculpture of an Ainu by Osamu Sonoda, somebody my brother respected, so he knew the name Shunsuke Murai. When I was accepted as a provisional employee in the Murai Office, he told me again, "Tōru, you're really lucky." It sounded to me as if he were telling himself that he was the unlucky one, stuck in what he was doing.

I felt a drop of rain on my forehead. Mariko, who must have felt the same, looked up. The next moment, as if the sky had fallen, rain was pouring down. We hurried through the door nearest the garden. Mariko finally smiled.

Even with all the windows closed, the sound of rain pattering on the glass filled the room. The katsura leaves quivered. A large puddle was forming in the garden. Sensei, who had come out of his office, was looking out of the south window.

In about an hour the rain stopped. When I opened a window to let in some cool air, a fresh, wet smell wafted up from the greenery. In the west the sky was oddly bright, the sun throwing its last rays on the forest. The leaves, now sinking into the evening, shone orange along the edges. Maybe the male cicadas had given up finding a mate, because with a short *bzzz* they left the katsura tree for other parts.

"I'll be back by Sunday morning," Sensei said soon after the rain stopped, and drove off toward Koromo in the Volvo. Iguchi, a pale linen jacket slung over his arm, was also about to leave. He was going to a little party that an old classmate of his, now the managing director of a large construction company, was throwing at his summer house in Kyū-Karuizawa.

"Just so you know—this isn't all fun and games," he said, looking only half-serious. "You can never tell where you'll pick up information that could make or break us. You guys had better stay on good terms with your classmates. You can depend on them a lot more than you can on people who were ahead of you at school, even if you used to look up to them." Since the party wouldn't be over until late, he was going to stay overnight at a local hotel and would be back by evening tomorrow.

Shortly afterward, Mariko left in her Renault. "See you Monday," she said, with a slightly stiff smile. And so people disappeared, one by one. The six who'd be spending that weekend at the Summer House all had work to finish on the two private homes before we got really busy with the new library: Kobayashi and Kawarazaki, Ms. Sasai and Yukiko, Uchida and me.

I was looking out of the workshop window, thinking about how much easier weeding the garden would be after the rain had loosened the soil, when Uchida came in, dressed in black leather from head to toe. He had a matte-silver helmet and goggles in his hand, and his jacket squeaked as he walked.

"I'm off too. The clutch on my bike's been acting up lately, and I want to take it into Oiwake for repairs. They said they could probably have it fixed by tomorrow, but I won't know till I get there. Sorry I won't be able to help with the gardening."

While the rest of us had come in the station wagons, Uchida had used his own transport, a black British motorcycle to get here. The crowded, humid summer streets of Tokyo weren't good for the engine, apparently. "British bikes need to escape the summer heat too," he'd said.

The Vincent Black Shadow had been a hot property in the 1950s. True to its name, it gave an overall impression of blackness, but even someone like me, who knew nothing about motorcycles, couldn't help admiring its style and sheer solidity. He told me he'd saved up for two years to buy it. His helmet and goggles were restored British originals from the 1950s, and he had bought his leather gloves and boots in England too.

By this time, the temperature had gone way down. I watched his headlights on the road into the forest until he rounded a curve and disappeared into the darkness. I stood there awhile, looking into the night, listening to the sound of the engine.

11

It was sunny that weekend. A quiet Saturday without mail, visitors, or thunder.

Kobayashi and Kawarazaki retreated to the workshop after breakfast, while Ms. Sasai, Yukiko, and I changed into work clothes and went out to the field.

This had been a vegetable patch since the 1960s. At one time there were apparently beehives and silkworms as well. I thought at first that it must have been the influence of Wright's farm at Taliesin, but according to Uchida, Sensei was probably just following the example of other summer residents, who used to spend a lot more time in Aoguri in the early days, and not only grew their own vegetables but kept a variety of animals: goats, chickens, and even ducks they made ponds for on their property. "Besides, when you think about it," he added, "there's architecture in beehives and shelves for silkworms."

The green field was waiting for us, soaking up the sunlight. Each took a row. Leafy suckers had to be broken off the tomato plants, and we needed the right size of cucumber to pick from the vines. If left too long, tomatoes crack, and cucumbers and zucchini grow too large and lose their flavor. It was still too early to harvest the corn, but we weren't the only ones waiting for it to ripen. Somewhere in the forest, bears and raccoons were waiting too. And they could smell it from a lot farther away than we could.

We surrounded the corn with a net to protect it from the trespassers. As one swipe from the paw of a hungry bear would destroy something so flimsy, we attached several big bells around the top, in the hope that the jangling would frighten them away. These were Yukiko's idea.

There were three kinds of potatoes: danshaku, May queen, and Andes red, plus a few ratte. The Andes red were a little yellower inside than the danshaku, with a sweet taste that made them good for potato salad and croquettes. Ratte ones are French; the year before, Mariko had brought back some seed potatoes for her uncle. They were small—about the size of a dormouse—but rich in flavor and smell, delicious whether baked or steamed. They were also good for potato puree, and Uchida claimed that they made much smoother, more delicate vichyssoise than the danshaku.

I dug up one row each of danshaku and Andes. Wearing green gardening gloves with rubber on the palms, I straddled the row and pulled at a vine with both hands. Danshaku potatoes came rolling out, one after another.

The moist, warm earth under my hands brought back the smell of the dark, cold ground in our garden when I was a boy. The white leghorns my grandfather kept would be pecking at their feed in the shadow of the old well. I remember squatting down, watching the rooster's comb move restlessly up and down. Before I started kindergarten, probably.

That may have been when I had my first asthma attack. I'd been playing tag with my brother and his friends until evening, and when the temperature dropped, I began wheezing. As my airways narrowed, it got harder and harder to breathe, until I thought I was going to choke to death.

I started going to an asthma clinic by bus once a week. When I had a bad attack at night, I would have to lie on my side with the mouthpiece of a glass nebulizer in my mouth, while my mother squeezed a bulb that sent vaporized medication down my throat. As she got sleepier, the pumping got weaker and finally stopped. Despite feeling lousy, I remember finding it quite funny, and sad too. I'd gently reach out to give her arm a push, and the pumping would start again. She'd doze and I'd push, over and over, until morning came.

From the time my visits to the clinic began, I was indoors more than out. I would draw, or build things out of Lego, or watch my electric trains run around the track. Though I sometimes played with a girl my age who lived in the house diagonally across from ours, usually I was alone. I used to lie on the sofa, staring up at the ceiling, listening to the voices of other kids playing outside. My grades weren't bad, but I missed more days of school than anybody else. I stood on the sidelines watching the long-distance race in winter, and rarely finished my lunch.

During the spring vacation before I started third grade, my mother's younger brother, who was still single, began taking me to the mountains. We went to Chichibu or Takao, where we walked along mountain paths looking at birds through his binoculars. At first, it was hard to focus on ones that weren't close by. My uncle taught me to recognize the calls of the meadow bunting and paradise flycatcher. He showed me how to scoop up a drink from a mountain stream, and how to tell the difference between two plants with similar names—*hitori-shizuka* ("one quiet alone") and *futari-shizuka* ("two quiet together").

One summer vacation we climbed Mt. Shibutsu in Oze, with an overnight stay on the way. A thunderstorm started just before we reached the summit; an earsplitting bolt of lightning struck a bush just four or five meters ahead of us. The pouring rain turned the path to running water as we started down. Soon I was sopping wet, yet it began to seem like fun, my squelching footsteps louder than the rain, leading me on and on. By the time we reached the elevated boardwalk above the Oze Marsh the rain was no more than a drizzle. We kept going until we got to Ushikubi Point, and by then blue sky had begun to reclaim the territory it had lost to the storm. I looked up and saw the arc a swallow made in the sky. That night we stayed in a simple wooden cabin. My uncle didn't talk much, but when our eyes met we smiled. He hung our wet clothes up on hangers, then rummaged in his rucksack and surprised me by producing two full sets of dry clothes, from underwear to breeches.

At home, I missed seeing and hearing the birds. Binoculars, by magnifying them to eight times their real size, allowed you to see living, breathing things you would have missed otherwise. A meadow bunting, its feathers standing up on its head as it sang. The dark eyes of an orange-flanked bush robin, repeatedly wiping its beak on a branch. A Bohemian waxwing, shuddering, then puffing out its breast. All living things with warm bodies one would never touch, in constant motion, their eyes darting here and there.

Summer ended, autumn came, and as the air began to dry out, my asthma attacks grew less frequent. That spring, just before I started fourth grade, the doctor at the clinic told me I needn't come anymore.

I put a bird feeder out in our garden, which I filled with flax and sunflower seeds; a bowl of water as well. I waited patiently, and in a matter of weeks the birds started to come. I collected illustrated guides, and by listening to recordings of bird calls, eventually I could identify all the species that could be seen in Tokyo, both by appearance and song. Membership in the Bird Searchers took me to Mt. Takao or Meiji Shrine on Sundays.

Meanwhile, my uncle left Tokyo for Hokkaido, where he got a job teaching at a small technical college, got married, and never returned.

As the soft brown earth coating the potatoes baked under the morning sun, its color faded. If I had pressed my nose to the back of a bear cub that had been lying in the sun, I'm sure it would have smelled the same.

You got the best view of Mt. Asama from this field of ours. Though now only a wisp of smoke drifted up from the crater, frequent eruptions had sent it billowing thousands of meters into the air. Even if mentally you could trace the mountain's history twenty million years back in time, unless you actually saw it erupt, you would know it only as a dormant volcano. Yet digging up the earth near the Summer House, your spade soon hit volcanic rock and debris, showing how firmly the earth held on to its memories of past eruptions. If the next one was big enough, the entire village of Aoguri would be destroyed. That might happen only once in a hundred or a thousand years, but if I were here when it did blow up, I would become part of this earth. Even so, I couldn't help wanting to see Mt. Asama erupt, just once.

Unlike the area close to the house, here in the vegetable patch you had to go deep to find igneous rocks. This was because the staff had been digging them up, one by one, for the last twenty years or so, then using them to pave the driveway leading to the yard. Our dark, rich soil was the result of years of sifting, and adding compost and bird droppings; it was alive with grubs when it thawed out in spring.

I learned a lot from Yukiko, who knew as much about farming as she did about wild plants and insects. She'd made friends with local farmers through the village youth group. Some of her know-how was picked up by helping them in the fields on weekends, and she'd come back with lettuce and cabbages on the front and back of her bike, riding slowly along to keep her balance.

While we were working, we hardly spoke. With the sun on my back, I kept my hands moving, my eyes on the ground. I could hear my breathing. A humid, almost oppressive odor rose from the earth and the harvest I'd dug out of it.

When I thought I was finished, Yukiko stuck her hand in and pulled out two or three spuds I'd missed. "Look, here's one... and another," she said. "You've got to be more careful." I couldn't decide whether these shirkers deserved to be dragged out of their hiding places.

Eventually we piled our baskets on a handcart, and feeling the weight in our arms, pushed it back to the storehouse next to the kitchen. Yukiko and Ms. Sasai each took a basket into the kitchen.

I opened the big door to the storehouse to cool air and a faint odor of fertilizer. Tools for gardening and farmwork lay still inside. Through the single horizontal window near the ceiling, only dim light reached the concrete that covered half the floor. In the semidarkness, hoes, spades, trowels, pickaxes, bamboo brooms, and a ladder and stepladder were propped against the wall, while thick straw ropes, garden clippers, and shears hung on hooks. There was also a blower to clear away fallen leaves, a string trimmer, a lawn mower, a chain saw, a can of gasoline, and some antifreeze. On the wooden flooring toward the back were the shelves used to raise silkworms in the 1960s, and next to a spindle and loom were hives, a honey separator, a smoker, and a honey tank. There was a mortar and pestle too. Along the wall were large and small bamboo strainers, baskets, work gloves, straw hats, and a neat pile of wooden boxes—I had no idea what they'd been used for.

I took out the string trimmer, set it on the block of Oya stone at the entrance, and topped it up with oil and gas. Then, after putting on a helmet with a visor, I pulled the starter. No reaction. I tried again, pulling harder. Finally, on the fourth try, it started up. The engine was about as noisy as a motorcycle. I picked up the vibrating machine and slung the leather strap over my shoulder. Now all I had to do was move it in a semicircle in front of me, holding the handle with both hands.

I liked cutting the grass. As the nylon cord sliced through it, tossing up gravel in its path, the trimmer led me forward as if it had a will of its own. The sound of the engine filled my ears. I couldn't hear anything else—not the rustling of leaves, or birdsong, or people's voices.

Within an hour, the approach to the yard and the area around the slope were mown. Why does clearing away crabgrass and weeds feel so satisfying? We like smooth surfaces rather than bumpy, uneven ones. Architectural concrete is definitely not bad to look at. But when did people begin to prefer flat surfaces? Was it the sight of a lake on a windless day, or a sandy beach after the tide has gone out, or a puddle frozen over? My T-shirt and jeans were wrinkled, bits of green leaves and grass sticking to them. I switched off the engine and took off my helmet. The sounds of the forest returned.

We had cold Chinese noodles for lunch, with some of the vegetables we'd just picked on top. With only half the usual number of people in the dining room, and the talkative ones—Iguchi, Mariko, and Uchida—gone, it was obviously quieter than usual, but what we were all most aware of was Sensei's absence. After he left, the atmosphere at the Summer House slackened, the rooms seemed empty.

Ms. Sasai got up, took an LP from the rack, and put it on the turntable. As if they'd been waiting for the needle to touch the record, wind instruments burst awake. Clarinet, oboe, horn, basset horn, and bassoon joined in Mozart's "Gran Partita." The light, open music transformed the atmosphere there. It seemed to be telling us to stay a while, motionless, on this quiet Saturday afternoon, even though we had finished lunch.

Kawarazaki spoke to me while I was washing the dishes. He had something to talk about, so would I mind coming to the workshop when I was finished? I sensed Yukiko's eyes on me as she stood beside me drying the plates.

"I hear you surveyed the Asukayama Church when you were a student." I was sitting at the big table in the workshop, across from Kawarazaki. Kobayashi was working at his desk. "Sensei said the chairs in the nave came up during your interview. What did you think of the rest of the church?"

I picked through my memories as I spoke. I mentioned the curved surfaces, which were uncharacteristic. And the combination of natural oak and plaster. The details of the cross, done by skilled craftsmen using traditional bentwood techniques. Though the methods used, in fact, were largely traditional, the overall effect was definitely modern, and yet I had felt no tension between old and new...

"With an oak ceiling and plaster walls," Kawarazaki said, "you'd never get a finish of that quality without the best workmen. The curving walls must have made it all the harder. And as you say, compared to Sensei's houses, that church seems much more modern." He adjusted himself in his chair, then lowering his voice, went on. "The library is a much bigger project than the Asukayama Church. But he'll probably use similar traditional techniques in the interior, and the finishing. Especially in the reading rooms, he'll insist on using wood. He may want plaster walls as well. Kobayashi agrees with me on this."

Kobayashi, who must have been listening, kept his eyes on his desk. When he was busy, he never spoke unless he absolutely had to. Kawarazaki continued:

"It wouldn't occur to Funayama to use traditional techniques—he couldn't even if he wanted to—so there's no chance his team will make that sort of presentation." I nodded slightly. For the first time I felt I was being treated as an equal. "If we get the commission, we'll naturally be using wood for the bookcases and counters."

"Wood goes best with books, Sensei himself said."

"The problem is, we don't have as much time as we'd like to spend on the plans." He cleared his throat as if preparing for the important part. "Kobayashi and I aren't at the stage where we can come up with a final plan for the bookcases yet. I've already talked to Uchida about this—we'd like you two to start doing sketches."

"Yes, certainly," I said, surprised how positive he sounded. But perhaps it was this sort of initiative that Iguchi was looking for in the two veterans.

"Have you read any of the books in the room where you're sleeping?" I cringed slightly.

"Take a good look in the northwest corner. That's where all the books about libraries are. There should be about ten on the Stockholm Public Library alone."

"Sorry—I'll look at them right away."

"We'll know what Sensei's plan is next week. After then, the office will be concentrating on this project till November, so be prepared for that."

"Okay."

"He hasn't actually said so, but I think you joined us this year because of the library project. So bear that in mind. That's all."

Leaving them with a slight bow, I went straight to my room. The books in Western languages were in the corner farthest from my bed. A closer look showed there were three whole shelves about libraries. On other shelves were quite a few volumes with PALACE or HOTEL or GARDEN in their titles. Almost all had been published in America or Europe during the 1950s or 1960s, so Sensei may have bought them when he was abroad. Just as Kawarazaki had said, there was a whole series on Gunnar Asplund's Stockholm Public Library in the LIBRARY section.

In fact, I found about as many on Asplund as on Sensei's mentor, Frank Lloyd Wright. Some were in Swedish. The collection must have taken a while to compile. Almost all Asplund's work was in Sweden, and unlike others of his generation—Le Corbusier or Mies van der Rohe—he wasn't known as an innovator who paved the way for a new type of architecture. I'd never even heard of him until my thesis adviser at university named him as a European who had been influenced by Japanese architecture.

Asplund was sixteen years younger than Wright. After Wright had built Taliesin West and had started making those long trips back and forth—in 1940, just after Sensei had become one of his apprentices—Asplund had died, at the relatively young age of fifty-five. His career as a practicing architect was less than half as long as Wright's.

I chose a large book about the Stockholm Public Library and put it on the little table by my bed. There was something nostalgic about the smell of sunburnt paper, and the raised feel of the print on the slick pages. The text was in Swedish, the photographs black-and-white, and there were cross sections and floor plans, as well as diagrams showing the surrounding land. From these a clear image emerged of a building, shaped like a two-sided L, enclosing a large, cylindrical reading room.

The library is on top of a small hill. The approach to the entrance is a gentle slope. When you go in, you find yourself in a dimly lit hall surrounded by black walls under a high ceiling. Up a flight of shallow steps, and just ahead you suddenly enter a bright, round area with white walls and natural light pouring down from above. Inside are three circular tiers lined with books whose varicolored spines make the bookcases look like a tapestry. I imagine the effect is something like walking into a baseball stadium for a night game. That feeling of openness, coupled with a contradictory sense of being in a secluded place.

The smallest of the books on Asplund was a fairly recent biography in English. On the brick-red cover was a gloomy-looking black-and-white portrait of the man in profile. I took it out and lay down on the bed.

When he was a boy, Asplund loved to draw. He wanted to become a painter, but his father, a tax official, strongly objected, so he studied architecture at the Royal Institute of Technology. What sort of painter did Asplund, a generation younger than the Impressionists, and living a long way from Paris, want to be? And what, exactly, is the difference between an architect and a painter? You can paint without being asked to. You're free to tell anyone you're an artist. There are painters whose work no one sees during their lifetimes, who are discovered after they die. But what about architects? You can design a building without being asked, but if it's never actually built, can you call the blueprints "architecture"? Can you call someone whose plan never becomes a finished building an architect?

From somewhere inside my head I heard a tapping sound. I felt my body floating, my mind somehow inside out. Another knock, a little louder this time. Then suddenly I was yanked up to the surface from the depths of sleep.

"It's Yukiko," a voice said, and I sat up, sending the book on Asplund sliding from my knees onto the floor.

"Sorry. Just a minute," I said, picking up the book.

"Were you asleep?" she asked from beyond the door. "There was a book I wanted to look at, but I can come back later."

"It's all right. Come on in." When I opened the door, she was standing there, looking slightly hesitant, suppressing a smile, I thought.

"Okay, then, if you don't mind." She went straight to the library section, where I'd stood a while before, and after looking the titles over, took one out and came back with a clear smile on her face. You always knew exactly who Mariko's smiles were meant for, but Yukiko's simply appeared, as if she didn't care whether anyone saw them or not. Rather like that sense of calm she had—I could never figure out where it came from.

"Thanks," she said. "I'm borrowing this one." She showed me the cover and turned to leave, then stopped as if she'd remembered something. "Oh, Ms. Sasai says let's have a barbecue tonight since the weather's nice." The stuff for it would need to be taken out of the storehouse.

Feeling calmer after being suddenly woken up, I went down to the storehouse and hauled the table and barbecue grill out to the terrace outside the kitchen. I also put a basket full of the pine cones and small branches we used for kindling next to the grill. Then, back in the kitchen, I took some steaks out of the freezer and left them on a metal tray to thaw. All that needed doing was cutting up some vegetables closer to dinnertime. So I brought a few deck chairs and a coffee table outside, and decided to read the Asplund biography there until evening. The weeping cherry, now a deep green, was swaying in the afternoon breeze. Before long, the cicadas started up again. They were probably *Ezo-haru-zemi*.

Asplund's countrymen probably remember him more for the Woodland Cemetery, including the Woodland Chapel and Woodland Crematorium, than for the Stockholm Public Library. Having won prizes in a number of competitions, he began to gain recognition in his twenties, and in 1915 won the competition to design a new communal cemetery in the southern part of Stockholm, to be constructed in cooperation with his friend Sigurd Lewerentz. This marked his true start as an architect.

The project was planned as Sweden's first burial ground for cremated remains. It was sited on some bare land dotted with pine trees; the scale was large, involving landscaping as well as architecture.

The history of cremation in modern Europe began in the late nineteenth century, principally in England, then spreading to other Protestant countries like Germany and Holland, as well as Scandinavia. Although cremation was long proscribed for being against the Christian doctrine of resurrection of the body, as urban crowding increased after the Industrial Revolution, governments began to seriously consider endorsing cremation and communal cemeteries.

Cremation was legalized in Sweden in 1889, a decade earlier than in England. The ancient view of death as a return to the forest, deeply rooted in people's subconscious, had never entirely faded away. If that old idea could be made visible in a natural way, it might soften their psychological resistance to cremation. This was partly why the two young men named their plan the Woodland Cemetery.

But it took a long time to finish.

Even if he had known this would be his lifework when he won the competition, it wouldn't have seemed particularly symbolic. But five years after work on the project began, Asplund's oldest son died of some illness. Death had come near. He drew a plaque on his sketch for the gate to the chapel, which was being built around the time of his son's death, saying "You today, I tomorrow."

12

I heard a car come into the driveway—the hard crunch of tires on volcanic gravel. Slipping on a pair of sandals, I stepped down from the terrace and got to the garage just as Sensei's cream-colored Volvo pulled into his parking place. Stooping slightly, he slowly reached into the back seat to retrieve his Boston bag. "I'm back a little earlier than I expected," he said with a smile.

"Welcome home." I reached for the bag. "We've been waiting for you."

"Thanks, but I'll carry this myself. We haven't had another power outage, I hope." He laughed.

"Don't worry. The refrigerator's nice and cold."

"Good." Looking up at the katsura tree, he started toward the house. "In the old days power outages used to last a week or so. Didn't bother us much back then, though, with no refrigerator, or television, or washing machine. There was a time when we didn't even get electricity here until after dark."

I caught a whiff of something herbal from his open-collared white linen shirt. His well-waxed brown moccasins looked almost new.

"Evenings by kerosene lamp are nice," he went on, putting his bag down. "It's much easier to talk in a dimly lit room." He seemed in a good mood. "Bright light from above doesn't do much for faces. Got to be something softer, like candlelight off to one side. Women look prettier too. Who's fixing dinner tonight?"

"Yukiko says we're having a barbecue."

"Then I guess you won't mind me joining in at short notice." As if he'd just remembered, he added, "Be sure to use the new charcoal. The stuff left over from last year is probably a little damp. You don't want sparks shooting out while you're cooking on the grill. Okay then, I'll see you after six."

He slowly climbed the stairs. His back reminded me of the father in one of those old black-and-white Japanese movies who comes home from work too tired to speak. He stopped halfway up and turned.

"Do you have a minute?"

"Sure."

When I followed him into his office, he handed me a sketch he'd done.

"I've been thinking about your idea of using stacking chairs in the new library."

He wanted to use bent laminated plywood, something along the lines of Alvar Aalto's stacking chairs or Arne Jacobsen's Series 7. But the shape was distinctively in the Murai style, with just enough curve in the backrest and arms to accommodate a body. I felt it demonstrated his philosophy, that design must serve the user. The removable leather cushion on the seat was his way of keeping comfort from falling by the wayside in the pursuit of practicality.

Seeing a question in my face, he answered it before I asked. "I understand why Iguchi wants to leave the furniture for later," he said, "but in architecture, you can't just make the overall plan and let the details come afterward. I'm sure Iguchi realizes that too. The smaller parts have to develop along with the main structure. Have you ever seen how the cells of a fertilized egg divide until they start to look like a human being?"

The image of a fetal face, looking like an amphibian, popped into my head.

"I saw an illustration once in a biology textbook."

He nodded. "The fingers develop at a surprisingly early stage. A baby is already scratching its cheek with those tiny fingers before it's born. And opening and closing its mouth. The details of a building are like that, no less important for being small. Those fingers make it possible for an unborn child to touch things; to learn about its environment, familiarize itself. Chairs are similar. While you're designing one, you sometimes get a sense of the entire space it's going to be placed in."

Nobody remembers being in the womb, except maybe subconsciously. Yet even then we're discovering the world. It isn't only thought that makes our hand move— moving our hand can give rise to thought. Sensei's style of architecture took both things into account. Looking down, I opened and closed my own hand.

"Would you like me to discuss this with Uchida?" I asked.

"Actually, I'd like you to handle it yourself. He's already got plenty to do. I'll take a look when you're finished."

I made a photocopy of his drawing, then put the original in a big brown envelope for safekeeping.

Downstairs, I got the stacking stools out of the walk-in closet in the ironing room and lined them up on the terrace. Sensei had designed them more than ten years earlier, when he built the artist Yamaguchi's summer house in Aoguri. Each seat, made of castor aralia wood, had a slight depression to it; Tagawa, the furniture specialist, had used a special wooden plane with a curved blade for this. The stools fitted neatly on top of each other.

I heard Yukiko from the kitchen door.

"Sensei's back, isn't he?" Barefoot, she stepped down onto the terrace and, taking the handle on the lid of the black barbecue grill, peered inside. The sun was setting, and a cool wind blew down from Asama. I went into the kitchen, where three of us started preparing the vegetables. The potatoes we'd just dug up were the color of new ivory when peeled. Onions, eggplants, green peppers, and carrots, all in cross section.

"You can start the fire now," said Ms. Sasai, seeing that I had the rice cooker ready.

"Now?"

"It takes a while for the charcoal to get red," she said. "Wait too long and we'll all be full by then."

Uchida's method was first to put balls of newspaper in the bottom, then lots of pine cones and twigs, with two long, thin cedar branches bent on top to get the thing burning solidly. I lit the newspaper. The flames spread quickly, smoke billowed up, and soon I had a good fire going. The charcoal went on last. Although it didn't seem to catch, when you looked closely you could see it was turning white around the edges. By the time the rest had turned to ash, the charcoal was finally beginning to give off heat—from the side, the air above it shimmered.

The kitchen door opened and Sensei stepped out. It was still only five thirty.

"Which chair would you like?" I asked him.

"Could you bring out the comb-back, the one by the fireplace?"

It was one Tagawa had made especially for him, according to his specifications. The name comb-back comes from the thin slats that line the back, like a comb. Apparently a good deal of skill had gone into it—using the bentwood technique for the arms, and carving the seat just deep enough for hips and thighs to settle comfortably into.

When Windsor chairs were becoming popular in eighteenth-century England, the parts were made by different craftsmen: a bottomer did the seats; benders specialized in bentwood; a bodger made the legs, which had to be turned on a pole lathe; a framer then put all these components together. At present, however, hardly any workshops parcel the work out. Skilled furniture makers assemble the chairs themselves. Sensei showed his appreciation by having used this Windsor chair for over a decade now.

He pointed to the spot where he wanted me to put it, on a corner of the terrace some distance from the grill, with the weeping cherry just behind. Its lush green leaves, some with holes eaten away by insects, almost touched the back of the chair. This was Sensei's favorite tree. He sometimes scattered ash from the fireplace around its roots.

"Of all the libraries you've used," he asked, "which one would you say was your favorite?"

I thought, looking down at the charcoal, which was now glowing red.

I often used the university library when I was a student, but once I'd found what I needed, I never stayed. In high school I rode my bike along the river to the local public library to study for my university entrance exams. The reading room was full of students like me; tables, chairs, air-conditioning, and quiet were provided, but not much else. My junior high school didn't even have one. There was a large classroom on the second floor that we called the library, but there weren't many books on the shelves, and I don't remember borrowing any of them. Going a bit further back, though, there was a library at my elementary school.

"It's not there now, but there was a library—a one-story wooden building—on the grounds of my old elementary school," I said. "We used to go there every Saturday. One hour a week was set aside for reading, the last class on Saturday."

The school was on the highest point in the area; our school song contained the phrase "atop the hill." Across the road was a small, dark Shinto shrine, with the sprawling grounds of a prison beyond, built long after our school. Back in those days, apparently no one thought of protesting as they would today. Several of my classmates lived in buildings for the prison staff.

Alongside the high concrete prison wall was a broad avenue, off-limits for cars, with a wide, grassy verge. For children it was a perfect place to play, and grown-ups walked their dogs there. I remember my brother explaining that the wall had been rounded off where it reached a corner, because a ninety-degree angle would make it easier for a prisoner to get a foothold, shinny his way down, and escape. We sometimes saw groups of them collecting trash outside or cutting the grass. Before the war, it had held a lot of political prisoners.

Tall fir trees, planted at regular intervals, shaded the area around the brick entrance to the prison. There was a small wooden building as well, a shop selling things for visitors to take to inmates. It was very different from the average Tokyo residential district, more like the American suburbs I'd seen in TV dramas. Of course, I knew what sort of place a prison was, but the surroundings still looked attractive.

The elementary school library was on the edge of the hill to the left, just beyond the prison gate, less than three minutes away.

"What sort of wooden building?" Sensei asked, sounding genuinely curious.

"It was all on one floor, with a gable roof. The floor was wood too."

"Was there a passage connecting it to the school?"

"No. When it was raining, we took umbrellas. There may have been a connecting passage sometime in the past, though, back when the school itself was wooden."

One Saturday, just when our reading hour was ending, there was a sudden storm. A bunch of us waited in the library for a while, but the rain showed no signs of letting up. One of the girls told the teacher, "We'll be okay if we run, Miss," so we all dashed out into the rain, holding the books we'd borrowed under our arms or shirts to keep them dry.

Talking to Sensei brought these memories back, along with the smell of the schoolyard, wet from the rain. The book I had had under my arm that day was about Otto Lilienthal, who experimented with gliders before the Wright brothers but died in a crash on his last flight.

"At the entrance, we used to put on slippers, then slide the glass door open and go in. The library was much smaller than the gym—the ceiling wasn't very high either. The top third of three of the walls was all windows, with bookcases below, all the way down to the floor. There were two rows of tables where you could sit and read, four in each row. I think they were probably zelkova wood. The color was slightly dark, and the corners were smoothed from use, sort of like tables you might see in a monastery, or some old British university. Our school desks were all marked up by kids with their penknives, but there was nothing like that in the library. The chairs were natural wood, too, so they were pretty heavy to pull out from the table."

Out in front was a huge cherry tree, its branches reaching down almost to the entrance. The shade in summer made the library the coolest place in the school, which wasn't air-conditioned. As soon as you were inside you sensed a change in the air. Perhaps it was the fragrance of wood and books that made us so quiet in there.

"If you remember it that well, it must have been well built."

The evening light, tinged with red, shone on the crown of the tree behind him. I saw the shadow of a bird fly across it. Heard its cry, *khii*. A kogera.

"Without something extra," he said, "like the numbers left over when doing long division, architecture can be awfully dull. What attracts people to a building, what they remember about it, often isn't in the basic design. But those extras aren't always something you can plan for. Sometimes you don't even think of them till it's finished."

I looked over at the grill and saw that it was ready. I could feel the heat from the glowing charcoal, carried on the wind, and the aroma it gave off.

Yukiko and Ms. Sasai carried a large platter heaped with meat and vegetables out onto the terrace.

"That old school library," I said, "was somewhere you could be alone, without worrying about what the other kids were doing. At least it was for me. Even with a friend sitting beside me."

Sensei thought for a while before saying, "It matters, that freedom to be alone. It's as important for children as for adults. Books carry you away—from your family, from the society you live in. Alone but not lonely. Discover that when you're a child, and you have a place to come back to for the rest of your life. In that sense a library is something like a church, somewhere you can go by yourself, that will always take you in, just as you are."

I heard the cry of a kogera again from somewhere, quiet but clear. Maybe libraries are quiet for that reason, not because of an unspoken rule against talking. If so, what sort of shape was Sensei planning to give that space?

"We're going to start cooking," Yukiko said, peering into the grill.

"Sounds good," Sensei replied, in a tone that suggested we'd talked enough. I got off my stool and went over to help.

As if he'd planned his arrival to coincide with the barbecue, Iguchi pulled up in his car. He walked through the garden from the garage straight onto the terrace.

"I see my timing was just right," he said cheerfully. Kawarazaki and Kobayashi were already putting vegetables on the grill. Kobayashi, who didn't usually show much interest in cooking, was always happy to do the barbecuing. He watched the meat carefully, plating it up as soon as it was quite done. He seemed to know which part of the grill was hottest, and where to put each kind of vegetable, taking them off before they were burnt and quickly adding more in the empty spaces. I couldn't help wondering if he saw the grill as a floor plan with circulation routes. Had Uchida been there I would probably have made him laugh about it, but there was no one to joke with now.

"You look happy," Yukiko said, coming up to me.

"Barbecue's really good if it's done right."

"What do you mean, done right?"

"The stuff I've had before was always either charred or half-raw—never as good as I'd hoped."

"If only there was a Kobayashi for every grill..." she laughed.

With a barbecue, there was no time to relax. Cooking, eating, watching the fire, everyone's mind seemed to be elsewhere. Even Iguchi didn't have much to say as he helped put potatoes on a plate.

"Anyone who wants rice can get it from the kitchen," said Ms. Sasai. "There's miso soup too."

I took my loaded plate into the dining room. Yukiko joined me. Her usual seat wasn't near mine, so I was a little nervous with her sitting right across from me.

"What did Kawarazaki have to say?" she asked before taking a mouthful of rice. I watched her mouth and cheeks move as she chewed.

"He wants Uchida and me to start making sketches for the bookcases."

"Really? Lucky you."

"No need to feel that way. He told me off for not having read any of the books in my room."

"You really were asleep, weren't you?" she laughed. "There are lots of rare books in there."

"Have you read many of them?"

"Sure. That was my room, too, the first year I came."

"I was surprised to see so many on Asplund. The only things of his I knew were the Woodland Cemetery and the Stockholm Library."

"It's hard to believe he was the same generation as Mies van der Rohe and Le Corbusier. They had their eyes on the future, but he seems to have been looking backward."

"Let's say he took the long way around, and didn't care how long it lasted. I can imagine people getting fed up, asking, 'Why didn't you do it that way in the first place?'"

"What do you mean?"

"Well, when you look at how the plans for the Stockholm Library, the Woodland Cemetery, and especially the Gothenburg Courthouse Extension developed, you see them getting more refined with each change, and all three follow a similar pattern. He'll start out with a plan that shows great respect for old, classical styles of architecture. The first sketches for the Courthouse Extension look more like he's doing maintenance and repair work than architecture. But as he continues to make more drawings, the plan gets more modern. Maybe this trial and error, doing it over and over again, was a process he had to go through. At first the Stockholm Library had a dome you'd expect to find in Florence, maybe, and his starting point for the Woodland Cemetery was a Greek temple. That may have just been the way his mind worked, but it makes you wonder why he had to go all the way back to the Renaissance, or ancient Greece."

"In that sense, our boss is a bit like him, don't you think? An interest not just in traditional Asian architecture, but its European equivalent."

"And yet he always ends up with something rational and modern."

"Yes, he isn't a true classicist." It was unusual for Yukiko to be so talkative. Lowering her voice slightly, she went on, "It seems a little strange to me that Sensei studied under Wright. Wright said that nature was his only mentor. That's like saying there were no architects worthy of his respect—which is incredibly arrogant, isn't it? He saw his own work as 'classical'—maybe that's why he called his students apprentices. It just sounds old-fashioned to me. Sensei seems like the exact opposite in every way—I think he has more in common with Asplund. He hardly ever mentions Wright, and I don't really see how his experience at Taliesin is reflected in his work now." I'd been wondering the same thing and wanted to talk more about it, but just then Sensei came inside.

"Would you like some rice?" Yukiko asked, getting up.

"If you wouldn't mind."

Yukiko got him a bowl of rice, with some pickles out of the refrigerator on a little plate.

"Thanks."

On the terrace, the outdoor lights were on. There was also an oil lamp on the table. Someone had turned on the light trap beyond the weeping cherry. It gleamed blue. The temperature had gone down a little more, and the wind felt chilly.

Ms. Sasai went into the kitchen and started making the leftover rice into rice balls. Kobayashi kept his post at the grill until the end. When I went to see how he was doing, Kawarazaki called after me, "You young people should eat more." I ended up helping the three who were still on the terrace polish off what was left of the meat and vegetables.

I realized that only Mariko and Uchida were missing from this Saturday night meal. After emptying the ash from the grill, I sat there on the terrace for a while, feeling the night breeze.

13

It was Sunday, and though I'd thought of sleeping in as I didn't have anything planned, and wouldn't be cooking, either, I woke up at about five thirty, Sensei's usual time. I read some more of the Asplund biography in bed. Then I went downstairs, fixed my own breakfast, and made some coffee, which I brought back to my room in the library. I turned on the reading light and opened the book.

Visitors to the Woodland Cemetery, Asplund's last work, walk straight down a path of paving stones along a low fence, perhaps looking at the gently sloping hill on their right now and then, each at their own pace, drawing closer to the world of death. The white fence on their left serves almost as the boundary between one world and another, not waiting far ahead but nearby. Beyond it, the chapel and crematorium gradually come into view. Past the crematorium is the forest, leaves rustling in the wind.

The crematorium was the last part of the cemetery to be built.

After Asplund became a professor at his alma mater and remarried (his relationship with his first wife gradually deteriorated after their son's death), his reputation as an architect continued to grow. Nevertheless, his plan for the Woodland Cemetery, which he'd begun working on in 1915, ran into financial and other problems, and came to a standstill just as he was about to start on the blueprint for the crematorium. With the plan for the chapel also shelved, more than a decade was spent devising the landscaping, including the long paved path with the white fence running parallel to it. This was overseen not by Asplund but by his friend Sigurd Lewerentz.

In 1934, the stalled plan for the crematorium began to move again. But this development unexpectedly placed Asplund in a difficult position. When the cemetery committee asked Lewerentz to show them his plans several times and were refused, they decided to remove him from the project. Asplund was forced to decide whether to honor his long-standing bond with his collaborator and quit, or accept the committee's ruling in order to complete work that had already occupied him for twenty years. After much thought, he chose to finish the project by himself.

The cemetery was finally ready in 1940, when he was fifty-five. As if some unseen presence had been waiting for its completion, Asplund had a heart attack that year. The circle had been closed. His body was burned in the crematorium he'd designed, and his ashes were buried in the Woodland Cemetery.

The first sketches for the crematorium, made around ten years before it was finished, show that initially he wanted an obelisk, rather than a cross, to stand by the entrance. The plaque on the obelisk was to read "I today, you tomorrow." When, I wondered, were "I" and "you" switched around?

The site was also impressive for its use of stone. Different textures were carefully chosen, each suited to its place: on the floor or in the walls, where hands would touch them.

Granite was selected for the long random-pattern path to the crematorium and the huge cross that appears on the right. In the main chapel as well, a granite floor slopes down toward the bier on which the coffin is placed. Depending on how they're handled, these massive slabs that once lay motionless in the earth can create a feeling of stark stability or quiet. In the floor of a smaller chapel, granite is combined with brick. Marble, sandstone, and limestone each have a role to play in the mourners' response to the funeral as it progresses.

Asplund loved stone. The land he chose for the summer house he built for himself and his second wife, whom he married when he was past forty, was below a cliff of exposed bedrock facing the sea. The house is nestled under the rock, as if carrying it on its back. When you look down on the house from the top of the cliff with the sea stretching out beyond its roof, it looks like a boat in a small harbor, tied to a huge stone bollard.

Although he was demanding, Asplund apparently developed close personal relationships with the stonemasons. A generally bad-tempered man, he was nevertheless always willing to listen to what they had to say. And while they thought of him as "a hard taskmaster," and tended to keep their distance, they recognized him as someone who loved stone as much as they did. It was these people who found and delivered the materials for a rock garden that would blend in well with his summer house.

At the dawn of the modernist age, when steel, glass, and concrete were changing the shape and scale of architecture, Asplund retained his affection for a material with which human beings have had a strong connection since ancient times, and used it extremely effectively. He knew how to combine the very old with some surprisingly functional innovations in the Woodland Cemetery.

When a funeral service was over, the bier—the focal point in the chapel—was lowered on a hydraulic lift, to suggest the lowering of the coffin into a grave. Asplund left strict instructions that it was not to be transported to where the furnace was waiting until the chapel was empty. A line of small, round windows in the ceiling directly above the furnace was to allow natural light to enter, much as afternoon sunlight might shine on an open grave. This was where the mourners were meant to see the coffin off. In deference to the resistance most people still felt toward cremation, however, the idea of having them actually watch the coffin disappear into the furnace was not put into practice.

I heard Sensei's voice at the open door to my room.

"Sorry to bother you on your day off, but are you free this afternoon?"

He asked me to go with him to Yamaguchi's house, the one that had been burgled. He'd left the blueprints for the place on my desk, and I was to ask Yukiko how to get there, though it wasn't far away. Message delivered, he went back to his office.

I found the blueprints in the workshop and went through them page by page. They felt quite heavy resting in my hand. I'd seen the design in compilations of Sensei's work, but the actual blueprints had pencil markings on them, and his signature. It was like having direct contact with one of his projects.

The thief had apparently broken in through the window in the laundry room on the first floor. This was in the northeast corner of the house, along with other rooms where water was used: the kitchen, the first-floor toilet, and the bath and toilet above it on the second floor. From the cross section I could tell that the window was quite high off the ground and not very big, so it was hard to figure out how someone got in. In a city, the northeast corner would usually be at the back of the building, where people would be less likely to see somebody trying to break in, but the summer houses, built on large plots of land, were in full view on all sides. Did this thief specialize in narrow openings?

While I was examining the blueprints, Yukiko, who was also up by this time, walked by. I asked her where the Yamaguchi house was, and she took out a memo pad and started to draw me a map, then stopped and suggested we go there by bicycle after she'd had breakfast. There were two bikes at the Summer House, but hardly anyone used them except Yukiko. I never had.

We left before nine. The sky was blue, and the sunlight already warm. Even so, with the wind I felt as I pedaled along, I was a little chilly in short sleeves. As we rode the bumpy, unpaved road, the saddle and handlebars shook, until we reached Aoguri's wide main street and headed north. It would have seemed a little lonely if we'd been on foot; there were no people or cars around.

Both sides were lined with larch trees, their leaves a deep green. From somewhere overhead I heard the song of a gray thrush. It sounded cheerful, as if the bird knew today was Sunday. When I first heard the blackbird at the end of the Beatles song in junior high school, I wondered if it might be a distant cousin of our gray thrush. The two birds resemble each other both in their quite-complicated songs and in the way they look when singing them, with their breasts puffed out. Could the blackbird have changed its coloring bit by bit until, after many generations, it turned into a different species, living far to the east? I wanted to stop for a while to listen, but seeing Yukiko pedaling on ahead, I gave up and followed.

Old summer houses from the time the village was founded began to appear on either side. There were chalets with well-tended thatched roofs, not a sign of any weeds growing in them, and others where the trees were untouched and the grass had been left to grow. Quite a few had their rain shutters closed. We were now deep in the forest. It seemed funny how the back of Yukiko's white T-shirt looked like the newest, flashiest thing around. As I followed silently behind, I caught the sharp smell of fir trees.

Yukiko's bicycle suddenly stopped. I quickly braked as well.

"Are you all right?" I heard her ask anxiously. An old woman in a kimono was sitting, leaning against the shoulder of the road, staring upward. The hem of her kimono was torn, and I could see her shin, like a dry branch, above her white tabi socks. Yukiko got off her bike and squatted down beside her.

"Had trouble breathing..."

"Don't worry, Sensei," Yukiko assured her. "We'll take you to the hospital." She then turned to me. "Could you ride back and get a car?"

The old woman was the novelist Harue Nomiya.

"I don't need a hospital," she said. "I get these spells now and again. They pass if I rest awhile, nothing to worry about."

Yukiko looked at me again. I nodded. "I'll be right back. Anything else I should bring?"

"Water and a towel. Oh, and could you ask Ms. Sasai to get out a pair of my pajamas? Bring my wallet too." The instructions were clear and straightforward.

"Are you sure we shouldn't call an ambulance?"

"That would take even longer."

"Hold on, you two," the woman broke in. "I really don't need a hospital. I'm feeling better already."

"I understand, Sensei. But at least let us take you home."

"Thank you, yes. Sorry to put you out... Who are you, anyway?" She looked at Yukiko, still squatting beside her, but the light through the trees must have been too bright for her, because she closed her eyes again.

"I'm Yukiko Nakao. From the Murai Design Office."

"Ah, Murai Sensei. So we're neighbors."

"Yes, that's right."

"No need to fuss, I won't be here much longer anyway." Yukiko frowned slightly. "No need, no need," she repeated. Her face was very pale.

"I'm off then," I said.

So that was the writer, one of the village's first residents, the person who'd taken the discovery that a tree had half destroyed her cottage so calmly. I was surprised to see how tiny she was. Had she been out walking alone? I pedaled furiously. I didn't listen to any birds on the way.

I found Ms. Sasai in the laundry room and asked her to get me the things I'd been told to bring. We might end up taking the writer to a hospital anyway. It was just like Yukiko to think of pajamas on the spur of the moment. After putting some water in a thermos for me, Ms. Sasai told me to wait a minute while she looked up the phone number of the old woman's relatives.

I used the Volvo to drive back to where the two of them were waiting.

Harue Nomiya was leaning against Yukiko, her eyes still closed. "Let's get you into the car," I said as I took her in my arms and carried her over, then laid her down in the back seat. Her body was as light and fragile as a child's. It was embarrassing to think I had never held a woman this way before, but I couldn't laugh.

From the driver's seat I could see about half of Yukiko's face in the rearview mirror, looking calm as usual.

"I'm fine," said Nomiya Sensei. "The water is good. If I can just lie here awhile I'll be all right."

"I'm sure you will," Yukiko said, "but just in case, wouldn't it be best to let a doctor check to make sure?"

"No, just take me home."

"Today's Sunday, so your maid won't be there, will she?"

"She'll be coming over to make my lunch."

"I see. We can talk about what to do next after we get there."

"My regular doctor's in Tokyo, but I've hardly ever been to the hospital here. Besides, at my age there's not much they can do for you."

Carefully, so as not to swing the car around too sharply, I made a U-turn and headed for the cottage.

Entering it was like walking into Aoguri just as it was fifty years ago. There was hardly anything in her room. With its walls of plaster and faded wood, it was as bare and still as somewhere used for the tea ceremony.

I gently put her down on the sofa in front of the stone fireplace, which was so clean I couldn't tell whether it had been used recently or not. She was beginning to get her color back.

"What was your name again?" she asked Yukiko.

"Yukiko Nakao."

"How do you write 'Yuki'?"

"With the character for snow."

"A good name."

The novelist had clearly taken a shine to her. I opened the window facing the garden to let some air in. Outside, some Oriental tits were calling back and forth as they pecked at the sunflower seeds in the bird feeder, or carried them off to the branch of a nearby tree.

Yukiko phoned the old woman's relatives, before telling me she would stay with her until the maid arrived, and I should go back, since I had to look at the Yamaguchi house that afternoon.

I later heard from her that after I'd left, a whole stream of neighbors—writers, poets, musicians—stopped by, some looking in from the doorway, others coming inside, to see how Harue Nomiya was. There was no knowing how the news got around, but the lady was clearly still an important member of the local community. Yukiko was worried that they would tire her out, but as Harue Nomiya talked to these mostly younger friends and acquaintances, who treated her with deference, she seemed to revive. She introduced Yukiko to everyone as "the girl who saved my life."

A doctor, who was also a novelist, came to listen to her heart through an old ivory stethoscope and take her pulse. He told her it might have been a mild heart attack, and advised her to see her regular doctor in Tokyo as soon as possible. "It gets chilly in the mornings and evenings, so be sure to keep your hands and feet warm. Stay away from stimulants like coffee and English or green tea—better to drink lots of *hōjicha* instead."

"I see, yes, I'll do that," she replied, now somewhat subdued.

Yukiko made her some *hōjicha*, brought chairs for the guests, cut up some watermelon from the refrigerator, which the doctor had said would be all right for her to have in the afternoon, then washed the plates and saw the visitors to the door.

"I've come back to life," Harue Nomiya said after a bite of the watermelon.

"You two had quite a time this morning," Sensei told me in the car on the way to the Yamaguchi house.

"If you hadn't been there, she would have been in real trouble."

"She kept saying she didn't have much time left," I mentioned, with my hands on the steering wheel, looking straight ahead, "but for someone so tiny, she makes quite an impression."

He chuckled. "A warrior, that one." We both laughed.

"She must be over ninety by now," I said.

"Way past. Ninety-six or -seven, I think. People born in the Meiji era are tough."

"You were born then too, weren't you?"

"At the tail end of it," he said, a hint of laughter still in his voice. "By the time I was old enough to know what was going on, the Meiji emperor was gone and it was Taisho."

I stopped on the way to load the bicycle Yukiko had left by the side of the road into the trunk. Yamaguchi's place was a little farther on, off to the left. It was less than three hundred meters from where we'd found Harue Nomiya by the side of the road.

After Sensei announced himself, standing in the entranceway, Gen'ichiro Yamaguchi appeared.

"I'm sorry to call you out on a Sunday," he said, a little too politely.

"No problem," Sensei replied. "You've had some bad luck."

Yamaguchi was a small man, almost delicate, but a commanding presence—he had this in common with the old novelist, I thought.

"This fellow here and one of my team found Harue Nomiya collapsed by the side of the road this morning, right near here," Sensei said, by way of an introduction.

"I'll be handling the repairs," I said with a bow, giving him my name.

"Is she in the hospital?" Yamaguchi asked Sensei.

"She insisted she didn't need to go, so we took her home," I answered in his stead.

"That sounds like her. I hope she'll be all right, though."

"Someone's still with her," Sensei said, "but apparently she recovered pretty quickly."

Yamaguchi turned to me. "You're very young, aren't you? Did you just join the office?"

"Yes, in the spring of this year."

"Our first new employee in three years," Sensei added cheerfully.

"That's good. Glad to know you."

There was a sort of calmness in his eyes. And he had a slow, cultured way of speaking. It was easy to believe that he and Sensei had been friends since they were students. Sensei was his usual informal self, but I detected an undertone, a certain reticence that wasn't there when he was talking to us. It reminded me that relationships between men weren't at all cut-and-dried, in ways that were hard to pin down.

"A long time ago," Yamaguchi said, walking briskly toward the interior of the house, "a bit of burglary wasn't uncommon in Aoguri." Just before he got to the living room he turned into the dining room, then on into the kitchen. "But I hadn't heard about anything like that for so long," he continued without looking back, "it never even occurred to me that it might happen here."

After a tour through the house counterclockwise, we reached the laundry room. In my mind I was comparing the rooms to the blueprints. The washing machine was on top of the dryer, with a chute next to them for clothes sent down from the second floor, where the bath was. Near the ceiling were two pipes to dry clothes on, and there was a heater fixed in the ceiling. Next to it was a small window, through which you could see only blue sky.

"The frame was removed from outside with great care," Yamaguchi said. "The police were impressed. Said they'd never seen such an efficient break-in. I'm not sure they should be admiring something like that, though," he laughed. "If he'd taken the trouble to put the frame back the way it was before, they probably wouldn't have been able to tell how he got in," he added, saying the police had reinstalled it later.

Sensei took me for a look at the laundry room window from outside. First-floor windows in all the summer houses were vulnerable. This was the only one in the house without a heavy wooden shutter, probably because it was so high up, and you wouldn't want to cut off a source of natural light.

Would he have used a ladder, or some sort of scaffolding? Either way, he'd have been far off the ground.

According to the police report, there were faint markings on the concrete wall, probably made by a ladder. I examined the window from both inside and outside the house, then after taking out the wooden frame, with a single, old pane of glass in it, put it back and fastened it with long nails as a temporary measure.

Mrs. Yamaguchi, small enough to match her husband, brought us tea and sweets in the living room.

"We'll put in a new window, with double glazing," Sensei said in the official tone he used at work. "But if there's iron grating on the outside it'll look like a prison. I could put something like a shutter on the inside, but do you think you'd bother to open and close it?"

"I'm not sure. It is a long way up."

"It might make you feel safe, but a really determined thief would just break through it."

Although he was sorry about what had happened, Sensei told Yamaguchi he thought it was best not to do too much to prevent it occurring again. Thieves can break in anywhere if they use enough force. Taking extreme measures to keep them out would be awkward, like walking down the street in a full suit of armor.

"If someone tries again, will double glazing be strong enough?"

"The frame won't come out so easily, and the glass will be harder to break. If somebody tried to take the frame out as cleanly as they did last time, it would take at least an hour, maybe more. Of course, with a crowbar you could break the glass in about thirty seconds, but if we use a thicker frame the opening will probably be too small for an adult to get through."

"I'll leave it to you then."

The two of them then started talking about old friends from art school. Yamaguchi told me I should feel free to look around, so I went to take a look at the other rooms.

Both men knew one another's taste, and there were signs everywhere that Sensei had felt free and easy when he designed the house. The ceiling in the atelier was very high, while the low ceiling in the bedroom gave it a cozier feeling. The living room, on the other hand, had large windows and a ceiling of medium height. In the music room, quite a distance from the atelier, there were only two small windows, but the cloth wall covering provided a relaxed, intimate effect, similar to the bedroom. Though it wasn't a big house, each room gave a different impression. And every corner was well used, lovingly, too, making it unmistakably Yamaguchi's house. Sensei's designs always matched his clients' lifestyles, leaving room for them to grow into the place, to make it their own.

Mrs. Yamaguchi was in the kitchen, starting to get dinner ready. I remembered the painting I'd seen on the wall of Mariko's summer house, with a wave washing away a child's footsteps. I'd heard that nearly thirty years before, their only son had died at the age of twelve.

"Protecting a house isn't easy," Sensei said from behind me on the way back. "You try to design it so that it's fairly fireproof, and make it sturdy enough to survive earthquakes. Safety is an important part of our job. But just imagine, if there was a really big earthquake that reduced the whole city of Tokyo to rubble, how would you feel if your house was the only one that didn't collapse or burn down? That's something worth thinking about."

I wasn't quite sure I understood. I didn't answer, so he went on.

"Imagine a wasteland, with only your house left standing. Most of your neighbors would be dead. And you, not only alive, but with a roof over your head, and everything unscathed. It would be unbearable. Could you recover from something like that? People make it through a disaster believing they were just lucky, right?

"A house that's completely prepared for any kind of disaster is a fort, not a home. Could you live comfortably in a place like that? I doubt it. You'd always be anticipating the next disaster."

Something about this didn't seem quite right to me. I couldn't explain it in words, though, so I kept quiet. Had seeing the Great Kanto Earthquake as a teenager led to this way of thinking?

The setting sun shone down on the Summer House. The dining room window and the one in the workshop upstairs were both wide-open. It had been a long day. I carefully backed the car into its usual space. I was now used to driving the Volvo.

"Let's do Yamaguchi's window quickly. Could you finish the design tomorrow? I'll check it then. Oh, and could you call Sugiyama, the contractor?" He then retreated to his office until dinner was ready.

After sundown, Mariko, who wasn't expected until Monday morning, turned up in her Renault. She was wearing a blue linen dress. Her arrival was like seeing a colored ball bounce down the Summer House floor.

"The smoke was really billowing out of Mt. Asama. Did you see it?" she asked.

"No, I was pretty busy today with this and that."

"On a Sunday? There were lots of people out in Kyū-Karuizawa. Quite a commotion."

Soon afterward, Yukiko came back from the old novelist's cottage.

After eleven, when everybody had had a bath and was ready to retire, I heard the low rumble of the Vincent Black Shadow's exhaust, sounding like a small tremor deep in the earth as it drew closer. A black bike in a black forest. There was the sound of tires on volcanic gravel, then quiet. I retreated to my room in the library and softly closed the door. The window looking out on the garden was open. I heard the screen door open and the inside door close; beneath my feet I felt the rattle of the inner door as it slid shut, and the thud of the bar being replaced. For a while I carried on with the biography of Asplund under my reading light.

14

The next afternoon, Harue Nomiya stopped by with her daughter, who had come to take her back to Tokyo with her, and left us an expensive basket of fruit. She also brought a signed copy of her latest novel for Yukiko. The India ink was still so fresh you could almost smell it; the brushstrokes wavered only slightly. Mother and daughter then climbed into a waiting taxi and headed for the station.

A towering white cloud that formed in the northeastern sky looked almost high enough to reach the stratosphere. Past noon, the temperature rose to over twenty-five Celsius. Then, unsurprisingly, a rainstorm drenched the Summer House soon after our tea break. The air quickly cooled. Watching these weather patterns made me begin to lose track of what day it was. Sensei was to present his plan for the Library of Modern Literature on Thursday.

I quickly drew a blueprint for the window at Yamaguchi's house, and when I'd finished negotiating with the contractor, concentrated on my full-scale drawings for the house in Ogikubo. At some point, I showed Uchida Sensei's sketch for the stacking chairs in the library.

"He doesn't like the finish to be too delicate," he said, after looking at the drawing for some time. "But if the drawing's too crude, the chair itself will turn out to be heavy. His lines are neither fine nor rough but somewhere in between, which actually makes it hard to draw the blueprints. I'm always feeling my way as I go, every time. But I've got the chairs for the reading rooms to do, so I'm glad I got to see this. Thanks for showing it to me."

Uchida must have noticed that Sensei had given me the drawing first, and I was grateful that he didn't comment on it.

Late that afternoon, when he had reached a good cutoff point in his work on the Ogikubo house, Uchida cleared his desk and set to work on sketches for the new library. I mentioned the furniture in the Stockholm Public Library. "What makes that a really great library," he said, his arms folded across his chest, "is the basic design, which is wonderful, but the quality of all the furnishings is definitely a factor. We probably won't be able to reach that standard, but we've got to do what we can." He sounded a lot more serious than usual.

For the next few days, Uchida and I used the blueprints from the Hokkaido University Library for reference as we considered sizes and types of bookcases, and came up with ideas for minimizing problems due to differences in the size of books, along with ways to keep moisture and dust from collecting at the back of the shelves. Uchida didn't stop to chat as much anymore, and started going straight to his room after dinner. I couldn't tell whether this was because he suspected something might be going on between Mariko and me, or if he was just absorbed in his work.

Iguchi, who'd been at the office in Tokyo, was delighted to be back. "It's hot as Hades back there," he said. "This is heaven."

Mariko and I continued our shopping trips, but we didn't talk about anything special or stop off anywhere on the way. I felt a little disappointed, yet relieved at the same time.

Thursday morning was unusually cold and wet. Perhaps the birds and insects were hiding somewhere, waiting for the rain to stop, for they didn't make a sound. After lunch, Sensei sat at the middle of the workshop table and explained his plan for the Library of Modern Literature. We listened, sipping tea Mariko had made for us.

Drawn freehand on a croquis whiteboard with a Staedtler Lumograph pencil, Sensei's plan was a combination of two hexagons, one larger than the other. It looked as if he had just replaced Kawarazaki's cylinder with hexagons, adapting them to Kobayashi's idea of having a bigger and smaller structure.

But there was a clear difference from either of those two plans.

The diagonal corridor that connected the two buildings was the same width as one side of the smaller hexagon, making the outline of the six-sided shape less distinct. Seen from above, they were connected not by a straight line but a mild curve, something like a treble clef. It was an organic shape, where one part suggests the whole, like part of a snow crystal, or the tuning peg of a stringed instrument.

As with the curved surfaces in the Asukayama Church, the shape of this building would immediately strike the viewer's eye. This seemed unusual for someone who believed that what was needed in the interior should determine a building's outward form, and who didn't like to surprise people with showy appearances.

It seemed even more so when we saw the cross section. The larger hexagon had three floors below ground and four above, while the smaller one had two below and three above. The corridor between them was a downward slope that connected two different levels. I had never seen anything like it in Sensei's work.

"This is a little off track," Sensei said, and began to explain the difficulties of the cylindrical form. "While it gives you access to a 360-degree view of the outside, a circle is actually closed. And it's a hard form to open up, so that it welcomes people in. When you need to gather them into a central space, for religious ceremonies, say, a cylinder can be effective, but it's not really suitable for a public building that has to be open to everyone. Besides, rectangular books don't fit into curved bookcases—you end up with gaps and leftover space. If the diameter of the circle is large enough, the curve on the grid of each individual bookcase won't be so pronounced, so this might not be much of a problem with the Kawarazaki plan. But with the Kobayashi one the grid is smaller, which means the curves will be sharper, so even though the way he's arranged the bookcases is interesting to look at, they might be hard to use. Anyway, cylinders are hard to deal with."

Having explained this much, he brought out another sketch to show us. It was of a hexagon enclosed in a circle, with all six points touching it.

"A circle on the outside is something else. The curve creates a gravitational pull."

Sensei's plan for using both circles and hexagons showed up clearly on the cross-section sketch. He had cylinders and hexagons alternating floor by floor. In the main building, the first floor was hexagonal, the second cylindrical, the third another hexagon, and the fourth a cylinder. Viewed from outside, the second and fourth floors were cylinders with small rectangular windows to let in light, while the first and third were hexagonal, with all six walls made of glass panels. Furthermore, these two hexagonal floors were about thirty degrees out of alignment, so the glass walls were a little off-kilter as well. In the smaller annex, only the second floor, which was to house the restaurant, was hexagonal with glass walls.

The arrangement of the tables and chairs in the reading rooms was different at every level. On the odd-numbered, hexagonal floors, there were long tables alternating with rows of sofa chairs in front of the glass walls where people could sit and look outside. There was plenty of natural light to read by. Behind them were two hexagonal rows of bookcases and, as on the even-numbered floors, two semicircular reference tables in the center.

Each of the two glass-paneled corridors connecting the buildings sloped down a floor, from the fourth and third floors of the library to the third and second floors of the annex. Sensei said he thought one of the most enjoyable things about the library would be walking down these shallow slopes from the library to the restaurant or auditorium. The corridors curved slightly just before they reached the annex; as you walked down you'd be able to see the extensive grounds of Aoyama Cemetery through the glass. The curve would resemble that of the pages of a large book open on a table. Users would be likely to stop for a while to enjoy the view.

The first floor of the annex was the auditorium. Its ceiling reached all the way to the height of the mezzanine in the main building, while the seats sloped down to the level of the upper of the two underground floors. You came down the slope from the second floor of the main building into the mezzanine overlooking the lobby of the auditorium. The passageway connecting the first floor of the main building to the first floor of the annex was also glass-paneled; as the passageway descended, the ceiling gradually got lower, until it led into the auditorium lobby.

If this library was actually to be built, it would undoubtedly be Shunsuke Murai's definitive work of the 1980s. Still, I couldn't help wondering: Why had he turned away from traditional Japanese architecture toward more modern designs in the mid-1970s? And there was something else that we all must have had in mind, though no one brought it up. This was the influence of Frank Lloyd Wright, whom Sensei had studied under briefly before Japan went to war with America. There had been no sign of Wright's influence in the buildings he had designed until recently, and he had never written, or even spoken, of his brief apprenticeship. Yet there were a number of discreet lines connecting this library to the Guggenheim Museum, completed after Wright's death.

Outside the workshop, the rain poured steadily down. It was even cooler than before.

"I see you've left a large setback space," said Kawarazaki. "Is that going to be a park?"

"There aren't many places near Aoyama Cemetery to take a stroll in, or stop to rest in the shade. I thought it would be nice to have benches too. It would be great if people happen to look up at the restaurant windows while they're sitting there and decide to go into the library."

"Museum restaurants are usually a real letdown," said Mariko, who had come for the teapot, from behind the table. "Please—try to get a really good one for this library." That loosened the tension in the room. Even

Uchida laughed. Mariko took the teapot, put it down on my desk, and stood there, looking out of the window.

"What do you have in mind for where exhibitions will be held?" asked Yukiko.

"I'm thinking of the first floor of the library. Since the walls will be glass, it'll be easy to see what's on display from the outside. And easy to access."

"What materials will be used in the interior?" asked Kawarazaki.

"The floor and ceiling will be wood. For the walls it will depend on the place, but I'm thinking of plaster for the underground floors. But the overall image will be wood. I'd like the users to feel like they're in a wooden building."

"What about the bookcases, tables, and chairs?" Uchida wanted to know.

"I don't have anything special in mind for the furniture. Of course, any ideas you have for features that'll be unique to this library will definitely be worth trying."

The visual impact of the building itself would be striking, but what the user experienced inside, wandering through the open stacks, then sitting down to read, would be quite orthodox. I was beginning to see what he was aiming at.

"Long ago, Europeans used to read and write standing up, at something like a lectern, while back in the Meiji period people sat on cushions at a low table on the tatami. Desks are sensible, and more recent. I myself like to read lying down, but we can't very well put beds in a library, can we?"

We all laughed. The small bed where I now slept had originally been put there for Sensei to read on, and sometimes to drift off to sleep on.

Iguchi, who had been silent all this while, asked Mariko, still looking out at the garden, if she wouldn't mind getting us another cup of tea. Yukiko got up to give her a hand. She always moved quickly. I watched them as they left the room.

While we were waiting for our tea, Iguchi casually mentioned that someone he knew from one of the big construction firms had dropped in at the office in Tokyo, apparently hoping to find out how the plans for the library were progressing. Iguchi knew a lot of people and was easy to get along with. The man probably thought he'd be able to get something out of him, as Sensei wouldn't talk to outsiders.

"The construction will probably be a joint venture," he went on, sounding a little more formal, "but I'd like us to have full control over the furniture as usual. For that we'll need to have a plan in place. We won't be able to just ask Tagawa to handle everything, as we did with the Asukayama Church."

"That's a good point," Sensei said. "Otherwise, the library might be finished before the bookcases are ready, and we can't use the extra workload as an excuse to shortchange our other clients either."

Reassured by this acknowledgment of the problems we might have further down the line, Iguchi didn't pursue the matter. Instead, he turned to the rest of us.

"There's less than four months left. We're now entering the crucial phase. I know you're all busy with your own projects, but you'll just have to discuss things among yourselves and work it out somehow. And if you're having problems, don't hesitate to talk to me. And one more thing—Mariko will be working at the Tokyo office in the fall, to help with all the extra paperwork."

Mariko was back in the workshop by this time. Putting a large plate of freshly baked scones on the table, she said, "Thank you for giving me a chance to help on such an important project." She did this with a little bow.

The same aroma I'd smelled at her summer house now filled the workshop. Yukiko, carrying the heavy teapot with both hands, went around pouring everyone a cup of tea. I felt acutely embarrassed, looking at the scones Mariko had placed in front of me. My ears felt hot. Yukiko, now seated, raised her eyebrows as if to ask me what was wrong, but I looked down, took a scone, and scooped up some clotted cream with it.

After pouring some milk in his tea, Sensei announced that he wanted Kawarazaki, Kobayashi, and Sasai to take charge of the design for the library, while the furniture would be handled by Uchida, Nakao, and Sakanishi. Hearing him say my name made me feel like a full-fledged member of the team. In something this small, I couldn't be the new guy forever.

I was in a boat without a life jacket, rowing with an oar I wasn't used to handling. If I looked off to the side, even for a moment, I would lose my balance. Before I knew it, the boat had left a calm, protected bay and was about to ride the waves of the open sea.

15

"I've got something to tell you," Mariko said, looking straight ahead, her hands on the steering wheel. "Promise you won't be shocked?" We had just finished the weekly shopping in Kyū-Karuizawa, and were sitting in the Renault, about to start back. It was the day after Sensei had presented his plan.

Not sure how to respond, I looked at her.

"Let's have tea at my place. I'll call Iguchi and tell him we'll be late."

She turned the ignition key a little more roughly than usual. The car slipped quickly between the others coming in and out of the parking lot. As we pulled out onto the back road, I breathed in the smell of fir trees through the open windows. I didn't hear any birds.

"Sensei will probably speak to you, just before we leave the Summer House." With no idea where this was going, I sat there, listening. "He'll probably say something like, 'Sakanishi, how do you feel about Mariko?'"

"How I feel...?"

There were very few people outside at this time of day. The car sailed along under a row of larch trees.

"He'll want to know how you feel about marrying me."

I stared at her profile. She didn't look as if she were joking.

"Sensei suggested it to my father, who talked it over with my mother. So my parents and the Murai brothers are all thinking about us two getting married someday."

This had never entered my head. I felt numb, my brain like a thick soup stirred with a ladle.

"Have you known about this for a while now?"

"Heavens no. I just heard it from Uchida." So that was it. Uchida had been with Mariko the weekend before.

"But how did he find out?"

"He was off somewhere with Sensei and heard him talking about it."

"Where?"

"At somebody's house, where he went to repair the furniture."

I had no idea what she was talking about. Uchida had told me he was going to have his bike fixed. Somebody's house? Whose?

"It's where Sensei goes every weekend."

My confusion was still hanging in the air when we reached Mariko's place.

We put the bags of food we'd bought into the big refrigerator, giving ourselves things to do, staying away from the subject of our interrupted conversation.

"I'll just be a minute. I'll make some tea."

I went into the living room, pushed back the curtain, and opened the window. The grass had grown quite high. It needs cutting, I said to myself, finding it odd to be having this thought. Marriage didn't seem at all real to me, and yet here I was, imagining myself mowing the lawn.

"If we have time, I could cut the grass," I murmured.

Whether she hadn't heard me or was only pretending, Mariko stood there at the threshold of the living room with her arms folded.

"Why do you suppose people are talking about marriage without telling you?" she said.

That was what *I* wanted to know. She stood without moving, waiting for an answer.

"I've never even thought about it, so I have no idea."

"You mean marriage is something you can't even think about right now?"

Her face was hard to read, perhaps because she was trying to hide her feelings.

"I'd always thought of marriage as something way in the future. Not for any special reason."

"The future is what Sensei and my father are thinking about."

"I've never even met your father."

Talking to her this way had dulled that first shock. I was pretty sure Mariko herself didn't want to get married. Maybe she was just trying to be fair, laying out the facts for me.

"Well, if they're thinking of me in that way... How can I put this?... I'm flattered," I said, my voice growing quieter as I spoke.

"What're you talking about?" She sounded upset. "That's not what I meant. I want to know why you think they consider you a suitable partner for me."

I didn't know what to say.

Mariko was three years older than me. I had just graduated from university, and had accomplished nothing. She was the only daughter of a well-to-do family, owners of a long-established confectioner's in Hongō, and I was the second son of an average, middle-class company employee. On a purely social basis, anyone could see that this wasn't an ideal match. Objectively speaking, she was sure to have plenty of suitors with a lot more going for them than I had. It was understandable for her parents to be worried about her still being single, but was this really a matter for her uncle to poke his nose into?

I hesitated to say what I was thinking, but looking at Mariko's face, I made up my mind.

"You're the Murai family's only heir. Sensei doesn't have any children. So are they hoping some man will join the family?"

"As an adopted son, you mean?"

Now that I'd said it out loud, this theory sounded fairly convincing, even to me.

"But you've joined the Murai Office, you're going to be an architect, aren't you?" she said angrily. "Surely you don't want to work under my father, as the shop's young master." She whirled around and retreated to the kitchen, where she poured some water into the iron kettle and put it on to boil.

Sensei, the oldest son of the Murai family, had no descendants. If Mariko didn't marry, both brothers would be left with no one to carry on the family name. If they wanted an adopted son to keep the name alive, what would that mean for my future as an architect? Would the shop be left for Mariko to run while I was free to practice architecture? I laid all this out for Mariko. "Maybe they're not thinking of anything quite that complicated, though," I concluded, sinking down into the wicker chair that faced the garden.

"You talk as if it had nothing to do with you," she replied.

We heard the kettle boiling in the kitchen. Mariko quickly made the tea and returned, and after putting two cups on the coffee table beside me, sat down on the other side. She stared out at the lawn as if she'd forgotten what we'd been talking about.

"Let it go just a little while and this is what you end up with," she said.

I realized she was talking about the lawn, something that seemed off-limits to me now.

"Could you get married and leave home?" I asked. "Without taking over the family business, I mean." For some reason, I now felt I could ask her anything. Suddenly I was thirsty. I picked up the cup nearest me and drained it. The tea, a rich golden color, without a trace of bitterness, was soothing as it went down.

"No, I would never do that. I don't know what my father's thinking, but even if I change my name when I get married, I've no intention of leaving our shop. In fact, once the extra work for the library is over with, I'm going to quit working for Sensei's office, so I can learn more about how to run it."

So, Mariko wasn't planning to stay long at the Tokyo office. I might not be able to see her much after she stopped working there.

"If you're that concerned about the family shop, then there's no reason to rush into marriage, is there?"

"*I'm* in no hurry myself, but my parents? I don't know. They've never put any pressure on me, but lots of girls I've known since grade school have already tied the knot."

I remembered the house Mariko had mentioned in the car, where Uchida had gone to repair the furniture.

"Who is this person you say Sensei goes to see every weekend?"

"A horticulturist."

"Someone he works with?"

"A client."

The word "client" caught me by surprise.

"Does this horticulturist have a name?"

"Fujisawa, Kinuko Fujisawa. She has a plant nursery on the other side of Mt. Asama, just beyond Oiwake."

"I know of two houses he designed in Oiwake, but I don't remember hearing the name Fujisawa. Why's that, I wonder."

"Because it wasn't official."

"Not official?"

"He designed the house himself, without going through the office. According to Uchida, he made all the arrangements with contractors too. So the blueprint isn't in the archives."

"When was this?"

"Back in the 1960s."

"But why would he do that?"

"Haven't you figured it out yet? She's Sensei's lover."

I had never imagined him having an affair.

"Do the others know about this?"

"He was a lot busier back then, so it seems people from the office helped out on the construction site. Iguchi knows all about it, but pretends not to. Uchida knows more about it than anyone now, because he's in charge of any extensions or repairs. When work needs to be done there, it's Uchida who's asked to take care of it."

I wondered exactly when and where Mariko had talked to Uchida about this. Had the conversation taken place right here, in her summer house, when the two of them were alone?

"What're you thinking about?" she asked.

"Oh, just wondering what sort of house he designed."

"It's on a little over eight acres of land. Most of it's either fields for growing things, or woods. There's a big main house and smaller ones for the people who work there."

I tried to imagine how big an eight-acre plot of land was.

"She's apparently starting to cut back on the work, though."

"Does she live alone?"

"Apparently so, now anyway. Shall I make some more tea?"

Mariko put our empty cups on the tray and went back to the kitchen. I followed her and put the kettle on.

"So what are you going to say?" she asked. Unable to come up with a good reply offhand, I kept quiet. "If Sensei brings up the subject of us getting married, what are you going to tell him?"

Looking down, she took the lid off the teapot. The hissing of the kettle sounded loud in the silence. When I finally managed to speak, I said, "Uchida..."

"Uchida?" She seemed surprised, as if she couldn't see what he had to do with anything.

"What about Uchida?" I asked.

"What about him?"

I said nothing.

"Oh, you mean Uchida and me?" she asked, sounding much brighter. "There's nothing between us."

"Really?"

"You're wondering if we have some kind of relationship—well, we don't, not at all."

"But you were with him last weekend, weren't you?"

"We had tea at the Mampei Hotel, that's all." She took the kettle off the heat, poured boiling water into a white bowl to cool it a bit, then emptied it into the teapot, her hands moving deftly all the while. "Uchida told you that an office romance is out, didn't he?"

I wondered what sort of talk had gone on between the two of them.

"As a matter of fact, he did."

"I heard from Yukiko that he told her the same thing, just after she joined."

"But he didn't make that rule himself, did he?"

"No, seems it originated with Iguchi. A long time ago a love affair at work got messy, and he decided once was enough. Uchida's actually a very serious guy. But he tries so hard not to act like it that people don't know what to make of him. He'll ask me out to dinner, or give me a ride on the back of his motorbike. He does things like that on purpose—I'm not sure why. Maybe he's testing himself, to see how much he can get away with." She laughed.

"What do you mean?"

"Well, I'm Sensei's niece. And he himself goes around telling people that it's forbidden." Sounding perfectly innocent, she went on. "He'll get drunk at a bar near the office and then offer to drive me home."

I stood there, just listening. Hearing her calmly deny any relationship with Uchida came as a relief, while at the same time making me feel a little guilty.

"He probably does stuff like that for fun, but if he keeps at it, it's bound to get kind of painful, don't you think?"

I had some idea of what she was trying to say, but thought it might be better not to know. I pulled out a chair and sat down at the kitchen table. Mariko put my cup of tea on the table and sat opposite, giving me a sympathetic sort of look. "Shall we head back when we've drunk our tea?" she said.

This chance was now slipping away. I thought about what she had said. If this talk about our getting married someday stopped sounding like a joke and gradually took on more reality... I couldn't think of any reason why I should try to resist it. I knew very little about the sort of life Mariko had led up to now, but we'd been sharing the same time and space all summer. We had cooked together, eaten our meals at the same table, had tea together, done housework together, traveled in the same car listening to the same music, done the shopping together, and occasionally been alone together. Her laughter and the way she walked were almost part of me. And I knew how she talked—straight, without putting on any airs. It would be easy for these feelings of mine to grow, to take shape. In fact, they were already beginning to grow.

But how much did Mariko know about me? Wondering about that brought back something I'd heard from Uchida. Before I joined the Murai Office, they had apparently hired an agency to look into my background. "Sensei said there's no need for that sort of thing nowadays," Uchida had told me with a wry smile, "but Iguchi, who's more of a realist, insisted on it, saying that since you'd be dealing with important clients, we had to make sure you weren't flaky."

So maybe they knew quite a lot about me, about my completely average family, that I'd never been in any kind of trouble with my university friends, or had a steady girlfriend. I must seem very meek and mild to them, without a hint of any risk.

"What're you thinking about?" Mariko's voice brought me back to myself.

Khii. I heard it, very softly, from the garden. A kogera. Maybe I'd be able to point it out to her. I quietly stood up and went into the living room to look out of the window. The little woodpecker was hopping up the trunk of the cherry tree. It stopped now and then to peck at the bark for insects.

"It's a kogera," I whispered, looking back at Mariko.

"Where?" She crept up, and lightly taking hold of my arm, stood there, half behind me.

"On the cherry tree—see that big branch that forks off into two? It's high up on the right-hand fork."

"Where?" she asked again, squeezing my arm a little tighter.

The kogera was busily pecking at the bark.

"I see it now," she said, her hand flitting down my arm like the bird down a tree trunk. Her cool, light, delicate hand slipped easily into mine. My eyes were still on the woodpecker, but I wasn't seeing anything. And all I could hear was the pounding of my own heart. Ever so slightly, just to make sure, I squeezed her hand. I thought she may have squeezed back, but only for a second.

"It's kind of cute," she said quietly.

Perhaps it was young, because it was smaller than the ones I was used to seeing.

"Is that a chick?"

"Maybe. But the adults don't get much bigger than that. It's a small bird."

The kogera suddenly flew away, a faint *khii* trailing behind it.

"It's gone." She sighed and let go of my hand. I went closer to the window and looked up at where it had disappeared. I began to wonder what Mariko's sigh meant, then stopped.

The two of us left the cottage as if nothing had happened. Mariko didn't put on any music. Abruptly she started talking about a beef-and-rice dish on the menu at a Western-style restaurant in Hongō she sometimes went to. Then she moved on to a tiny confectionery shop run by two old ladies who were twins. I told her about a place that used to be near my house where they sold fresh eggs lined up on rice chaff, and about the jar of peppermints that for some reason was always by the cash register in a record store in Aoyama where I used to go when I was at university.

As we drove back to Aoguri, Mt. Asama looked down on us, a plume of smoke above its crater, its outline clear against the blue sky.

16

Just as the Tokyo office was closing for O-Bon, the festival of the dead, preparations for the library competition got serious up here at the Summer House. We constantly heard Sensei's deep voice discussing his plan with Kawarazaki and Kobayashi at the big workshop table, talking not in the abstract but about specific things like length, height, width, thickness, and angles.

Ms. Sasai kept in close contact with our affiliates—an office of architectural design in Akasaka, and an independent contractor who had started out by working for us—informing them about the schedule and explaining where we would need their cooperation. She also proved to be a capable secretary for Iguchi, who had to negotiate with the Ministry of Education. She was good at framing each problem as it came up in concrete, practical terms. She knew when to hold back and when to nudge, without making waves. For the rest of us, it was reassuring to have her overseeing the project with Iguchi.

Uchida, Yukiko, and I set to work making sketches for the bookcases in the open stacks, tables and chairs for the reading rooms, reference counters, and lighting fixtures. We used the detailed drawings on file for the Hokkaido University Library as a reference. When asked what improvements he thought could be made, Sensei would quickly draw things on the spot, which were then pasted into a croquis sketchbook whose cover had "Modern Library" and "Furniture" underneath in Uchida's handwriting.

Much later, when I looked again at the drawings and notes Uchida had added in this book, I immediately remembered what we were working on back then: "Dealing with dust," "Folding bookrests," "Chairs that can be pulled out quietly," "Reading tables where a wheelchair fits," "Tables for two or four, not three." Sensei's demands were summarized one to a page or across facing pages, along with particular points concerning design, and illustrations of human figures using the furniture, close-ups of hands—things that made it fun to look at.

The large reading room was not only to be easy to use and move around in—it should have a comfortable, homey feel, so we were encouraged to come up with ideas for more-casual furniture in addition to the basic stuff. Sensei showed us what he had in mind: high counters with bookrests where a user could look through something standing up, to be placed at intervals along the circulation route, and sofa chairs nearer the bookshelves for people who wanted to flop down with a book. We recognized how these effects were also meant to soften the angular sameness of the bookcases.

What Uchida worried about most was how modern to make the furniture. While the plan for the library wasn't a complete break from Sensei's designs up to now, the exterior leaned strongly toward modernism. What, then, should it look like inside? Should we stick to the established, as Sensei had suggested in his presentation, or aim for something more unconventional to match the outside?

These days, to include the architect's design for original furnishings in a plan for a public building would be considered excessive, both in terms of maintenance and finance. One alternative was to have original designs produced by a company that manufactured office supplies. Something like this library would open up possibilities for the company to work on other public projects, so the architect was helping to secure its cooperation in the future. Kei'ichi Funayama, being good at this sort of give-and-take arrangement, could be expected to leave the furniture to a collaborator so that he could concentrate on his presentation.

Sensei, however, believed that desks, chairs, and bookshelves were at the very heart of a library, and how they were made would directly affect the users' experience. How could we make the library a memorable place for the people who came there to spend time with books?

At the Stockholm Public Library, Asplund's attention to detail is already apparent at the front door, where the handle is decorated with a small sculpture of Adam and

Eve. Adam, about to bite into the forbidden fruit, isn't yet ashamed of his nakedness, so there's no fig leaf provided. A sense of mischief must have been behind choosing this biblical scene for a doorknob. Other details, scattered throughout the library, seem playful, yet carefully designed. People seeing and touching them would remember them, as part of their experience in the place.

In the great circular reading room, for example, the strips of walnut paneling between the bookcases have a brass Art Deco inlay suggesting the stamped gold lettering on leather bindings. And the handrails along the shallow steps leading from the entrance to the reading room are tightly wrapped in tanned leather. Everything, including the tiny human figures on the faucets of the drinking fountains, is original, designed more for decoration, surely, than any practical purpose. There is a variety of different tables, chairs, sofas, and benches, and about ten types of lighting fixtures. From reading lamps to window sashes, all these things are custom-made.

This devotion to detail doesn't seem to show perfectionism so much as the sheer pleasure Asplund took in the art of design. Perhaps architects once saw these finishing touches as the most enjoyable part of a project: surface as opposed to framework, like the luxurious lining of a coat, or the dessert that tops off a meal. Fashioning fiddly little things may have been fun precisely because they were costly and impractical, a small area where the architect could play with ideas. Sensei perhaps inherited the memory and texture of work undertaken from an older generation's perspective.

During our afternoon break, Uchida and I took glasses of some lemonade he'd made out to the back garden. We sat on the bench under the wisteria trellis, looking out at Mt. Asama. No smoke was coming from the crater now. Sunlight lay on the mountain's reddish-brown surface. There were no clouds in the sky. From somewhere higher up we heard a blue-and-white flycatcher, a migratory bird that summers in Japan. A high, clear voice, something like a thrush. We couldn't see it, though. I'd seen this kind of flycatcher only once, on Mt. Takao, during summer vacation when I was in elementary school. The blue on its back and breast shone like silk, its head was a deep black. Here, on a branch somewhere facing the sky, the bird, its blue feathers standing out from its surroundings, was singing away, throat quivering.

"When you try to do something new with chairs, the process always gets more complicated," Uchida said. "You want to keep it simple so they'll be finished on time, and so they won't need much maintenance down the line. But if you want comfortable chairs, you have to be careful to get the seat just right."

"What about the chairs in the Asukayama Church?"

"They were supposed to be folding benches at first. People stand up and sit down again a lot during services, so comfort seemed to me less important than having something simple. But those plain chairs go well in a Protestant church. And there's a dip in the seats, so they're probably easier to sit on for a long time than flat benches would have been."

"Seats of braided paper cord would creak, wouldn't they, when people start to fidget? Kind of noisy in a church."

"The creaking might actually suit a church service. Sort of like the hand straps on a commuter train that all squeak when it rounds a sharp bend—not a bad sound, really."

I remembered Sensei once talking about how the rattle of heavy wooden rain shutters being pulled shut used to tell you it was evening. "Kids playing outside would go home when they heard that," he'd said.

"Plain wood is too hard for the seats of library chairs," Uchida went on. "And leather or cloth can get dirty or marked up. There's the summer heat too. Sensei says that since the place will be air-conditioned, leather will probably do. It's easier to replace than paper cord braiding too. But anyway..." He paused and looked at me. "What's the worst kind of chair you've ever used?"

I thought a while before answering, "The swivel chairs in my professor's seminar room at university. The ball bearings and casters were always coming loose, and the backrests broke in no time. I couldn't believe how quickly they fell apart. It was kind of shameful, having such badly made chairs in the architecture department."

"Anyone who thinks he's saving money by using ready-made chairs is kidding himself. They're not made to last. You have to keep buying more—that's how furniture companies stay in business. Wooden furniture costs a lot up front, but if you take care of it you can use it for fifty, maybe even a hundred years. So, you end up saving the cost of dozens of ready-made things. But people nowadays don't think of repairing things, and there's no telling whether fifty or a hundred years from now they'll even want to use what we make now. Nobody thinks that far ahead anymore. Everything's calculated to fit the annual budget."

"Is there any chance of using laminated plywood?"

"For modern designs it's easy to work with, and you can bend it into interesting shapes. But plywood's kind of dull—you can't get away from that. The chairs Alvar Aalto designed for the Paimio Sanatorium look cool at first, but after a while you get tired of them, and they're not that comfortable either. They take up too much space too. I guess modernism and furniture don't go together very well."

"Hans Wegner's chairs are modern, but orthodox too."

"He's fantastic. He wasn't an architect, but a craftsman. A genius at what he did. That modern-looking three-legged shell chair of his is very comfortable. That's because he put a nice, sturdy leather covering over the plywood seat and backrest. Which goes to show that while it's hard to get modern furniture right, it's not impossible." Uchida looked thoughtful. "I think natural wood would be best for a more orthodox design. But for tables and desks, laminated wood is more practical. Natural wood is heavy, which can be a problem, and it can warp or crack. It gets nicked and scratched more easily too."

"In the lower grades at my elementary school the desks were natural wood, and kids carved their names in them, or gouged out holes you could fit a pencil through. Each desk sat two, and some kids even carved a boundary between each other. Made a real mess of them."

"They probably wouldn't even think of doing that nowadays."

Sensei had given Uchida four sketches of chairs for the reading rooms. Two were quite modern, while the others were orthodox, more like previous designs.

"He wants us to think along both lines," he said ruefully. "I wasn't expecting his plan for the library to be so strikingly modern. There's actually a lot of new stuff in the Asukayama Church, but it doesn't stand out—that's his way, or at least it was until now." There was no denying this. "His designs have a kind of reticence. A lot of architects are just the opposite, always showing off, trying to surprise people. Sensei keeps the best things hidden. Until this library, that is—you can tell how new it is just by looking. It'll attract attention. If Funayama saw it, I bet it would make him nervous. It's hard to say if that will work in Sensei's favor in the competition, though. The committee will be expecting plans that are typical of each participant's work."

"But if you look closely, it actually is typical in a lot of ways, isn't it? It's comfortable for the users, and easy to move around in."

"True."

"Do you think orthodox furniture would be better?"

"I don't think anything, really. Both are okay, and I can do either one. I'm just concentrating on what he wants."

I was surprised to hear this. Yes, he listened to Sensei's instructions, but hadn't he always tried to put something of himself in his work, and been a little scornful of the kind of single-minded devotion he saw in Kawarazaki and Kobayashi?

Uchida drained his lemonade. Pieces of ice tinkled in the glass.

"I'd planned to tell you this later, but after the library's finished I'm going to quit," he said calmly. "I've been thinking about it for some time—I have a feeling that if I don't quit now, I'll lose my chance. Not that I'm dissatisfied or anything. You couldn't find a better place to work. But if I stay here working under Sensei another ten years, I'll never make a go of it on my own."

We heard Yukiko and Mariko laughing in the kitchen. Did Mariko know that Uchida was planning to leave?

"Are you going to set up your own office?" I asked.

"I suppose so, although it'll just be me at first," he replied, looking as if he didn't want to say any more.

"One more thing—there's somewhere I have to take you before the summer's over." I immediately knew where: the woman Mariko had told me about, who lived on the other side of Mt. Asama. "There's a client of Sensei's I've been doing work for, and I'd be grateful if you'd take over for me. It's near Oiwake, so less than an hour from here. Think you can go this weekend, if we leave in the morning?"

"Sure. Does Sensei know?"

He nodded. There was no change in his expression. Just then, Yukiko called to me from the back door of the kitchen.

"Could you come here a minute?"

I got to my feet. Uchida slowly stood up and stretched.

"Nomiya Sensei is here. She's come all this way to tell us she wants a new bookrest. I talked to Sensei just now, and he said he wants both of us to see her."

I followed Yukiko inside, and found the old woman sitting on the sofa in front of the fireplace. It had been less than a week since she'd gone back to Tokyo with her daughter. In a neat-looking kimono, she looked remarkably healthy for someone who had recently collapsed.

"It's a relief to see you looking so well," I said.

"Thank you. Tokyo was so hot I told the doctor I'd faint again if I stayed any longer, and rushed back here." There was laughter in her eyes. This sweet-tempered side to her was a surprise. "Unfortunately," she went on, "I can't retire just yet. I need you to make me a new bookrest, that's why I'm here."

Apparently she leafed through large-format art books from time to time, as well as things from the Edo period, their soft covers sewn up with thread. She also occasionally read foreign books. Until now she'd been using a bookrest bought in Germany before the war, but after over a half century of use, it was wearing out.

"A little thing like that is still architecture, isn't it? It's a support—one that folds up and opens out again. It's got to balance. Whether it's easy to use depends on the design. I hesitated to ask Mr. Murai since I only know him to say hello to, but after Yukiko here helped me out, I thought there was a connection."

The old woman looked over at Yukiko, then me.

"Actually," Yukiko said quietly in her clear voice, "we were just about to start designing new bookrests for something else."

It seemed to me that the timing couldn't have been worse. We simply didn't have time to take on anything new. Yet Yukiko had cheerfully accepted her request. Though dismayed at first, I later saw that in giving us this small assignment, Sensei may have been thinking it might serve as a model for the library.

"Would you like to see my old bookrest?" the lady asked, so Yukiko and I set out for her cottage. She led the way, walking very steadily for someone well into her nineties.

17

The study was, like its owner, tiny, with all the wall space except the window and door taken up by bookcases. Six of them, made of paulownia wood, held only Japanese books. There was also a single bed, small enough for a child. Hardly any of the books looked new. The faded spines seemed weathered by the passing years, along with the house itself.

Nomiya Sensei showed us her large, rickety bookrest, which she'd mended with sticky tape, and demonstrated how it could be adjusted to four settings by placing first a large book of paintings by Piero della Francesca on it, then her thick, heavy *Oxford Dictionary of Quotations*. She said that when she was working on the proofs for a novel, she lowered the bookrest to a fifteen-degree angle, practically flat. Yukiko took a few notes, asking questions from time to time. While we were talking, a shy-looking woman in her mid-thirties, whom Nomiya Sensei introduced as her granddaughter, brought in some tea. Kazue Nomiya had a quick look around, then left without saying more than her name.

Though the old novelist didn't waste words, she didn't leave anything out either. The reason you never got tired of looking at della Francesca's paintings, she said, was that he had no illusions about people being virtuous; he brings out the ways we have of deluding ourselves. His paintings may appear to be concrete, but they're actually depicting humanity in the abstract. "He was a mathematician," she said, "and an architect too. Architects should be hardheaded, like him. Emotion is useless when you're working with wood and stone, building in three dimensions. Japanese people are sentimental, and we've paid a heavy price for it. The war could have been stopped much sooner, but we kept on fighting even after we'd been bombed to ruin. That failure came from turning against cool, rational thought." She said all this succinctly, without a pause.

I got the feeling that the bookrest was secondary, that a more important task was to receive this old woman's moral instruction.

When the lecture was over, she told us a simple supper was ready, and not to feel shy about staying. I looked at the clock. It was nearly six. Dinner would be starting at the Summer House, so I thought we should leave, but she insisted: She had told Kazue to make *gomoku-zushi* according to a recipe that had been in the family for generations, and since she herself never had anything but tea and toast for breakfast, the sushi had to be eaten tonight, and so on...

Yukiko, finally worn down, called the Summer House. Iguchi answered the phone and cheerfully told us not to worry—since we'd been invited to stay, that's what we should do.

The flavored rice mixed with seafood and vegetables had the taste of an old, traditional Tokyo dish. The *kanpyo*, strips of dried gourd, was soft and sweet. Shiitake mushrooms, thinly sliced carrot and lotus root, shrimp, pieces of saltwater eel, tuna, and flounder, shredded egg crepes, and cherry-colored flakes of cod were scattered over the rice. Though the granddaughter barely spoke, she smiled as she served us.

After tea and ice-cold sweet dumplings for dessert, we took our leave. Nomiya Sensei was clearly getting sleepy. It was much cooler now.

In that village, you couldn't go outside at night without a flashlight. The occasional streetlamp was obscured by trees, and the summer foliage made this the darkest season of the year. Since the road led straight back to the Summer House, we could have managed, but the ground was rough, with stones to trip over and hanging branches hidden in the darkness. Kazue, realizing that we hadn't brought a flashlight, took a big, old-fashioned one off the hook on the side of the wooden shoe cupboard in the entranceway and handed it over.

There was no moon that night. Until I turned on the flashlight, we were surrounded by a darkness so deep we couldn't even make out the ground at our feet. I slid the switch on, and moved the pale circle of light back and forth until I found a well-trodden furrow by the side of the road. Following it, we set off, heading for the speck of light from the Summer House that appeared and disappeared through the trees.

The chirring of insects filled the space around us. So loud it seemed to be spilling out of our own ears.

"I really like old houses," Yukiko said, apparently not the least bit nervous about walking in pitch darkness. "Wood looks lighter when it's dried out."

"Yeah, but I think that house would be hard to spend the winter in."

"Nomiya Sensei's stayed there every winter since before the war, so it can't bother her. But life was hard for her generation, she's a lot tougher than we are...Hey. Wait a minute." She stopped. "Did you hear that?"

"What?" I said quietly, also stopping.

"An owl?" she whispered.

I listened carefully. The insects seemed even noisier than before. And then, for just a second, a low call cut through the noise. I stood there awhile, and again heard *hoo, hoo, hooooo* beneath the chirring, like the low tones of a flute from behind.

"I'm not sure," I said. "The only night bird call I know is the gray nightjar."

"Is 'night bird' a category?" She laughed. "I wonder if it's the same owl Ms. Sasai heard that time."

Hoo, hoo, hooooo. No wonder people used to think owls sounded ominous. This one was like a voice from another world.

Every time there was a major eruption, once every century or more, this whole area turned into a wasteland where neither animals nor birds could survive. Ash and debris from Mt. Asama had been known to reach as far south as Maebashi, in Gunma Prefecture. Then, as rain fell and sunlight poured down, the wind carried seeds to where the village of Aoguri now stood. They sprouted, their roots reaching hesitantly down into the soil. The scalding stuff thrown up by the volcano provided a lasting supply of nourishment for the young plants. Trees stretched their slender branches across the empty fields, in time becoming groves. Insects and birds gathered, drawn by the foliage. As fallen leaves became compost, the groves grew into a forest, which attracted small mammals first, followed by foxes and owls that came to hunt them. How many times had this forest Yukiko and I were walking through been destroyed and come back to life again? Like that owl we'd heard, we knew next to nothing of the past the land had had.

On the way ahead there was only the wavering, bluish-white oval where I pointed the flashlight, surrounded by pitch black. Like water pressure, the darkness seemed to be pushing at its blurred edges. It wasn't only living things that gave the darkness its power. I looked back and saw that the light from the old lady's cottage was now very small. Yukiko suddenly stopped again with an "Ah!" of surprise. "Fireflies," she whispered.

I looked around.

"See? Over there, to the left."

I didn't need to look hard to see specks of fluorescent green blinking as they floated through the air.

"Turn off the light a minute," Yukiko said.

Sliding the switch to off produced a second of complete blackout. But to our left, right, ahead, and behind, the air was filled with those ephemeral green lights, winking on and off.

"Look how many there are."

"I wish Nomiya Sensei could see them."

She, more than anyone, was worried about the decrease in their numbers, yet right near her cottage we were startled to see so many, drifting silently through the trees.

One of them passed right by my hand. It looked like a tiny glider that would be carried on the slightest breeze. The fluorescence left a rhythmic sort of haze on my retina, a larger creature breathing in and out.

"Why don't we try walking like this, with the flashlight off?" She sounded like a child inviting me to join in a game.

"We might fall down."

"If we do there's a road to catch us. It's not like we're walking along the edge of a cliff or anything. Don't worry, we'll be fine."

"Let's stay close together then."

"Are you scared?" Though I couldn't see her standing beside me, she sounded amused.

"No, I just don't want to stumble." I put out my right hand where I thought she'd be. My fingers touched hers. I reached a little further, took hold of her left hand, and pulled it toward me.

"Okay, let's go."

Without hesitating, she kept her grip as we started off.

"It's summer, so you'd think there'd be more people around."

I turned my head, but her face was invisible. Only the feeling of her hand in mine grew in the dark. After a while, she said quietly, "Like my cousin."

"Huh?"

"My cousin held my hand like this the first time I went ice-skating. I was in fourth grade and he was in junior high. I remembered that just now."

I imagined a much smaller hand than now.

"I never knew boys could be so nice," she went on. "The kids at school were so rough and mean." Remembering how I'd envied my classmates for daring to be nasty to the girls, I didn't say anything. I was surprised at myself, how easily I'd reached out and taken Yukiko's hand. The distant speck of light we'd been heading for gradually took on the shape of a window and then, as it got nearer, the outlines of the Summer House. The number of fireflies had gradually dwindled on the way until they completely disappeared. In the dim light we saw the path leading to the entrance. I let go of her hand.

"Thanks," she said.

"That's okay," I replied.

There was the fresh, green smell of the cedar as we approached. Then light from the incandescent lamp in the dining room shone on the leaves of the katsura tree spreading overhead. The tree looked as if it were floating in midair. It felt good to be standing here in the dark, looking up at the building. We couldn't see anyone inside. Still, the light surrounded them, letting us know they were there, waiting for us.

As we stood in front of the door, the outdoor light shone on Yukiko's face. We had made it through the darkness, I thought. She was smiling.

When we went in, the noise of insects receded like a wave, even though the windows were open. The smell of the lamb Uchida had roasted with rosemary lingered in the dining room. The night stayed outside. Houses have always been a means of escape from the dark.

"Welcome back," said Mariko. She, Iguchi, and Sensei were sitting on the sofa in front of the fireplace. No fire was lit. Mozart's Sinfonia Concertante for Viola and Violin was playing, turned down low. The others were probably in their rooms or having a bath.

"You were there a long time," Sensei said with a sympathetic smile.

"We had a really good dinner," Yukiko replied cheerfully.

Iguchi was already a little drunk. "She must like you. I've never heard of her asking anyone to stay for a meal. She's one tough cookie, I can tell you. Gets up real early and writes till about noon, then reads till it gets dark and goes back to writing after dinner. Keeps to that schedule every day. Never has visitors at night, or so I've heard."

"Really?" Yukiko looked surprised.

"Strange, getting an order like that just before the library competition," Sensei remarked. "Seems like a sign. You'd better get it done quickly."

"We'll do it right away. I'd never seen a German bookrest before," she added, a little less seriously. "Hers is over fifty years old."

Sensei nodded, then turned to me and asked for details. Mariko was next to him, her knees bent, those long legs scrunched uncomfortably up to her chest. I tried to ignore them, but felt her eyes on me as I explained that the bookrest was a different size from ones used in Japan; that even someone like Harue Nomiya, who isn't very strong, could easily adjust it; that there was a stop to keep your fingers from getting pinched or the book from falling off; that it could be adjusted to four levels; and that though it was a little rickety due to lost screws and the wood being worn away, I thought it would be better to make a replica rather than design a new one for her.

"What kind of wood was it?" Sensei asked.

Yukiko answered quickly: "It was so dark with age I can't be sure, but I think it was chestnut. I noticed wormholes in it." Sensei nodded, as if that sounded right.

Insects are drawn to not only the leaves but the trunks of chestnut trees. They make black pinpricks in them that are easy to miss if you're not looking for them. I'd been watching the old lady's hands, so hadn't seen them.

"Chestnut can warp or crack while it's drying," Sensei said, "but once that's settled down it's a strong wood, even if you cut it thin. Perfect for a bookrest. I guess you'll be making a replica, then."

"I'll show you the blueprint when I have it done," I told him. He then asked us to make one more like it, for Tagawa, the furniture maker in Yatsugatake, as a model for the library, saying "Let's use oak for that one, then we can compare it with the chestnut."

When this was over, Yukiko went upstairs. I poured myself a glass of Perrier and joined them on the sofa. Then Sensei, watching his niece bring a long-necked bottle of grappa from the dining room cupboard, said "I'm going to bed" and disappeared. Mariko, wearing linen Bermuda shorts with a Sea Island cotton sweater that looked as if a red-wine stain would ruin it, poured some grappa into two long-stemmed glasses and gave one to Iguchi, who'd been drinking wine and nibbling on slices of pickled beet. We listened to him start rambling on about Harue Nomiya.

Firefly Pond, he told us, was a man-made lake that she and other early residents of Aoguri planned not long after the village was established in the 1930s. It was one of a whole string of projects completed in rapid succession during those first few years: a clubhouse, tennis courts, an archery range, and a gym, along with a post office to serve the village. Around this time someone—it's not clear who—got the idea for a lake. Nomiya Sensei, who hadn't shown much interest in the plans for the new buildings, was very enthusiastic. But the year after it was finished, Mt. Asama erupted, setting off an earthquake that seriously damaged the embankment. Just when it seemed that Firefly Pond was going to dry up, Harue Nomiya, still in her forties back then, used her connections to raise money, and got it repaired. "Saved the pond almost single-handedly," Iguchi said. He and Sensei were still students while all this was going on.

In time, Firefly Pond became a symbol of Aoguri. In winter it was covered with a thick layer of ice, and there were ice hockey games on it. Nomiya Sensei herself was quite a good skater; never keeping pace with anyone in particular, ignoring the children, she would glide elegantly around the long circumference. There were always people around back then, partly because the village was still young, but also because of the lake, it seemed.

"Have you ever seen any fireflies?" asked Mariko, who had been silent until then.

I didn't want to answer if I could possibly avoid it, but thinking Yukiko might innocently tell her sometime, I said as casually as I could, "Yeah, we saw some tonight."

Before she had a chance to react, Iguchi blurted out, "Fireflies out there tonight? That's good news. Haven't seen any in a while. I wonder if Nomiya Sensei knows."

"It was after we left her place, on the way back."

"We used to see them right here, by the screen door." He meandered back to the previous topic. "Ever heard of Shigehisa Shinozaki?"

"The art historian? He specialized in the Italian Renaissance, didn't he?"

"That's the one. You're well informed. He's before your time—died in the early 1960s. They say he was her lover."

"When I said she had a lover," put in Mariko, sounding a little miffed, "you pretended not to know anything about it."

"That so?" Iguchi replied, feigning innocence.

"The place where she collapsed is right near where Shinozaki's old cottage was, on the lakeside. She probably still remembers, and that's why she felt bad there."

"I don't know about that. Shinozaki's house *was* right by the lake, though." Trying to keep Mariko from taking over the conversation, he went on to talk about how someone now well past ninety must be feeling her strength slip away even though she tried not to let on. "If you and Yukiko hadn't found her that time, there's no telling what might have happened. But her wanting a new bookrest is a good sign. You can learn from copying the old one, but anyway, be sure to make it good and sturdy." By this time, he was slurring his words, and though I thought he'd gone to the toilet, he must have headed back to his room, leaving the area around us silent.

"Iguchi has a way of suddenly disappearing like that," Mariko said, draining the last of the grappa in her glass.

"Let's clear these things away then," I said, moving away from the sofa with Iguchi's plate and half-empty wineglass. Stretching her bare leg out, Mariko stepped lightly on my right foot, making me lose my balance. I almost fell.

"Are you okay?" she asked.

I definitely wasn't. Without answering, I took a paper napkin and started wiping up the wine that had spilled on the floor. I couldn't tell whether she was drunk or not; she didn't look very different as she watched me from the side. I could still feel her foot on mine. Like the palm of her hand. Thin and light.

"Why aren't you angry?" she demanded, crouching down beside me and taking hold of my arm. I stopped wiping. Then, on her back, she worked her way directly under me. Looking straight up, she said quietly, "Kiss me."

I would have, even if she hadn't told me to. As I gazed down at her sleepy-looking yet wide-open eyes, my arms relaxed and, propped up on my elbows, I eased myself down on top of her. Her arms, cheeks, and lips felt cool. We kissed for a long time. When we heard the door to the bath on the second floor opening and closing, we finally drew apart and sat up.

"Shall we clean up?" she whispered.

Side by side, we washed the plates and glasses, dried them, and put them back in the cupboard. "Can I come to the library later?" she asked. I nodded. "Okay then," she said, looking up at the kitchen clock, "I'll be there at a little past one." She turned around, cut through the dining room, and went upstairs.

I went up, too, and took a bath. Soaking in the tub, I looked out toward Mt. Asama. The mountain was sunk in darkness.

Back in my room, I found the section on Kita-Asama in the bookcase, took out a slim volume from a local publisher, and sat down at the desk to read. Just a few years earlier, the remains of two people who had died in the eruption of 1783 had been found. They were trying to climb to high ground, but were covered by lava and debris before they reached safety. They were thought to be a daughter with her mother on her back, who died just as they were starting to climb the steps leading to the Kannon-dō Temple. The village of Kamahara had a population of almost six hundred at the time, but about five hundred perished—those who hadn't taken refuge in the temple. Kamahara was about twenty kilometers from Mt. Asama. Kita-Asama is closer, within ten kilometers.

1783. About two hundred years ago. The village had been destroyed on the eighth day of the seventh month, according to the old lunar calendar, which would be right around now... And that was as far as I got. I closed the book. A gentle breeze brought cold air in from the north. Feeling chilly, I shut the small window that looked out onto the garden.

At a little past one o'clock, Mariko quietly opened the door and came in.

18

I had never been given a ride on a motorcycle before. Seeing me fumble with the helmet and goggles he'd handed me, Uchida fixed the strap firmly under my chin and adjusted the goggles. I straddled the seat behind him, and as soon as my arms were around his waist he started the engine. The Vincent jolted into motion so suddenly I was thrown backward. The Summer House was soon far in the distance.

Until we reached the highway, we were on a dirt road riding under trees, with sunlight filtered through the branches. On the asphalt, though, the glare was blinding. As we picked up speed, pressure from the wind made it hard to breathe. Whenever we rounded a bend, I clung to Uchida, my grip tightening until my fingernails dug into his leather jacket. I was embarrassed, letting him know how scared I was, but even more scared of falling off. Nearer the Sengataki area, the road swerved uphill and down through a series of hairpin turns. Our bodies lurched left and right, our knees almost touching the ground. I began to suspect him of actually trying to throw me off, and though I knew it was unlikely, it didn't help me to relax.

Past Hoshino Hot Springs the road leveled off, with more traffic, so our speed dropped. My arms and shoulders finally eased up. Just before we reached Route 18, we even stopped at a traffic light for the first time since we'd set out. We then turned right, heading for Komoro, and after the Oiwake intersection I could see a long slope over his shoulder. Abruptly the bike took off at high speed and I grabbed on to him again, pressing into his back. I thought I heard muffled laughter, but may have been imagining it.

A wide curve to the right revealed Mt. Asama in front of us. This was the back of the mountain, the side we never saw in Aoguri. Though its surface was about the same color, it seemed much brighter with the sun on it. It also looked much bigger from this angle, its sheer weight bearing down on us. The cloud of white smoke from the crater, drifting eastward, didn't seem to be moving at all.

After a while we saw a field of sunlit corn up ahead, and another with green wheat swaying in the breeze. This road of slight curves, dips, and mounds cut east to west along the foothills of Mt. Asama. Like the Summer House, the plant nursery we were headed for was at the foot of the volcano.

The bike turned onto a narrow farm road with cracks in the asphalt. Nearly an hour had passed since we left.

When we had climbed about two or three hundred meters, we were surrounded by fields, as far as we could see. Through the stillness, we could hear a faint muddle of sound from lower down. To the south was the town of Sakudaira, and beyond it the Southern Alps. Feeling a dry wind on my face, I turned my head and saw the mountain behind me, its reddish-brown surface bathed in summer light.

"This whole area and on up the hill belongs to Ms. Fujisawa's farm," Uchida said. "I couldn't tell you exactly where the boundaries are, but she owns a lot of land."

The bike headed farther north, up the hill, along a hedge to our left. We came to a slight break, like a breathing space; this was the entrance. Two deep furrows in the unpaved lane gave off a smell of rich earth and grass. At the top of a slope was a low stone wall to our left, and beyond it, a field of flowers: an array of color—blue, yellow, white, purple, pink—across the southern slope. Though the plants were of different heights and sizes, the field had a sense of order and balance. How much labor had gone into creating it? There was no sign of a human presence anywhere.

A little farther on, to our right, was a stone gate. We turned into the gravel driveway and saw a small wooden house on the left, and beyond it another, similar one on the opposite side. I could tell at a glance that Sensei had designed both. Fields of flowers spread out behind them. Uchida drove up to the second house and switched off the engine under a huge Sargent's cherry tree, its leaves drooping over the roof. Standing in the shade, I took off my helmet and goggles, to cool, dry air.

Kinuko Fujisawa lived in the big house at the end of the drive. Birches and poplars stood on the neatly mown lawn. It was a cool sound they made, like waves coming in to shore. The breeze never felt this unconfined in Aoguri.

"We're now in the heart of Lapillus Farm," Uchida told me.

I now know that the name came from lapilli, little drops of molten lava.

"That cottage was the first one built," he said, turning back toward the place we'd passed on our left. "Nobody lives there now, but the inside is still in pretty good shape. I've stayed overnight in it once or twice. The people who work on the farm use this one," he added, pointing to the wooden house in front of us. "They'll take a nap here, or have a cup of tea and a snack. There's a shower too. Four women work here, but only two come every day, and they all commute. I heard that long ago they used to raise silkworms too. They've still got some mulberry trees around here—they get incredibly leafy in summer. Remember those shelves for silkworms in the Summer House storeroom? They're probably from around the same time."

Uchida walked slowly toward the main house along the drive, which made a wide curve toward the entrance, then just before reaching the front door, swung clockwise around the cherry tree and back toward the start—the same sort of circular approach as we had at the Summer

House. The cedarwood siding had a reddish tinge. It smelled good when you got close. The ruddy outdoor walls of the house stood out against the white birches, the greenery of the farm, and the blue sky.

The wooden door was simple, like most of Sensei's doors—the first thing you noticed was the brass doorknob. There was a horizontal slit at just about eye level, but perhaps because the entranceway was dark, I couldn't see anything through it. I sensed Sensei's love of order in the neat pile of firewood under the eaves.

"She must be out in the fields," Uchida said. "Let's wait here."

Not even bothering to knock on the door, he sat down on a wooden bench over to the left, which Sensei must also have designed. I wondered if there was an "I'm not in now" sign I hadn't noticed (I later learned that there was a wooden flap inside that Ms. Fujisawa lowered over the glass when she went out—the entranceway wasn't dark after all). I stepped back to look up at the place from the driveway.

"About what year was this built?" I asked.

Judging from the doorknob, the wooden window sashes, and the way concrete was used, I thought it was probably from the late 1960s at the earliest, or maybe the early 1970s.

"Around 1969, I think. The two little houses down the road are earlier, though. One was built in 1958, and the other in 1963. Around the same time as the Summer House."

Sitting on the bench near the front door, we could see Mt. Asama. A black-eared kite was circling overhead, its eyes trained on the ground. Its head swiveled back and forth. Was it searching for prey, or sizing us up—two intruders?

"Ms. Fujisawa moved up here around 1968, during the student riots in Tokyo. She was in her late fifties then. This was originally her summer house, but then she got serious about horticulture, planted more and more flowers, and started spending most of her time up here. If I stayed in a place like this for a week, I probably wouldn't want to go back to Tokyo either." He sounded much less complicated than usual.

I was bowled over by the whole scene—the expanse of land, the dry air, a big house Sensei had designed—all tucked away in the hills.

We saw a woman walking toward us. She was dressed for gardening, in overalls and a wide-brimmed straw hat, carrying a woven bamboo basket over one arm. She walked slowly but with a certain dignity. Her back was straight. She didn't look like a woman in her seventies. I hurriedly got to my feet. Seeing Uchida, she broke into a smile and called out, "Hot today, isn't it?" An intelligent-sounding voice. He slowly stood up, stretching.

"Yeah, but the air's dry," he said, "so it feels good." He obviously knew her well.

Not knowing quite what to do, I introduced myself, even though she was still fairly far away.

She removed her hat as she got nearer, and took a good look at me.

"So you're Mr. Sakanishi. Welcome. I'm Kinuko Fujisawa."

Silver-gray hair and clear-cut features. Her eyes were tinged with brown.

"Come on in." The door was unlocked.

We stepped up from the entranceway and followed her down a dark corridor to a staircase, well lit by the skylight above. She climbed the stairs easily. There was a large oil painting on the wall just before the staircase. The upper half of the canvas was white, the lower maroon. A Mark Rothko? Unable to stop for a closer look, I walked by, wondering if that was possible.

At the top of the stairs was an incredibly spacious living-dining room, filled with natural light. While it was much too large for someone living alone, everything in it—the furniture and all the accessories—clearly came from one person, Kinuko Fujisawa. On the floor was a pale-yellowish short-pile rug, and the walls were plaster. Another big oil painting hung on the western wall, the one that had the most space. This was definitely a Rothko.

Next to the grand piano was another of Gen'ichiro Yamaguchi's seascapes. In the one at Mariko's cottage, the wave was coming in, here it had just receded. The smooth, wet sand shone dully in the light. A child's footsteps, the three closest making dips in the sand, grew shallower as they neared the water until they disappeared.

The ceiling was very high, especially on the west side, where it was double height, though it gradually got lower toward the east, where the kitchen was, as if following the slant of the roof. The kitchen ceiling was the standard height for one Sensei had designed.

Uchida, seeming completely at home, walked straight to the big dining table, pulled out a chair, and sat down. I could clearly see the outline of Mt. Asama through the horizontal northern window. I went over to look out at the deep-green forest that covered the foot of the mountain.

"You came by motorcycle, didn't you? Do you want to wash your faces?"

"Good idea," Uchida said, standing up. I followed him to a sink behind the kitchen, which was long enough for two to stand side by side, with a lamp whose shade Sensei had probably designed. The amber-colored soap had a nice smell. It felt good to wash my face and hands. There was a stack of white towels in the cupboard.

"Can I use one of these?" I asked.

"Sure," said Uchida, his voice muffled because he already had his face buried in one.

When we got back, I noticed that the dining table was maple wood. It was smooth to the touch, without a mark on it. Uchida, or perhaps Sensei, must have waxed it regularly. Ms. Fujisawa brought a glass plate of peaches and grapes on a big tray that looked like cherrywood. The plate was a frosty white.

"Have some fruit."

She had changed into a linen blouse with a long skirt. Her hair was tied behind. There must have been a side room somewhere behind the kitchen. In big houses, Sensei sometimes put one near the kitchen, like a getaway. "A woman might want to take a break while she's cooking," he'd said, "or duck in to fix her makeup if she has guests." I couldn't tell from the dining table where the door to it was.

The ripe peach melted in my mouth and slid coolly down my dry throat.

"You're going to be taking care of my house from now on," Ms. Fujisawa said, looking straight at me.

"I don't know if I'll be as good at it as Uchida, though."

"You'd better be. I'm counting on you." She laughed out loud. There was something about it that must have been there since she was a child—it was that sort of laughter. "This house is fourteen years old, so it's starting to wear out, as we all are. The sun, wind, and rain are much stronger up here than down below. I'm really grateful to you"—she turned to Uchida—"you've never complained about coming when I need you. Thanks for everything."

"No need to thank me," he said. "It was Sugiyama who actually did the work."

Sugiyama, the contractor in Oiwake, handled almost all of Sensei's work in Karuizawa. His father had run the business when the Summer House was built, so they had been working with Sensei for a long time.

"But if it was something simple you always fixed it right away. That was a big help." She opened the big window that looked out over Sakudaira. The wooden sash looked a little heavy for a woman, but like all Sensei's work it had a nice simplicity. A cheerful gust of wind blew in. She then moved toward the north window.

"Shall I open it for you?" I asked, starting to stand up.

"That's nice of you—thanks."

Unlike the window she'd just opened, which reached all the way to the floor, this one was horizontal, with a sill to rest your elbows on. Through it you could see Mt. Asama to the right and Mt. Kurofu to the left. The brass lock attached to the sash was the same type as at the Summer House and Mariko's cottage.

Ms. Fujisawa gave Uchida a teasing look. "He may seem brusque," she said to me when I returned to the table, "but he's actually very kind. So don't be shy—pester him with questions. He'll tell you what you need to know, plus lots of other things into the bargain. But maybe you *are* shy, and you wait for the other person to speak first."

"Afraid so," I said, startled that she'd read me so well.

"It's hard to tell with quiet people, isn't it?—from the outside. I always talk to the flowers I grow. They look a lot prettier than they used to, when I kept my mouth shut. Really—it's true." She smiled. "But he never talks while he's working. He fixed my oven frame, and the range hood, and my kitchen drawers—gave them all a complete overhaul."

"I don't do that for everybody," Uchida said, looking slightly embarrassed. As I listened, I was thinking about Mariko. Just as this lady said, I always waited for the other person to make the first move.

"So, the Library of Modern Literature will be your last job with the Murai Office?"

"If we lose the competition, that is. If we win, I'll stay till the library's finished, so I'd have a place at the office for another two years."

"Have a place? It's not like anyone's trying to throw you out—you're the one leaving."

"I know. I'm throwing myself out," he said, looking at her rather than me.

"Well, as I said earlier, if you have trouble setting up your own office in Tokyo, you can use either of my little houses. There's plenty of work for you around here." She got up and went back into the kitchen. I heard her put the kettle on.

"Do you mind if I take a look around?" I called.

"Of course not," she said without turning. "After we have our coffee, I'm sure Uchida can give you a guided tour."

I looked down through the big southern window. There were fields of flowers on either side of the drive. Someone was bent over, working. Off in the distance I could see buildings and a river with a bridge—a scale model of the town of Sakudaira, about one-hundredth the actual size, bathed in soft sunlight. It must be beautiful at night too.

"We're about a thousand meters above sea level," Uchida said from the sofa by the window.

"Seems higher, but about the same height as the Summer House?"

"In midwinter, even with central heating you can feel the cold in your back. The temperature goes down to about twenty below, so without some kind of heating you wouldn't survive."

I smelled coffee from the kitchen.

"Talking about winter?" Ms. Fujisawa asked as she brought in a coffeepot and put it on the low table in front of the sofa. The sofa was a type Sensei often recommended to his clients when they came to discuss furniture. I had never seen one like this, though, covered entirely in leather.

"Yes—I was just saying it gets to twenty below."

"Five below, twenty below—there's really not much difference. I sometimes get a cold when autumn comes around, but in midwinter I'm fine."

"It's best not to overdo the brandy, though," Uchida said as if he knew how she spent her winter days.

She ignored this. "It hardly ever snows in Tokyo anymore. The air just gets terribly dry."

"I like Tokyo in November and December," he countered.

"Really? Come and get your coffee," she urged, "before it gets cold." I went over and sat next to her on the sofa.

"The smell of brand-new wool sweaters, and good leather jackets, and sweet potatoes baking," he said. "All floating in the cold, dry air as you walk around town. People say Christmas decorations are tacky, but I like them. The air is much clearer then, so the lights look pretty at night, even from far away. Late fall to winter is the best time to be in Tokyo."

"Maybe for someone like you who's got a girlfriend," she teased. So, Uchida has a girlfriend, I thought. Surprised, I looked at him.

"I don't have a girlfriend. Why do you think I do?"

"For someone like you, not having one would be like landing in jail in Monopoly."

Uchida drank his coffee in silence. Ms. Fujisawa then turned to me.

"I hope you'll really poke around, since you'll be taking care of things."

The building may well have been as big as the one Sensei had designed for the American millionaire Thompson in the late 1960s. Both were built around the same time. Because it was on such a huge expanse of land, its size didn't overwhelm you, but in the city a house this big would look out of place without at least half an acre of land around it. Sensei believed that homes should be in harmony with their surroundings—only somewhere like this would Ms. Fujisawa's place fit in with that way of thinking.

The living-dining room was the largest in the house. Ms. Fujisawa apparently had lots of visitors, especially in summer. Parties for twenty or more were not unusual. Uchida, who had joined me in the kitchen, said that the kitchen counters, long enough for a whole crew to work at, and the huge dining table had been designed with these parties in mind.

Many of her guests must have stayed overnight, because there were three bedrooms on the first floor, each with its own shower. There was also a Japanese-style room with a sunken *kotatsu*—a small table with a heating unit underneath covered by a quilt, and an open space below so you could sit on the tatami with your feet dangling. Compared to the living-dining area upstairs, the light was dimmer on this floor, having smaller windows. The ceiling was much lower as well. These rooms were closed in, suitable for rest and quiet. Sensei didn't think a house needed to be bright and airy throughout. Where he wanted a spacious area, he opened it up all the way, while keeping other places snug and private. "When people are happy, they want friends around to talk to," he once said. "Then again, they need peace and quiet sometimes, and when they're down, they'll hide under the covers. Ideally, a house should be designed with rooms for each of these moods."

Ms. Fujisawa's bedroom was beyond the dining-room fireplace on the second floor, next to the sink where Uchida and I had washed our faces. It had a small fireplace of its own, directly behind the larger one. You could see Mt. Asama through the window in her bathroom. And there was a boudoir, just big enough for one. Though the house itself was huge, the part where the owner spent time in private was fairly confined.

To the south, on the other side of the kitchen, was a comfortable-looking study.

The third floor was storage space, with cardboard packing cases for paintings lined up along the wall. There was also luggage of various sizes. Among it was an old leather trunk of the kind taken on cruises.

Outside the southern wall of the storage room was a tiny balcony. Just big enough for two people to stand on side by side, but too small for a chair, much less a table, it looked about the size of the basket in a hot-air balloon. I wondered why Sensei had put it there, because it didn't seem to serve any practical purpose. I slid the door open and stepped out. There was the smell of fields warmed by the sun. With my hands on the railing, I was looking down at the flowers when a little black object cut straight across my line of sight from right to left. I looked back in that direction and knew immediately where it came from—a wasp's nest, hanging under the eaves about two meters away. As big as a basketball, it was covered with a pattern of pale-brown and white swirls. Several yellow-and-black wasps hovered angrily around the single opening.

A low humming drew nearer. One of them came close, its wings buzzing as it circled me.

"What's wrong?" I heard Uchida's voice from behind. I took a step back and slid the door shut without quite slamming it. The wasp headed straight into the window. I heard it knock against the glass twice, three times.

"So they've made another nest," he said calmly. "I'll have to call the exterminator."

The insect had stopped headbutting the window, but was still flitting suspiciously back and forth outside. It looked about three centimeters long. For wasps, this had been a good year, Uchida told me. You were likely to find nests when there were lots of hot, clear days, but in wet summers there wasn't a sign of them. They built them not only under the eaves, but on the trunk of a larch, or in a hollow tree left where it had fallen, or between large stones in the garden. Even though she'd been badly stung once, Ms. Fujisawa didn't seem very worried about them.

"I just happened to be here that time," Uchida mentioned, "so I took her to the hospital. But wasp stings are much worse the second time around. The doctor told her to be careful—one more sting and she'd be in real trouble—but she just laughed it off." He said this with some exasperation.

After we'd toured all the rooms, I realized how well positioned the fireplaces were. On the second floor, the big one in the main room and the smaller one in the owner's bedroom were back-to-back. And there was another pair on the first floor, one in the living room, back-to-back with the one in the biggest guest bedroom. This design could serve as a model for how to put multiple fireplaces in rooms of completely different sizes and proportions, each in exactly the right spot, all feeding into the same chimney.

There was a large boiler room in the basement. It was dark, with bare concrete walls. From somewhere, I heard a low-pitched humming. The boiler wouldn't be on in midsummer. I turned my head, listening carefully, until I saw a swarm of honeybees outside the screen door. I went over for a look. They had built a nest large enough to fill about half the space between the screen door and the heavy wooden rain shutter. When I blew on them through the screen, their wings started quivering all at once, sending them up and down in waves as the buzzing got louder. With the screen between us, they couldn't sting me. Like a nasty kid, I blew on them again and again.

The wasp's nest was about ten meters above this spot. A house this size, built at the foot of a mountain, had to share its space with various other creatures. Woodpeckers had drilled holes in the cypress siding. Snakes or field mice might be finding shelter in the attic or in the hollows of the woodpile. The lives of the rain-shutter bees were balanced precariously between danger from the wasps above and the feast of flowers outside. If the wasps attacked, the whole hive might be wiped out. Or would they band together and fight back?

Why was the house on this scale, though, if Ms. Fujisawa was the only one living here? Even if she needed plenty of room for large parties, she wouldn't have one every week. And in winter, with fewer visitors, how did she spend her days here by herself? There didn't seem to be any dogs or cats around, not even an aquarium or a birdcage. She would cook for herself, make tea, listen to music, read, and go to bed. I wondered if it was the scenery that kept her from getting bored or lonely—but no, best not to oversimplify. Until now, I could never have even imagined a place like this.

England had a class of people with time on their hands, great wealth, and more land than they needed, all to themselves, which helped explain the knowledge that country had of natural history and biology. I remembered a professor making this point, and thought of Ms. Fujisawa again. Perhaps this farm, where she hired people to grow whatever flowers she liked, provided her with her own private field of study. But how had she prepared herself for this sort of life, so far away from the city?

Uchida's father ran a well-known import business specializing in Scandinavian products, and I'd heard that his family home in Shinagawa was huge, a real mansion. That must be why he wasn't as astonished as I was to see how Ms. Fujisawa lived. In that sense, Mariko was more like him. Uchida would be a better match for her; I could imagine them side by side. Uchida probably thought so too. Why, then...? I felt myself sinking back to that same question I'd had swirling around in my head ever since that day at Mariko's cottage.

Despite this unsolved problem, my relationship with her was starting to change. I found her irresistible. The tone of her voice crept into my ears and stayed there.

The feel of her light, soft hands and slender fingers, the way her hair fell over her neck and shoulders when she moved, those long legs of hers, the way she tensed up in protest, or relaxed and accepted things.

The wooden door to the boiler room, faded to gray, suddenly swung open. Ms. Fujisawa was standing there with the light at her back. "You've been down here so long," she said cheerfully. "My old boiler can't be that interesting. It's time to leave this gloom for the outdoors. Come on, I'll show you around."

Uchida had been hard at work the whole time, fixing a little fan in the wall and checking some pipes near the ceiling to make sure they were properly connected. Looking relieved to see her, he brushed the dust off his sleeves and headed for the open door.

The flowers, planted along dead-straight ridges, were full of heavy-looking buds pointing upward. Half-open blooms seemed to be warily checking the outside. Some flowers had a strong scent, while in other beds you smelled the earth first. Among the tall plants were much smaller ones, with flowers like the palm of a baby's hand. All were from abroad, things I had never seen before.

"Only the ones who found this soil and climate to their liking survived. I don't do much for them—they do very well on their own."

The paths through the beds were only wide enough for one.

"Do you know what this is?" she asked. She was squatting over what looked like an empty patch, some distance from the flowerbeds. Beside a pile of discarded leaves were clumps of tiny flowers, only a centimeter or so high. "You have to look carefully to see them."

I squatted down next to her. Yellow, purple, and pale blue, they looked like miniature pansies. Their flowers and leaves were delicate, quivering.

"These are the original violets. They're called *Viola tricolor*," she said. "I leave them alone, don't fuss over them at all."

We walked to the eastern edge of the field. Not knowing I was the villain who had been blowing on them just a while before, bees flitted right by me in different directions. Along with the fragrance of flowers and earth, the smell of herbs like rosemary, mint, and thyme floated past on the air.

Then a human figure emerged from one of the neighboring ridges. "Sensei," the voice called out, "there's a bee's nest in the stump in front of the apricot tree, so be careful." The speaker was an old woman in a straw hat with a thin towel tied under her chin. Still bent over, she raised her sunburnt face to look at us.

"Thanks for telling me, Nori-chan. I'll watch out for it."

Nori-chan looked at me.

"Who's this? A nephew or something?" she asked, her eyes widening.

"Heavens no. I couldn't very well have a nephew this young, could I?"

"I didn't mean *your* nephew," the old woman laughed. "I thought he might be a relation of Murai Sensei's—he looks just like him."

"Who, me?" I asked.

"Yes, you. You look like Murai Sensei when he was young."

Ms. Fujisawa was laughing too. Uchida had wandered off, apparently to check the location of the bee's nest.

"Murai Sensei has such a nice, deep voice, like an actor. And when he was young, he was very handsome." She was laughing so hard she had to press her eyelids with a corner of the towel under her chin. "Still is, of course," she said, then chuckled again.

"She's telling you you're good-looking," Ms. Fujisawa said, looking a bit nonplussed. "You needn't stand there with your mouth hanging open." The old woman must have known all about her relationship with Sensei.

Uchida said it was time to leave.

Ms. Fujisawa came with us as far as where we'd left the bike. "Come back anytime on your own," she said to me.

"I will. Thank you for everything," I replied with a bow.

Uchida, already gripping the handlebars, started the engine the moment I climbed on behind him.

"Well, Ms. Fujisawa, I guess this is it. Thanks, it was a pleasure."

"But surely you'll be back sometime?"

"Probably, but from now on Sakanishi will be in charge."

"I understand. But I hope you'll come for a visit anyway."

As if paying his last respects to the farm, Uchida slowly released the clutch and headed for the gate at a crawl. We went down the private lane, and when we came out onto the asphalt, he stopped the bike. Mt. Asama was right in front of us.

"Be sure to remember where we turn, and look for landmarks so you can come by yourself next time," he said, leaning back toward me.

I nodded and said again, "I will."

19

By the end of August, the whole village of Aoguri seemed in a hurry to leave for home. The days were still hot, but in the evening a forest breeze swept all trace of the heat away. Sensei now wore a light cardigan when he went out for his morning walk.

I was permanently in search of chances to be alone with Mariko. After finishing the cleaning, or laundry, or work I had to do in the vegetable patch on Saturday mornings, I would take the bus into Kyū-Karuizawa, where I met her at a coffee shop near the roundabout, and from there she drove us to her cottage. At night I took the last bus back to the Summer House. Since the *mizu-yōkan* sweets her father's shop was wholesaling to a department store were selling much better than expected, he'd given up his summer vacation to take care of this. Mariko had been told to mow the lawn, but I did it for her.

On weekdays I sometimes said I was going to do research at the Karuizawa Library and met her there, or we'd stop off at the cottage after our weekly shopping trip. As if trying to squeeze through any narrow crack we could find, we were always looking for spare moments we could spend together.

Taking a shower at her place was when I'd start worrying. What if we were found out and I had to quit the office, as Uchida had warned? The anxiety was worse at night, the moment I opened the door to the Summer House. Maybe everyone, or no one, knew what was going on. While either seemed possible, I couldn't decide which was the case.

As summer came to an end, I got a great deal busier. I had to get the window at the Yamaguchi house repaired; Uchida made me redraw the blueprints for the furniture in the Ogikubo house; the estimates from the contractor needed checking before I could contact the clients for their approval and place the orders. When clients asked me what sort of washing machine and refrigerator would be best for their new house, I ordered catalogues of the latest models for them. And while all this was going on, I was afraid that any new ideas of mine for the bookcases in the Library of Modern Literature would slip away before I could do anything with them. Also, I still didn't have a blueprint for the stacking chairs Sensei had sketched for me, because I couldn't get the angle between the seat and legs right, or the positioning of the legs.

I did, however, have an idea for preventing dust from collecting on bookshelves, and protecting books from mold and insects. When Uchida told me to try it out with a model, that's what Yukiko and I set out to do.

People constantly moving in and out of a building inevitably bring some dust in with them. From fall to winter, woolen clothing makes the problem worse. Little by little, it collects on books and in the narrow space at the back of bookshelves. Controlling humidity as well as temperature is obviously important, and during the rainy season, air-conditioning can only do so much. In summer, when hands are sweaty, the moisture that stays on books encourages mold, and a layer of dust makes a perfect environment for insects. Our hot, damp, monsoon-like climate makes dehumidifying an essential factor in library design.

Air currents keep dust and mold from collecting, and make it hard for pests like silverfish and deathwatch beetles to survive. Bookcases designed so that air is constantly moving through them would be protected from all this. A solid board across the back keeps air from getting through. But what if the boards were open, with space at the top and bottom of each shelf to let air in, and exit grilles installed in the floor behind the bookcases instead of in the ceiling? The lowest shelves in the Diet Library are raised about twenty centimeters above the floor for better maintenance, so the idea of suction from below makes sense. Air flowing down through the bookcases would carry the dust toward the floor, to be drawn into the grilles. A constant current would also make life miserable for pests and mold. This was my idea.

Yukiko and I worked on our basswood plywood model at the big table in the workshop. The mock-up included a grille in the floor, with a pipe underneath that had a small extractor fan at the end, driven by a Mabuchi motor. We cut down some paperbacks we'd bought from a secondhand bookstore at ten yen each to a quarter of their original size, to make miniatures to fill the shelves. Incense sticks of various heights were to be placed at several points in front of them so we could tell from the smoke how well the ventilation system was working.

It was Yukiko's idea to use basswood plywood rather than styrene board. Using a handsaw she'd found in a corner of the storehouse, she cut the pieces we needed in no time. I was amazed how skillfully she did this, oblivious to the sawdust that was getting in her hair and all over her arms. "I'm a carpenter's daughter, you know," she said, turning to me, looking pleased with herself. "In grade school I used to make my own toys."

When she was finished, we took the pieces back to the workshop, where we spread some newspaper out on the table and set to work. We were sitting side by side, gluing them together, when Yukiko reached over for the piece I was holding, brushing against my arm. "It's best not to do it that way," she said. "You don't want to start at the top—here, try putting these together." As she reached across, her upper arm touched me again, on the back of my hand.

I sensed that Mariko had come into the room. I could tell it was her by the rhythm of the footsteps. Yukiko looked at me for the first time since we'd started working. She was smiling.

"I'll be making some tea soon, so come downstairs," Mariko said loudly.

I didn't turn in her direction. I heard Iguchi say, "Will do," and Uchida get up from his chair.

"Thanks," Yukiko said, sounding upbeat. "We'll come as soon as we get to a good stopping place."

"Okay," Mariko answered briskly, and went back downstairs.

Yukiko and I were still at it when we were supposed to stop for the afternoon break. Working on this model made me feel like a kid again. Before I knew it, I was babbling away, and Yukiko's laughing got louder.

"You two certainly seem to be having a good time," Ms. Sasai said when she brought us a tray with our tea and snacks. "What's so funny?" she asked. I looked at Yukiko. Her face flushed with laughter, she started to say "He just..." and then dissolved into giggles before she could finish the sentence. "Sounds like you need a break now and then," we were told. Without any further comments, she left with the tray under her arm.

By the time the tea break was over, we had finished the model bookcases. When I went downstairs to take our cups to the kitchen and get the incense we needed for our experiment, I passed Ms. Sasai in front of the dining room. She stopped and looked straight at me.

"Don't try so hard to please," she told me in a low, clear voice.

An "Ah?" came from deep in my throat, not even really a voice.

"You know what I mean," she said. Then promptly, as if blowing a candle out, she went back to normal and started up the stairs.

Mariko wasn't in the dining room. I checked the ironing room, thinking she must be there, but it was empty. Feeling uneasy, I got a box of incense sticks from the shelf in the storehouse, and without even a glance at the ironing room when I passed it on my right, went back to the workshop. I could hear pencils on paper, drawing lines I couldn't see. Lines pointing at me; for something I hadn't told them about. Yukiko, the only one not using a pencil, looked up and smiled. With Ms. Sasai's words echoing in my head, I looked away.

We lit the incense and began our experiment. Pencils and rulers were put down as the others came over to watch. Smoke from the incense was drawn through the open part at the back of the bookcases, filled with miniature books. The drawing power seemed stronger on the lower shelves. Yukiko bent over to watch from a short distance away. As the smoke gathered by the grille and came out of the end of the pipe, the clean smell of incense—Sensei's favorite brand—filled the area around the table. When the two bookcases, placed back-to-back, were too far apart, the drawing power decreased, but when pulled closer together to about the width of the grille in the floor, the speed of the smoke was noticeably faster. It was the same principle Sensei had shown me in the fireplace, how the flames flare up or die down depending on how far apart the logs are. When logs, bookcases, or people are just close enough, their energy makes the air move.

"Looks like this'll work all right," Uchida murmured to himself, then turned to me and said, "You'd better explain it to Sensei yourself."

I went to the director's office. There I told him about my idea and showed him a sketch. "We've made a model—you can see it anytime," I added.

He frowned. "Have you done that blueprint for the stacking chairs?"

I felt myself tense up. "I'm sorry. I should be able to show you one quite soon."

"You're very slow. What seems to be the trouble?"

I explained that I hadn't been able to get the angles between the seat and legs right.

"Is that really something you have to work out by yourself? Why didn't you show me what you had, and tell me about it?" He sounded unusually cross.

"I'm sorry."

"You've got clients and deadlines. That's the way things are for an architect."

"Yes, I understand."

He took off his bifocals and looked straight at me.

"There's no such thing as a perfect structure, without a single fault. No one can build something like that. Is it worth making the client wait forever while you're fiddling around with the blueprint? That's what you need to ask yourself when you're designing a building." Nothing I did at this point would be worth keeping a client waiting for. "I'm not saying you should do whatever the client says," he went on, "and just concentrate on meeting the deadline. But what if you're working on your design till the last minute and then suddenly have to change something the client doesn't like? Or you find you've made a mistake. To prevent emergencies like that, you've got to keep track of how much time you have. In that sense, architecture isn't art at all. It's function, pure and simple." After stopping to rub his eyelids with a finger from each hand, he continued. "One of the reasons for having an office like this is so that I can have more people working, to make up for the limited time. Two can finish a job that would take one person a whole day in half the time. If I had to do a big project like this library by myself I'd still be at it five years from now. I ask you to do certain jobs, and others you leave up to me. This kind of cooperation has nothing to do with who's boss. There's no pecking order here. It's a matter of trust. Without that, how can we work together?"

Unable to raise my head, I concentrated on the dull sheen of his old wooden desk, with his hand resting on it.

"There's no need to hang your head," he said. His frown loosened into an awkward attempt at a smile. The anger was gone from his eyes, which looked almost diffident now.

"Well then," he said, "I'd like to see this experiment of yours." Putting his glasses back on, he stood up.

Sensei spoke quietly, but what he had to say was clear: as dust and moisture always collect at the bottom, it was best for the downdraft to be strongest on the lower shelves. Still, improvements could be made in the design. Bookcases should look good even when they're empty. Open spaces at the top and bottom would make the shelves look unstable and rather cheap—sort of like the swinging doors in an old Western saloon. Why not divide the backboard into three pieces—top, middle, and bottom—and pull the middle piece slightly forward, to make slits above and below? The slits wouldn't be visible from the front, but should increase the speed of the air moving through them, as in a fireplace. "So, try again—something along these lines," he said, handing me a rough sketch he'd made in the interim.

"Where you put the grilles is always a problem," he went on. "They usually end up in the ceiling or on a crossbeam, but drawing air out through the floor is actually practical, and if you do it right, maintenance should be pretty easy, too. With this plan, you're not just keeping the air moving. If you work out the details carefully, you'll have a new way to protect books that doesn't look awkward, and makes almost no noise. It just needs a little more work. But it's a good idea. Thanks."

Yukiko grinned at me.

"Sakanishi, could you come back to my office for a minute?"

I followed him there.

"I hear you went to Ms. Fujisawa's place," he said from his sofa chair.

"Yes, I went with Uchida."

"Have a seat," he said, motioning toward the chair across from him. "How was it?"

"I was surprised to see how big it is. But the study, bedroom, bath, and little side room are all pretty close together, north and south of the kitchen, so considering how much space there is, the owner doesn't need to walk very far."

His face softened.

"She gets enough exercise working in the fields during the day. In the winter I thought it would be nice if she could spend most of her time in that small area on the second floor. She's an intelligent woman, so don't worry, but there's more maintenance work to do as the place gets older. You may end up going there now and then, I'm afraid."

"That's fine, sir."

"The central heating isn't working all that well. She really needs a new boiler, but whether or not you put one in this year is up to her."

He sat there massaging the corners of his eyes, with an expression that was hard to read. I decided to ask him about something that still puzzled me.

"About that balcony on the third floor..." I started to say.

"Yes, I hear the wasps have made a nest again this year."

"Why did you put a balcony there?"

"Why?" he laughed, and after some thought, started to explain. "There's an old city hall in Copenhagen. Do you know it?"

"No."

"Well, it's not just government offices. It's an impressive-looking redbrick building, with a tower over a hundred meters high. Since they have a rule against building anything higher than that in Copenhagen, it's become a symbol of the city. Nowadays it might look like a very Scandinavian building, modeled on medieval Danish architecture. A man called Martin Nyrop designed it. But back in 1905, when it was finished, most architects hated it." He rubbed his chin with the palm of his hand.

"Actually, there's little traditional about it. For instance, it has a glass roof. From above it's a real eye-catcher, and it makes the inside much lighter. The pitch of the roof is steep, to keep it from leaking. There're all kinds of handcrafty touches inside, and he's used different materials, like wood, brick, granite, and steel, in ways that bring out what's best about each one. Nyrop really let himself go—did whatever he wanted." He laughed. "The chairs were all designed from scratch too. He made them comfortable to sit in, rather than ornate, which would have been conventional back then. I think his chairs helped Scandinavian furniture break out of its traditional mold and find a new direction. But most architects then were academic types, and conservative. Nyrop was more practical, more of a craftsman, really. Nobody's complaining about the building now that it's become a landmark. It took some time, but Danes caught up with his way of doing things.

"People have weddings there, and when a Danish prince or princess gets married, the citizens have a celebration for them at city hall before the actual ceremony. And the square in front of it is just the right size for the proportions of the building. In Japan we don't have anything like the European town square. Open on all sides, so anyone can use it. It's nothing special, really—definitely not a gift from the royal family. If there was a revolution, it would probably become a meeting place, because it belongs to the public. The Japanese have never tried this—probably never will."

He shifted in his chair as if getting back on course.

"In the center of the third floor there's a wooden door with an arch that opens onto a balcony where the royal family come out and wave to the people below. Sort of like the figures that come out of a cuckoo clock on the hour. The balcony's that small."

He was lightly tapping his left thumb with the pencil in his right hand.

"When I saw that city hall for the first time, it showed me a way of using a balcony that I'd never thought of before. The one at Ms. Fujisawa's house is the same—somewhere for her to come out and greet... her flowers," he said with a chuckle. "That's just a joke. But I did want a place with a view of all the fields, and since it's such a big house, I thought a playful touch somewhere would be nice. When you go back there, try looking up at someone standing on that balcony from somewhere out in the fields. It's an interesting sight. From far away, people look tiny. And with a pile like that in the background, they seem even tinier, more fragile."

Looking as if he'd just remembered something, he sat there quietly for a moment.

"Better not to go out on the balcony while the wasp's nest is still there," he said finally.

"I could call an exterminator to get rid of it."

"No hurry. When autumn turns to winter, they'll leave. If there's no immediate danger it's better to wait till it gets cold and remove the empty nest. Talk it over with her before you do anything."

He spoke of Ms. Fujisawa as if she were just another client. He didn't seem about to broach the subject of Mariko either.

I stayed in the workshop late that night, finishing my blueprint for the stacking chairs, which I handed to Sensei the next morning, when he came back from his walk. He pointed out several things that needed fixing, so I spent all morning redoing it, after which he told me to make several more adjustments. When I finally gave him the new blueprint that evening, he looked it over in silence for a while before saying "It looks good. If we win the competition, these are the chairs we'll use."

If they actually got made, they would be the first bits of furniture I was responsible for. I made an extra copy of the blueprint and took it back to my room. He had chewed me out, and then approved of my work. This blueprint would remind me of both events.

There was one more problem to solve concerning the bookcases. How many different heights should the shelves be? In other words, what percentage should accommodate books considered to be of average size—about thirteen by eighteen centimeters—and how many should fit books of larger or smaller format? After spending some time holed up in the Karuizawa Library checking the size of books and their publication dates, I discovered that the variety of different shapes was decreasing year by year. By the late 1970s, large-scale books that came in a cardboard case were hardly being published anymore, except for sets of authors' complete works, and there were also fewer oblong-shaped volumes, or those that were either slightly larger or smaller than normal. I suspected that as time went on, there would also be fewer books with carefully designed cloth or foil-stamped covers.

If we used removable shelves that could be adjusted to different levels with shelf rests, the result would inevitably be some wasted space, and would give the huge bookcases a random, inconsistent look. "I think fixed shelves, as in the Hokkaido University Library, would be best,"

Sensei had said, "There must be a way to arrange books on fixed shelves without wasting too much space—that's what I'd like you to figure out." We hadn't even started working on it, though.

Harue Nomiya's new bookrest was almost finished. I had sent the blueprint to Tagawa, the contractor in Yatsugatake, and discussed the details with him on the phone several times. When it arrived, I was planning to talk to Sensei about how bookrests would be used in the new library.

To call Tagawa, I used the phone in the ironing room, where Mariko had her office. She didn't even smile when she saw me. The last time we'd been alone together was three days before. There were still plenty of homegrown vegetables left, so we had skipped one of our weekly shopping trips. Standing there with the receiver in my hand, I felt her perfume tickling my nose, making it hard to relax. The smell brought back the sensation of her hair and skin.

"I should be able to send you the oak bookrest by next week," Tagawa said on the other end.

"Thank you. That's a big help," I replied, barely conscious of what I was saying.

After I'd put down the phone, Mariko said, "You don't go in for small talk, do you? I mean, you never ask, 'How are you?' or 'What's the weather like over there?'"

"You think I was rude?" I asked.

"You sounded brusque—like Sensei," she told me, flicking her long hair back over her shoulder, uncovering an ear.

Unable to find a way to keep the conversation going, I just mumbled, "Really?"

We were the only ones on the first floor. Knowing I could reach out and touch her held me back all the more.

"Thanks for letting me use the phone," I said, as usual. I wanted to talk to her about the weekend, but couldn't find the words.

"No problem," she replied.

Now who's being brusque, I thought, as I reluctantly left and went next door to the kitchen, where I poured myself a glass of cold tomato juice. After grinding some pepper into it, I drank it in one gulp. While I was washing and drying the glass, I looked over at the ironing room, and saw that Mariko had lowered her head onto her arms, folded on the desk. Her soft hair looked like a curtain, closed to me. Without speaking to her, I left and went back to the workshop.

At dinner that night, she was very quiet. For some time now, Uchida hadn't been talking much either, so there wasn't much conversation.

Sensei broke the silence. "Now that you've got the window over at Yamaguchi's place fixed, why don't we plant a pepper tree by it? That should keep the thieves away."

There was a row of five *sanshō* trees in the back garden at the Summer House. Four had apparently grown from the seeds of one. They were about two meters tall, their lush leaves covering the nearby white *Enkianthus* shrub. The branches were heavy with peppers, like little green grapes, and just walking by you could smell them. But if you reached a bare arm out to pick them, long, sharp thorns would make you sorry you had. Yes, a pepper tree was a good burglar repellent, but Yukiko was against the idea of transplanting one right away.

"It's too late now," she said. "The rainy season is the best time to transplant them, but if you want to do it this year, you should at least wait till autumn."

"Okay. Let's take a couple of our trees over to his place in the fall then. How does that sound?"

"Fine. I'll come and help." She turned to Ms. Sasai to talk about picking the peppers. Every year the two of them looked forward to this, then boiling and freezing them, or simmering them in soy sauce and mirin to make *tsukudani*. I was a little miffed that they didn't ask me to help pick them. Mariko was silently eating her penne arrabbiata as if all this had nothing to do with her.

A while before, I had bought a 50cc motorbike. I'd told Uchida I needed a way to get to Ms. Fujisawa's house, and it would be convenient for local errands as well. "Two can't ride on a such a small bike, you know," he pointed out, looking me in the eye. "I don't mind that," I said, "just so long as it has enough horsepower to get up and down these mountain roads." He told me about a place he knew in Karuizawa that sold secondhand bikes. Their prices were reasonable, they were good at doing repairs, and they considered a sale to be long term, which meant you could trust them. So one evening I caught the bus into town, reaching the shop just before closing time, and with no hesitation bought the red bike the owner recommended. Now I'd be able to go to Mariko's cottage on weekends without worrying about the time, as I could come back in the middle of the night or early in the morning. Iguchi had mentioned that in certain places the bus route followed the track of the old Tanasaka Light Railway, which had taken the long way around to avoid having to go up and down steep slopes. A 50cc engine would surely be able to handle that route.

"Here, you can have these, I don't use them anymore," Uchida said when I had registered the bike and was about to go and pick it up. He handed me a helmet and goggles, made in England, of much better quality than the contraption I'd be riding. Down in Karuizawa, I put them on, straddled my machine, and rode it back to the Summer House, with Mt. Asama sometimes right in front of me or off to the side, taking about twice as long as I would have by car.

Mariko, who had retired to her room after dinner without saying a word, slipped a small envelope under my door late that night. Inside was a note saying simply "Can we spend Saturday and Sunday together? Mariko." A whiff of her eau de toilette came from the thick, soft paper.

On the morning of the last Saturday in August, Yukiko and I were making breakfast. The outside thermometer showed that it was twelve degrees Celsius.

I'd been planning to make something simple by myself, but then Yukiko came down, saying she wanted to make hash browns. In a well-worn blue T-shirt with a dark-brown cardigan over it, she moved quickly around the kitchen.

She was sliding the crisp shredded potatoes out of the frying pan onto a plate when I heard her give a little gasp. Looking outside in the same general direction as her, I saw branches moving up and down. Three turtledoves were in one of the pepper trees. The thorns must have been pricking their legs, since they kept flapping their wings, perching precariously on one branch after another as they stuck their necks out to peck at the small round peppers. It looked painful, but quite funny.

"Do you mind them stealing your fruit?" I asked, my hands resting on the coffee mill.

She was planning to pick the peppers after breakfast.

"There's lots, so they can have as many as they want. Caterpillars love the leaves too. Even thorns can't protect those trees—they taste too good."

The birds leaned over sideways, utterly undignified as they stretched for a berry.

"Like a bed of nails," Yukiko said, "but they still want to eat."

Watching them flap clumsily around, I felt as if I were watching myself. There was something ridiculous about my buying a motorbike this late in the summer just so I could be with Mariko. But I was too wrapped up in her to look at what I was doing objectively, and change. After breakfast I was going to ride my bike into town, then go on to Kyū-Karuizawa, where Mariko was waiting, to spend the weekend with her.

"Morning," said Uchida as he came into the dining room. The turtledoves took off all at once. The pepper branches swayed, then were still. Only four of us—Ms. Sasai, Yukiko, Uchida, and I—sat at the table. This was the smallest number for breakfast since I had come to the Summer House.

"I woke up to the smell of hash browns," Uchida said, looking happier than he had in quite a while.

"You have me to thank for that," Yukiko replied.

Kawarazaki, Kobayashi, and Iguchi would all be at the office in Tokyo until Monday. Sensei had left the previous evening. He was probably at Ms. Fujisawa's farm.

When our quiet meal was over and we were having another cup of coffee, Uchida straightened up in his chair and cleared his throat. "Since you're all here, I have an announcement to make." He tried to smile, but looked stiff. "I know this is kind of sudden, but after we're finished with the library, I'll be leaving the Murai Office."

A cloud came over Yukiko's face.

"You're going to start your own office?" asked Ms. Sasai, obviously surprised.

"Yes. But it's all still up in the air."

"If we win the competition you'll be staying till the library's finished, won't you?" Yukiko asked.

"Of course, I'd like to, if we win."

"Then we'll be working together for a while yet," said Ms. Sasai, trying to sound cheerful.

Uchida got up to put more water in the kettle. "Who knows what'll happen," he said with his back turned to us. "If Sensei's plan gets a fair hearing, they'll surely see that it's the best one—the one that deserves to be built—but it's hard to tell how the dynamics work in the selection committee."

He went on to say that Sensei was the only one he'd told about his plan to quit, and that although Iguchi probably knew by now, for the time being he hoped we'd keep it to ourselves. He didn't mention Mariko, which was natural enough, though it seemed to me he was deliberately leaving her name out of it. Nor did he look at me once the whole time he was talking.

After I'd finished cleaning up, I got ready to leave. I'd told the others that I was going to visit a friend in Karuizawa. I got my bike out of the garage and put on the helmet and goggles Uchida had given me. They didn't go with the bike at all, but I felt the mismatch suited me.

I switched on the engine. It sounded distinctly lightweight, less than one-hundredth the power of the Black Shadow. I felt Uchida's unseen presence beyond the katsura tree as I slowly moved out, then gave the throttle a good sharp twist.

20

It was evening.

Old photo albums were lined up on the record rack in the living room.

"There're some pictures of Sensei when he was young somewhere."

Mariko took one of the albums out, and holding it in both hands, sat down next to me on the sofa. She reached back to turn on the Le Klint floor lamp. It was still light outside, but the record rack was in a dark corner, away from the window facing the garden. A round pool of bright light now shone down on her hands.

The smell of old paper was noticeable as she turned the pages. The black-and-white photos were carefully arranged, each mounted with triangular corners. In the middle of the first page was a family snapshot with Mt. Asama in the background. The little girl in the center was wearing a Tyrolean hat with a long-sleeved shirt, breeches, and sturdy climbing boots. The father and mother were also dressed for climbing. Smiling slightly, the girl looked dazzled by the sunlight, but you could clearly see the pride in her face. The caption below, written in blue with a fountain pen, read "August 5, 1962, Mt. Asamakakushi, Mariko's first climb." The writing was probably her father's. I saw a definite resemblance to Sensei, although his face was softer. A broader forehead, with more space between the eyebrows. A mouth that looked as if jokes would slip easily out of it. The mother's climbing gear looked borrowed somehow, and perhaps because she was tired, her smile was rather stiff.

"It was a really tough climb," Mariko said. "I thought I was going to die, but my father kept cheering me on. 'Look how far you've come,' he'd say. 'We're almost there!' When we got to the top and I put my rucksack down, I suddenly felt so light I could've been blown away by the wind."

In the album, Mariko as a first grader looked as delicate as a twig. She seemed unaware of how thin her arms were, though; her eyes were focused on the outside world, not on herself. Squatting down by a stream, staring into the water. Hiding one eye with a red maple leaf as she grinned to show off her missing front teeth. All dressed up in the dining room of the Mampei Hotel in grown-up clothes her parents had picked out for her, with hairpins holding her combed-back hair in place. On the first page of another album of about the same time, she was running away from the camera past some summer cottages, on a path lined with larch trees. The movement blurred her into a double image.

"Can you guess where this was taken?" Mariko asked, shifting the album onto my knees.

"Not in Karuizawa?"

"No, in Aoguri."

Surprised, I looked more closely and saw, in the unpaved road, a sort of rustic openness not at all like Karuizawa. A carefully laid out series of family snapshots taken in Aoguri followed.

An old building. You could tell at a glance it was a station. The characters for "Exit" were written from right to left, rather than the other way around, as has been standard since the war. Far below the exit sign was Mariko, too small even for kindergarten, standing by the turnstile, looking up in amazement at something in the sky. She was wearing a white blouse with embroidery on the collar, a checked skirt, and black shoes with straps. Her hair was a mushroom cut, her cheeks round and plump. This must have been taken at Kita-Asama Station, on the old Tanasaka Light Railway. There was a single car on the track, which was a little lower than the platform. Perhaps the train had just let Mariko and her family off, and was about to go on to Kusatsu. Aside from the pentagraph sticking out of the top that gave it the nickname "Horned Beetle," the whole train was less than half the size of an average passenger car.

There was also a shot of Sensei holding Mariko in his arms outside the station, smiling at the camera. Wearing an open-collared shirt, he looked much thinner yet tougher than now, with short hair.

There were more pictures, taken at the Summer House. Little Mariko standing beneath the katsura tree, only about half as tall as it was now, the trunk still slender. Another showed her coming down those stairs I knew so well, all by herself, her hand barely reaching the handrail. Puffy little bare feet. In a snapshot of Sensei with Mariko's family in the back garden, you could see Mt. Asama, a blurred silhouette beyond a row of young trees lined up at regular intervals like spindly youths. Both the people and scenery looked faded and fragile somehow, as if they were about to disappear.

A photo taken more than two decades earlier showed lots of exotic-looking flowers in the Summer House garden. I thought I'd seen some like them at Kinuko Fujisawa's nursery, but when I tried to remember which ones, they didn't match. A bench now stood where the flower beds in these old photographs had been. The pictures all looked very quiet. No sounds, or smells, and you couldn't tell which way the wind was blowing. No birdsong either, of gray thrush or Oriental tit.

"Looks completely different from now."

"That's only natural—he was still in his fifties."

"I didn't mean Sensei. Aoguri. The village seems so young somehow."

"The sky was bigger back then," she said, nodding, "and the whole village was open and breezy. The sun was brighter too."

There were several close-ups of her in profile. Her father must have thought she looked especially cute from that angle. I could see something of the intensity of that childish profile in her even now.

"What were you looking at in this picture?" I asked.

"I have no idea," she laughed.

By now it was completely dark. White moths bumped against the screen door and fluttered away. The air from outside was cold.

We went into the kitchen to heat up the wintermelon soup Mariko had made, and to fetch some pickled vegetables and *pitan* tofu to lay out on the table. We then boiled a big plateful of gyoza. They were crescent-shaped, with neat edges.

Watching me dispose of the slippery gyoza, pausing only to say how good they tasted, she told me more about the time she'd spent at the Summer House as a child. It was as though she was pulling out memories one by one, holding each in the palm of her hand to examine it. When Iguchi talked about the old days, she'd mostly sat there quietly listening, so I was hearing her stories for the first time.

In Kyū-Karuizawa the adults always came first, with their offspring tagging along, but in Aoguri the children had their own world. There were kids Mariko had known since kindergarten, so during summer vacation she had much more fun in Aoguri than in Karuizawa.

She climbed Mt. Koasama, a much smaller mountain near the volcano, with her parents. The water in the stream flowing through the village was always cold. She learned how to row on Firefly Pond, and she and her friends had a "ghost hunt" around the pond one summer night. With lanterns to light the way, they looked for tennis balls hidden in the mailboxes of various cottages, and the first one to find four ran back to home base. She'd always looked forward to autumn in Aoguri. She used to bring home a basket of chestnuts from the big tree in a corner behind the clubhouse. In winter they skated on Firefly Pond, and played ice hockey with sticks Sensei and his staff made for them, with a wooden puck wrapped in leather.

Mariko seemed to accept the hollowing out of village life as inevitable. "My mother hates the country," she said, "so she stopped coming long ago, but by the time I was in high school, I hardly came anymore either."

As they aged, the generation that had first built the cottages started finding the trip to the hills too much trouble, and their children, too, left this faded world behind for brighter, newer places. Gradually, the light went out of the village.

"I used to see Nomiya Sensei when I was little. She hardly ever smiled, so even back then she seemed different from the other women."

"Did you talk to her?"

"No, never. I don't think she's very interested in children—wasn't then, isn't now. The only time I saw her looking happy was at the assembly hall one time, sitting next to some dour-looking old guy. She was wearing a summer dress with blue flowers on it—I can picture it even now," she said as if this was somehow funny. "I remember thinking, wow, she has arms and legs. She always wore a kimono, so I'd never seen them before. Smiling and laughing like that, she looked like a completely different person."

When we'd finished dinner and washed the dishes, Mariko put a record on. Bach preludes, played on the guitar.

"Sounds different from the piano," I said.

"I like guitar music."

There was a Steinway grand piano in the next room. I wanted to ask her if she still played, but didn't. We sat back down on the sofa.

In the last of the old albums, there was a picture of Sensei, dressed for farmwork, lifting a bundle of branches full of leaves off the back of a small truck.

"What's he doing here?"

"Those are mulberry leaves, for silkworms."

"They were raising them at the Summer House?"

"That's right. There were trays of them in one corner of the storehouse."

"So, you were there back when they were doing that?"

"I was still little, and I liked watching the tiny white worms munching away at the leaves. That only lasted for two or three years, though. It was just a hobby, but very time-consuming. Some disease killed them all off, and that was that."

They must have brought the mulberry leaves from Ms. Fujisawa's place. Perhaps Sensei drove the truck there and back.

"Tell me about when you were in grade school," Mariko said, looking up from the album. I couldn't think of anything worth mentioning. "You used to go bird-watching, didn't you?"

"Yes—when I didn't have school, I was always either in the hills or the forest. During summer vacation, when there were more species to see, lots of kids used to come on the Bird Searchers' outings. That made things livelier, but the added noise drove some of the birds away. I always wanted summer to be over so things went back to normal, with just a few of us, walking as quietly as we could through the trees, on the lookout."

"What did you do besides look for birds?" she asked.

"Sometimes we went on family trips. To the beach on the west side of the Izu Peninsula, or to stay with my cousins in Yokohama. But most of the time I was at home. I had swimming lessons at school, or got together with kids from the neighborhood to take turns bashing a watermelon with sticks till it broke open. I let the days go by, and always put my summer homework off to the last minute. I'm sure my summers would have been different if we'd had a cottage in Aoguri."

Mariko looked at me and shut the album.

"Has Sensei said anything about us?" she asked, sinking back into the sofa, looking up at the ceiling.

"No, not yet."

The record was over. With no more Bach on the guitar, the room was very quiet. I got up to put on the other side, then sat back next to her.

"Maybe I shouldn't have told you that in the first place," she murmured, looking down, sounding disappointed.

I didn't know what to say. She slipped her hand under my arm and pulled her legs up to her chest. I could feel the warmth of her body.

"I guess it's bothered you a lot."

"Not at all."

The guitar music filled in the silences.

"I wish you were still a little kid," she said.

"Huh?"

"We'd go walking in the hills. And every time we heard a bird sing, you'd tell me whether it was a kogera, or a blue-and-white flycatcher, or a thrush. You'd look through your binoculars, then hand them to me, and tell me exactly where to look so I could watch it sing."

"You mean I'd be a kid and you wouldn't?"

"Of course. I'd be the age I am now. You'd be a shy little boy in grade school, much shorter than me, but guiding me."

"When I was in second grade you were in fifth. So why don't we try meeting at that age?"

"Yes, let's do that."

Little Mariko's pudgy cheeks and nose had thinned out as she grew up, revealing the fine bone structure underneath. As she learned to keep her will and emotions in check, the childish lips that had opened whenever she was fascinated or surprised stayed coolly closed. That little girl, light enough for Sensei to easily lift up, was now a good weight in my arms. And yet the child hadn't completely vanished. The shape of her head under my hand, the soft hair between my fingers, the straight back, the round shoulders—something of all that had always been there. The woman beside me now, breathing, talking, was... precious. A feeling quite different from sexual desire was growing in me.

We could hear the insects outside Mariko's bedroom. Our hands moved together, our bodies touched, our mouths closed when words stopped coming, then opened slightly once again. Feelings deep inside us were shaken loose and floated to the surface. Where did it come from, this sensation that arose again and again, just as strong each time? No matter how deep you sank, no matter how hard the shocks, even when you felt you were going to disappear, you knew you would eventually come back. Wasn't it because it was connected to a darkness deep inside us all, from our conception? A familiar kind of darkness, one not to be afraid of. Hearing each other breathe, then breathing together, we descended into that warm darkness.

21

A water stain had appeared on the cloth wallpaper on the side of Ms. Fujisawa's study. Sensei asked me to go and check.

"I'll be in the fields until about three," she told me after I arrived on my motorbike the next day, "so come and get me if you need me."

The study was one of the smallest rooms in the house. Except for the door, the northern wall was all bookcases. The neatly arranged books, about half Japanese and half in Western languages, included illustrated field guides to flowers, plants, and fruit trees, and volumes on botany, plus novels and poetry. I could tell from the worn-looking spines that the field guides had been thumbed through over and over again. I noticed an old book on beekeeping as well.

A small photo in a frame was propped up in a corner of one of the shelves. Ms. Fujisawa, her black hair pulled back, was standing next to a smiling girl who looked about high school age. She had the same curved eyebrows and nicely shaped ears as Ms. Fujisawa. Uchida hadn't said anything about a marriage, or a daughter.

From her desk, she had a fine view of the town of Sakudaira through the southern window. The wood was fine grained, probably maple. There was a pocket dictionary on the desk, along with a stone paperweight and a stone pen tray the same shade of blue as William the hippo, mascot of the Metropolitan Museum of Art in New York, with an assortment of pencils, an eraser, a fountain pen, and an Opinel knife, all neatly lined up in it. The pencils, though, were Uni rather than Staedtler. A dark-red one, freshly sharpened, lay across a notebook with a blank cover.

To the left of the desk, a display of butterflies in a glass case with a narrow wooden frame hung on the wall. I wondered if they'd been collected hereabouts. The butterflies, both large and small, had patterns and color combinations I hadn't seen before. Then came that pale-brown stain, infused with the tinge of wood. Running my hand over it, I found it was dry, which suggested that water had seeped in only once, not repeatedly over time.

I went up to the third floor. There was no sign of a leak on the eastern wall of the storeroom. I opened the small door in the ceiling Sensei had told me about, pulled down the collapsible ladder, and climbed up into the attic. A hatch there led to the roof. I stuck my head out and looked around. Still no sign of a problem. I put my hands on the edge and hoisted myself onto the roof. I felt the wind on my face.

The only thing up there besides the chimney, which was slightly north of center, was the skylight. It was a shallow gable roof, and as there were no gutters to get clogged with fallen leaves, the rain would flow unhindered down the east and west sides. Below the eaves I could see where the ground had been paved with black volcanic rock from the mountain.

Standing on the roof, it didn't seem like such a big house, perhaps because there was nothing under that expanse of sky to compare it with. I moved around in a half crouch, looking for signs of corrosion from wet leaves, or to see if one of the metal sheets had come loose. Because the skylight was almost directly above the study, I lay flat beside it to examine it more thoroughly, but didn't find anything out of order.

"When a typhoon whips the rain from the side," Sensei had said, "you get leaks in unexpected places. Sometimes water seeping between the clapboards is drawn up by capillary action into an inside wall. You have to watch out for things like that."

By the time Ms. Fujisawa's house was built, outside walls would probably have been waterproofed and insulated, so it didn't seem likely for rain to have leaked in that way. From what I'd seen on the roof, I figured the problem must be connected to the chimney. Strong winds and rain from the typhoon that tore across Nagano Prefecture late in July, when we were coming to the Summer House, would have beaten against the side of the house for two days straight. Maybe rain had seeped in through a crack near the chimney, then run along the sloping ceiling until it was right above the study, and with nowhere else to go, trickled down into the room. It seemed odd that there were no water stains on the storeroom walls, but for the time being all I could do was put in caulking around the chimney, and just in case the skylight as well, and see if that worked. If I told Sensei my findings, then phoned the contractor, the work could be done in a day or so.

When I started down from the attic, Ms. Fujisawa was standing at the bottom.

"Okay up there?" she asked.

"Afraid not," I told her. "I think rain may have found a way in near the chimney."

I climbed the rest of the way down and pushed the ladder back up.

"That's not what I meant," she said, smiling. "I thought it might be a bit frightening, walking around on the roof."

"Well, maybe a little."

I had felt kind of nervous—it was a long way down—but much more than that, I'd felt free up there. Besides, as daylight hours were long and there wasn't much heavy snowfall in this area, the roof had a shallow pitch, so there was little chance of falling unless I stumbled or slipped.

"Uchida was afraid of heights, so he just stuck his head out through the hatch and looked around," she laughed, adding as she headed downstairs, "I've made some tea, so come on down."

She poured the tea into two deep-blue cups. She was someone who looked straight at you, and didn't seem bothered when you looked back either. Though she and Mariko weren't related, there were certain things I felt they had in common.

"Some flowers will start pushing all the others out of their way if you let them," she said out of the blue. This was the horticulturist speaking. Though I was only meeting her for the second time, for some reason I found her easy to talk to.

"I guess in the right surroundings any flower can go wild."

"The ones I'm talking about aren't that passive—they're pushy without any help from me."

There were fine wrinkles in the hand that was pouring milk into the tea. She wore no rings. The long fingers looked strong and nimble, more suitable for playing a piano than digging in the earth.

"It's not just that they drop a lot of seeds and before you know it there're a lot more of them—they'll actually move into the space where another plant is quietly growing, as if they're mobile. The flowers look so sure of themselves."

"Only the flowers? What about the rest of them, the roots?"

"It's funny, but the rest of the plant never seems to have as much drive. The stems are wobbly, the leaves have odd spaces between them, like they've been thinned out. It's as though the petals have used up all its energy. They're the first ones to wilt after heavy rain, and as soon as I cut even one stem to put in a vase, the whole thing sort of collapses. Sassy flowers need others to push around."

Though what she said seemed exaggerated, she was fun to listen to. I couldn't help laughing.

"How did we get on this subject anyway?" She chuckled, as if amused by her own vehemence. "It's the same with people, you know," she added. "The ones with strong opinions and loud voices take over. The quiet ones lose out."

We sat there a while without saying anything.

"What's your favorite kind of flower?" I asked.

She answered my not-very-original question immediately. "The *Viola tricolor*. Not pansies. The little plants I showed you the last time you were here. Remember?" She was looking straight at me again. "They're wildflowers, only about a centimeter across, and about this high," she said, showing me with her bent fingers. That brought the memory back. Tiny things with purple and pale-blue petals, and some yellow around the stamens, next to a pile of cuttings on the dark earth. "The original violets," she'd told me. So delicate they looked as if a dog could wipe them out with one paw.

"I always try to choose flowers I can devote myself to," she said, "but the *Viola tricolor* is special."

Pansies are hybrids, apparently, created early in the nineteenth century when Scandinavian horticulturists started crossbreeding several types of violets. *Viola tricolor*, the species that gave rise to the pansy, grew wild throughout Europe, on farmland and in open fields. Also called heartsease, it was known as a medicinal herb used to treat asthma and skin disease. Horticulturalists, thinking of its looks rather than its medicinal properties, wanted bigger, brighter flowers that would bloom in profusion, so they created one new hybrid after another. By midcentury, multicolored pansies several times larger than the original *Viola tricolor* had spread all over Europe. Around the same time, greenhouses were becoming popular ("The nineteenth century was the age of iron and glass," she reminded me), and leaving their wild parent with its tiny, unassuming flowers far behind, pansies became famous for their showiness.

"Have you read any Shakespeare?"

"Only *The Merchant of Venice*."

"Everyone should read him—architects, scientists, pianists, no matter who."

A Midsummer Night's Dream, she told me, is a comedy set in motion by juice from the heartsease, which, when sprinkled on the eyelids, makes a sleeper fall madly in love with the first creature she or he sees on waking. This mischief is done by fairies who live in the forest. A seventeenth-century audience might well have thought of the *Viola tricolor* as they watched tiny hands holding the flowers on the stage.

They also appear in *Hamlet*, in the scene by Ophelia's grave. While trying to hang "fantastic garlands" she's made from nettles and daisies on a willow branch by a brook, Ophelia slips, falls in, and drowns. When her grieving brother, Laertes, prays at her graveside, saying "from her fair and unpolluted flesh / May violets spring!" he means the *Viola tricolor*. Mozart and Scarlatti both wrote songs called "The Violet."

Ms. Fujisawa first saw the plant in Switzerland while living in Europe during the early 1950s, and was immediately taken with it, so began looking for it everywhere—in fields, parks, or on riverbanks. She then brought some plants and seeds with her when she returned to Japan by ship. But it proved to be temperamental. The plants didn't find the soil and water of Tokyo to their liking, as not one took root. After moving up here, she remembered the places in Switzerland where she'd seen *Viola tricolor* growing, and tried planting the seeds in the sunniest spots she could find. Although most never came up, a few did, and in the second year, they bloomed. She expected them to spread little by little, but because they're an annual, in some years there were no flowers at all. Finally, in the fifth year, nearly all of them were gone and she was about to give up when, though she hadn't planted any new seeds, several flowered in different places, all at once. She said she'd never forget how happy this made her.

"The seeds of wild plants don't like you to fuss over them," she told me. "They started growing much more steadily when I let them get on with it, wherever they pleased. *Viola tricolor* are the only things on this farm that we just ignore."

The leak in her study was never mentioned. "Oh, I almost forgot," she said as she disappeared into the kitchen and came back with a fresh pot of tea and a large tart covered with different kinds of fruit. On a bone-china plate, it looked like a miniature flower bed.

"Flowers are to enjoy, but when you start looking into their origins and the sort of terrain or climate they thrive in, you get a sense of how and why they came to be as they are," she said. In the *Viola tricolor*, for instance, she felt she could see something of the ancient plant that had survived the Ice Age.

"You know how flowers tend to get bigger as you move from the temperate zones to the tropics," she went on, "and in cold climates, or at high altitudes, you find more species with tiny flowers? They use less energy that way, and wind and snow don't affect them so much. I can imagine that little violet eons ago, bravely surviving on a sliver of earth between lumps of snow."

When a wild species is bred for improvement, its delicate features tend to get blown out of proportion, and the flowers lose much of the beauty they once had.

"Pansies have the basic pattern of the *Viola tricolor*'s petals, but little of its grace. If the breeders had had their wits about them maybe they could have come up with something new without losing what was best about the original. That's awfully hard to do, though."

Every shape has its own origin. I thought of this woman's daughter, her ears and the curve of her eyebrows in that photograph.

As if she'd just noticed it, she took a bite of the tart in front of her. "Fruit tastes really good in summer," she murmured almost to herself. I imagined Sensei, who wasn't so talkative, sitting next to her, listening.

It occurred to me that skyscrapers were also the product of selective breeding, with iron and glass being shaped into a new sort of building that gains in utility what it loses in beauty, whisking you up and down fifty or a hundred stories, however feeble your legs are. This was architecture developed in the brain rather than in nature—regardless of nature. You can build it anywhere, in the middle of a desert or deep in a tropical forest.

We went downstairs, down the two steps from the terrace facing south, and out into the fields.

"There was a village here during the Jōmon era," she said. "At first I was always finding old clay pottery and stone tools."

Wondering if she meant there might still be some right here, I looked down at the ground around my feet.

"Not here—when you have time I'll show you the place," she said. "Sometimes there've been obsidian arrowheads. I found the stone ax on my desk in the study there too. Just right for a paperweight."

I remembered that long, heavy stone I'd seen.

"I really ought to get some archaeologists to do a dig. But if this area was designated a historical site, I'd have to give up farming at least for a while, and pay for the dig too. Since I'm not ready to do that yet, I've left things as they are. I've saved some money to have the site investigated, though—even put it in my will... When I die, all the flowers will be sold except the *Viola tricolor*—that'll be carefully transplanted—then the whole place will be open to archaeological research." She laughed. "I wonder how people made it through the winter here, a thousand meters above sea level. They say the Ice Age was coming on late in the Jōmon, so the human population was way down; fewer than ten thousand people in the entire Japanese archipelago, apparently. Even if they could keep a fire going all the time in those old pit houses, the cold must have been unbearable."

"Mt. Asama probably erupted too."

"Yes... What's surprising is that this part doesn't seem to have suffered much damage, even back in the Jōmon. Still, lapilli—little bits of molten lava—must have come raining down... Twenty thousand years ago, Mt. Asama was much bigger than it is now. See that tall crag sticking up on the western side?" Looking where she was pointing, I saw a peak that looked like the nose of a witch lying on her back.

"In prehistoric times, that's where the base was. The center of the mountain was blown away by a gigantic eruption, and that peak is what's left of the bottom bit. There must have been other big eruptions, but apparently that old base served as a wall that protected this area. Just a little east of here the volcanic ash and lava came pouring down, because there was nothing standing in the way.

Which is why hardly any Jōmon relics have been found there.

"All the same, it doesn't mean we'll always be protected here. Another big eruption could wipe all this out. Who knows, hundreds or thousands of years later, somebody may dig through layers of ash and find seeds or fossilized flowers, and realize that this was once a plant nursery."

A large butterfly I couldn't identify was fluttering around me.

"Is that your daughter in the photo in the study?"

"Yes, it is. How did you know?"

"Well, you don't look exactly alike, but there are similarities."

She laughed. "What, for instance?"

I paused. "The eyebrows, and the shape of the ears."

"Everyone says she looks just like her father, but you're right—she has my ears and eyebrows. You're observant."

"I was looking carefully."

"Weren't you supposed to be seeing about the leak?"

"Sorry." It occurred to me that there was no trace of a father in the Fujisawa house, just as there was no sign of a mother at Mariko's cottage. "Is your daughter living in Tokyo now?"

"No, she's in England. At Cambridge, the Laboratory of Molecular Biology." She pronounced the words "Laboratory," "Molecular," and "Biology" rather carefully, with a slight pause between them.

"A subject that unlocks the secrets of eyebrows and ears."

"Really?" She laughed again. "I haven't the vaguest idea what's involved, but she tells me she's analyzing the smallest units of life, which is pretty much the same as what I do."

That made sense to me.

"'You look at flowers and butterflies from the outside,' she says, 'but I do it from the inside—that's the only difference.' She's come to believe there may be a God after all. Only God could create such rational, detailed, beautiful forms."

Abruptly she squatted down in front of the delicate, pale-purple flowers of some *Viola tricolor*.

"I think she may be right," she added.

Look at this violet long enough and you start to see a face in it. An innocent face, looking up at you from just above the ground. I squatted next to her.

"You know, I'm a bit worried about Shunsuke," she said, looking at me. There was a shadow of concern in her voice that hadn't been there before. "He seems to be in such a rush. He's always worked at a much more leisurely pace, sort of like an afternoon stroll."

"He's got the deadline for the competition pressing on him."

"He showed me his plan for the library. I thought it was wonderful. But the design didn't seem like him somehow. When I asked why he'd made it that way, he got really angry. I was shocked, because I'd never even heard him raise his voice."

The smell of earth and flowers surrounded us.

"I only asked because I thought it was so beautiful, but he lashed out at me. 'You don't like it, do you?' he said. He was fuming."

A mixture of uncertainty and grim determination may have been building up inside him, hidden from us. I stood up, and for a moment felt a little dizzy.

"I think Sensei is probably getting tired."

"It's the competition. I wish it was over," she murmured.

I turned around to see the big house looming there. Under the eaves was the wasp's nest. I imagined the little figure of Ms. Fujisawa standing on the balcony to the right of it.

"I'll leave the wasps until winter. They'll eventually leave on their own."

One wasp, then another would take off toward the east, straight as bullets. For the first time since I'd seen Sensei's plan I had a vaguely uneasy feeling.

22

Aoguri had taken on completely different colors. It was now late October, and Sensei and I were alone at the Summer House. The temperature was lower than normal, and several days before, snow had fallen on Mt. Asama's summit, the earliest on record. Signs of winter, yet to appear in Tokyo, were already here in Aoguri.

The forest, a solid wall of vegetation when we left in mid-September, was now divided into patches of yellow, red, and green, the size and shape of each tree distinct. Some had already lost nearly all their leaves in preparation for winter. Now that the foliage had thinned out, the trunks and branches looked like the framework of houses under construction.

A little over a month before the competition, there had still been problems with the corridor that connected the library to the annex, but after several sessions with the contractors, the broad curve, with its mild slope and glass sides, now looked positively elegant. When Kawarazaki spread the final blueprint out on the big workshop table, a quiet current of surprise and admiration ran through us. The floor plan brought to mind the curve of a G clef, and the elevation the rounded spine of a leather-bound book—a modern image that stimulated the eye yet had a smooth, natural beauty, as if sculpted by long years of wind and rain.

Why had Sensei, past seventy, decided on this new form, unlike anything he'd done before? Even now I couldn't help wondering about it, but perhaps he couldn't have explained it himself. If natural colors and shapes were determined by logic alone, would there be so many different species of flowers, or trees, or birds? An Oriental tit has no way of knowing why the feathers on its breast make that black-and-white pattern. Color and form don't belong to the individual creatures that wear them. They develop over time, beginning in the distant past, and are passed down from generation to generation.

Uchida, Yukiko, and I were almost finished with our plans for the furniture and counters. We were waiting for Sensei to check them to make sure they were in balance with the library as a whole; then we would make the blueprints, perspective drawings, and models to use in the presentation. But our boss, who had been working through the weekends, meeting with clients and supervising at construction sites, was looking haggard.

One Thursday, when the citrusy fragrance of *kin-mokusei* was starting to fade and its orange blossoms were dropping, he announced, "I'm going to the mountains tomorrow. Sakanishi, can you drive me?"

"Yes, of course," I replied.

"I want to concentrate on finishing up the plan over the weekend. I'll never get it done here in Tokyo."

He needed three days, from Saturday to Monday, apparently. I'd been planning to see Mariko then, but knowing she, too, was worried about him looking so tired, I didn't hesitate.

I went into the office early on Friday morning and quickly made a model for the counters, which I hadn't yet started on. Iguchi, hearing that Sensei was going to Aoguri, advised him to take either Yukiko or Mariko along, but he wouldn't listen. "I'll be fine with just Sakanishi," he said. Yukiko, who'd overheard their conversation, left her own work to help me with my model. At times like this, she could be counted on to quietly lend a hand. Uchida made a few final improvements on the model bookcases, desks, and little human figures, after assembling some cardboard boxes to transport them in. He put a lot of work into the figures: some sitting at reading tables, others standing reading a book in front of the case from which they'd just taken it, or squatting down looking through the lower shelves, with tiny parents and tinier children in tow wandering through the stacks.

The models were all finished before lunchtime. While looking them over from every angle, Uchida advised me not to carry the boxes into the Summer House as soon as we got there. "Open the rain shutters and have a cup of tea first," he said. "Wait till you feel relaxed. If you're in a hurry you're bound to knock the box against something.

A man in haste a smashed model makes," he warned, putting his hand on my shoulder.

    After lunch, Uchida and Yukiko loaded the stuff into the station wagon for me. "Take this for a snack," Mariko said, handing me a canvas bag. I was beginning to feel the weight of responsibility I'd been given. Sensei looked rather relieved as he climbed into the back seat, carrying only his Boston bag.

    That Friday afternoon there wasn't much traffic on the expressway, or on the highway after I got off at the Fujioka interchange. We crossed Usui Pass before evening. As we entered the village of Aoguri, a light truck driving along some way ahead stirred up a flurry of red and yellow leaves as it went. The leaves shone for a moment in the last rays of sunlight before falling back to the ground.

    Sensei, who had been dozing in the back seat, woke up and looked out at the late-autumn scenery. He had yet to say anything about Mariko and me. We'd continued seeing each other on weekends since returning to Tokyo in September. On weekdays we sometimes had dinner outdoors at a café in a narrow street near Meiji Shrine, then walked back to my apartment. She took a taxi home if she missed the last train.

    Yukiko, who couldn't have hidden it if she knew what was going on, still got along fine with Mariko. She seemed a bit livelier at the Tokyo office, while Mariko was slightly quieter than she'd been in the mountains.

I switched off the engine and got out of the car, prepared for the cold air outside. A pair of jays squawked as they flew by, low down, then suddenly landed and flapped up again, moving off to one side. Patches of bright cobalt blue showed whenever they opened their wings. They made short flights around the garden, picking up acorns. Jays are as intelligent as crows. This pair had probably eaten enough and were gathering food to store for the winter. Butcher-birds impale insects or small frogs on sharp twigs and leave them there for later, but jays will choose a hollow tree or a niche in the roots to use as a storehouse. They are observant, so were probably watching us go into the Summer House.

All the foliage on the katsura tree had turned bright yellow. Without even a breeze, the tree seemed to have absorbed all sound as it stood there in the evening light.

The house felt almost abandoned. The wooden floor creaked in places as we walked across it. I opened the kitchen and dining room windows one by one. The trees where Yukiko and Ms. Sasai had collected peppers, avoiding the thorns, looked denuded. I heard Sensei opening the door to his office on the second floor. Upstairs, I opened the big window in the workshop and looked down on the katsura's yellow leaves. The empty workshop was like a classroom after school. Next was the men's bath, where the western window let in the last of the day's light. As if urging the Summer House on toward winter, the harsh cries of the jays split the cold air.

Before I cleaned the bath, there were several desiccated camelback crickets to dispose of. They must have wandered in, fallen into the tub, and when even their highest jumps weren't quite high enough, died there. I brought bath towels, facecloths, and a bath mat from the linen cupboard. After putting clean sheets and a pillowcase on the bed in the director's office, I went down to the kitchen to put a kettle on the stove.

The door of his office was open, and I could hear him talking on the phone, probably to Ms. Fujisawa. I wondered if he was planning to go over there.

I decided to make some tea, a brand he liked from Dimbula, Sri Lanka. Four spoonfuls. The whistling of the kettle was a welcome sound in the chilly air. Just as I was wiping the cups, Sensei came downstairs.

"Tea?" he said cheerfully. "I was about to ask you to make some." I hadn't seen him smile like this at the Tokyo office for days. As if to make a fresh start, he took a deep breath, exhaled slowly, then looked out of the window.

"It's beautiful here from fall to winter," he said. "The colors may be at their best this weekend."

We had a good view of the katsura tree and its bright-yellow leaves from the dining room window.

"Lovely," he said.

"Painful too," I said. The ache I'd felt seeing the autumn leaves tossed up under the wheels of the truck ahead came back. I picked up the teapot and poured, watching the reddish liquid fill the cup. Sensei sipped his tea and began to talk.

"At this time of year, I always think of people back in the Jōmon. How busy they must have been, getting ready for winter. They'd have to stockpile wood. Collect nuts before the animals got them. Probably hunt rabbits and squirrels, maybe set traps for things. And weave cloth for heavy winter clothes. They must have felt that nature was putting the pressure on when the leaves started to turn."

He stopped to munch some small rice crackers, then took another sip of tea, savoring it.

"You know those old pit dwellings? They'd build a fire in the center with stones around it, and stay close by. They cooked over the fire and ate around it, the women did their weaving or played with the children, then everyone went to sleep right there. Bigger pit dwellings have been found, but generally a family lived in one room—about sixteen square meters."

I imagined a house with a fire alight in the middle of the floor.

"They were the first people to build their own houses rather than live in caves or under a cliff. With it getting cold, everyone would be in by sunset to sit by the fire."

He took a few little crackers in the palm of his hand and popped them into his mouth, all at once.

"In Tsuburano they've found lots of old Jōmon settlements. The river would have made it a good place to live, but like here it's a thousand meters above sea level, so winters must have been incredibly tough. Makes you wonder why they decided to settle there, but they must have thought it was worth it, because there was plenty to eat. Of course, people feel the cold differently—age has something to do with it too. Back then they only lived on average about fourteen or fifteen years. Even with infant deaths bringing numbers down, you can bet there weren't many old men around who felt the cold as I do. Someone your age would have been a leader, a wise old man." He chuckled. "We live a lot longer now, but we've gone soft."

I could picture him with Ms. Fujisawa, talking about the Jōmon relics she'd found on the farm.

"No matter how many children were born, most would have died in infancy. And lots of women died in childbirth too. Illness would have been a big problem for everybody, so banding together in settlements was the only way they could survive."

It was unusual for him to go on talking this way.

He said that children's bones were never found among the remains of a communal graveyard. A child's body would be put in an urn made for that purpose and placed in a separate grave somewhere near the house. Infants were sometimes buried on the threshold. It was believed that a child's soul could return to the mother's womb when she stepped over it, to be born again.

"Have you ever made one of those O-Bon fires, to welcome back the dead?" he asked.

"We do it at home every year, in July. We're the only ones in the neighborhood who do—everyone else has given up. You pile up a few hemp sticks in front of the entrance..."

"And after you've lit them, what then?"

"You douse a *misohagi* plant in water and sprinkle it over the fire to put it out."

"And when the fire's out?"

"You step over the wet ash and go back inside."

He nodded slightly. "Stepping over the ash is probably basically the same as stepping over the threshold of a place where a baby's been buried."

As a child, I'd always wondered why we did this.

"Of course, we're talking about the distant past, so we can't be sure what they really believed..." He smiled, tracing the contours of his cheek and chin with his hand. "But there's one thing that hasn't changed since then: the entrance to a house separates but also connects the inside and out. A dead baby couldn't be let into the house, but instead of leaving the body outside, they buried it in the space in between. It tells us something about how they felt, doesn't it? I think I can trace a line from what was in their hearts to what's in mine, anyway."

He drank some more of his tea, now nearly cold.

"In traditional teahouses they drew a sharp line between inside and out by forcing people to crawl through a little square door into a room the size of two tatami mats; but it's basically the same in an ordinary house—you go in because you're allowed to, leaving those who can't or won't behind."

"Like after a funeral, you sprinkle yourself with salt at the doorway before going in."

"Right. What you leave outside are the dead, whatever lives in the dark, in the rain and wind, under the night sky—the outdoors. Thinking in terms of inside and out is what gave people the idea of a self—the beginnings of an inner life—and it seems to me that building their own houses had a lot to do with that."

As he talked, I recognized the connection he saw between early customs and things like the front door of a house—whether it should be pulled or pushed open—or the boundary between an open kitchen and a living room, or how a master bedroom and the children's rooms should be arranged. Variations in human emotion were what his architecture was based on. That was part of what he meant when he said that architecture wasn't art but function.

"So, people who lived in pit houses had a different way of thinking from cavemen or cliff dwellers."

"Probably. Earliest man had to spend much of his energy finding shelter when he was caught in a howling storm, or the sun was beating down, but in a pit house he had more time to relax and look outside, or just stare into the fire. Perhaps that's when he started thinking about things, having inner feelings. We're just the opposite—we can't bear being stuck inside too long. We want to go out, take a walk under the trees, look at flowers, or the sea. I suspect that's because our hearts have been left behind. Too weak for us to live entirely inside. Needing things in the outside world, rather than within ourselves, to move us emotionally."

"Up here in the mountains, though, I feel I could live entirely inside."

"That's because you can look out and watch things change. But if you were snowed in for a month, you'd get cabin fever."

There was no more tea left in the pot. I got up to boil some more water.

"Thanks, but I've had enough," Sensei said. "Could you put the floor plan on the table upstairs, and set up the model?"

"Certainly."

Remembering Uchida's warning, I carefully took the cardboard boxes out of the station wagon and carried them up to the workshop one at a time. The air outside was biting cold. I heard the muffled *khii, khii* of a pygmy woodpecker behind me. Holding the box with both hands, I turned and saw a little bundle of black and white hopping up the trunk among the varicolored leaves.

For dinner we went out to a local restaurant. "Let's have supper at the Asama, near the roundabout," Sensei had said before we left Tokyo. The Asama, along with a general store, a post office, and a liquor store, was near the old wooden Kita-Asama Station on the Tanasaka Light Railway line, no longer in service. "Their pork cutlet with egg on rice is really good," he said, "and so are the mustard greens they serve as a starter." "Just average" was Uchida's assessment.

The TV was perched high up in a corner, where families used to put their home shrines; the NHK news looked grainy due to poor reception. There was a big photo on the wall of Mt. Asama erupting. A gray stream of ash several times higher than the mountain itself rose from the snow-covered summit. Though it was a color photograph, the sky looked muddy, the blue almost faded out. A glass cooler held only beer and orange soda. A middle-aged woman in a white apron, soft from many washings, came to take our order: pork cutlet with egg over rice for him, chicken with egg over rice for me. The air smelled of soy sauce and dashi. Two young construction workers dressed in work clothes came in, ordered extra-large portions of pork and rice, and got magazines from the rack to read while they waited.

As we ate, Sensei told me he wanted to start checking the blueprints for the furniture as soon as we got back. Tomorrow he would look at the model and floor plan, and decide exactly where each piece of furniture would go. "If we finish early," he went on without looking up, "maybe I can take you to Tsuburano." That gave me a jolt.

"Okay," I said.

It was pitch-dark when we left the place, the only light coming from the general store. The smell of the food we'd eaten still clung to our clothes.

When we got back, I made a fire in the living room, doing it in the way he'd told me to. Flames leapt up between the logs. Sensei came down and asked me to make one in his office as well. When I took some firewood up, cut to fit the smaller fireplace, I saw that he had the desk lamp on but not the floor lamp. I was surprised to see him working by such dim light, too weak to reach into the corners of the room.

I built up the short logs in the usual way and struck a match. A whiff of sulfur, then lively crackling as the wood caught fire.

"You're pretty good at that now." His voice came from behind.

I turned to see the flames reflected in his glasses.

"Smells good," he added. "Those are good logs."

The wood was oak. I cut the wire around a bundle with a pair of pliers and stacked the logs alongside. Silently I asked him why he had hired me, but couldn't get the words out. Why did he want Mariko and me to marry? When I swept up the stray slivers with a brush and sprinkled them on the fire, they sent out sparks like firecrackers.

"I've brought four bundles from downstairs. Should I bring more?"

"No, that's plenty. I'd like to take a bath sometime after nine, though."

"I'll get it ready."

"Thanks a lot," he said, looking up at me, then turned back to his work.

After dealing with the bath, I went to my old room in the library and got out the photo collection of Asplund's works I'd looked through often during the summer. I laid it on the desk.

There again was the huge granite cross overlooking the grounds of the Woodland Cemetery. Also, the approach to the Stockholm Public Library. Both were designed to guide people straight in through the front entrance. The library Sensei had designed had an open space, a sort of square in front of it, which meant it could be approached from several directions rather than one clearly defined route. People would be drawn toward it by its unusual shape and the ramp leading from the main building to the annex. The straight paving-stone path down to the Woodland Cemetery, on the other hand, seemed to attest to the word "covenant"—a straight line as an appropriate representation of the personal relationship between an individual and God.

There was a photograph of the waiting room for mourners to use before the service started. A long bench built into the wall, facing a large, horizontal window. No other decoration whatsoever. It was an odd sort of place. A chapel is a chapel even when no one's there, but this room had no focal point; it took on a purpose only when people gathered there. Three old women dressed in black sat on the bench, staring through the window. Sisters of the deceased? They looked as if they might start whispering among themselves, maybe share a joke. It might have been in a station, for a single-track train traveling across the wide Scandinavian countryside. A train to carry a dead soul away.

Bright afternoon sunlight spilled across the floor. The white ceiling, rounded at the corners, sloped down to meet the wooden wall, which curved inward at a certain point to form the back of the bench. The bentwood bench had a rounded edge to fit under the sitters' knees. This room had no square corners or sharp edges. Knowing how hard grief is to accept, had Asplund given them only soft, smooth surfaces to see and touch? I remembered the details in the Asukayama Church, the way the wooden ceiling and walls gently surrounded the altar.

I heard Sensei open the door to the bath upstairs. From inside came the faint sound of him scooping hot water into a basin and splashing it over himself. I had hardly noticed this sound when we were all here together during the summer. I thought of offering to wash his back, but had neither the timing nor the courage to actually do it.

The phone in the workshop was ringing. I rushed out of the library to Iguchi's desk to answer it.

"Hello." It was Mariko.

"Oh, hi," I said, trying to sound both friendly and detached.

"What were you doing just now?"

"Sensei's taking a bath."

"And what about you?"

"I was looking at a book in my room."

"Asplund? He's your favorite, isn't he?" She was trying to show how well she knew me, which set me off-balance. Hoping she wouldn't notice, I changed the subject.

"Why are you calling?" I asked. "Has something happened?"

"I just wanted to hear your voice," she said, ignoring my efforts to sound businesslike. "Are you enjoying your evening alone with Sensei?" There was a hint of laughter in her voice.

"I get to hear him talk a lot more than usual."

"That's because he likes you. He has things he wants you to hear."

"Oh, I don't know..."

"Well, I do. Is it cold up there?"

"Yes, very. I just made a fire in the living room and in his office too."

"You're good at that."

"That's because he taught me how."

"Your piles of firewood are very neat too."

"Don't know about that either."

"Well, I do. Make sure Sensei keeps warm. Getting chilly straight after the bath would send his blood pressure up."

"Okay. I'll watch out for it."

"All right, then. Work hard."

"I will. Thanks."

"And don't catch cold."

I quietly put the receiver down. One of the windows in the workshop was open a crack, so I pulled it shut and turned the latch. Then I went downstairs to lock the front door and check the windows. I put more wood on to stoke up the fire, and placed the screen in front of it to keep sparks from flying. Surprisingly, some still found a way past, sailing up in an arc but then petering out in midair, turning to black ash as they fell to the floor. They wouldn't set the place on fire. And since the logs were dry, they wouldn't hiss or crackle too much. The fire was burning well now, the flames lapping eagerly at the wood. I listened to it burn, felt the heat, breathed in the smell. Back in the Jōmon era, too, people must have watched the flames, felt their skin getting warmer, and listened to the sound of the wood burning. I kept the door open so that the heat would rise upstairs.

When I went upstairs myself, Sensei had just finished his bath. His face was slightly flushed.

"That felt good."

"Would you like something to drink?"

"I could do with a nice cup of *hōjicha*, if you don't mind."

"Sure. I'll bring it when it's ready."

"Thanks." He turned to look at me. "I heard the phone ring."

"Yes, it was Mariko."

He looked a little surprised, then relaxed. "What did she want?"

"She told me to make sure you didn't get cold when you got out of the bath."

He smiled. "I'll have to be careful then."

After I made his tea, I took a bath too. I opened the window to let in the cold air, and sank deep in the hot water. The insects that had been so noisy on summer evenings were now silent. When I closed my eyes, thoughts of Mariko filled my head. She always sent the ball straight at me. But when I tried to count how many I'd returned, I wasn't sure. If things went on this way, we might break up... I suddenly felt cold and opened my eyes. My head was clear. I got out of the tub and closed the window.

Before going to bed, I thought I should check the fire in his office. I knocked softly on the door. There was silence on the other side. "Excuse me," I said quietly, then went in.

Sensei was lying in his bed at the back of the room, hair tousled, without his glasses. His face looked a little flushed in the light from the fireplace. He was asleep. The open paperback on the edge of the bed had probably slipped out of his hand when he drifted off. It was Schumann's *On Music and Musicians*. I put a bookmark in it and laid it on the bedside table where his glasses were. The cup of *hōjicha* I'd brought him was untouched. There was a pair of bookshelf speakers here on which he listened to piano music with the sound turned down while he was working. As Mariko's uncle, he may have hoped she would become a professional pianist.

As I watched him sleep, I felt uncertain. There was a slight crease between his eyebrows, as if he were trying to remember something. His breathing was regular, so he didn't seem to be in pain. Until I could be sure, though, I stood there watching, holding my breath, listening.

I turned off the bedside lamp. The only light in the room came from the wavering flames in the fireplace. In an hour or so the logs, now glowing red, would burn up completely. Careful not to make any noise, I left the room.

The following morning, I looked up from the window in the workshop at a perfectly clear sky, an almost otherworldly blue. Though it was still very cold, the temperature would probably rise as the day went on. The light was strong. The air was dry. Unusually for him, Sensei slept late; while I was waiting for him to come back from his walk after breakfast, I washed the dishes, made my bed in the library, and opened the living room window to let in some air.

Back from a short walk, Sensei was still slightly out of breath when he sat down at the big table in the workshop. Picking up pieces of the model, comparing them to the blueprint, he checked the positions of the bookcases, reading tables, chairs, and counters, one by one. Though he had his notebook at hand, he didn't write down anything that needed doing.

But at some point he stopped and thought a while. The plan was to have three concentric rows of hexagonal bookcases starting from the wall, with the same distance between each one.

"Remember on sports day at school, when you raced on a track," he said, "didn't the curve on the inside lane always feel tighter than the one on the outside?" He was right about that. "Well, with the same distance between the outside and inside rows, the bookcases on the inside are going to feel squeezed in. When we start making the detailed design, we'll have to check this on a slightly larger model."

While he was talking, he moved the model around several times, lowering his head to peer between the rows of bookcases. He bent way over as if following the path of a mouse as it ran through the aisles. Then he sat down again, arms folded across his chest.

"This isn't just a problem of distance," he said, still staring at the model. "Because the bookcases are all the same height, it looks as if you're being closed in as you move toward the center."

At first I couldn't see what he was getting at.

"Would you mind making each row one shelf shorter, moving inward?" Lowering the height of the inner bookcases would relieve that oppressive feeling, he assured me.

We had started by making an estimate of how many books of which format we had space for, and then made sketch after sketch, showing them to Sensei and asking his advice until we had our final plan. If we took shelves off the top of the two inner rows, we'd end up having much less room for average-size books. That meant we'd have to recalculate the total amount of space and how to use it efficiently. I was sure Sensei realized the implications of what he was asking me to do.

I began after lunch. If I simply cut the model down, traces of glue would be left showing, so I decided to make a new one. Thinking back over all the calculating I'd done to figure out the capacity of each shelf and how many books it would hold, I felt too discouraged to start. But finally I took a deep breath, found some empty space on the big table, and got to work. While I was cutting parts out of styrene board, I began to understand why he'd asked me to come, and got absorbed in what I was doing. Work can be comforting when things go wrong, the simpler the better.

"There's no need to hurry," he told me. "You have all day, so take your time."

I heard the strains of Mahler's Fourth Symphony from the living room. He must have been sitting on the sofa. Alone in the huge workshop, I listened along with him as I worked. When I looked up, I saw the yellow foliage of the katsura in the noonday sun gleaming like an incandescent bulb.

The new model was assembled and glued together before teatime. I went downstairs, told Sensei it was finished, then went into the kitchen to put the kettle on. Unusually for him, he said he wanted coffee, and followed me into the kitchen.

"I make a pretty good cup of coffee," he said. "Don't know if it's as good as Uchida's, though." He looked rather pleased with himself as he ground the beans. The rich aroma filled the air. We sat at the kitchen table, not talking much as we drank our coffee and ate the cheesecake Mariko had given me before we left, then went back up to the workshop.

I lined up the model bookcases from the center outward. With each row growing progressively taller, the model now looked like the tapering layers of a shallow cone-shaped bowl. The inner bookcases no longer seemed so closed in. That alone completely changed the impression you got from the model as a whole. Looking outward from the middle, the catwalk built into the wall behind a bookcase over four meters tall, with two more shelves than the one in the center, was visible.

"Not bad," Sensei said.

We bent over together, peering at it from various angles. Though it didn't really show in his voice or his face, I could tell he was pleased.

"Let's go with this. The blueprint for the bookcases will need a lot of work, which will be tough on Uchida," he said. "Let's hope Yukiko doesn't object." He smiled, then coughed several times. "She's pragmatic, so if there's something we've overlooked, she'll catch it."

Sensei relied on Yukiko. He obviously depended on Kawarazaki, Kobayashi, and Uchida too, but the trust he placed in her was different. If there was something unpleasant he needed to hear, she was the one he'd listen to.

"She and Uchida started working out the seating plan for the auditorium yesterday."

"We'll have to finish that by next week."

"By the way," I said as if I'd just remembered, "Mariko was wondering if the library restaurant will be Italian or French."

"Oh? Which would she like it to be?"

"Well, whichever it is she doesn't want it to have a kiddies' special for lunch, or harried waitresses, or serve cold, hard bread," I said, reciting what she'd told me the week before. "And she definitely doesn't want it to be one of those places where you buy a coupon for what you want from a vending machine at the entrance."

Sensei laughed out loud. "Restaurants in museums and public libraries can be pretty tacky. As long as it turns a profit nobody's going to complain, though, so why not make it really nice? I could talk to the guy who runs Hana, where we had your welcome party, and see if he's interested. Or would that look like a backroom deal?"

I couldn't tell how serious he was.

"If Hana sets up shop in the library, Mariko'll go all the time," I said. "She'll be able to ride there by bicycle from the office." I wondered if I was talking too much about her, while also half hoping Sensei might say something about her and me. But he just went on cheerfully talking about the library.

"The auditorium shouldn't just be for lectures and movies either. They could have concerts there. The Library of Congress in America has an auditorium where you can hear the Juilliard Quartet sometimes. They archive not only books, but images and sound as well. The aim is to collect everything that's ever been recorded, in whatever form. Their collection of maps is world-class—as you'd expect from the country that produced *National Geographic*. Even if we can't go that far, maybe we can have an archive for LP records—they'll be rare items someday—and TV programs too, so people can come and watch them. Designing a library isn't enough. Whether it really works depends on what it provides."

He finished his coffee. "Well, we've finished our work a lot faster than I thought. Which is a relief," he said, then started coughing so violently his face turned red.

"D'you want some water?"

"No, I'll be okay... Fasten your model with tacks so we can take it back to Tokyo. It's getting late, and we don't have to hurry back. How about taking our time, and going back tomorrow?"

I didn't mind at all. Tomorrow would still be a day earlier than we'd planned.

"Let's stop by Tsuburano, then spend the night at Koromo, at a hot spring. My back and shoulders ache, and I've a bit of a headache today. A hot spring bath should do me good."

By "stopping by Tsuburano," did he mean going to see Ms. Fujisawa? While I was washing the coffee cups he came into the kitchen to say he'd reserved a room for us. "I'll tell you how to get there," he added.

The sun was going down. I drove the Volvo, with Sensei in the back seat.

In just one summer I had become thoroughly familiar with the road down to Naka-Karuizawa. When we reached the intersection for the turnoff to Shiraito Falls, Sensei spoke for the first time.

"I guess you've heard about Uchida."

"Yes," I said after a slight pause. I could see in the rearview mirror he was looking out of the window.

"Too bad, but it can't be helped. He's certainly good enough to make it on his own. And I'm sure he'll be a fine architect—no doubt about that. Still..." He thought for a bit before going on. "There's something sort of guarded about him."

I listened in silence.

"Sometimes in this business you have to deal with difficult people, who insist on having their own way."

The only sound was the humming of the engine.

"Uchida walls himself off at times like that. He tries to take it as it comes, without feeling anything. That may be a defense mechanism, but he'll come out of it all the worse off."

He seemed to be talking not to me but to the person not here.

"If he keeps on just taking the nonsense instead of standing up to it, he'll lose sight of what he really wants to achieve and what he absolutely doesn't want to do. You see what I mean?"

"I think so."

"Sometimes you'll be pressed into accepting something that doesn't make sense. Because there are always certain people an architect has to deal with. But even if you get steamrolled, you need to explain your position as clearly as you can. If you don't, it's as though your conception of architecture never existed. You won't even be able to remember what it was."

I knew that although there were few postwar architects who spoke publicly or wrote as little as Sensei did, he always said what he needed to say in the clearest possible terms. Uchida knew it too. So did the entire staff at the Murai Office.

"If you ask what good explaining yourself will do," he went on, "all I can say is, possibly none at all. In the end, all that's left are the final blueprints and the building itself. How about it, Sakanishi? Think you'll be able to speak up and defend your position when the time comes?"

His tone had softened.

"I'm not sure yet, but I understand what you're saying."

"You look friendly but you can be surprisingly obstinate." He chuckled. "Hang on to that obstinate streak of yours."

The car was just going around a hairpin curve. I concentrated on driving carefully so he wouldn't be thrown about in the back seat. I couldn't even nod until we'd come out of it.

"Very few clients who make unreasonable demands are willing to stake their lives on them. What they're saying isn't based on firmly held convictions. They're repeating what they heard someone say, or are afraid of what people will think, or they have fixed ideas about how the world works. If you're ready to dig your heels in, you can usually bring them around to your way of thinking.

"But there are those who insist on having their own way. When you have to deal with people like that, your principles as an architect are at stake. How successful you are at explaining yourself is really just an extension of the work habits you've developed all along. You may think you have a pool of inner strength that will be ready when you need it, but unless you develop it through the work you do every day, it's not going to just suddenly appear."

The dim shape of Mt. Asama, lit from behind, lay ahead to the right. Snow had already fallen on the peak once, but it now looked bare.

"I guess there won't be an eruption this year," he said. "It spewed out a lot of smoke during the summer, but it's settled down now." He was looking up at the mountain through the car window. "It's hard to tell what a volcano's going to do. Something mysterious about them." He was silent for a while. "They say that after it snows three times on the summit, you get the first snow down in the village."

"Then I guess there won't be any snow down here for a while."

"I hope winter will hold off for a while. The autumn's so beautiful."

I rounded the last of the bends.

"Turn right when you get to the end of Route 18, then go straight for a while."

"Got it."

He hadn't said we'd be stopping at Ms. Fujisawa's farm yet.

"You should keep in touch with Uchida after he quits."

"I will."

"It gets warmer when we're on lower ground."

We were already several hundred meters lower than Aoguri. The leaves here were only beginning to turn.

"Shall I open a window?"

"Could you put on the air-conditioning a little?"

I turned the dial to a low setting.

"Thanks. Think I'll take a nap." He coughed again in a choking sort of way.

"Do you want me to wake you up later?"

"Before you get to Oiwake, there's an intersection on Route 18 called Maseguchi. Wake me up after we pass it."

I could see in the rearview mirror that his eyes were already closed. Hoshino Hot Springs appeared on the left. It wasn't far to Route 18.

Ms. Fujisawa had offered Uchida the use of one of her small houses in Tsuburano. Was that her idea? Or had Sensei suggested it? Either way, Uchida was obviously important to both of them. Sensei must have wanted him to hear what he'd told me today. Knowing he couldn't, he'd said it all to me instead.

If we were to win the competition for the National Library of Modern Literature, Uchida would stay at the Murai Office a while longer. If we lost, he might quit after the New Year. But looking at the plan, now so near completion, I simply couldn't imagine there being a better one anywhere. Iguchi had said Sensei was almost certain to get the support of Michio Kajiki, the minister of education. And the selection committee for the competition was bound to have some contact with the minister, so although Uchida was afraid Sensei's backing was too weak, I didn't see how it could be.

We were now starting on the long downward slope toward Oiwake. I turned the air-conditioning up a notch.

Sensei had started snoring. A low, deep sound. He had worked without a break, then come to Aoguri, and now, finally, the end was in sight. All we had to do was finish the final blueprint and model.

I stopped at the Oiwake intersection. He was still snoring. When I turned toward him in the back seat, his head was leaning against the window on the right side. Looking at his face, I had an awful feeling about this. The traffic light turned green.

"Sensei, we've passed Oiwake. A little earlier than I thought we would."

He was still snoring. I spoke to him again, louder this time.

"Sensei... Sensei, wake up."

No reaction. I pulled the car over to the side of the road and shouted, "Sensei, are you all right?" I reached back and grabbed his right knee.

With the engine off, the snoring sounded even louder than before. He wasn't napping. He was unconscious. I'd have to get him to a hospital. But I didn't know where one was. There didn't seem to be a pay phone around anywhere. I decided to take him to Ms. Fujisawa's and ask her to call an ambulance. I released the hand brake and slowly drove off.

"Sensei," I said, half to myself, "we'll be at Ms. Fujisawa's place in a little while. Hang on a little longer. You'll be all right. We'll get you to a hospital, and you'll be all right."

I turned off the highway and went up the hill toward Mt. Asama. Ms. Fujisawa was standing alone in a field in the evening light. As I pulled into the driveway she stopped working and turned around. She smiled. But as she walked toward us, pulling off her work gloves, I saw doubt in her face. I stopped the car. She came running over.

The air through the car door was much colder than inside.

Since it was a weekend, the hospital corridors were almost empty. I looked up at the clock on the wall and saw that it was past eight.

I had come in the ambulance with Ms. Fujisawa, and after watching Sensei being taken into intensive care, I called Uchida. He told me he would contact Sensei's wife, Iguchi, and Mariko. "It's a good thing you were with him," he said calmly.

Sensei had been in the ICU for over two hours now. Ms. Fujisawa and I were waiting outside. Neither of us said anything.

A doctor came out and looked first at her, then me, sitting side by side.

"Are you his wife?" he asked her.

"No," she said, then after a brief pause, added in a clear voice, "I'm his partner," with a trace of English intonation on the last word. I explained that I worked in his office. The doctor spoke carefully, with consideration for the strangers to whom he was about to deliver some bad news.

"He's had a severe cerebral infarction, a stroke. Considering his age, we can't be too optimistic. It would be better if you stayed at the hospital tonight. And please inform his family as soon as possible. We're doing everything we can for him, but he could take a turn for the worse anytime."

"His family has already been notified," Ms. Fujisawa said, looking directly at him. "He's in your hands now." She bowed. For a while afterward she didn't move.

"His family's in Tokyo so it might take them a while to get here," I added.

The doctor nodded and said, "It all depends on whether he makes it through the night." He turned and went back inside.

23

From the waiting room, we could see Sensei's bed at the back of intensive care for a few seconds when the door slid open to let a doctor or nurse in or out. In that huge room, much bigger than I'd imagined, the wires and tubes he was hooked up to looked flimsy, as if they might easily fall out. Cold fluorescent light flooded every corner. Sensei hated those white tubes, lined up on the ceiling like plumbing. I remembered him standing on a station platform one afternoon, looking up at a row of them, all turned on though the sun was out. "Where the hell did they get the idea, the brighter the better?" he'd said.

"Poor Shunsuke, with those lights he can't stand all glaring down on him," Ms. Fujisawa murmured.

It had been over a month, and he was still in the ICU. Alive, but unconscious. The stroke had affected a large part of his brain; the areas around the cerebellum and the part that controls language appeared white on the CT scan.

Kajiki, the minister of education, suggested transferring him to a hospital in Tokyo known for treating stroke patients, but his doctor advised against moving him until his condition stabilized, and his wife, who was also a doctor, agreed with this opinion. He was put on a breathing machine, his ECG, pulse, and blood pressure under constant surveillance.

His wife, who ran a private pediatrics clinic in Yoyogi-Uehara, made the trip to the Asama Central Hospital to see him twice a week at first, which involved taking several trains and a twenty-minute taxi ride; but with him still in a coma, and the instruments, charts, and brain waves showing no signs of improvement, she must have decided there wasn't much point in just sitting by his side. The round trip took a lot out of her, and after several weeks, she stopped coming.

As Mariko usually came with me to the hospital on weekend afternoons, we decided she should go to Yoyogi-Uehara once a week to report on Sensei's condition. Having no children of her own, his wife was delighted by her niece's visits. The third or fourth time, she was even waiting to open the door for her. "Well, hello there! I'm so glad to see you," she'd said, her face wreathed in smiles. Mariko had felt her own face stiffen at this enthusiasm, and she started phoning her instead, saying she was too busy to go in person.

Intensive care had visiting hours twice a day, in the morning and afternoon, limited in principle to family members. After Sensei's wife stopped going, though, Mariko's father asked Ms. Fujisawa to go in her place;

with the doctor's permission, she dropped in once every three days.

Iguchi may have been the hardest hit. When he arrived at the hospital with Uchida the day after Sensei's stroke, he was frowning and only gave me a slight nod. While he was at work, answering the phone or meeting people who'd come to ask about Sensei's condition, he went through the motions, and could even sound cheerful depending on who he was talking to, but when the phone stopped ringing and everyone left, he holed up in the director's office.

Since the basic design had been completed before Sensei was hospitalized, there was no reason to withdraw from the competition—or at least that was what most people thought. Kawarazaki and Kobayashi both said that if Sensei recovered, he should be able to take charge. Iguchi listened in silence.

During our meetings, the white model of the new library sat on the table in the Tokyo office in its clear acrylic box, waiting for its debut. Making it had mainly been Uchida's responsibility, with Yukiko and me assisting. Starting from the top, each floor could be removed. No matter how often I looked at them, I was struck by the finesse of those hexagonal rows of bookcases, arranged concentrically, descending in height toward the center. Uchida's little human figures added a touch of reality and humor. The model in a box, unseen by anyone except the staff assembled here, seemed to symbolize

Sensei himself, unconscious, inert. Once the image got into my head, I couldn't get rid of it.

After several private talks with the officials handling matters concerning the competition at the Ministry of Education, Iguchi got permission to submit our plan "for reference" only. As the invitation was extended to the Murai Office rather than to Murai himself, his being in the hospital shouldn't have been a problem. Nevertheless, Iguchi, having decided the staff were not quite ready to take full responsibility for the project without Sensei's guidance, gave the ministry detailed reports on his condition. Until the competition was over, he told only Kawarazaki and Kobayashi that our submission was "for reference."

The news about Sensei spread quickly. Bouquet after bouquet was delivered to the office, the smell of flowers only reminding us of his absence. Yet prospective clients were still contacting the office to commission a house. Iguchi explained the situation, telling them that as his boss still needed treatment and rest, he had no idea when we'd be able to accept further work, which was much the same as a refusal.

The office faced a critical situation. Sensei had fallen ill before Iguchi had a chance to take his plan for a new order any further. If things went on this way, we would eventually go out of business. Yet Iguchi didn't see Sensei's absence as an opportunity to restructure the office along the lines of another Taliesin.

One day late in November, when Mariko was down with a cold, I left her in Tokyo and headed for the Asama Central Hospital alone. I happened to meet Ms. Fujisawa there, and in the car on the way back to her place, we were caught in a heavy rainstorm. Even with the wipers on the highest setting, the windshield turned opaque every other second. I drove slowly, with the headlights on. Over toward Sakudaira the sky was split by several bolts of lightning. The scale was quite different from anything in Tokyo.

"The river used to overflow every time it rained like this. Since my fields are on a slope, mud and stones would come pouring down, uprooting flowers, washing bulbs away. I'd have a terrible time clearing away all the mud after a storm. That's why I had a stone wall built."

The Tsuburano area was on a hill between two rivers. It was the proximity of a river that had attracted the earliest settlers. They got their water from it and caught fish. They picked watercress. Maybe they splashed around with their children. But their houses might be washed away in a flood. How had Jōmon people balanced the violence the river could inflict with the benefits of living beside it? Tales of the worst floods were probably passed down through generations, but people can't live in dread if they want to survive...

Now and then, on a whim, a downpour would overturn the soft, cultivated earth to expose traces of their lives: bits of broken earthenware pots, stone tools, arrowheads— pieces of obsidian shining in the light when the rain had stopped.

I parked as close to the entrance as I could, darted around to her side, and opened the car door, holding out an umbrella for her. Though I was outside for only a moment, I got drenched. Inside, as soon as we shut the door, the rain was much quieter. Thunder rumbled in the distance. I put the bath towel she handed me over my head and dried myself off. The towel had the same whiff of something herbal I had once smelled on Sensei's shirt.

"I hope Shunsuke can be transferred to a hospital in Tokyo," she said after putting two cups of tea and some apple pie she'd warmed up on the dining table.

I agreed, thinking at the same time that she probably wouldn't be able to see him then. I drank my tea with milk, a taste I was now used to. I could tell that it was Dimbula, Sensei's favorite. The English teapot was just like the one at the Summer House.

"He called me that day, asked if I'd mind if the two of you stopped off here for a while."

He had said something about "stopping by Tsuburano," but hadn't mentioned her name. Now I knew what he'd meant.

"And then to have a stroke on the way here..." She sighed.

"I'm sorry."

"What do you have to apologize for?"

If I'd taken him straight to a hospital, they might have started working on him a half hour earlier, and he might have regained consciousness. That was another thought I couldn't get out of my head.

"He complained a lot about headaches this summer," she said, "but he was always moaning about some ache or pain, so I didn't take it seriously. If only I'd taken him to the doctor before it got to this stage..."

The rain had stopped. The sun was already streaming through breaks in the clouds, falling in columns of light over Sakudaira.

"He swore he'd never do any public buildings again, and then for some reason he took on this Library of Modern Literature. He worked so hard on it. He'd hardly ever discussed architecture with me, but this time he showed me his plan and told me all about it."

She opened a living room window, the one facing south. A gust of air blew in, cold and washed clean by the storm. From a branch somewhere we heard the call of a grosbeak: *hinrikokirii*, a high-pitched whistle you often heard thereabouts.

"I have a feeling he'll never work again, even if he does come out of the coma," she continued. "It's a shame, but there's nothing anyone can do about it... We never know how long we have left. Every morning I think this might be my last day, or maybe tomorrow. You're still young, so you needn't worry, but it's unavoidable."

The sky was growing clearer, the wet stone wall she'd built gleaming in the sunlight.

"There's a favor I'd like to ask you."

"What is it?"

"I've never been to the Summer House, not even once. Shunsuke used to ask if I'd like to go, but he never got around to actually taking me. Never said, 'Okay, let's go now.'

"He sometimes took flowers from here, but I never knew where he planted them, or how well they got on, because he never told me. When he phoned, I couldn't picture the room he was calling from, whether he was sitting down or standing up. I don't really know anything about the place.

"And if he doesn't wake up, I'll never have a chance to find out. Just once I'd like to see the room where he worked, the chair he sat in, the view he had from the window. Since he's been in a coma, I've been thinking a lot about that house. But I can only hear his voice; I can't actually see him there."

"I understand. Of course I'll take you."

"Sorry to put you to the trouble. It doesn't have to be right away, and if Shunsuke recovers, you won't have to do it at all. But if winter comes and then spring, and he's still unconscious..." She looked as if she was about to lose control.

"Would it be all right if Sensei's niece comes along?"

"You mean Mariko?" she said, her face immediately brightening up.

"You know her?"

"She's been here lots of times, since she was little."

I had no idea they were close.

"Shunsuke wanted to see the two of you marry. Hadn't you heard?"

"No, he never said anything about it."

"Really?" She seemed surprised.

"But Mariko heard something about it from Uchida," I added.

"That's because I told him," she said.

"Why him?"

"Because he kept making passes at her, in a half-hearted sort of way. He'd take her out, but he was really just playing, fooling himself. Keeping things light, so he could always back off and say it wasn't serious, both to himself and to her. That's really the worst thing about him."

"How do you know all this?"

"I heard it from Shunsuke."

He'd seemed uninterested in things like that, but all the time he'd been watching.

"It doesn't matter about Uchida," she said. "The thing is, Shunsuke took a shine to you, right from the start." She laughed. "But it's not for him to decide. It's up to you and Mariko. There's no hurry, though. You're both so young."

I didn't know how to reply.

By the time I left, her usual smile was back as she said "Goodbye. Thanks for the ride."

24

The competition for the National Library of Modern Literature was held on November 25. First prize went to the plan submitted by the Kei'ichi Funayama Office of Architectural Design.

The Funayama library was shaped like a compact but very thick Bible standing up, open at the middle. A typically Funayama form, it drew the eyes straight up. Parallel rows of bookcases lined the trapezoid-shaped east and west wings, with the counters and administrative offices in the center—the area that on a book would be the inside margin. A librarian sitting at a counter would have a full view of the aisles between the bookcases. The focus appeared to be on management, keeping track of the books, rather than on moving the users smoothly through the place. In that sense, it reminded me of the lobby of a large hospital. Anyone with the slightest interest in architecture would immediately recognize the façade as a Funayama design, the way it seemed to look grandly down on the street below. And if grandeur was what they were looking for, no one could have objected to the selection of this design.

Setting my position and personal preferences aside, I still thought Sensei's plan was superior in every way. But in his absence, the plan was headless, like a teapot without a lid. For us, Sensei's stroke was such a blow that the disappointment of losing the competition just dissolved and sank away.

In December, winter came to Tokyo with a string of very cold days. One weekend evening, seven weeks after Sensei's stroke, Mariko and I, plus Yukiko, who had shyly asked if we wouldn't mind her joining us, headed for the Asama Central Hospital. Before leaving Tokyo, I washed the Volvo in the office parking lot and gave the windshield, rear window, and side mirrors a good rub with a dry cloth.

We brought with us a tape of one of Sensei's favorite piano pieces, which I'd asked Mariko to play in advance. This wasn't just for sentimental reasons; information about brain damage indicated that because hearing is a primitive function that developed very early in the evolutionary process, the ear can sometimes identify sounds even when a person is in a coma.

The only sounds in the intensive care unit were the compressor on the breathing machine, the low hum of the air-conditioning, snatches of conversation between doctors and nurses, the monotony of meters and gauges, and the occasional opening and closing of automatic doors. No wind blowing through the trees, or birds calling to each other, or wood crackling in the fireplace. Right now, Sensei's consciousness was deep underwater, but Mariko's piano playing might stir some memory in those depths.

He had gone to all his niece's piano performances when she was in elementary school and junior high. Pupils were allowed to pick which piece they would play from among several their teacher chose for them, but Mariko always asked her uncle's advice first. When she was in fourth grade, for example, he had suggested one of Schubert's impromptus.

I knew almost by heart the music Sensei often listened to in the living room or his office. Some were things Mariko had played at school recitals. But he never talked to her about music, at least while they were at the Summer House. If not for his stroke, I doubt I would have had the courage to ask her to do this recording. She hadn't seemed very enthusiastic about the idea, and sounded almost angry about one of Schubert's piano sonatas she'd decided on.

"I've been practicing every day, and I'm finally at the point where I can play the first movement. It's about twenty minutes long, though, so that's all I can manage."

She said she didn't mind recording only part of it, but wanted to start on Friday evening, alone. The piano at the cottage in Kyū-Karuizawa was the one Sensei had helped her pick out after she'd finished junior high, going with her not only to the showroom but to the storage warehouse as well. When they finally narrowed it down to two pianos, she still couldn't decide. "They're both fine instruments," Sensei had said. "One has a sharp, clear tone, and the other is softer, rounder."

"They sound so different. Which is better?"

He laughed. "You're split between them because each has a part of you in them."

"Which makes it all the harder to decide."

"It doesn't have to, though," he'd reassured her. "If you choose the one with the sharp, clear sound you can still play soft, rounded notes on it. And vice versa on the other one. It all depends on your ability."

After wavering a while longer, Mariko had finally opted for the gentler-sounding piano. That had been over ten years ago.

Mariko told me she wanted all of Saturday morning to do the recording as well. "Just set up the tape recorder," she said, "and tell me which button to push."

"It's easy. The sound should be pretty good too."

The machine was a Sony Cassette Densuke I'd borrowed from a friend from university. I was planning to have Sensei hear the tape on the Walkman I always used.

"I want to stay at the cottage on my own," Mariko said, "so can you and Yukiko pick me up at around noon on Saturday?"

As I hadn't planned on staying alone with Yukiko, some uncertainty must have shown in my face.

"What's wrong? What are you worried about?" she wanted to know.

"I was just wondering..."

"Wondering what?" she asked fiercely, reaching for my neck, lightly enclosing it with her slender fingers.

After the three of us had dinner at a Western-style restaurant in Kyū-Karuizawa, I set up the tape recorder near the piano for Mariko. Leaving her at the cottage, Yukiko and I then headed for the Summer House. The moon was nearly full. On our left, the outline of Mt. Asama appeared in the moonlight, its surface covered with a layer of powdery white snow. The only sounds in the dark interior of the car were the engine and the heater. The orange light of the instrument panel glowed in the dark.

Winter had come to the village of Aoguri. The trees were bare, and our headlights, passing through leafless branches and trunks, reached far ahead.

On arrival, while Yukiko was opening the front door, I walked around the house, fallen leaves rustling under my feet, to turn on the four water mains. A slightly sweet odor rose from the katsura leaves. By the time I got inside I was freezing, so I immediately lit the kerosene heater and brought some logs over to the fireplace. The thermometer outside the kitchen window showed that it was below zero. To take my mind off the fact that I was alone with Yukiko, I turned on the radio on the dining room chest. The news had just ended, and the weather report was coming on. "The low tomorrow for Ueda will be minus one degree, for Matsumoto minus two, for Karuizawa minus five..."

"One bath will do for just the two of us, don't you think?" said Yukiko.

"Sounds fine to me," I replied, and went up to get the men's bath ready. Looking down at the tiled floor, I wondered what Mariko would think, but assured myself that we were doing nothing wrong.

When I returned to the living room, the fire I'd made had gone out. The logs must have been damp, because however many times I relit and fanned it, I got only billows of smoke. Yukiko brought me a cup of *hōjicha*. After numerous tries, I finally got some weak flames going. As the logs heated up, the moisture expelled from the cut end made tiny bubbles with a faint sighing sound. We sat at opposite ends of the sofa in front of the fireplace, staring into the fire. Even here in the living room we could see our breath.

"God, it's cold tonight," Yukiko said.

"All we can do is take a bath and go to bed."

"I guess so," she said absentmindedly, adding, "I wonder if Mariko's playing the piano now. I'd really like to hear it." I nodded in agreement. "Have you ever heard her play?" she asked.

"Me? No, never."

"Oh..." As if prompted by her voice, one of the burning logs slid down and rolled off the pile. I picked it up with the tongs and put it back. The flames grew stronger. Yukiko silently watched them glow.

"The bath should be just about ready, so why don't you go ahead?"

"Mm," she murmured, but I couldn't really tell whether she was listening or not. Only the crackling of the fire broke the long silence. Just as I was thinking I should say something, there was a loud pop and a burst of flames. We turned to each other. Smiling, she seemed to look at me a little longer than usual—or was it me who was looking at her?

"Okay, I'm going upstairs," she said, standing up as if she'd remembered she had this to do.

"Take your time—it'll warm you up," I said with my back to her, arranging the logs in the fireplace.

"Thanks. I will."

Though it stayed with me, her voice told me nothing. As if glued to the spot where I knelt in front of the fire, I kept putting logs on. Not only to warm the room up—I was hoping to make the flames strong enough to burn away the half-baked feelings that had collected inside me. If a fire is burning well enough, even damp logs will catch soon after they come in contact. I added an extra layer to the firewood frame. Before long, the fire was so hot I jerked my hand back when I used the tongs. My face, too, felt as if it was being grilled.

Yukiko, back from the bath looking happy and refreshed, plunked down next to me on the sofa. She smelled of a different soap and shampoo from Mariko's. After draining her cup of *hōjicha*, now cold, she said, "There was a constellation on the back wall of the fireplace just now."

"A constellation?"

"Yes. When sparks stick to that black wall it looks like a constellation. You can use it to tell someone's fortune—Sensei showed me how once."

"And did you see anyone's future this time?"

"No, not really." I watched her profile as she stared into the fire. Still sitting there, she said, "Think I'll go to bed now." I nodded, but could find nothing to say.

She stood up, turning away from me. "Good night."

"Good night," I said to her back. She climbed the stairs without turning around.

I stayed for a while, then suddenly remembered Ms. Fujisawa and decided to call her. I wanted to keep that promise I'd made.

When I went into the ironing room and turned on the light, I saw the little glass vase Mariko had used during the summer, next to the pencil sharpener on the edge of the table. The last thing she'd put in it was a thistle flower.

Ms. Fujisawa answered the phone right away. "Thanks for remembering," she said when I let her know my idea. "Is Mariko there with you?"

I told her she wasn't, and hung up without mentioning Yukiko.

Though the window was still white with steam, the room was clean and neat. The smell of Yukiko's shampoo lingered in the air.

"Mariko says let's have lunch together and then go to the hospital," she told me next morning. They had talked on the phone.

"Did the recording go all right?"

"She didn't say. Maybe she's not done yet." That smile again.

It was a bright, sunny day. Mt. Asama looked whiter than it had in the moonlight. We still had plenty of time before we had to pick Mariko up, so after breakfast I suggested we walk to Firefly Pond.

Even in a duffle coat and a scarf, I felt the air sting my cheeks. Yukiko was dressed for the Yukon: a Cowichan sweater, white and fluffy as a polar bear; a tousled wool scarf over her mouth; dark-brown corduroy slacks; Maine hunting boots; woolen hat; and mouton gloves. The katsura's bare frame looked like a skeleton. The sun was much lower than it had been in the summer. Cutting diagonally across the tops of the trees, the light was almost blinding. Hearing the cry of a kogera, I looked up and saw it take off from a branch.

There was no one around in the village. No cars either. We followed the straight road until we reached the spot where we'd found Harue Nomiya that summer. The dip where she'd been sitting was now filled with fallen leaves. As her family had finally convinced her to spend this winter in Tokyo, she had mailed the new bookrest we made for her to her home in Setagaya Ward. Beyond a turn to the left up ahead was the lake.

I smelled wood burning somewhere. This sign of another presence came as a relief. Leaves under our feet, we walked down the slope toward the water. Since I'd forgotten my gloves, my hands were freezing, as was the tip of my nose.

We were soon on the path around Firefly Pond, where Mariko and her elementary school friends once had their ghost hunt. The light shone dully off the edge, where the water had frozen. I heard the harsh cry of a redheaded woodpecker. A warning not to enter its territory.

"I hope Sensei..." Staring down at the ice, Yukiko let her voice trail off, then continued in a drier tone, "...at least regains consciousness. Mariko says he may not be able to talk again, though."

"He's pretty tough, and his heart is strong, so I'm sure he'll come out of the coma," I said, not mentioning Mariko's prediction.

"I wonder what's going to happen to the office."

"It'll be hard to keep it going the way it is now."

"You're right," she said gloomily. "Something's got to change."

A duck flew up from the middle of the lake, which wasn't frozen over yet. As if chasing it, another flapped across the surface, then rose into the sky. Calling to each other, the two flew in circles over our heads. We stood there for a while watching them, listening to their lonely cries.

Golden afternoon light streamed into the back of the car, where Mariko and Yukiko were sitting.

"Do you mind if we listen to the tape of you playing the piano?" Yukiko asked as we were leaving the Kyū-Karuizawa area.

"It's not very good," Mariko replied, looking out at the scenery, "but if you really want to..." She got the cassette out of her handbag.

"Thanks." Yukiko removed the case and handed me the tape.

When I slid it into the player, what we heard first wasn't the piano but Mariko's voice.

"Hello, it's me, Mariko. How are you feeling today? You've been lying there for such a long time I'm afraid your back or your bottom must be sore. If it hurts somewhere, let me know. Just move the tip of one of your fingers, on the left or right hand, it doesn't matter which, and I'll tell the nurse.

"It's winter in Karuizawa now. Mt. Asama looks beautiful, white with snow. Yukiko told me that when you had Sakanishi's welcome party at the Ristorante Hana, there was a big Mont Blanc for dessert. That's just what it looks like now, she says. She and Sakanishi are both with me today.

"I'm going to play the piano for the first time in ages, so you can hear some music.

"It'll be on the one at our cottage, which you helped me pick out just before I started high school—more than ten years ago. I can't believe how fast the time's gone by. You said it had a nice tone when I finally chose the softer-sounding one.

"It's a piece you like—Schubert's Piano Sonata no. 21. I haven't had enough time to practice, so it's not up to scratch. Think of it as my way of saying hello, just for now. When I'm in better form, I'll let you hear it again.

"Well, here goes." There was the sound of her pulling out the chair in front of the piano.

As I drove down Route 18, the music filled the car. Mariko had a light, sure touch. She was certainly no amateur. My surprise at how good she was soon faded, though, letting me concentrate on the music. It wasn't the times Schubert lived in, or a close friend or lover he was addressing. He was alone, the melody a dialogue with himself. Did he know how little time he had left when he wrote it?

I saw Yukiko's face in the rearview mirror. She seemed to be keeping her head up, eyes forward, to stop any tears from falling if she looked down.

We passed Oiwake and had almost reached Tsuburano. The tape was still playing. In a little while, we should be able to see the windbreak trees on Ms. Fujisawa's farm from the road. When I'd told her that Mariko and I went to the hospital every weekend, she had said only, "If he knew you two were coming to see him, I'm sure it would make him very happy."

Sakudaira appeared on our left. These were parts of the countryside Sensei had seen many times. Wisps of smoke rose here and there on the broad slope leading into the area. The car continued along the gentle ups and downs of the road past Tsuburano, heading farther west.

The faces of the ICU staff were all familiar to Mariko and me. "It must be hard, coming from so far away," said a nurse in her late thirties. The name on her badge was Koide. "Mr. Murai's color is much better today." As she turned to go, I called her back and told her we wanted to play a tape for him, of my companion playing the piano.

"That'd be fine," she said. "How long will it take?"

"About twenty-five minutes," said Mariko.

"Actually, I was wondering if you could play this tape for him once a day—if it's not too much trouble."

"That's a good idea," she said. "I'll make sure he hears it." Unsmiling, she added, "Once in a while we'll have a patient who hears everything that's going on even though he seems to be completely unconscious."

Mariko looked at me.

"I'll let the doctor know you're here so he can fill you in on Mr. Murai's condition afterward." Nurse Koide then hurried away.

We put on white coats, masks, and hats, and sterilized our hands and arms up to the elbow before entering his room in intensive care. Though the room had four beds, Sensei was now the only occupant, in the bed farthest from the door.

Mariko went straight up to him, and as usual lightly squeezed his right hand. He was still on the breathing machine, his eyes closed. The crease between his eyebrows wasn't as deep as the week before. I thought his color looked better too.

Mariko bent over him and whispered in his ear: "It's Mariko. Today Sakanishi and Yukiko are both here with me." She gestured for Yukiko to come over.

"Sensei, it's Yukiko Nakao," she said, putting her hand on his arm. She didn't say anything else.

I put the Walkman by his pillow. He was clean-shaven, his hair neatly combed. "I'm going to put some headphones on your ears," I told him. Then I pushed the start button, and the tape began to move. He should be hearing Mariko's voice. In a minute or two, the piano sonata would begin.

We stood there in silence, watching him. Neither his face, nor his hands, nor his fingers moved. After a while, Mariko started stroking his shin.

I looked at my watch, and when the tape was just ending I pushed the stop button and took the earphones out. Mariko reached out to smooth his hair where I'd mussed it.

The only things ostensibly moving in the room now were the hands of the clock, the instruments he was hooked up to, and his chest, gently rising and falling. The man we knew and respected was there and yet not there.

The doctor had nothing new to tell us. He looked apologetic, as if he were trying to warn us, in a roundabout way, not to get our hopes up. When we'd heard what he had to say, we bowed and left. Outside, a sharp north wind was blowing. The car was freezing cold. As soon as I had the engine running, I turned the heater right up.

Before driving out of the parking lot, I announced, "There's a place I want to stop at on the way. It's the home of Kinuko Fujisawa, a friend of Sensei's who says she'd like to see the Summer House." Even to me, this sounded rather too formal.

I could have seen Mariko's face in the rearview mirror, but didn't look.

"So, she's never been there," she said casually, skipping lightly over the part Yukiko didn't know about. Yukiko didn't ask who Ms. Fujisawa was, perhaps because she'd gathered from Mariko's tone that this was someone she knew.

When we pulled into the farm, I could tell that Yukiko was gawking at the expanse of land outside.

"Does all this belong to one person?" she asked. "Or is it some kind of huge farm?"

"It's a huge farm that belongs to one person."

As I drove slowly past the two small houses on either side of the driveway and on toward the big house, Yukiko, who must have recognized all three as Sensei's design, was silent. I cut the engine, got out, and was about to knock on the door when it opened from inside. Ms. Fujisawa was standing there, wearing a long beige down coat.

"We've been to the hospital."

"No change, I suppose."

"Right—no change."

While she was locking the front door, the other two got out of the car and came over.

Mariko greeted her, calling her Kinuko.

"Hello," Ms. Fujisawa said, "it's been a long time. You're looking well."

Yukiko then introduced herself.

"I've heard about you from Sensei. Glad to meet you. I'm Kinuko Fujisawa."

With Yukiko beside me in the front, I drove for about an hour through the snowy landscape toward Kita-Asama. What, I wondered, would Sensei have thought if he could see the four of us together in his car, heading for the Summer House?

I took a cassette tape out of the glove box and put it on. It was a piece Sensei often listened to while he was driving. He had written "Haydn, The Seasons" neatly with a fountain pen on the label.

The tape began with part three, "Autumn." It was music that might have been written to accompany a journey to the north along a winter road. By the time we got onto the winding road up the mountain with all its hairpin turns, the final chorus, a bright, lively hymn to the pleasures of good wine, was starting. The music became much quieter as I came out of the last turn and the dark introductory adagio of "Winter" began.

"Seems much colder," said Yukiko, looking out of the window.

The outside air temperature indicator said minus three degrees Celsius. "It's below zero," I said, looking straight ahead.

In the back seat, Mariko and Ms. Fujisawa were talking about piano music. There were two pianos in Ms. Fujisawa's house. The lid was always up on the baby grand, with sheet music on the stand. Sensei must have heard her play.

The wind blew sheets of light snow off the shoulder, sending them sliding across the straight road ahead. On the tape of *The Seasons* the prelude to "Winter" had ended, followed by the more encouraging "Weaver's Song," about making veils for young girls. This gave way to a slightly bawdy love song. The entire oratorio was filled with Haydn's desire in his last years to affirm everyday life and nature, both when it helps and when it threatens us. Sensei had never tired of listening to it while he was driving.

We reached the village of Aoguri. The music had ended a while before. Bare trees stood out black against the white forest floor. I felt slightly comforted by the fact that it wasn't spring, with flowers opening and green leaves stirred by a breeze.

The Summer House stood perfectly quiet in the winter scene. Wanting Ms. Fujisawa to see everything, I didn't stop the car at the front door, but swung around the katsura tree and parked in the garage. I backed it in slowly, just as Sensei used to do when he returned from spending the weekend at her farm.

Ms. Fujisawa was the first to open the car door and get out. There was a light coating of snow on the driveway. She stopped under the katsura tree and looked up at the house. Her eyes were trained on the workshop window. Instinctively I looked in the same direction.

Sensei might have been gazing down at us from up there. Though his face seemed stern from a distance, if you looked carefully you'd see that he was smiling slightly. This was how he always appeared to us: a kind face we would never forget.

She stayed there a while without moving. Mariko and Yukiko stood silently beside her.

Time seemed to have stopped.

We didn't hear any birds singing, or the sound of the wind, or Sensei's voice.

25

Architecture always has a life expectancy. Unlike art that's there to be looked at, buildings are inhabited, used, and gradually suffer damage. Hands and feet soil them, wear them down, exhaust them. Fingers make smudges on white walls, wallpaper starts peeling from corners, wax fades from wooden floors, leaving them pale and dry. After doors are opened and shut thousands of times, the hinges loosen and eventually break. Baths, sinks, toilets, and kitchens—places where water is used—age especially quickly, and often need repairs. From outside, sunlight, rain, and wind play their part. Roofs and window frames, exposed to the weather, start to leak, and before anyone notices, things rust, adding to the decline.

The moment a building is completed it is out of your hands, its fate left up to the client and the passage of time. Even clients willing to spend time and money on the upkeep of their house will eventually want to modify it to accommodate changes in their lives, such as an increase or decrease in the size of their family. You might be asked to do this work, or the client may hire an entirely different architect or contractor whose plan has no connection to your original concept and will alter the form of the building. And if a house is sold, the new owners may either warm to it, and continue to live there, or tear it down.

It's only natural for the value of a house to change dramatically with new ownership, or different inhabitants. A well-known architectural work, viewed from a different angle, can seem like nothing more than a worn-out, inefficient, inconvenient waste of labor. It's possible to restore a house to its original state, but once it's been torn down, there's really no hope of rebuilding it just as it was, on the same plot of land. The life of that particular piece of architecture ends there.

Yet strangely, hearing that a building has been razed can be a relief. At least to me.

Clients rarely contact the architect directly when they're having their house pulled down. The news usually comes from the contractor, or an enthusiast, or occasionally from a student, who'll say "That building you designed..." in the hushed tones used with the bereaved. When that happens to me, I'll sit down at the archive I've got stored on my computer, after finishing the day's work, and look at the floor plan, elevation, cross section, and detailed design, one by one. Comments and criticisms start to rise in my head like bubbles. The layout of the rooms on the first and second floors was off-balance; the route between the kitchen and the dining room wasn't quite right; I wouldn't do the ceiling baseboards this way now. . .

On the other hand, sometimes I'll be impressed by a design I did twenty years ago. "I bet no one noticed what I did there to keep the rain out," I'll think, or "I wouldn't have the patience now to design a three-story house on such a tiny plot that met all the client's demands and yet was so well proportioned." Or "My specifications for that handrail were so detailed. Whoever actually made it must have been really fed up with me. I wonder if the client even noticed how much trouble I took over it—I wish he'd leave it to me as a souvenir after he has the place rebuilt." When I was young, I'd get totally absorbed in one part of a plan, forgetting about time, aiming for an unreasonable level of perfection, not even noticing things I was neglecting, things I hadn't even started on.

Successes and failures disappear equally when a house is destroyed. Deep down, though, I don't really regret this. Buildings are replaced for a reason, or, to put it more dramatically, each has its own fate, and you just have to accept that.

When I look back over the relationships I've had with these clients, they all seem to have been rather cool, or difficult, with the two of us usually talking past each other, which seems strange, but in a way quite natural. He wants a house, has it built, and lives in it, so the result—how well it turns out—should contain some trace of the connection between that person and whoever designed it. Yet now that I think of it, in each case there was a change in ownership, and the land was disposed of along with the house. Regardless of how well or poorly something is made, the economic value of architecture in Japan eventually comes down to zero.

After you've designed about a hundred homes, and worked on a number of public buildings, every five or ten years or so requests for repairs, extensions, and maintenance, such as replacing the wiring, suddenly start arriving at irregular intervals. As maintenance jobs often have to be dealt with immediately, they tend to take precedence, and you end up feeling that building new houses is only about half of your actual workload. For the past several years, I've only taken on a few new commissions, always discussing things thoroughly with the client first, and yet the amount of work I do each day seems to increase year by year. I've kept the staff in my office small, so there's a limit to the number of jobs I can take on anyway.

When I'm no longer able to go on working, I will reduce my staff of ten people by stages and shut the office down within four years. All the employees are aware of this. After we close, I plan to have the maintenance jobs we now handle taken over by a new office under my two chief architects, set up with capital and operating funds from my medical and life insurance. My current key people are the third pair I've hired. They knew from the outset that I expected them to take over our maintenance jobs after I bow out.

Though at first this seemed like a cold, dry sort of plan, it didn't turn out that way. The staff work hard to acquire the skills necessary for them to start out on their own at some stage. After a building is finished, they're more careful than we were about maintenance; they've come to see that the work they do now will affect their future. Rather than working under a "sensei," they're cooperating on projects for a limited time only, knowing they will eventually benefit from what comes out of current assignments. This motivates them, and I think it's actually improved the atmosphere in the office. These young architects need to see what lies ahead as a chance to develop. Each needs to be independent.

In my fifties, preparations for my eventual absence took on rather more urgency. If I hired a lot of people in their twenties, I would feel I'd let them down if I were forced to close the office much earlier than expected. I didn't want to put recent graduates through what I had experienced myself. What happened at the Murai Office after Sensei had a stroke led me to plan for closing down my own firm well in advance.

Sensei had the stroke in mid-October of 1982, and was still in the ICU in Nagano at Christmastime. When the swelling in his brain went down, relieving the pressure, he was able to move his left hand, very slightly. Then his left foot twitched. Next his head moved a little from side to side, and finally, after a long period when we almost gave up hope of any further improvement, without warning, he opened his eyes. They looked as if they weren't really seeing, though. He moved them aimlessly around, unable to focus on anything. From the expression on his face, I imagined this was something like a blind person recovering his sight. Until the things he sees take on a meaning, connected to words, it's as if he's not really seeing them at all.

After a while he was taken off the machine and could breathe on his own. Though perhaps through a thick layer of mist, shafts of light began to reach his consciousness.

The tubes and wires he was connected to were removed, bit by bit. In due course he was moved to a private room. Though he occasionally nodded when we spoke to him, it wasn't clear how much he understood. He still couldn't speak at all. Eventually a faint, raspy "Ah" emerged from deep in his throat, and he was able to respond more often, in the affirmative or negative, to questions.

His upper body was gradually raised in his bed, and when the inflammation in his trachea from months of being on the breathing machine had subsided, he started taking food orally. His first meal was two spoonfuls of thin rice porridge. His right side was still paralyzed.

Late in January 1983, it was decided to move him to a hospital in Tokyo. That day, I called Ms. Fujisawa.

"I see," she said, and for a while I heard only silence, as though down a long, dark tunnel.

"I'll call again as soon as I see how he's doing there," I told her. She thanked me and hung up.

I drove the Volvo back to Tokyo, with Sensei and his wife in the back seat, and Mariko beside me up front.

When we reached the expressway I put on the tape of Haydn's *The Seasons*, but saw no sign of recognition. I'd wanted to ask him sometime about the tape he'd heard on the Walkman, of Mariko playing, but looking at his face, I thought better of it. What, and how, was he feeling, now that he could no longer speak? I sensed sadness, and irritation. How long would it be until we saw even a trace of pleasure? The music idly filled the car as it raced along the expressway. Music no one listens to is just a long series of notes strung coldly together. When the chorus of "Summer" was over, I turned it off.

There was no dramatic change in his condition at the Tokyo hospital. The words he managed to get out were still garbled, the voice weak. He couldn't really read either. When a newspaper was placed in front of him, he merely glanced at it but didn't pick it up. He tried writing with his left hand—the one he could still use—but produced only meaningless lines that stretched out, curved, wavered, then stopped.

"His vision will be patchy on the right side, so be careful he doesn't bump into things, and the damage to his brain might make it hard for him to keep his balance," the doctor told us before we took him home, adding "We shouldn't give up, though, so let's continue with the rehabilitation program."

I drove him to his house in Yoyogi-Uehara, where a woman carer was already waiting. After making sure he was settled in a chair, his wife went back to her clinic. Mariko visited him every other day. Aside from twice-weekly trips to the hospital with the carer for rehabilitation, he sat silently in his wheelchair in the living room, looking out at the trees in the garden as music played.

About a week after Sensei went home, Mt. Asama erupted.

Pictures on the news showed a pillar of smoke and flame above the crater, and fires on the opposite side of the mountain from the Summer House. Worried about Ms. Fujisawa, I phoned her.

The voice on the other end sounded much more cheerful than I'd expected. "Thanks for calling," she said. "I'm fine. The fire's quite a ways off." She told me that since the main explosion, she'd seen smoke coming out of the crater now and then, but no sign of another big blast. "It woke me up in the middle of the night. There was a boom, loud enough to shake me. I dragged the sofa over to the window and just sat there, looking out at the mountain. It was frightening, of course, but eruptions are also rather beautiful. It had been a long time since I'd seen fire spewing out like that. I saw lightning in the smoke too. Apparently the wind carried volcanic ash off to the west, so it may have affected the Summer House. There might be some broken windows as well, from the blast of air pressure."

When I told her how Sensei was spending his days at home, her voice got much gloomier.

"If all he can manage is going back and forth between Yoyogi-Uehara and the hospital, there's not much chance of him coming to Aoguri this summer. I can't phone him, and I can't very well send him a letter either... Even if I did, I doubt he'd be able to read it. Does he know Mt. Asama erupted?"

"He watches the TV news every day, so he probably knows."

"I wonder what he thought. No matter how long it takes him to get the words out, I wish he'd say something."

Westerlies carried the ash over a wide area; it fell as far away as the Pacific coast of Fukushima Prefecture.

Mariko was at Sensei's house on the day of the eruption. She told me later that he had sat there, not moving, staring at the TV screen while the news was on. The two of them were alone in the living room. He had slowly raised his left hand to point at the television, then looked at Mariko. When the news was over, he had looked down and closed his eyes.

"When he looked up again, his eyes were filled with tears. He was trying to wipe them away with his left hand, so I gave him my handkerchief." She said she didn't even want to guess at all that was behind those tears.

That evening, Mariko had stayed with Sensei until his wife returned from the clinic, sometime after nine. She told him about how she was practicing the piano again, about a new product that was selling better than anything else at their shop this spring, about how all her father's socks had suddenly disappeared, and he later found out that her mother had thrown them away without telling him... When he heard about the disappearing socks, Sensei had laughed, slowly, "Ha, ha, ha."

On her way home, Mariko stopped at a pay phone in Yoyogi-Uehara Station and called Ms. Fujisawa to see how she was after the eruption. She didn't mention that Sensei had cried as he watched it on the news, though. Out of coins, she'd put her last ten yen in when she remembered something she had to tell her. "Sensei laughed today, the first time since the stroke," she said quickly.

"That's great," she heard, before the phone went dead.

It was now early summer.

Work continued at the office. Although no one had quit, there were far fewer meetings, and increasingly the place was as quiet as a library. In a normal year, things would be getting busy around this time, as everyone got ready to go to the Summer House.

Then one day, Sensei appeared at the office in his wheelchair; Mariko had driven him. Seeing us gathered at the entrance, he tried to smile, but since the right side of his face was still paralyzed, it looked more as if he was in pain. Each of us spoke to him in turn. He nodded all the while.

Uchida, who had decided to stay on for the rest of the year, picked up the back of the wheelchair, while I took the front, and together we carried him up to his office on the second floor. His face was very pale, and he had lost a lot of weight. It was painful to find how light the wheelchair was.

Installed there, he moved the wheelchair forward slightly with his left hand and tried to pull open one of the desk drawers. While I was hesitating, wondering if he should be left to do it by himself, Uchida said, "Here, let me open that for you." Sensei looked up at him, raised his left hand, and nodded, thanking him in his own way.

He then took a white envelope from the drawer, picking it up between the fingers of his left hand, and put it on the desk. He pointed at Iguchi, again with his left hand, nodded, and touched the envelope.

Iguchi took out the letter, written on stationery, and read it silently. It was over ten pages long. "I understand," he said with a deep bow on finishing it.

Uchida and I carried him back down the stairs to the car, where Mariko was waiting. All twelve of us went out and silently saw him off. We watched him raise his hand to us through the car window.

Sensei's long letter had been written a year earlier, on the day before we had left for the Summer House. It began:

> *Dear Iguchi,*
> *This is to tell you what I would like you to do about the office in the event of my death or incapacitation.*

What followed was very specific. The Murai Office should continue to operate for a fixed period of time, and if possible, close within two years. Provided they agreed, Kawarazaki and Kobayashi were to set up a new office, which would take over maintenance work for Murai Office buildings. Funds for the new enterprise, as well as severance pay for staff members and other expenses, should be covered by selling the office building and the land on which it stood. In accordance with the terms set out in the letter, staff members' salaries should be fully guaranteed for a year after proceedings to shut down began.

Further instructions for dissolving the company were laid out plainly and in detail. These ended with a personal message for Iguchi:

> *There might have been ways, including the plan you had in mind, to keep the office going. But any effort to carry on when the end is unavoidable is bound to peter out before long. My decision has come after a great deal of thought.*
>
> *You made it possible for me to do good work over many years, and for that I am very grateful. Without you, I could never have accomplished as much as I did. Once again, all my thanks.*
>
> *I have also been lucky in having such a good staff to support my work. I would have liked to write personally to each of them, but as there is no way of knowing who will still be around when you read this (if you are the only one left, this will seem like a bad joke, won't it?), I'm asking you to convey my gratitude to them as their*

representative. They have all been a great help. Thank you.

I'm afraid I'll still need your assistance in closing down the office, which will be laborious, but I'm depending on you. Please make sure everyone understands and accepts this. Their work is in their own hands, not ours.

Hoping all of you will continue to be fine architects,

*Shunsuke Murai
July 28, 1982*

A red Staedtler pencil, a 4B lead pencil, an eraser, an ash-wood ear pick with a white cotton puff, and his favorite Montblanc fountain pen were lined up in the leather tray on the desk as usual. The letter had probably been written with that pen. Like his architecture, the blue-black lettering was neat but original, nothing like the aimless lines he'd drawn with his left hand in the hospital.

Three days after he came to the office, Iguchi handed a copy of the letter to each of us. The date was July 28, 1983, exactly one year after Sensei had written it.

A little over two years later, the Murai Office of Architectural Design closed down. As Sensei had specified, we were all given time to decide what we were going to do next. When someone found a new job or a new employer, duplicates were made of the work that person had been in charge of, and Iguchi sent letters to the clients, telling them what was happening. Then the leaver sorted through his or her things, packed, and cleaned the desk drawers. Sensei had provided new employees with a Staedtler Lumograph pencil, a French curve ruler to use when making blueprints, and an Opinel knife on which he carved the newcomer's name himself. "You can take these with you if you like, as souvenirs," Iguchi offered, but even if he hadn't, no one would have parted with them.

Each departure meant another farewell party at the Ristorante Hana. The sound of pencils being sharpened with Opinel knives in the morning grew a little fainter each time.

Kawarazaki and Kobayashi rented one floor of a multitenant building in Yushima and set up their business there. Ms. Sasai was invited to join them, which she did. Apparently they asked Yukiko as well, but she was hired on a fixed-term contract as curator of an architectural gallery established by one of the major construction firms.

After Uchida quit, he went alone to Denmark. With an introduction from a friend of his father's, he joined a medium-sized architectural firm, and three years later returned to Japan with a Danish companion, to set up his own design office. A year later, they married.

Mariko stopped working for the Murai Office right after Sensei had his stroke. She gave piano lessons at home to the children of customers, and also helped her parents in the shop, and took care of her uncle.

There was no more talk of the two of us getting married. Mariko herself stayed off the subject. The summer ended, Sensei was hospitalized, and by the time Mt. Asama was covered with snow, our marrying already seemed a thing of the past, receding like a station glimpsed through the window of a moving train.

Only once, Mariko talked to me about having children. As the weather was nice and the cherry trees were in full bloom, she suggested a walk through Aoyama Cemetery. It was a Sunday afternoon, not long after Mt. Asama erupted. We passed through the chilly cemetery grounds toward Aoyama-Itchome, looking up at the flower-bright branches forming a tunnel over our heads, then crossed the street onto an unfrequented road lined with plane trees, facing the plot of land where the National Library of Modern Literature was to be built. We walked right past it without stopping. Discovering an old coffee shop that had classical music to listen to, we dropped in.

"I'd like to have a child by the time I'm twenty-eight or so," Mariko said quite casually, as if she were discussing plans for a summer vacation with a friend. We were sitting on a sofa upholstered in white, after eating the cream puffs a uniformed waitress had brought. When I asked Mariko why, she said, "Well, my dad's getting on. He'll probably retire in another ten years. If my child isn't in grade school by then, I don't see how I'll be able to run the shop."

For a while I couldn't find anything to say, only wonder what the woman sitting beside me in a gray knit top with matching cardigan was going to say next. She wasn't thinking of me as the father of that child, was she? From this distance, dozens of years after the fact, I would have given my twenty-three-year-old self some encouragement. "You've still got a chance," I would have told him. "It's up to you." But dozens of years afterward is usually too late to do anything about it.

We did keep seeing each other. We spent time together on weekends: had dinner at a restaurant, did some shopping, saw a movie, or went to a bar she knew. Although I always turned bright red, I'd started to drink a little. By the fall, Mariko was working full-time at her family's shop. Weekends became Saturday only, and in time she couldn't see me then either, because the shop was open. If we met when it was closed, before long she was telling me apologetically that she had to get up early the next morning.

As time went on, we'd have minor arguments and not see each other at all for a couple of weeks. A trace of her scent from a cardigan or scarf she'd left at my apartment would bring on a bittersweet ache in my chest, a loneliness that gathered in my throat, making me want to cry out loud. Yet at the same time, deep inside me, a sense of resignation was growing stronger as I realized that Mariko was drifting away and I would never get her back.

In the spring of 1984, she called to tell me she was engaged to a man her own age, a schoolmate of hers from elementary to high school. His name was Takeshi Shigihara, the son of a salesman at a largish insurance company. I imagined a *shigi*, a shorebird scurrying along a beach. I hadn't seen her since December of the previous year, so when she suddenly told me she was getting married, I managed to sound calm on the phone.

A week later, I happened to have dinner with Uchida, who was home from Denmark for a visit. We ended up in a bar I'd been to several times with Mariko, and for the first time in my life I got dead-drunk. I had no idea how I managed to get back to my apartment, but when I crawled out of bed around noon the next day and crept into the bathroom, a bloated face I'd never seen before looked back at me from the mirror. Uchida, who was staying with me, said, "Carbohydrates are the best thing for a hangover," and gave me a bowl of slightly salty congee he'd whipped up. It came with little spears of fresh ginger and a pickled plum.

"How old are you anyway?" he asked.

"Twenty-four."

"How many women do you think you'll meet from now on?"

With my head feeling like a dry, cracked wall, I didn't even want to think about women.

"Keep Mariko as a good memory," he said. "Don't hold it against her. First on your agenda for today is getting rid of that hangover," he laughed.

Mariko's wedding took place in the Scandinavian Cultural Center in Daikanyama, which Sensei had designed twenty years before. I wasn't invited, but Iguchi and Yukiko were. Yukiko told me about it the next day. Sensei had also attended, in his wheelchair. After the ceremony, Yukiko, who hadn't seen him in a long time, went over to greet him. Though he didn't speak, he looked up at her, nodding again and again. She couldn't tell whether he understood everything people said to him, but anyway, speaking slowly and plainly, she told him all she knew about what the other members of his staff were doing. He listened carefully, trying to catch every word, then nodded deeply. There were tears in his eyes. When he offered her his left hand, which she took in both of hers for a gentle handshake, she was surprised how firmly he squeezed back, while making a sound like "Un, un," deep in his throat. That was the last time she saw him.

Late in the year Mariko got married, Iguchi introduced me to one of Sensei's former employees who ran a small architectural design office, which I joined. Though my salary was half what it had been, the people were friendly and considerate, which made it a comfortable place to work. I left after three years and started an office of my own. I was twenty-seven. Mariko was already a mother.

After all the old team were safely employed, Iguchi sold the building to a small publisher of architectural items with whom we had once had dealings. The new owner let him use the director's office for a small fee. Iguchi started commuting to work, serving as the copyright agent for Sensei's blueprints and other materials. Aside from an occasional visit from Kawarazaki and Kobayashi, however, he hardly had any customers. More and more of his time was spent dozing in the chair where Sensei had once sat. On the side table by the window was the model of the National Library of Modern Literature in its acrylic case.

There, apparently, he had a dream: he was riding on the old Tanasaka Light Railway, bound for Aoguri. Snow lay thick on the ground. Iguchi and Sensei were the only passengers. Except for a low, muffled hum inside the car, the snow absorbed all other sounds of travel in the little electric train.

"Think we'll make it to Aoguri?" Iguchi asked. "It's snowing really hard."

Sensei smiled but said nothing. Big white flakes stuck to the windows.

"It's no joke. We're the only ones on the train. If it stops here, we'll have to get out and help shovel it clear. D'you understand?"

Still smiling, Sensei looked out at the flurries of snow. As everything turned white around them, Iguchi was getting scared, until, with a sudden jolt, the train stopped. A beam of yellow light came toward them through the storm. It was a station attendant, holding up a lantern as he peered through the window. They had reached Kita-Asama Station.

The day after Iguchi had this dream, Sensei, who had been back in the hospital for a while, died of pneumonia. It was January 21, 1985.

I heard about the dream from Iguchi himself, who got drunker than anybody else at the wake.

Ms. Fujisawa didn't appear at either the wake or the funeral.

26

I stood in front of the Summer House.

I'd first come here twenty-nine years ago. Though I always intended to drop by when I had business in Karuizawa, I had only made it to Aoguri twice since then. The last time was over ten years ago.

The forest in Aoguri was even denser than before. Quite a few cottages were shuttered and overgrown with ivy, the garden strewn with leaves, the grass and weeds left to grow, then wilt. Although it was a sunny autumn day, the light here was dim, cut off by the trees.

I was surprised how huge the katsura tree by the driveway had grown. The trunk was twice as thick as I remembered, and it was now tall enough to overshadow the roof. What hadn't changed were the leaves. Just as on that day when Sensei had the stroke, they were bright yellow, from top to bottom. The sweetish smell took me back. I walked across the untidy driveway, took out the key I'd been given by Mariko Shigihara, and opened the door.

Soon after Sensei died, Mariko's father had bought the Summer House, but as he had his own cottage in

Kyū-Karuizawa, he and his family hardly used it, so it had been left to the elements. Then, when the owner himself, who lived much longer than his older brother, died one spring, my wife was the first person Mariko had called. She wanted to know if we were interested in buying the place. The price, much lower than I'd imagined, was more or less within our reach.

I had come now with my wife, who was also a partner in my firm.

I stepped up into the dark house, so long unvisited that the air was stale and heavy. Taking care to avoid splinters, I went around the first floor, opening the rain shutters. For the first time probably in years, light poured inside. Motes of dust moved in the air like a silent stream. Long ago, I never could have imagined that the house would no longer be used.

I saw the bare pepper trees through the kitchen window. After two of the original five were transplanted to Yamaguchi's place to prevent burglars from getting in, seeds from the remaining three had sprouted until that part of the garden was thick with their branches. The weeping cherry which had been Sensei's favorite tree was now hemmed in by them, struggling for breath. Pale-green palm ruffle lichen grew on its trunk and branches. If I didn't prune the pepper trees right back, get rid of the lichen, and sprinkle ash from the fireplace around its base as Sensei used to do, it might rot and die.

There were three blackened logs in the fireplace, left from the last time someone had made a fire. On the shelf beside it, catching the long rays of the afternoon sun, was a row of big glass jars: seven of them, each filled to the brim with pencil stubs, too worn down to be used. All came from the Murai Office. Some of my pencils must have been mixed in toward the top of the jar on the far right.

"Quite a sight, aren't they?"

"I'd forgotten all about them," said Yukiko, standing beside me.

We went upstairs. The handrail brought back memories. I remembered that photo of Mariko as a toddler, standing on tiptoe to reach it. I opened the shutters on the second floor. The desks and chairs in the workshop had been left as they were. A layer of fine dust had collected on the desks. Desiccated insects were scattered in the bathtub, and there were cracks between the tiles in places. The water heater looked like an antique now, and waterproofing for the whole area would probably have to be redone.

In the library, books had been taken out here and there, leaving spaces like wormholes; several volumes were leaning over, or had fallen flat, covered with dust. The bed where I had slept that summer when I was twenty-three had been stripped down to the bare mattress. Had Yukiko known back then that Mariko and I used to lie together on this narrow bed? I saw the spine of the book on Gunnar Asplund that I'd looked through again and again, just where I remembered leaving it.

The director's office, too, was just as it had been.

The old dial telephone was there, though it had obviously been disconnected long ago. Sensei had used it to call Kinuko Fujisawa. When I brought her here for the first time, she had stood there, looking at that black phone. I held the receiver to my ear, feeling its heaviness, then put it back. Ms. Fujisawa had been dead for over a decade now. A much younger sister had inherited the farm. I'd heard that Uchida was renting one of the two small houses on the grounds, and often came to stay during the summer. He was in his sixties now.

On the big table in the empty workshop sat the model for the National Library of Modern Literature.

Five years after Sensei died, Iguchi got cancer of the esophagus. As radiation wasn't enough to deal with it, he'd had an operation, losing not only his esophagus but his vocal cords as well. When I finally plucked up the courage to visit him in the hospital, he was waiting for me with a memo pad, on which he furiously scrawled messages. As soon as I replied, he was back at it, writing away. Still as talkative as ever, he had no trouble keeping up his end of the conversation. Like his speech, his notes rambled on, and were just as cheerful.

He had his favorite Lebanon Shaker rocking chair in his private room there, along with a huge poster of Marilyn Monroe on the wall, and a Danish mobile Uchida's wife had brought him, made to look like autumn leaves, hanging from the ceiling. With all these furnishings, it didn't seem like a sickroom at all. In one particularly vigorous note, he told me that the head nurse, whom he was very friendly with (or so he said), even let him order grilled eel for dinner from a place he used to go to when he was working at the office in Kita-Aoyama.

Before I left, he picked up his notepad again. On it he wrote: "I've had the model for the National Library of Modern Literature taken to the workshop in the Summer House."

He nodded several times, looking straight at me. I searched for something to say, the look in his eyes making me feel I couldn't keep the lid on my emotions otherwise.

"I'll take you to see it," I finally came out with, "when you're out of here."

Iguchi died about six months later.

After carefully wiping the dust off the case, I examined the model from various angles. Aside from a few places where the glue was starting to wear off, there was no real damage. I walked around to the other side of the table and leaned over to look from a lower angle, remembering how Sensei had done the same thing, at this very table.

I picked up the case in both hands and gently set it aside. Never have I seen such an intricate yet sturdy model, before or since. Uchida, Yukiko, and I were able to finish it in that short a time because our hands and fingertips worked in tandem without wavering a millimeter on the most delicate work, or missing the tiniest gap. We were young, so not really aware of it, but we were close to being the perfect tools that Sensei had in view.

Starting at the top, I removed each floor of the main library building. Uchida's little figures were still where he'd put them, between the bookshelves, at the reading tables, sitting in chairs. I picked up one that had fallen over in an aisle, and stood it in front of one of the bookshelves. My fingers trembled slightly.

This was the project that we had all worked on together twenty-nine years before, never doubting that it would take first prize in the competition. We imagined construction starting soon afterward. We pictured ourselves in helmets and work clothes, commuting to the site. As the basic design became the detailed design and then the final plan, we saw ourselves negotiating with contractors, then watching over the actual building of this library.

Yet strangely enough, though I still had vivid memories of how I felt back then, even with the model in front of me I no longer regretted the fact that a plan this good had never actually become reality.

I had been any number of times to the library that Kei'ichi Funayama designed. The previous month, I'd gone three days in a row to see a series of movies based on the novels of Harue Nomiya. Two years before, after the first major renovation in the twenty-five years since the library had opened, the number of reading tables and chairs had been halved, while three times as many sofas were added, leading to a marked increase in the number of users who stayed for hours to read. A lot of new restaurants and secondhand bookstores opened nearby, changing what had been a lonely street near Aoyama Cemetery into a lively area crowded with people, even on weekdays. The library was fulfilling its function on perhaps an even larger scale than was originally intended.

When a building is completed, architecture comes alive. That's how I've come to think of it. It's the people who use it, and their way of life, that give it life and keep it going. The Nishihara St. Peter's Cathedral, once thought to be in such bad taste, had settled in over the years as the central point in the landscape, and seemed much quieter now. People and time had mellowed it. Sensei's library never had a chance to really exist. The passage of time hadn't breathed the least bit of life into this model. Sensei's plan hadn't lost its value, it simply never got going.

As I stood there staring blankly at the model, I felt an irrepressible urge welling up inside me, directed at the Summer House. From long before I got my start here as an architect, it had a history, of renovations and extensions, and in the memories of all those who had gathered around its builder, it was still alive. Though it had been asleep for years, I told myself, it hadn't been lost. Its breath hadn't been cut off. All I had to do was reawaken it.

"Architecture isn't art at all. It's function, pure and simple." His voice came back to me now, sounding exactly as it had all those years ago.

I reassembled the model, putting each floor back in order. Someday I would repair the places that were starting to come apart. Meanwhile, I would return it to its acrylic case and find somewhere to store it in the house. Yukiko, who had been standing beside me, silently looking on, helped me put it away before leaving to explore the rest of the house.

From the workshop window, I could see her walking through the women's wing, opening and closing doors, after spending a while in the room she'd once slept in. I looked up at the ceiling where the original part of the building, built in the 1950s, joined the east and west wings, which were added on during the 1960s. There were stains at the dividing line, probably from a leak in the roof.

Yukiko came into the workshop.

"Might be better to put it back the way it first was," I mumbled, half to myself.

"First was?"

"We probably won't use it for our staff during the summer like the Murai Office did. And the two of us don't need such a big place."

She stood there quietly, thinking.

"It may be ours now," I said, "but we'll end up passing it on to someone else in twenty or thirty years."

We had no children.

"So restoring it to what Sensei first put together might be best. It would be nice to see how he used it as a cottage, sleeping and waking up in the rooms the way he arranged them—actually experiencing the original house. And if it's small, that'll make it easier when we sell it, for us and for the buyer."

"That's a point. But it's strange to be thinking about selling a house you haven't even started living in yet," she said, laughing. "You're always thinking about how things will end."

Her eyes were examining the part of the ceiling I'd been looking at.

"Endings are important, you know."

"True, but some endings aren't knowable. Let tomorrow worry about it."

Yukiko sometimes said things that sounded vaguely religious.

"The ceiling was so carefully finished you'd never notice where the wings were added. I used to think they'd always been there."

"Really? You were tricked, then."

"That's right—Sensei had me fooled."

We went down to the living room and stood in front of the fireplace. It had been here from the beginning, the center of the house, its oldest part. I stuck my head up the flue and opened the damper. Checking to make sure there was no backflow, I took some logs and arranged them in a square frame, as I'd once been taught to do. I got a sheet of old newspaper, rolled it into the shape of a baton, and lit it with a match to see if the flue was drawing. A steady stream of smoke rose up through the damper. I put more newspaper under the firewood and lit it. Flames immediately started lapping the wood. When she saw the fire crackling, Yukiko went around closing the windows.

I heard a bird singing somewhere. My first summer here, I'd heard it almost every day. I couldn't remember the bird's name, though, and the sound disappeared when the windows were shut.

"I never imagined the Summer House might be ours one day," I said to her.

"Really? I had an inkling..."

I looked at her. She was staring into the fire.

"How come?"

"Can't really say, just a feeling I had."

The logs were really starting to burn now. They had looked so old and tired, but now were eagerly feeding the fire.

Air from this room was being drawn up through the chimney and on outside. The years of emptiness seemed to be stoking the flames—as much fresh air would come into the Summer House as was now being drawn out. I could feel the cold of autumn and the warmth of the fireplace driving the humidity out of the room.

I pictured smoke rising from the chimney, surrounded by yellow leaves.

Evening came, and even after it was dark outside, we sat silently in front of the fireplace until all the wood was used up. We never tired of watching and listening to the flames as they rose and fell.